HIGH
PASSION

||||||||||||||||||||||||||||||||||||||||||||||||||||||||||||||||||||

VIVIAN AREND

BERKLEY BOOKS, NEW YORK

THE BERKLEY PUBLISHING GROUP
Published by the Penguin Group
Penguin Group (USA)
375 Hudson Street, New York, New York 10014, USA

USA | Canada | UK | Ireland | Australia | New Zealand | India | South Africa | China

Penguin Books Ltd., Registered Offices: 80 Strand, London WC2R 0RL, England
For more information about the Penguin Group, visit penguin.com.

HIGH PASSION

A Berkley Book / published by arrangement with the author

For information, address: The Berkley Publishing Group,
a division of Penguin Group (USA),
375 Hudson Street, New York, New York 10014.

ISBN: 978-0-425-26334-1

PUBLISHING HISTORY
Berkley mass-market edition / September 2013

PRINTED IN THE UNITED STATES OF AMERICA

10   9   8   7   6   5   4   3   2   1

Cover art by Gene Mollica. Cover design by Lesley Worrell.
Interior text design by Laura K. Corless.

This is a work of fiction. Names, characters, places, and incidents either are the product
of the author's imagination or are used fictitiously, and any resemblance to actual persons,
living or dead, business establishments, events, or locales is entirely coincidental.
The publisher does not have any control over and does not assume any responsibility for
author or third-party websites or their content.

ALWAYS LEARNING   **PEARSON**

Praise for the novels of
New York Times bestselling author

VIVIAN AREND

"An adrenaline rush of fiery, all-consuming passion and breathtaking romance."
—Jaci Burton, *New York Times* bestselling author

"The bitter cold of Alberta, Canada, is made toasty warm by the super-sexy Coleman brothers of Six Pack Ranch . . . skillfully written erotic passion." —*Publishers Weekly*

"Vivian Arend pours intense passion into her novels."
—*Library Journal*

"Arend once again proves that no matter what the genre, she's a master." —Lauren Dane, *New York Times* bestselling author

"This is a new favorite cowboy series, and a must read!"
—*The Book Pushers*

"[A] rare combination of romance, adventure, humor and screaming hot sex, all in one." —*Long and Short Reviews*

"Arend instills humor and heart into a story."
—*Book Lovers Inc.*

"I have fallen in love with this paranormal werewolf shifter series by Vivian Arend. With her humorous writing style, the off-the-chart chemistry and love scenes, and the endearing and wonderful characters, this series has become auto-buy." —*Pearl's World of Romance*

Special people helped guide this journey: Elle Kennedy, Dee Tenorio, Barb Hancock, and Nicole Synder. You tossed me lifelines when I needed them most. Thank you.

Bree and Donna—you're my safe place during the storms. Thanks for being there.

And to my husband, who has always believed in me and is even now plotting new adventures for us to experience so I can have the perfect settings for more disasters.

CHAPTER 1

,,,,,,,,,,,,,,,,,,,,,,,,,,,,,,,

Sweat slicked the curve of his biceps as his arms flexed above her. He hung there for a moment, beautifully suspended, before lowering an inch at a time, total control in his every move.

Alisha Bailey licked her suddenly dry lips. She attempted to tear her gaze away, but she'd been mesmerized. Spellbound by the pounding beat of the music surrounding them and the ambience—overwhelmingly masculine, perhaps, but as if she were going to complain. He exhaled, and she breathed with him. Unconsciously their bodies moved in sync.

A lock of blond hair fell over his forehead, and she was tempted to reach out and push it away. To drag her fingers over his shoulders and caress the ridges of muscle. To tug him closer until he wrapped all that leashed power and passion around her.

A metallic crash rang from their left and broke her fixation on Devon's half-naked body.

Reality set in far too quickly. She was on the treadmill,

the belt flying underfoot as she secretly ogled Devon. He hung from a horizontal bar not even five feet in front of her while he cranked out pull-ups one after the other.

People interrupted their workouts to eye the bodybuilder who'd lost his grip. Devon dropped lightly to his feet, pulled a towel from the crossbar, and wiped sweat from his face and neck as the weight lifter in question shrugged sheepishly and replaced the plate.

The low-level testosterone hovering in the air of the hard-core gym, a mix of dust and perspiration, made Alisha wrinkle her nose. With every gasp she took, the odor flooded her senses, and those breaths were coming far quicker than usual.

She wanted to blame her accelerated panting on the steep incline of the treadmill and her rate of turnover, but it probably had more to do with the eye candy than she wanted to admit. No matter how annoying Devon Leblanc was, how exasperating he was to work with, the entire aggravating package was a mighty fine one.

Not that she'd ever let him know. He had a big enough ego as it was. He didn't need her stroking it. As much fun as *stroking* might seem some days.

The machine under her beeped a warning before powering up yet another notch. Alisha focused on keeping her balance at the near all-out sprint. After a full summer of climbing rescues and spending all her spare time off hiking in the Banff area, she was in peak condition. Working to stay that way was now a way of life.

When the treadmill finally shifted to a slower pace, she gulped a mouthful of water, forcing herself to finish the run strong. Follow through, all the way. No shortcuts, no sympathy.

As the smallest person in her business, and often the only woman, Alisha didn't allow anyone to cut her slack, especially not herself. Her *never give up* attitude had gotten her through training that had left older and larger men in puddles on the search-and-rescue school floor. By graduation, her work ethic had sent her to the top of the list and earned her an invitation to join the most elite SAR team in the Canadian Rockies.

Maddening how her gaze automatically darted to Devon, who'd been her only real competition back in the day. The fact that the two of them had been hired straight out of school onto Lifeline still made a few tongues wag and bitter comments fly.

As if she cared what the gossips said.

She cleaned the treadmill before dragging herself to the stretching mats. The noise in the oversized area was a lovely distraction from the throbbing lactic acid in her limbs. One of the reasons she enjoyed using the local gym instead of the weight room at the Lifeline building or the school.

She enjoyed her job, but didn't need to live in her team-mates' pockets 24/7.

Once again Devon came into view, and she debated throwing something at him. The one person she wouldn't mind getting away from, and yet he constantly showed up. Damn him for being her tagalong shadow.

Probably did it to piss her off.

"Alisha."

She scrambled to her feet, pulling her blond hair tighter into her ponytail in prep for hitting the weight room floor. The three guys headed in her direction might know her name, but she wasn't sure who they were. "You looking for me?"

The two slightly behind their leader smirked and made some low comments, and Alisha's heart fell.

Oh goody. Another muscle-bound Neanderthal looking to impress her. The signs were everywhere as the one in front swaggered his way into her personal space. "I hear you're pretty good at climbing things."

"You heard right." She tilted her head to maintain eye contact, refusing to look away while he took a leisurely gawk down her body. It was like clockwork, in a way. The scum always appeared this time of year as new people filled the resort town in prep for the seasonal winter work.

This? This was the reason working out at the public gym

wasn't fun. What was it with guys thinking she'd make a good trophy?

Mr. Annoying leered. "You want to have something of substance to climb?"

Good grief. This one was stupider than usual. Alisha's watch went off, reminding her she had two hours until her staff meeting. "You know, it's been fun and all, but I have things I need to do. So, if you'll excuse me."

She shifted her body to one side, but he leaned with her, blocking her path. "We should get together. I want to find some of the tougher climbing routes in the area."

"Buy a book." Of all the things she hated, guys who acted as if they had some privileged right to access her time and knowledge pissed her off the most.

He didn't take the hint, remaining in her path. "You're not being very friendly."

Screw. This.

She glanced up to make sure she had the ceiling height to play with overhead. Other than that, Alisha didn't bother to see who was around. None of the locals would condemn her for what she was about to do. She bent her knees slightly to get momentum, grabbed a handful of his shirt, and leapt upward.

He swore, scrambling backward as she basically walked over him. One foot landed on his thigh, one somewhere in his groin area—she didn't worry about exact placement. She pushed her hands down on his head to get the final height needed to place one foot on his shoulder and dive for the chin-up bar Devon had been using moments earlier. A gentle swing turned her momentum and she landed on the path between the stretching area and the exercise machines, now on the opposite side of the guy who'd gotten in her way.

The asshole cursed, but she didn't care, simply strode forward as if he wasn't there.

Devon eyed her from where he'd been holding up the wall, sipping from his water bottle as if watching a circus performance. He straightened to vertical, clapping softly as he gestured her into the main weight room.

"Having a good day, Alisha?"

"Bloody idiot." Wrapping her fingers around a set of dumbbells and heading for the mirrors gave her a physical outlet for her frustration.

Devon chuckled. "Him or me?"

She paused for a moment. If Devon insisted on hanging around and driving her crazy with unanswerable longings, maybe he could actually help her for once. She looked into his laughing eyes. "Do me a favour and keep him from bothering me?"

Devon raised a brow.

She paused. "Please?"

"This your boyfriend?"

Alisha tensed as she realized the brute squad had moved in behind Devon. Only he didn't seem concerned. He winked, in fact, before he faced the jerk who'd interrupted her.

Devon checked out the three men. "I'm her friend."

The ass in front shifted his weight. "You're gonna keep me from bothering her?"

The last thing she expected was for Devon to burst out laughing. Full-out laughing. When he stopped, he was still shaking his head.

"You think this is funny?" The asshole stepped in closer.

"You have no idea how hysterical." Devon moved aside, opening a path to Alisha. "You want to mess with her, go right ahead. I have a paramedic on speed dial. I'll deal with your two friends if need be. She doesn't need my help."

Whoa. That was a vote of confidence she'd never expected to hear from Devon. Ever.

It was enough to make her grin.

Maybe she looked scarier than she thought, because Mr. Annoying faded away, his buddies with him.

"That simple, huh?" Alisha caught Devon by the arm and squeezed. "Wish they'd gone away the first time I told them to."

"Yeah." He glanced at his watch. "Finish your workout. We have a meeting to make."

He turned his back, once again becoming a barrier between her and the rest of the room. For a moment she stood motionless, wondering at the compliment Devon had paid her.

Wondering why exactly he was there, *again*, underfoot.

She sat and struggled to focus on her arm workout. It was far too tempting to use the mirrors to track the location of Devon and the creep she'd crawled on instead of checking her form on each lift.

Maybe her response to the newcomer had been, well, over the top, but she was tired of having to fight for every damn inch of respect she got. She thought it would get easier over time, acting as if she didn't care. Pulling on a *screw it all* attitude like armour.

She loved her job with something close to obsession. Why people couldn't recognize that and respect her for it was beyond her understanding.

The noise calmed as the athletes settled into their routines. The newcomers vanished, and Devon took an unobtrusive spot at the edge of her peripheral vision.

Alisha put her irritation aside and focused on her body. On making it strong enough to handle anything tossed her way.

If only she could train her heart and soul as easily.

Devon watched.

It seemed he'd been watching forever.

Across the room, Alisha sipped from an oversized water bottle as she visited with the Lifeline pilot, Erin Tate. Alisha and the black woman next to her looked far too small to be lifesavers, but they were both forces of nature, and that knowledge made Devon smile more than the disparity in their sizes from the rest of the team.

The team winch man, Anders, lay sprawled over two-thirds of the couch discussing the latest mountain film he'd seen with Xavier and Tripp, their paramedic and avalanche specialist, respectively. The three guys were about as far apart in physical appearance as possible, but together they were a hell of a team.

Together they saved lives.

Whatever things made them stand apart didn't matter to Devon, as long as they worked together when it counted.

The door opened and their boss entered the room. Marcus Landers was a legend in his own way. Not that Devon would ever say that—Marcus would tie him up and leave him dangling from a rope for mentioning how much he'd inspired Devon early in his career. And working for the man?

His level of hero worship at first was embarrassing to remember. Devon had finally put that reverence into what he considered good use. He'd joined Lifeline and committed to making a difference.

Marcus glanced around the room. "Damn. You're all here."

"Ha." Erin flashed him a one-fingered salute. "You're late. We should make *you* do training circuits to make up for keeping us waiting."

Marcus grinned. The man was notorious for his creative training methods. And his creative punishments. "Just keeping you at the top of your game."

"You enjoy it too much," Tripp drawled. "We know better than to be late without a note from the hospital or fresh stitches."

Everyone shuffled into position around the massive boardroom table. Alisha curled herself in a chair across from Devon, ignoring him to face Marcus. "This must be an important meeting. You didn't bring us any doughnuts."

Erin leaned forward and picked up the roll of paper Marcus had dropped on the table. "But he did bring us a treasure map."

Marcus folded himself into the chair at the head of the table. "Treasure beyond your wildest dreams, Erin."

She raised a brow. "I can dream pretty big."

"Hey," Anders interrupted. "Before you get started on the official meeting, what's happening at the Banff training school? I bumped into your brother the other day, and he was grinning far too hard."

"Probably still gloating over having Becki James as a head coordinator," Devon suggested.

Marcus's smile deepened at the mention of his lover. "The school is damn lucky to have her on full time. The grin, though, is because he got a new sponsor who set the school up with a couple of scholarships plus enough cash to revamp the entire training centre."

Tripp whistled softly. "Sweet. Unnamed benefactor?"

"Some Toronto bigwig with more money than God. Said he wanted to help support *the ongoing development of excellence.*"

"Should see if he wants to pour some cash this direction," Xavier suggested. "Because you know this place could use a little sprucing up, and we are excellent ourselves."

Across from Devon, Alisha had stiffened, watching the banter, but no longer participating. The tightness to her body hadn't been there moments before.

Conversation continued around them about what they'd do to fix up the staff quarters of Lifeline if they had a spare million to play with. Devon ignored them and instead thought through all the reasons he could for Alisha's strange tension. She'd grown up in Toronto. That was the only connection he could come up with without doing more research.

Marcus tapped on the table to get their attention. "Okay, put your speculation about the Banff SAR school aside. I have news."

"Raises?" Erin teased.

"Actually, yes." Marcus waited until the hooting and hollering died down. "You're a horde of wild animals this morning. What the hell did you have for breakfast?"

"I don't know what she ate, but Alisha went climbing over a gym rat." Tripp held his hands up in surprise as Alisha whirled on him in exasperation. "Well, you did, right?"

"How is my business all over this town in less than an hour?" She glared across the table at Devon.

He hated how quickly she looked at him to be the cause of her troubles, but then, being annoying was his usual ploy to distract her from the truth. "Don't blame me. I have better things to do than gossip about your choice of workout equipment."

"Nah, it wasn't Devon." Tripp held up his phone and showed Alisha the screen. Her face grew red as she stared.

Devon grabbed Tripp's wrist and pulled the phone to himself to look. Facebook. Someone had taken a picture of Alisha and Photoshopped it so she appeared to be climbing over King Kong.

"Enough." Marcus shook his head. "Bunch of children, all of you. You want the news, or should I take you to the nearest playground for a while?"

His grin remained firmly in place. Marcus knew the truth. The teasing and joking—it was all part of dealing with the stress of life-and-death decisions. They played hard, they worked even harder.

Marcus looked them over one by one as he spoke. "It's been a good summer, guys. I'm proud of you and the way you've operated. There have been a couple of nasty situations we had to deal with, and you pulled together and made it happen. Thank you."

Goofing aside, Tripp relaxed in his chair, his expression full of pride. "Did you hear back from that rescue we did up at Twin Falls? Did the dad pull through?"

"He did." Marcus gestured down the table. "And that's what I mean about good work. That man would be dead without you. All of you, working together."

"It's what we signed up to do." Xavier shrugged.

"It's what we love to do," Alisha corrected.

"And it makes a difference. Don't ever forget it. Last year you won awards. This year, you quietly did your job, and got it done. So again, thank you."

"Easier without the media in our bloody faces all the time, anyway," Erin muttered. She focused on the roll, giving it a poke. "I take it your secret news has something to do with this?"

Devon agreed. Curiosity ate at him. "Enough cheerleading, Marcus. I want to see what's on the treasure map."

Marcus gestured. "Go for it."

Eager hands reached forward and unrolled the paper, securing the edges in place.

"A map of western Canada?" Alisha tilted her head. "Oh, cool. You've marked the locations of our rescues."

Everyone leaned in, pointing to markers and commenting on the toughest parts of the rescue they remembered, or the most memorable.

"This is like a scrapbook, Marcus." Erin eyed him. "Who knew you had it in you?"

He grinned. "Becki's idea."

"Go, Becki." Alisha dragged a finger over the mountain range to the east of Banff. "It's an awesome idea."

"And, what's more exciting? We'll have markers in a much wider range over the coming months and years. This is my news." Marcus leaned over the table and laid his forearms on a section of the map, his prosthetic left hand on the divider line between Saskatchewan and Alberta, his right arm down the center of British Columbia. "This, to date, has been our corridor. Now?"

He opened his arms wider and settled his right hand off the coast of Vancouver Island.

"Holy shit." Erin leaned forward. "We're taking over coastal duties?"

"Pacific rescues have been added to our list. With cutbacks to the government, donors decided to chip in to make sure we keep our nonprofit work going. We're now on call to assist with any extreme situation between here and Port Tofino. As far north as needed."

A thrill of excitement shot through Devon. "Does this mean I get to break out the scuba suit a bit more often?"

Marcus nodded. "In coordination with naval SAR, but yes. Your reputation as a guppy is now official."

The grin stretching his cheeks felt awesome. Devon glanced at his teammates, pleased to see the same thrill on their faces.

Erin waved a hand in Marcus's direction. "Does this mean you're getting me a bigger, better chopper? Because those are some long-ass hauls you're talking about."

Marcus tossed her an oversized envelope. "Try a man in every port. You'll have a chopper on the island to access—we'll add a plane to the team here in Banff. And yes"—he caught her with her mouth still open—"you get a bigger bird to base here in Banff."

Erin danced in her chair as she pulled out a manual.

Tripp and Xavier were debating which of them would get to drop from the new chopper first. Devon laughed, then glanced across at Alisha to see her response.

She stared at the map, her pasted-on smile so fake he could have peeled it off and put it on the shelf. "Alisha?"

She blinked at him before shaking off the cloud. "You and your scuba suit. I thought you were over that fixation after the time you got stuck in the kayak."

He laughed. "That was a long time ago, and say what you will, it was a blast."

She raised a brow. "Oh, yeah, so much fun as we hauled the entire kayak out of the pool on a winch system. I still have the newspaper report. The one with you as front-page news."

"Hey, when you got it, flaunt it. The *Banff Crag and Canyon* needed my extraordinary good looks to peak sales that week."

"So giving." Alisha made a face as she rose to her feet, taking her empty glass with her. "Marcus, I need a refill."

Their boss waved her off, busy arguing with Erin about what upgrades the pilot was allowed to get on the larger, brighter, faster helicopter.

Devon . . .

He watched.

Like he always watched, especially Alisha.

The tension in her body as she'd walked away? The lack of gushing at Marcus's big news? That wasn't the Alisha he'd been around for the past four years.

She should have been vibrating in her seat, asking a million questions. Usually her reactions would have driven him crazy as she poked and teased in what he'd come to consider the longest foreplay session in the fucking universe.

Walking away quietly? Something was beyond wrong.

Curiosity drove him, as did the need to get them to the next stage of the game. Which meant he needed to find out what the hell was wrong.

So he could fix it.

She'd shot him down once, a long time ago. Probably didn't even remember she'd told him to grow up and get a life. To stop goofing around and wasting his opportunities.

The cutdown had actually sunk in, and he'd decided to do just that. Done it so well, in fact, that her taunt had changed his future.

It was time for a little positive payback and an end to their sexual frustration. He was going to find out what had put that sadness behind her eyes. Find out, and help her deal with it.

No turning back.

CHAPTER 2

||||||||||||||||||||||||||||

After years of reacting instantly to all kinds of life-and-death situations, Alisha thought she was beyond panicking without proof. The trembling in her hands proved otherwise.

It was the one topic guaranteed to throw her over the edge, though.

Somehow she got through the rest of the meeting. Smiled and nodded in all the correct spots, and kept her concern to herself. She'd fooled everyone in the room other than maybe Devon, who had her fixed in his gaze every time she took her eyes off Marcus. She slipped out of Lifeline headquarters ahead of the team and was in her car headed home before she could be invited for lunch, or a workout, or whatever else they came up with.

The short trip from the industrial area where their SAR base was located to her apartment wasn't enough time to distract her. The summer had been incredible—in that, Marcus had been correct. It wasn't only the successful rescues. Alisha had been a member of Lifeline for two and a half years now, and this was the first summer she'd felt she'd grown closer to all the members. Even Erin seemed to more than tolerate her, although the prickly woman often wore an expression of amusement as they did things.

Being a part of something as exciting and big as Lifeline was what Alisha had wanted from the start, and she'd become more successful than she'd dreamed possible.

Wasn't all you wanted to achieve . . .

Alisha stormed into the tiny kitchen and grabbed herself a glass of juice, ignoring the urge to go fill a cart with nothing but junk food so she could have a nice pity party.

She wandered to the window and stared over the street, the uneven rooftops and towering pines turning even the civilized city into a kind of wilderness. Inside, the rustic roof timbers and her thrift shop furniture added to the surreal effect. This inelegant setting was home, vastly different from what had been home for so many years.

Alisha flopped onto the couch and pulled out her phone. She tapped in the familiar number and waited to run the gauntlet.

"Mr. Bailey's office. How can I help you?" The words snapped out. Crisp. Cold. The woman hadn't cracked a smile in all the years Alisha had known her.

"Hello, Marilee. It's Alisha. May I please speak with my father?"

"Alisha."

No *So good to hear from you*, or *How are you doing?* but Alisha hadn't expected more than polite distance. Efficiency was the name of the game, after all.

Marilee finally continued, "He's in a meeting, but as soon as he's done I'll have him call you. Did you need me to arrange anything else? I haven't received your response regarding flights for Thanksgiving."

Drat. She'd been avoiding answering that particular e-mail as long as possible. "I'm afraid I still don't know my schedule for early October yet. I'll have a decision made within the week."

"Very good." In spite of the words, Marilee's tone dripped with disapproval. It was hard to not laugh. Alisha knew very well which of them had Marilee's loyalty—her or her father. "Thank you for calling."

The loud click triggered images of the perfectly coiffured secretary slamming down the phone hard enough to crack the case flitted to mind. Not that anyone in Bailey Enterprises would ever act out of line, but it was fun to picture.

Alisha shoved her phone in her pocket and went to deal with her workout gear, double-checking that her emergency clothing stash was in place. If she was called on short notice to work a rescue, searching for socks was the last thing she wanted to waste time on.

In some areas being efficient was necessary, but her family took it to ridiculous extremes, especially outside the office doors.

Enough moping about her father, at least until he called. Alisha turned up the music and poked through the fridge, but nothing looked interesting. Nor the cupboards. She'd lost her appetite during the morning meeting, and it seemed there wasn't much of a chance to get it back soon.

Coastal rescues? The advancement was a huge honour, and definitely something to celebrate, but would her family even register that the team had set another milestone?

Frustration flared again, this time at herself as much as them.

By now she should know better than to expect accolades, or even a brief *hurrah*. That the longing for approval still rose seemed cruel.

The phone rang and she checked the screen, almost hoping for a SAR call to pull her away from having to speak with him.

No such luck.

"Hello?"

"Your father will speak with you now." Marilee put Alisha on hold to make the connection.

Because heaven help it if Mike Bailey had to wait on the line for a moment or two, even to talk with his own daughter.

"Alisha. It's about time you made your Thanksgiving plans." His soft-spoken tone hid his stubbornness. What he called *willfulness* when she displayed the same tenacity.

Well, she wasn't ready to cave. "I'm not sure yet that a trip east will work with my schedule. I didn't call about that, I called to find out if you'd been making donations to the Banff SAR school or Lifeline."

"The corporation makes donations to all sorts of worthy causes, Alisha. I'd have to check the records—"

"Please do. I specifically asked you to stay out of my business here in Banff. I'd like to confirm you're honouring that agreement."

Her father's sigh echoed through the speaker. "I promised not to interfere, and honestly, as far as I know, no, Bailey Enterprises has not made a donation to your old school or Lifeline. Even though I'd imagine they'd enjoy receiving one."

"They probably would, only there are enough rich pockets to scoop into without diving into yours. I need this to be my—"

"Yes, Alisha. You want to do it on your own. Fine. You did. You're now a climber and ski bum instead of part of the family business. It seems to make you happy, so good for you."

The really sad thing, he wasn't being sarcastic. Just out of touch and oblivious, as usual. "I *am* happy here. By the way, Lifeline is now the premier search-and-rescue team for all of western Canada."

"It's . . . fine. Good for you," he repeated. Distraction blurred his voice.

Her father was no doubt simultaneously signing paperwork as Marilee placed it before him, unable to stop and listen to his only daughter for five minutes. He'd never allow himself to be that unfocused if she were a business contact with real important news.

"Yes, it is good. In fact, it's incredible." The idea of an expanded territory thrilled her and sent shivers down her spine at the same time. Wasn't it enough to impress him? "I got a raise."

He actually laughed, and bitter frustration rushed her as he stomped on her wishful dreams. "Well, now you can afford your fancy lifestyle, can't you? Alisha, enjoy yourself. Get it all out of your system so when you come home next summer we don't have to put up with more of your gallivanting."

There was a point in every conversation with her father when Alisha's blood pressure got too high to continue. This was five minutes past when she should have given up. "I don't think I'll make it home for Thanksgiving this year. Tell Mom I said hello, and I'll e-mail her soon."

Alisha didn't wait for his farewell. Best-case scenario, he would offer platitudes in an attempt to smooth the conversation over. Worst case would be an attack, shaming her for her lack of feminine compliancy.

She paced through the tiny attic space, feet unwilling to stop, her furious energy needing some outlet of escape. She fidgeted with everything she passed as she walked in circles.

She wanted to scream. Wanted to throw things. Wanted to beat her body into submission with another workout, but that was unreasonable. It would be stupid to punish herself when her father was the one who should be apologizing.

Although the one positive from their discussion—*ha! discussion*—he didn't seem to have tossed the money their direction. Not that she wanted Banff SAR to go without funding, but having her father dump money on them would only add to the pain of fighting for her position and standings. People found it hard enough to believe she'd achieved what she had on her own. If it were discovered that Daddy Dearest had poured money into the school coffers, even now after she was gone, all her accomplishments would be suspect. She could have the fastest times on the stopwatch and gossips would still believe she'd bought her way into the placements. And her current job.

Her job—a member of an elite, highly trained, kick-ass rescue squad. Thank you very much.

She growled her frustration at the walls. It was no use. She wasn't going to be able to relax, not for a while.

A visit to Tim Hortons to nab an entire box of doughnuts was looking far too attractive. She needed a diversion. In spite of the clouds hanging low over the mountains, she grabbed her hiking boots and yanked them on. Maybe if she burned off a little steam, visions of using the toe of her boot to kick some sense into her father would stop dancing through her head.

She grabbed her emergency gear bag and trundled down the stairs to her car.

His curiosity got the better of him. There might be other ways to find out what he needed, but the first solution that came to mind was the simplest.

The sneakiest as well, but whatever.

Sneaky required Devon to wait until the rest of the team had left headquarters. Alisha was gone in a flash—again, atypical for her. The others poked around for a while. Chatting, teasing, and carrying on. Xavier flirted with the new part-time call-centre-worker-slash-receptionist before leaving with a shouted challenge at Tripp for darts that evening.

The newest employee Marcus had hired to Lifeline, Lana, had arrived in the middle of their meeting, gliding past the giant boardroom table to hide out of the way in the administration area. The dark-haired woman had worked silently through all the discussion and recaps and the planning for the team's shoulder-season training and rescue setups. After the meeting she continued her tasks, nodding attentively while Marcus gave directions for ordering new materials.

Devon ignored her as he wandered through headquarters in a deliberately casual manner. Lana would work with Marcus during emergencies to gather information, and the rest of the time she would play a more relaxed administration role. It was a position that required someone trained in search and rescue but not one who joined the team physically on the field.

Marcus had made Lifeline HQ into an environment that was both efficient and relaxing, but it wasn't Devon's choice of hangouts. He'd prefer to head home, hit the gym, or call up a couple of his buds and see if they were free. As it was, for over an hour he found tasks to keep him busy. Organizing gear, straightening supplies. There wasn't any problem finding reasons to stick around.

Although, as the others all left, his continued presence became more noticeable.

"You know, I've already promised you a salary increase," Marcus teased.

Devon grinned. "Thanks for that, by the way. It'll come in handy. Thought I'd get some work done while it's quiet. I've already finished my workout for the day, and the weather's crap for hiking or anything."

Marcus gave Devon's shoulder a squeeze before turning on the lone remaining Lifeline member. He shooed Erin out of the building. "Enough. Do your research, and stop asking me impossible questions about your new chopper. Get."

"Meanie. See you later, Devon." Erin snatched up the pile of materials Marcus had offered her.

Marcus slipped out the door, walking rapidly to escape as Erin followed and kept badgering him.

As the door latched behind them, Devon glanced to check where Lana had gone. She was nowhere in sight, so he pushed his way past the call desk and into Marcus's private office.

He closed the door most of the way. Okay, what he was doing at the moment wasn't strictly kosher, but it wasn't as if he were snooping for tons of information. Just a hint to help him explore Alisha's background more thoroughly.

The cabinet that held their employment records stood in the far corner. He carefully slid the metal drawer forward and flipped through hanging files until he hit Alisha's name. He didn't even pull the envelope out, simply opened it and skimmed down to where the emergency contact numbers were listed. Father's name. Mother's. A phone number. He memorized them and stuffed everything away how he'd found it.

Discovering that Lana now blocked his path to freedom proved he'd make a shitty undercover operative. Unless he wanted to spend the next however long hidden in the office until she left the room again, he was about to get caught. He went for nonchalant and headed for the door.

Her chair was tight enough to the wall that his hips bumped it as he eased past.

"Were you lost, Devon?" Her lips twisted into a smirk. "Or did you think I wouldn't notice you?"

"Well, I was hoping . . ."

He winked. Damned no matter what he said, Devon fell back on charming her into silence. If his track record were anything to go on, he'd all too easily persuade her not to tell on him.

Lana shook her head in amusement, turning to face her desk. "If you get caught where you shouldn't be, it's your butt. Marcus won't yell at me." She slipped another set of papers into place. "And I might have only been here for a week, but even I've figured out he's a good yeller."

"A very good yeller," Devon agreed. "Only, *he* didn't catch me."

She snorted but didn't say anything else, her focus on the papers.

"Efficient," he complimented her.

"I try." She spun her chair and gave him a long stare. "You, too. You weren't in there for very long."

Devon waved a hand easily, attempting to put his actions into a better light than it might seem. "I wasn't doing anything terrible, only—"

"I didn't see anything, remember?" She completed her task before picking up her purse and rising to her feet. "I have no idea what you're talking about."

Amusement mixed with relief washed over him as he grabbed his coat and headed out the front door. Lana left as well, locking up behind them. He slowed his step as he realized his truck was the only vehicle left in the parking lot. "You need a ride into town?"

"That would be great. Catching the bus takes forever."

Lana paced at his side, her long legs easily keeping stride with his. "My car is at the shop while they figure out why it's making weird noises. And their diagnostic machine is down, so I have to wait for them to get a replacement part before they can tell me what replacement parts I need."

"Typical. The higher the tech, the longer it'll take."

She slipped onto the bench seat of his truck and tossed her purse at her feet. "Usually I don't mind. Walking around Banff isn't a hardship, only the Lifeline building is a little far out of town to hoof it to work."

"I can give you a lift if I'm around and headed in," Devon suggested. Only made sense to offer her a hand, seeing how she was now part of the team.

Her face lit up. "I'd appreciate that. If it's no problem, you could drop me off at Safeway. I'll grab a few groceries and walk home from there."

As he drove, Lana rambled about the move from wherever she'd come from, and how her U-Haul truck had been, as she called it, *hijacked* at one of the gas stations along the way. Devon tried to respond at the proper moments, but he was distracted, his focus once again returning to the mystery of Alisha and what had upset her so much.

They'd worked together for years, been in school before that, and the amount he knew about her private life was minuscule.

The way she'd avoided sharing anything about her family had to be deliberate.

"I hope there's a good place for wings in town." Lana broke into his mental ramblings. "Funny how we all have our vices, right? I spent my time at training school taking such good care of my body, but put an order of wings in front of me and I'm putty. I picture them at times, teasing me and calling my name."

Devon dragged his mind off memories of Alisha's ass while she worked her way up a vertical wall. "We do get addicted to the strangest things."

He pulled into the grocery store parking lot and paused to let Lana off. Familiar faces turned his way to greet him, the guys checking his passenger out with more than a little interest as she slipped from the cab and waved her thanks.

Devon kept his grin hidden. She wasn't going to lack for company. He looked her over as she walked away, chatting with one of his buddies who'd rushed the truck to help her. She was older than him, probably closer to thirty. Lana was in good shape—most of them in the field were a bit fanatical about conditioning, but that was what happened when your body was a part of your equipment.

Even observing another woman couldn't stop Alisha from popping to his mind, though. While Lana might have the long, lean thing happening, Alisha made Devon heat up far beyond reason. She had muscles while remaining feminine, but it was her attitude that fired his desire to the point where he had to fight for control. He had to be a bit of a masochist if being pushed by Alisha to the edge of his endurance during a challenge turned him on more than the fluttering lashes Lana was using on her current mark.

He headed home more determined than ever to find a way to break through Alisha's constant rebuffs. He wanted her in his bed, and it was past time for her to admit that was what she wanted as well.

CHAPTER 3

''''''''''''''''''''''''''''

There was an unwritten law that most emergency calls arrived an hour after you went to bed or an hour before you were ready to wake up.

The alarm blaring across the room jerked Alisha from a dream that shredded away like a cloud in high wind, leaving behind only the uncomfortable sensation of watching eyes and hungry wolves.

She snatched up her phone and acknowledged receipt of the call, gazing out the window into the darkness of the backyard as she checked the sky for weather conditions. Something flashed near the fence, catching her attention for a split second before she stifled her curiosity and hurried into routine. There was no time to be distracted. She jerked on her clothing and was out the door in less than five minutes.

Her rapid response still wasn't quick enough to make her the first to arrive at headquarters. Both Erin's and Devon's vehicles were already in the parking lot, with Marcus pulling in behind her.

"What's the location?" she called to Marcus as she reached into her backseat and pulled out her bag with the rest of her gear.

"High alpine in the Monashees Range. Rock slide surprised a research team, and they're still missing a couple of members." Marcus got ahead of her and held the door open. "I'll know more in a minute."

Inside the building, the bright overhead lights made her blink as she hurried into the sorting locker to join Devon. He was already stacking ropes and bags in preparation for loading into the chopper.

He smiled, his blue eyes looking far clearer and brighter than hers felt at the moment. One section of his hair stood straight on end again, taunting her to try to make it behave.

"You slept in," he teased.

"You know who's leading the rescue today?" Ignoring him was her only defense when he was borderline more adorable than she could stand.

Devon shook his head as he brought down a set of climbing cams and passed them to her. "Tripp is up on rotation, but depending on the exact location, Anders might call the shots—there are glaciers in the area."

"I knew that." She used two hands to accept gear, keeping everything untangled while stowing it away. With a bag slung over each shoulder and another in each hand, Alisha twisted to escape.

She raced out the door and across the tarmac without looking back. She kicked herself for being rude to Devon when he'd simply been sharing news like a teammate was supposed to—she had to pull herself together before she made any more mistakes.

They were in the air in less than twenty minutes. Erin lifted the chopper while the sky remained dark, the pale glow of sunrise only a thin line against the eastern horizon.

"Everyone gets thirty minutes to wake up before I brief you on details. Marcus is back at base, finding out more. Once he knows what we're into he'll update me, so I'll go over expectations and set up then." Tripp spoke over the headset speakers, his voice rushing past her ears like a soft zephyr.

He held out a thermos, and Anders, seated to his right, grabbed it eagerly. He opened the lid and took a deep sniff. "Whoa, now that's a nice surprise. Who had time to make coffee before heading to HQ?"

"New gadget Lana installed." Tripp beamed. "Timer or computer controlled—when we got the bug-out call, I triggered the on button using my phone. It was ready to go when we were."

"If it's always prepped, we'll never do a rescue without caffeine again." Xavier held up a hand and high-fived Tripp. "Nice. Now hurry the hell up and pour, Anders."

Banter continued as Anders filled everyone's travel mug. There was no way to stop a smile from lifting her lips as Alisha observed her team.

They had all developed coping strategies to deal with the nervous anticipation that slipped in en route to a rescue, let alone the flat-out shock of being dragged from their warm beds. Some of them sat quietly, slowly letting themselves come alive. Others like Xavier seemed to have nothing but an on/off button. He chattered nonstop to anyone who would listen as he flipped songs on his MP3 player, occasionally singing along.

Alisha found it harder to wake up this morning than usual. Her restless wandering the previous afternoon had tired her out, all right, but she still hadn't fallen asleep at a decent hour.

She straightened her coat, preparing for the hour-plus flight. She adjusted her gloves and cupped her hands around her travel mug, but even with the heater blasting overhead there was no way to completely ignore the cool temperatures clinging to the interior of the chopper.

Transports were overheated in summer and cold the rest of the year. She had to be slightly crazy to want to be a part of it all. Part of the discomfort of being woken willy-nilly, and all the other inconveniences that went with being search and rescue.

She probably *was* slightly crazy. So be it.

Beside her, Devon laughed at something, and she pulled her coat hood up to hide her face. Watching him made something inside flutter and ache, if it were possible to have those two conflicting emotions. He had so much life in him—so much enthusiasm. Sometimes she felt he'd pulled her through the roughest moments of training school with his sheer exuberance alone.

Striving to beat him at challenges had made her stronger. She'd admit that to herself now.

He didn't need to know she was attracted to him, though. The player didn't need more ammunition. Besides, it wasn't as if he needed more playmates. He was already making a move on the new receptionist. As she'd headed out to the trailhead yesterday she'd seen Lana in his truck, the two of them laughing as they waited at the lights close to Devon's house. She wouldn't comment on how quickly the two of them had gotten cozy.

The wall needed to stay up. Solid. Attraction firmly ignored.

The daydreams about his strong hands and his rope-handling skills—those were simply a nice way to pass the time during a long rescue approach.

Devon glanced her way. Heat spread though her fast enough that if she weren't careful, she'd be too toasty for her coat and the rest of her gear, and stripping prior to a rescue wasn't a good idea. Wasn't a good idea *ever*, not as far as Devon was concerned. It was unfair that he turned her on, since she certainly didn't want her name added to his harem list.

Thirty minutes passed far quicker than she expected, and she'd relaxed, drifting off to better fantasize. A soft touch to her thigh jerked her to full alert to find herself staring into a pair of bright blue eyes. His hand on her leg was hot through the fabric, and instant tingling shot through her core.

Devon's voice carried over the headset. "Are you ready?"

Sexual fantasies evaporated in a rush of indignation, and she stiffened. "Of course. What makes you think I'm not ready to do a rescue—?"

Rapid motion to one side caught her attention. Tripp's soundless clapping ended as he held up two fingers. Alisha flushed and switched her headset to channel two.

"Sorry, Tripp, don't know how I got flipped to a different setting." She gave Devon a sheepish smile. "Thanks for getting my attention."

Devon shrugged, then focused on Tripp.

"Everyone ready?" the older man asked. "We still have flight time, but I thought we'd go over a couple plans now so we can get into position quicker."

"There's already a rescue team in the area?" Anders asked.

Tripp nodded. "They've marked the perimeter, and they've contacted the RCMP K-9 division to get a dog brought out. Right now they suspect a couple of new cracks that opened might be the trouble. And none of them are climbers, so we'll be the ones going, only down, not up. Questions?"

Everyone had trained and worked together on far too many rescues to need to be babysat through procedure. Only one subject still remained as far as Alisha was concerned. "Partners?"

As lead hand, she would be the first to head into any climb, or the first to drop from the chopper into position. Up until the start of summer her partner at the other end of the line had always been Anders. During boot camp week, though, she and Devon had been partnered up, and since then it seemed they were always paired together.

"You and Devon, Anders with Xavier. I'm sticking close to Erin with the chopper in case you find the victims and we can winch them out. Deal?"

"Deal." Everyone acknowledged their positions and chatter resumed over the headsets.

Alisha went back to mentally prepping for the rescue.

Getting into the right frame of mind to crawl down a rock wall into the darkness. To have only a rope and a headlamp as the connection between her and the outside world.

A rope, and the man on the other end of it.

She caught herself staring at Devon's hands again. Strange. She trusted him completely when it came to belaying her. He held her life in his hands, and she didn't feel the need to worry one bit.

When it came to her heart? He was simply another man she refused to allow to hurt her.

The chopper banked and she snuggled deeper into her coat. Much more awake, but no further ahead in solving her major dilemma.

Thank God for the distraction of a rescue.

Nothing was wrong, but something wasn't right.

The equipment was fine, as were the steps they'd taken so far since reaching the rescue site. A sense of foreboding hovered over Devon, though, and he could find nothing to explain why.

It wasn't some mystical foreknowledge, only he knew not to ignore the sensation, either. It had been the topic of many a late-night drinking session during training school when more experienced recruits would stop to share stories from the field. They'd all had times when they'd felt a warning ahead of time, for whatever reason. It would make sense later, but for now? He kept his guard set higher than usual.

Efficiency built from years of training and working together had Alisha slipping out of sight as the morning sun peeked above the low mountain ridge to their east. Shadows reached crooked fingers toward the rock slide, creating patterns of light and dark emphasized by variations in rock. Pale grey slabs and darker black chunks mixed with clumps of freshly exposed soil and ragged splashes of green pine needles. Devon ignored the strange beauty found even in the middle of the devastation and focused on the changing weight on the rope in his hands.

"Take," Alisha called from below. "Devon, tie off and descend to meet me. I've found something. There's a tunnel opening to one side. I want you to anchor me from here before I try it."

"On my way." Devon signaled Anders to his side. "Alisha's got a lead. I'm going down."

Anders nodded. "Xavier's dealing with the two victims we spotted from the air at the edge of the slide. I'll take over up here."

A few quick adjustments switched his ropes from belaying to rappelling. Devon twisted his headlamp to high before leaning back on the ropes and allowing them to support his weight. A ray of sunshine hit him like a spotlight a second before he stepped over the edge.

The walkie-talkie link on his chest allowed him to hear Alisha without her shouting. "You've got a thirty-foot path—nice and clear. If you move slightly to the right when I warn you, you'll find a set of footholds to get you to my ridge."

"Let me know. What did you find?"

"Jacket shreds and a shoe. Some blood." Report was clear and precise, but there was a touch of disgust in her voice any time she had to discuss bleeds. "I'm guessing someone got carried along with the rubble for a bit of a ride before they hit the crack. This is a fresh opening—I haven't found any old growth."

Devon agreed. He worked his way down the slope rapidly, even as he flipped on his speaker. "You're not going to believe this. The research team was testing for seismic activity. They have clear records that show when the slide happened, and yeah, there was a bit of underground quiver."

"Head right. And really? Tell me they're not expecting any further activity."

Devon followed her guidance, rock dust hanging in the air between him and the wall, blurring his vision. "Agreed. In a fresh hole while things are still shifting? Not a great idea, but there's nothing on the equipment. Like zero activity. We're safer down here than up top where the fall is still shifting and finding its balance."

He landed beside her, the glow of his headlamp highlighting her cheekbones and making the bits of her hair that were visible under her helmet shine like an angel's.

Alisha checked him over quickly, then pointed to the left. "This way. I set anchors already, but I'll need to swing around a gap, then get some lights in place."

Devon tied off to the wall anchors she'd set. "Nice and bombproof. Well done."

"Thank you." Alisha pulled a rope from her shoulder and passed him the loop he needed. "I'll check the needed length. Hold me tight so I can lean out."

He motioned for her to wait as he hooked the safety line in place. Once they brought back their target, or if they needed it themselves, the way out would be a matter of grabbing the rope and signaling Anders to haul them to safety.

Devon adjusted his footing and slipped in directly behind Alisha, tightening the ropes to hold himself in place, fine-tuning the ones attaching them together. Then he threaded his fingers into her climbing harness. "Lean away."

Alisha had grabbed a high-power flashlight, the backup strap leashed around her wrist. She pushed forward, upper body hanging over the inky blackness at their feet. Light reflected from closer protrusions, skipped out into eternity in other spots as the holes ended too far back for the light to reveal the depth.

Dust particles hovered in the air around them. The taste of dirt skidded over his tongue. Peering through the haze caused by the wide dilation of his headlamp didn't help him see much better. "Anything? Worthwhile going forward?"

Alisha stretched a hand to him, holding out the flashlight. "There's a part of the wall to the left that's got . . . skid marks? I need to slide around the corner to be sure."

That would put this rescue one step further up the danger scale. Devon took the lamp and placed it aside, pulling her to vertical, their bodies tight together as they rearranged gear.

At some point soon he needed them in this position when

they weren't covered from head to toe. Naked. Naked would be marvelous.

He slapped himself mentally, pulling back on track and thinking about the four rules his team had been built on. The first two were opposites, seemingly. Have patience, or move decisively. Was this a time to wait or move? "Do we have what we need to proceed?"

"We do for me to go around the corner. I'll know more at that point." Alisha took a deep breath. "On belay."

He adjusted his hands. "Belay on. Careful, Alisha."

She glanced over her shoulder, teeth flashing white as she smiled. A second later she was gone, the rope twisting in his hands as she used him as a fulcrum to find footing and scamper deeper into the darkness.

"Give me slack, Devon."

He let out a foot of rope. Then another. Tension remained on the line, and everything was going well, when his earlier uneasiness returned in a flash.

"Alisha, what's happening?"

"I found a trail. Correction. I found him." Excitement rocked her voice, not only over the microphone now but shouted into the darkness. "Hello. Are you okay? I'm coming to help you."

A muttered reply, nothing comprehensible, but thrilling to hear nonetheless. Devon hit his mic to the surface. "Alisha's found the mark. Anders, get in position. We're not far from the surface."

"Stretcher?"

"I'll let you know."

Alisha had continued to talk to the lost, now found, researcher. Devon fed out line and worked to get extra ropes in place for Alisha to secure the victim.

The speaker connection between them crackled. "Conscious and alert. He's been bumped around but he's good to move without a stretcher. Bring him up, Devon."

For the next fifteen minutes Devon pulled and worked his muscles to the maximum as he lifted the man to the midlevel platform. He was dirty from head to toe, his jacket and pants cut in places from the rocks he'd slid over. One foot in a boot, the other in a dirt-streaked sock. Blood marred one side of his face, the wound on his temple already covered with a quick bandage Alisha must have slapped in place.

Devon checked him over quickly, shining his light into the man's eyes to watch his pupils react. "What's your name and how are you feeling?"

A momentary flash of panic faded as the man pulled himself together. "Paul, and dark places aren't my favourite. Otherwise, I'm okay."

Devon nodded. "We'll get you out of here as quickly as possible. Hold tight."

He wasn't going to leave Alisha waiting in the dark any longer than he had to, either. It was a bit of a teeter-totter, making sure the researcher was roped to the wall, then adjusting lines to get back to Alisha to hoist her up. Devon worked as rapidly as possible, the occasional comment over the microphone the only thing assuring him Alisha was safe.

It seemed like forever before Devon finally was in position. "You ready?"

"No worries. I was doing my nails."

The researcher chuckled, and Devon smiled. Yeah, everything would be—

Static shot out from his handset followed hard by Xavier's overly loud response.

"Crap. Lock into position guys, incoming." His breathing increased in tempo as if he were running. "We lost another chunk of the mountain and it's rolling in."

Devon held a hand to Paul, keeping his voice calm and controlled in spite of the unknown factors barreling toward them. "Don't panic. We're good here. Let me get my partner, and we'll all bunker down."

Paul nodded, his fingers white around the ropes holding him to the wall.

"Haul ass, Alisha," Devon ordered.

"Already halfway there, sugar." Alisha peeked around

the corner, her bright purple helmet shining at him. "I'm ready to fly."

Fly she would. Devon gave her the word, then put all his strength into not just supporting her as she headed into the wide arc between them. He lifted her, making her cover the distance in half the time it had taken for her to leave him.

The rock underfoot shook slightly; sounds of the secondary rock fall carrying to them from the surface. Deep underground in the darkness where they were—that was all he concentrated on. On getting Alisha to safety. Like he'd promised . . . like being a partner always promised.

His biceps were screaming, but he brought her all the way up until he could catch her chest harness and lock her against him.

She blinked, half in surprise, half delighted, it seemed. "Well now, that was a lot of fun."

God. Devon would have laughed at her enthusiasm if they hadn't had a wide-eyed witness. They hurriedly shuffled toward Paul. "Anders, what's happening up top?"

"We had to retreat for a minute. Cover your heads, and I'll be back as soon as the leading edge settles."

"We're all fine." Alisha answered this time, totally calm, as if she'd been suntanning on the beach all afternoon with a relaxing cocktail in hand. "Anders, Devon and I are going to take a break for a minute, then you can lift Paul, okay?"

"No prob."

Devon stepped around Paul, putting the man into the middle of the huddle. Even as he worked like crazy to secure them all, Alisha carried on talking to Paul. She caught Devon's eye for a second and winked before teasing Paul about his girlfriend and the added value this adventure would give him.

Alisha was incredible. Once again proving she deserved every single accolade she'd gotten.

Above them the sunlight faded, and a torrent of dust and debris slipped into the crack. Devon turned his back on the surface and covered Paul. Alisha did the same on the other side, their arms cocooning the man as small rocks found their way into the opening and bounced off the walls.

"Slide mainly to the left of you," Anders informed them. "It's pretty dusty up here, but give it a minute and we'll be in position to get your new buddy up."

"There, see? Not bad at all." Alisha smiled up at both Paul and Devon.

Devon was distracted by a new sound, one not coming from the surface, but from the wall behind them. "Alisha, take over tying Paul in. I need to check something."

She frowned, but nodded.

He didn't do anything stupid like unrope and go explore, but he did loosen off enough to step away from the others.

Devon placed his ear to the rock. The rumbling increased.

At the same moment his headlamp caught a glitter in the distance. Devon's mouth went dry, but he forced himself to speak normally, no matter that everything inside was screaming for him to rush. "Alisha, is he ready?"

She gave a thumbs-up, patting Paul on the arm as she spoke into the mic. "Anders, take it away."

Usually Devon would be intently watching the victim until the man had reached safety, the way Alisha was doing.

Only not this time.

This time something else demanded his attention.

Devon swooped in on Alisha, looping his rope around her twice. Her verbal protests cut off when he pointed at Paul to warn her not to scare the victim, but she didn't simply give in.

"What are you doing?" she bit out in a whisper.

"The slide opened a stream. Brace yourself." That glitter in the distance was approaching faster than they could escape. "Once the first rush is past us I'm betting there will be enough room that we can climb out."

Her eyes widened, mouth gaping open until she snapped it shut. "A stream?"

She turned her head back toward the tunnel, headlamp shining out, and Devon swore. The glitter was no longer in the distance.

"Hold your breath, Alisha." He caught the back of her neck and held her face to his chest. His other hand wrapped tight around the anchors while he hoped like hell the rock lip they were crouching beside would deflect the worst of the first impact.

CHAPTER 4

''''''''''''''''''''''''''''''''''

The dull echo that had surrounded them since they'd lowered into the cavern increased, the voices above them growing fainter as the building roar of water raced toward them. Devon used the rush of adrenaline surging in his veins to take a tighter grasp on the ropes, and to surround Alisha more firmly as the whistle in the distance became a thunder.

Alisha caught him around his torso, burrowing in even as she shrank against the wall, trying to protect him in reverse. Drawing him close enough that they would present the smallest possible surface area to the impending deluge.

A fine mist hit before the light vanished and icy coldness poured over them. The current swept from left to right, crashing into the rock and breaking like a wave overhead, dousing them a split second before the rest of the torrent surrounded them. Devon tucked his face into the crook of his arm, pinning Alisha against the rock. Darkness enveloped him, as if he'd leapt from a dock and plunged to the bottom of a lake. Only in contrast to the lake, however, here there was no calming silence, no peaceful bubbles. Instead, dangerous currents attempted to claw him from his perch. Watery fists pounded them, attempting to sweep them from safety into the endless fissures threading through the roots of the mountain.

With his eyes squeezed shut, there was nothing to see but the ghostly echoes of their headlamps. Alisha shifted position, and he caught her harness. One of his feet slipped from the ledge for a second before he jerked himself back into position. Small rocks crashed into them, carried by the current, but the swell of pressure had already lessened. He ignored the buzzing sensation in his lungs that had begun to call for air, instead concentrating on Alisha, on keeping them both safe.

Once the first wave was past, the water rapidly dropped, filling the crevices and cracks at their feet. As their heads broke the surface, he and Alisha gasped for air. Devon loosened one hand from the ropes, wiping his mouth and spitting out dirt-filled water as he glanced up to check the sky and their route to freedom.

Another fifteen seconds passed, maybe twenty, and the water continued to ease off, finding its level as water always does. He was thankful to discover that the water was around waist level.

"A bath was not on the agenda for today," he joked, reaching to undo the first of the ropes binding them in place.

No answer.

Devon snapped his attention downward to discover that Alisha's face had gone ghostly white. Her eyes were squeezed close and her lips pressed into a thin line.

"You okay?" he asked.

The roar of the water was still loud enough to prevent voices from traveling from the surface, but he was close enough to Alisha that when a low whimper escaped her, he heard. Her body jerked hard enough to rock them both, a seemingly involuntary motion.

Fear was an ice-cold blade at his throat, more frigid than the water numbing his limbs. "Dammit, Alisha, are you hurt? Did you get hit?"

He edged away to examine her, to see if one of the rocks that had grazed him had slammed her harder and caused an injury.

His attempt to adjust position was thwarted by increased pressure on his harness straps. Her fists clenched tighter as she once more hid her face against his chest.

What the hell was going on?

He calmed himself even though he wanted to shout. Years of training forced him to offer reassurances instead of panicking along with the elephant tangoing in his belly. "Alisha, I need to check you. You've got to let go."

"No."

The word burst from her, high-pitched and totally not typical Alisha.

His heart rate, which had begun to drop along with the water level, raced back up.

The water continued to disappear, falling to midthigh. The current pushing against them had slowed enough that he could stand without needing to brace himself to remain vertical. Devon caught Alisha by the forearms and, though he hated to do it, used his superior strength to break her hold. He ducked down and caught her chin in his fingers, lifting until he could look her in the eye.

"Alisha. Tell me what's wrong."

She continued to shake, pupils dilated as she stared into the darkness past him.

She'd gone into shock. Devon slapped at his chest to turn on his microphone connection to Anders. "I need a rope lowered now. Alisha's—"

Her hand shot forward and slammed the button, effectively cutting him off.

"No." The word was barely audible, but she repeated it again and again, getting louder as her lashes fluttered hard. Her eyes focused on his as the tremors shaking her body slowed. "Don't tell them."

"What the hell is going on?" Devon demanded. "You're hurt, or in shock."

She grew stronger even as he spoke, pulling herself upright. Her feet splashed in the now ankle-deep water as she attempted to move away. "I'm fine. I'm fine."

His speaker crackled. "Devon? Alisha's *what*? You got a problem down there?"

Devon reached to answer, but Alisha blocked him again, her hand cupped over his transmitter to stop him from engaging the on button.

At least her reflexes were back up to speed. "Alisha, do we have a problem?"

She stared at him with begging in her eyes. "No. No problem. Don't say anything. Please."

That she was coherent enough to ask was the only reason he hesitated. Did he give her a break, at least for now? It was all kinds of wrong, but this was *Alisha*, dammit, and it seemed he had no brains when it came to her. He nodded once, and she reluctantly slipped her hand away.

Devon clicked the on button. Paused. Then did the only thing he could do under the circumstances.

"Alisha's . . . mic isn't working." The lie fell from his lips, leaving behind a dirtier taste than the deluge that had blasted them. With one sentence he'd as good as stepped into the void. "Send the rope down. We're soaking wet—a little help hauling our asses up would be appreciated if anyone has extra hands."

The entire time he spoke, Alisha kept her gaze fixed on him, wordlessly pleading.

He was going to be in so much shit for passing this situation off if something was really wrong with her.

Anders's instant response fell from above. "Affirmative. Look sharp."

A rope snaked down the rock wall, a narrow beam of light highlighting its descent.

Devon ignored the rope, focusing on a far more important target. Alisha had switched her attention away, intent on the wall and removing the gear they'd set in place. She unlatched cams and linked carabiners onto her waist clips as if her soul depended on it.

He caught her by the wrist and forced her to stop. "Look at me."

She twisted in slow motion, lifting her chin high. He ran a hand over her cheek, noting with approval that her skin had warmed, a deep crimson flush marking her cheeks. He checked the response of her pupils to his headlamp. All her physical responses were back to normal, but her eyes were haunted. He let out his frustrations in a long sigh, the sound mixing with the continuing gurgle of water past their feet.

Alisha caught his arm.

"Thank you." The words came out ragged and rough, as if she'd been screaming for hours.

It wasn't enough. After all the high-test emotions of the past minutes, anger rushed in and replaced them all. "This isn't over. I won't say anything now, but once we're home, we're going to talk about this more. Understood? Or I will question you in front of the team."

The hurt and betrayal in her eyes at his final words nearly killed him, slicing to the core, but she nodded her understanding.

Needed distraction came from the thump of the rope end landing beside them. Devon watched her tie up, stepping in to examine her knots.

"Stop fussing, Devon," she snapped. "I can climb. I'm fine."

"Arguing with me right now is not an option," he retorted. "Deal with it."

Alisha snapped her mouth shut, hanging on to the rope and glaring as he double-checked her harness bindings. Soaking wet. Freezing cold. Pissed off as all get-out, and worried like crazy, he shouldn't have been so damn aware of her curves as he tried not to touch anything other than her ropes and harnesses.

When he stepped back, she jerked her chin up. "Happy?"

"Not remotely."

She hit his microphone button. "Anders, on belay."

"Hey, girl. Belay on. Got your high-speed elevator ride all ready for you."

She twisted away, but not before Devon saw the moisture in her eyes. She rose rapidly, walking her way up the wall as the team lifted her from the depths.

Devon waited for the rope to make its return descent. Plenty of time for guilt to pour in as hard as the water had earlier. Alisha's behavior wasn't something he should have ignored or brushed off. She'd reacted in an unexpected manner. What if it happened again, at an even more risky moment? She'd be a danger to both herself and the team, not to mention the people they might be rescuing.

By keeping her secret, he'd put himself into a compromising position. He could only hope her reasons were something he could live with down the road.

Only feet from the top of the crevasse Anders extended a hand, and she grasped it eagerly. The warmth of his fingers was as welcome as the smile on his face.

"Good grief, what were you two doing down there? Mud wrestling?" Xavier stepped up, dropping a blanket over her shoulders. "Let me untie you."

"Devon?" Alisha twisted toward the cliff lip, but Xavier held her in place.

"Anders will get him. The other SAR team is dealing with the injured, and Paul checked out fine. You're soaked, though, so we need to help you before you have a reaction." Xavier loosened the rope at her waist as the chill in her bones shook her. "Yeah, like that."

"I'm cold." Admitting that was as far as she wanted to go right now.

"Come on, lean on me and I'll get you to your spare gear." Xavier looped an arm around her and guided her toward the chopper.

She hovered between reality and a dream. Fear threat-

ened to overwhelm her as she remembered the water surrounding her and Devon. Then the ensuing adrenaline rush
stopped her from going catatonic again.

She didn't want her breakdown to be revealed, and only
the terror of being discovered would give her enough
strength to get through the next hours without giving herself
away.

"You need me to give you something?" Xavier asked.

The man with the chemicals. God, asking for a sedative
was out of the question, but could she ever use one right
now. That, or a shot of whiskey straight up.

Hmmm. "You got your flask?"

"Shhh." Xavier glanced around sheepishly. "That's
strictly for medicinal purposes."

Her teeth chattered. "I think this counts."

Erin wasn't at the chopper, so Xavier helped her into the
transport area, standing her directly under the heater, which
he cranked to high. "Strip, and I'll get your gear bag from
the back."

She fumbled with the straps on her harness, fighting to
unthread the thick webbing from the metal hoops. Either
the fabric had swollen with the river water or she'd lost more
dexterity than she'd thought, because nothing seemed to be
cooperating.

Familiar hands pushed her fingers away, tugging the harness free far too easily and mocking her. She shivered in
place and refused to look up. She didn't want to see the
accusation in Devon's eyes.

"You need to get changed, too. I can take care of myself,"
Alisha insisted.

"Hush." Devon stripped away the final buckle holding
her harness in place. "We're a team. We help each other as
needed."

God, she was so going to lose it if he kept up being all
supportive and understanding. It was easier when he'd
flashed his disapproval. His anger. Those emotions she could
deal with far better than his disappointment.

She peeked up to make sure they were alone. "I'm sorry."

Devon pulled his sweater over his head and tossed it aside. "Save it for later."

"Just—"

"Later, Alisha, unless you want everyone to know."

Damn, she was out of control. He was right. She pulled off her outer layers, adding them to the pile at their feet. Heat poured from above, but it was another sort of heat that filled her now. No challenge against the cold in her extremities, but washing her face with heat and starting a pulse deep inside.

He was down to bare skin from the waist up, goose bumps on his chest as he rubbed a towel briskly over his torso and head. Alisha couldn't stop staring, fascinated as he left the towel draped over his shoulders and reached for the button at his waist.

Something had to have warned him because he stopped, button open, zipper halfway down. He glanced up and their gazes connected.

Devon swore, then closed the gap between them. She didn't think he was going to do what she wanted, which was press her to the wall and kiss her senseless. Kiss her until all the fear was so far gone that she'd never have to face it again.

No, she didn't think he'd do that, but she'd certainly never imagined he'd grab her shirt and strip it off her.

Alisha crossed her arms over her chest instinctively.

Devon laughed. "No modesty around here. Get out of the rest of your wet things. Xavier will be back in a second with our dry clothes."

"Xavier is back, dry clothes in hand. You two need help?"

"Alisha does," Devon responded before she could issue a denial.

Xavier was by her side in a flash, her spare clothing bag set on the bench. He knelt at her feet, untying laces and pulling her boots and socks from her one foot at a time. "I'm a professional. You can consider me like a doctor. You don't have to be shy."

"You pervert. You just want to see m-m-me naked," Alisha stuttered through chattering teeth.

He lifted his head and waggled his brows.

Good grief. "If I weren't so damn cold I'd d-do a strip-tease f-for you."

"Now that I want to see." Xavier turned her to face the back of the chopper, unhooking her bra and stripping off her pants with barely any effort. He had the blanket around her shoulders without making it apparent he'd seen her naked at all. "But since I'm a gentleman and all, I suggest the next time you want to go swimming you do it in the pool, or wear a wetsuit."

With the cold, soaking clothes removed and the furnace blasting overhead, Alisha at least wasn't getting any colder. "Thanks, Xav."

"No problem."

More voices joined in—Erin at the chopper door, Anders returning to the transport area and tossing up gear bags. He glanced around. "You guys stay here. I can grab the rest of the shit in a couple trips, and we can be headed home."

"I'll join you," Xavier offered. "Well done, everyone. Erin, let Tripp know we can leave within the next thirty."

"Got it."

Through it all Alisha worked slowly. Precisely. Pulling on dry clothing one article at a time. With a towel wrapped around her head she sat in her flight chair and dealt with socks and shoes. Beside her Devon had done the same. Flashes of firm muscles covered without false modesty, but no lingering over more sexual possibilities. The two of them had basically been side by side and naked, but this time he stayed silent, none of the usual teasing that would have accompanied such an event in the past.

Even the heater blasting overhead couldn't stop the shiver that took her.

Devon knelt in front of her. He caught her chin in his firm grasp. He refused to let her look away as he examined her. He checked her eyes, brushed a hand over her forehead.

Alisha met his gaze steadily, the terror that had grasped her gone.

He darted a glance away, but there was no one near to hear.

"Tell me you're okay," he said. "Promise me I don't need to worry about you going into shock on the ride home."

Could she guarantee that? Alisha dug deep and assessed herself as best she could. Fear wouldn't stupefy her anymore, not unless Erin flew them into a lake or something insane. Fear of her team finding out she'd panicked—that would keep her from saying anything reckless.

"I'm really cold right now. That's all."

"Me, too. We should probably share body heat. That would be the most effective cure, you know."

Her tongue wasn't working—whether he'd intended it or not, his words were an effective distraction. The wink he gave her a second before rising to grab blankets from the storage cupboard made her heart skip.

That was when she spotted Anders in the doorway, him and Xavier back with the rest of the gear.

So that was how they were going to play it. "Yeah, right. You're as cold as I am. No way am I cuddling with you. Xavier now, I bet he knows how to warm a girl."

Anders tossed bags into position and hooked up webbing to hold them in place during the flight. Up front Erin had the blades turning, preparations begun for taking them skyward. "You two never stop bickering. Think the noise alone would be enough to warm you."

"Hey, I have no objections to offering my body. Willing sacrifice and all." Xavier grinned at her.

"Oh, good," Devon cut in, patting his lap. "I'm cold, too, Xav. Come cuddle *me*."

Xavier blew a raspberry, and suddenly the team made it all very normal and ordinary. Xavier helped her strap in, rubbing her fingers momentarily in his palms before piling blankets on both her and Devon. For the entire journey home they were teased about going for a swim.

Chatting about the rescue—typical return stuff that distracted her.

Except that every time she met Devon's gaze there was a question there she knew she'd have to answer.

And how to answer? The trip home wasn't long enough to figure out a solution.

CHAPTER 5

'''''''''''''''''''''''''''''''

Marcus was waiting at headquarters to debrief them. Usually this part of the process excited Devon—a way to celebrate their victories and learn for the future.

Today he'd had enough. He was cold to the bone, even after a shower at HQ, but worse was the guilt at keeping silent regarding Alisha's strange behavior. Keeping up the façade of lighthearted bantering they were known for, and accepting taunts in return, was pushing him to his limit.

He wanted answers, dammit, and now.

It seemed like hours later they were finally headed out of the building, with orders shouted after them to get a load of calories and a good sleep.

"Next time I'll pack flippers for you," Xavier teased, the door closing on his words.

Yeah, yeah. Devon caught Alisha by the elbow as she attempted to sprint away.

"My place or yours?" God, he'd wanted to ask her that before, for far better reasons than the current ones. What a fucked-up situation.

She paused. "Now?"

"Now."

Alisha nodded slowly. "I have a lasagna in the freezer. We can eat. Follow the boss's orders regarding carb loading."

He wanted to say he wasn't interested in food, but his stomach gave up that lie too easily. "I can't beat that."

She snorted, and he had to join in, their history of never-ending contests raising its head again.

Within minutes they were at her place and up the stairs. She cleared her throat, flushing a little. "Lasagna is in the freezer, if you want to get it in the microwave. I'll deal with my wet stuff."

Retreat, obviously, but Devon let her go, struggling not to stare at her ass as she walked away. He'd done it so often over the years it was now instinctual. The time apart wasn't a bad thing—it gave him a few minutes to cool off further before he gave in and simply shouted at her, which would get them absolutely nowhere fast.

He got the food heating and dug into her fridge for something green to accompany it. Normal, everyday things, made all the weirder by the fact it was her apartment and they were about to have some kind of *come to Jesus* discussion.

All of it was so fucked up, he didn't even know where to start.

She was back before he'd managed to calm himself, but also before he'd worked himself into more of a frenzy. The normally confident woman he'd worked with for many years stood in the doorway of the tiny kitchen, twisting her fingers together.

"You want to talk?"

He followed her into the living room and took the easy chair. Not looming over her was the only concession he could make, his annoyance wanting to push her hard.

Alisha continued to pace. "I'm sorry."

He shook his head. "We're way past sorry. I've now

compromised my job by not telling the team that you freaked. What the hell happened back there?"

Her fingers had gone white-knuckled, she was squeezing them so tight. "I don't know. I've never . . ."

Devon bit back the urge to growl. "Dammit, Alisha, we've known each other for four years, and I've never seen you cringe away from anything. You were scared fucking shitless, weren't you?"

A crease formed between her brows. "Stop swearing at me. This isn't easy to figure out."

Oh hell, no. "It's not going to be easy to tell Marcus I fucked up and didn't report you, but if I have to, I bloody well will—"

"Yes, I was afraid," she shouted, cutting him off. She wrapped her arms around her torso as if putting up a barrier between them. Blocking herself off. "When the water hit, it was as if I weren't there anymore. I panicked, but it was only for a moment. I got over it, Devon. You can't tell me being plunged into a subterranean river is a normal, every-day experience. Not even for us with our record of twisted rescues."

A shiver rolled over her hard enough that he saw it. He was on his feet in a flash, stepping in closer. She lifted her gaze to his, sheer misery in the depths.

He didn't know if he should hug her or shake some sense into her. "You panicked. While you did snap out of it, we work in search and rescue. Don't you think this might be a bit of a problem?"

Her pause answered that, a second before she straightened and pulled on bluster like a coat of armour. "We work in the high Rockies. We climb and hike, and in the winter we ski. I've never had a lick of trouble in those settings. So, no, I don't think it will be a problem again."

"You don't think—God*dammit*, Alisha. That about sums it up. You're *not* thinking. At any time we could be called to do a water rescue. What will you do then? Put up your hand and ask to be excused? When people's lives are on the line? Hell, when your *teammates'* lives could be on the line?"

"I can get through it," she insisted. "I just . . . today was all kinds of wrong. That wasn't a normal situation, Devon, and don't tell me it was. We've done water rescues before, like that rescue at the falls last year—I didn't freak out then, did I?"

Frustration and fury mixed like a horrid poison in his veins. The fact that she had managed the rescue she'd mentioned calmed him slightly. "Fine, so you're not going to kill us all the first chance you get. You're still a walking time bomb."

She reached for him, laying a hand on his arm where he'd crossed them over his chest. "Then give me time to prove I can deal with this. You can't tell anyone on the team."

Devon tore himself from her, dragging a hand through his hair. "You don't ask for much, do you?"

"Please, Devon."

Shit. He confronted her again. "We're taking over coastal rescues. How the hell will you cope with that?"

Her hands balled into fists. "What part of *Let me prove myself* do you not understand? You don't have to worry about it anymore."

He laughed. "Right. Bullshit on that." Spots of colour returned to her cheeks. It didn't make her look happier, though, not with that death glare she directed his way. "Look. Your problem is now my problem. When I skipped out on telling the team how you went unresponsive in the cavern, I *made* myself have to worry. Which means either I go tell Marcus what happened and hope he doesn't fire us like he should, or I keep worrying alongside you."

"Telling Marcus doesn't do either of us any good at this point." She spoke softly this time, body still rigid but the fight fading from her eyes. "I don't want to give up my position with Lifeline, but I'm not stupid, Devon. If it turns out I've got a major problem I will be the first to admit it."

They stared at each other for a moment, Devon mentally sifting through all sorts of catastrophes that could come crashing down on them at any time. Tension was more than a wall between them; it was a living thing. Swirling like a wind in the room, chasing away the physical attraction he'd been fighting until all that remained was them. Two people, one huge disaster to deal with.

The beeper on the microwave went off, and they both jerked in surprise. Devon laughed in spite of the tension. "Ten more minutes."

She nodded, collapsing onto the couch and burrowing her head in her hands. When she spoke it was toward the floor. "I mucked up hugely."

"Hey, I'm not even going to argue with you on that one."

She snorted. "Great. We're finally in agreement about something. I'm an idiot."

Devon paced over, looking down as she leaned on the sofa. He took in the utter misery in her expression, the defeat in her body language. This wasn't the overconfident cocky woman who'd been driving him crazy for years. This was someone on the edge of breaking.

"Dammit, Alisha. I want to stay pissed off, but I can't." He joined her on the couch, figuring that looming over her wasn't helping matters. She had screwed up, but if they were going by protocol, so had he. "We're now officially in this together."

"Sorry for dragging you into it. I never intended to make life miserable for anyone."

"It . . . was an accident." He caved that far. She was right; the situation had been over the top and incredible. And her willingness to take responsibility meant a lot. It was also typical—she never gave herself a break. *That* Alisha he was familiar with even if the package was usually tied up tighter in cocky arrogance. "Okay, we've established what happened. What are we going to do about it?"

"You're not telling Marcus?"

He shook his head. "Not this instant. If we can come up with a way to test your boundaries that doesn't endanger you, me, or the team, we'll be okay. But if we can't, then I expect you to tell him yourself."

|||||||||||||||||

The bitter taint of disappointment stroked the back of her tongue. He was right, of course, in insisting she be the one to confess, but considering it made her nearly as ill as the idea of being crushed again by the river . . .

Devon caught her wrist, taking a firm grasp. She didn't bother to ask the question forming on her lips when she noticed he was eyeing his watch.

Taking her pulse. He'd probably check her pupils next. "There's nothing physically wrong with me, Devon. I had a panic attack."

"Humour me," he drawled. "You were there and then you were gone, and since we didn't let Xavier know anything happened, I'm your medic for the next few hours."

Alisha snapped her lips together to hold in the protest, because again, he was right. "Ways to test my boundaries? Can you think of any?"

Devon fell silent as he pulled out a Leatherman with a light attachment. Sure enough, he checked her pupils. "Have you had inklings of panic like this before? Do you have any specific triggers? I mean, you did manage the rescue by the falls."

She thought back. "I didn't have issues. Not then, or when we were by the Bow River. Today was a freak event."

"Maybe, but we need to logically eliminate what we can. I know you haven't had trouble with water before, but we could start at the simplest situation and work through them one at a time."

Alisha refrained from rolling her eyes. "You want me to hit the swimming pool to prove I'm not afraid of water?"

Devon nodded. "Hey, it's a place to start. We'll hit the pool, do a few laps, try a few rescues. You know the drills— you did all the same training at school I did. Well, you weren't nearly as fast as I was, but still."

His momentary attempt at lighthearted humour was appreciated but also put her back up. "I wasn't an ex-swimmer jock. I came far closer to kicking your ass than I should have a lot of the time."

Devon shook his head as he gently ran his fingers through her hair. "In your dreams, girl. In your dreams."

His skilled examination was over quickly, but the sensation of his hands on her scalp and neck lingered far too long. She didn't want to talk about the things that had been invading her dreams, since most of them involved him. "Fine. We can hit the pool. And then are we going to jump in a lake? Dive into a waterfall?"

"You have told me to go jump in a lake a few times." He flashed his grin, the high-voltage one that should come with a warning label. "Now I get to return the favour."

She rose from the couch, escaping because the heat from his body was far too distracting. "I don't want to quit the team. Maybe that's selfish, or stupid, but it's a reality. I've worked so damn hard to prove I can do this, that to have my career ripped away is . . . wrong."

"Your career is not over." Devon was on his feet. "But psychoses can be a bitch. So you need to trust me. Let's deal with this and then we can get back to happily working for Lifeline for years to come."

Alisha stared past him out the window as his words shot another blade into her. Frustration at her current dilemma and fear of her long-term predicament blended into an impassable morass.

The microwave buzzer went off, and Devon stepped around her without a word. He moved through her small kitchen area with a confident stride, filling two plates high.

Usually that was her. Full of confidence in herself. In her abilities.

Now? Having to prove she wasn't one step away from a panic attack was more than annoying—it made her want to scream.

He was back too quickly, pushing her toward the couch. "You're upset, and I'm starving. Eat, and after we'll come up with some other solutions."

She took the plate with fingers that had gone numb. "Right. You're right."

He laughed. "See, if you'd simply acknowledged that sooner, we'd have gotten a lot further in this conversation already."

Devon rested his plate on the couch arm, then ignored her and strode toward the television. He grabbed a DVD and had it playing within moments, the volume turned up loud as James Bond filled the screen.

Even with the confusion in her brain, her body had no trouble telling her what she wanted—starting with the food he'd served. Between the demands of the rescue and the adrenaline overload and its lasting effect, she was ravenous. Devon ignored her, settling on the couch and diving into his meal. The wild action of the movie was distracting enough that all she saw was her plate and the screen.

Until the one urge was satisfied. With the hunger in her belly sated, it was harder than before to ignore that Devon was in her apartment. No matter that he'd come over to give her hell, he was still there. He wasn't going to tell Marcus about her issue.

He wanted to help her.

For years she'd fought her attraction to him, but today, she wondered how many of her reasons for avoiding him had been valid. The actions he'd taken so far today weren't those of a mindless, inconsiderate playboy.

She put her plate on the coffee table and snagged the blanket from the back of the couch, draping it over herself. Devon rose and refilled his plate.

She turned down his offer for more food. "I'm full."

Full and getting sleepy as she finally relaxed off the rush that had flooded her system. She was going to crash hard in a bit.

Without a word Devon dropped beside her.

It was crazy. The heat in her body rose as the food fueled her and the blanket trapped it in. She caught her eyes closing a few times as she fought to stay awake.

Watching the movie caused problems of other sorts as a

love scene filled the screen. She hadn't thought it possible to become even more aware of Devon at her side.

In her peripheral vision his hands were far too noticeable as he placed his plate next to hers. His strong fingers and muscular forearms. She could picture him touching her, running his fingers over her body with the same confidence with which he seemed to do everything.

Alisha jerked herself upright, blinking to change the mental paths she'd started down. She tucked the blanket around her shoulders and faced him straight on. "Sorry, I'm nearly falling asleep and that doesn't help matters."

He examined her again, an intense gaze that seemed to dive into her soul. "One step at a time, Alisha. This isn't a moment we need to rush into anything."

Patience. The first of the team rules. "Right. You're right."

He laughed, following her into the kitchen with the dirty dishes. "I'm going to assume you have a concussion, or are seriously injured, if you keep agreeing with me so easily."

She pushed him from the room. "I'll deal with those later. I should let you go."

"Still waiting to hear if you think you have any triggers that caused your attack in the first place," Devon reminded her. "You were fine during our years at Banff Search and Rescue. I seem to remember doing open-water training a few times, and you never had any issues."

They'd gone over this. "I don't know of any. I mean, when I was little I had nightmares about the dark, but that's kid stuff."

He paced away, over to the window, and stared out for a while. When he turned he looked more impressed than pissed off. "Well, it was dark down there."

She nodded.

"Are you afraid of the dark now?"

A shrug was her only possible response. "No more than the average person. If I hear strange noises at night, sure, but otherwise, it's not as if I sleep with a night light or anything."

"Maybe this isn't as big a deal as we think."

Now that was an unexpected outlook. Alisha moved closer. "Really?"

He held up a hand. "Now, I'm not saying you're scot-free, or that I'm not still pissed off as hell, but there was a lot going on today. Maybe it was a bad combination."

"I don't think—"

He laughed. "How come all of a sudden I'm the one reassuring you everything will be fine? Today was enough to freak anyone out, Alisha."

She stood motionless, now shocked for new reasons. "I am surprised. I thought for sure I'd have to tie you up and hide you in the attic crawl space so I could keep my job."

He raised a brow. "Tying me up? We are getting somewhere. You never told me you had those kinds of fantasies. I would have loved to know that sooner."

Her mouth went absolutely dry, not only because he'd gone there, but because the idea of tying him up and getting to take advantage of him was a hot dream she'd partially had once.

Devon hooted with laughter. "God, you should see your face. No, Alisha, I'm not really propositioning you. At least not right now. You're dead on your feet, and I'm still cold from the rescue. I'll save the seduction for later."

He didn't seem to think she was psychotic anymore. She could tell by the way he was back to his normal, flirtatious self. "You're being way too reasonable."

"I now have food in my stomach. Does wonders for the average male."

She had to smile. "We'll play Test Alisha's Limits tomorrow?"

"Sure thing." He paced across the room, and suddenly she was wrapped in a firm hug. Nothing sexual or demanding, just a forceful, breath-squeezing embrace that he ended within a couple of seconds when there was a loud knock on her door. He grinned as he stepped back. "I'll sneak out of your way for a minute."

He ducked into the kitchen. Alisha stood for a moment,

amazed at the turn of events. Things were going to work out fine. Miracle of miracles.

She peered around the edge of the door before opening it. The glass she held in her hands fell unminded to the floor. The plastic bounced once and rolled toward the kitchen, but she ignored it, far more disturbed by the man standing on the stoop.

So much for her day taking a turn for the better.

CHAPTER 6

,,,,,,,,,,,,,,,,,,,,,,,,,,,,,,,,,

It wasn't proper to eavesdrop, but Devon didn't care about niceties at the moment. Her gasp of surprise had stopped him at the kitchen door and swung him into the small entrance to stand at her side.

"Problem? You got a collection agency tracking you down or something?"

"I wish," she muttered. "Just, don't be rude to him. But don't be too nice, either, okay?"

What the hell kind of comment was that? Curiosity rose in a flash, but he stepped back as she swung the door open to reveal a dark-haired businessman in an outfit that probably cost as much as Devon's truck. Maybe midthirties, the stranger smiled at Alisha and reached to give her a hug, pulling to a stop when he noticed Devon.

"Vincent. What are you doing here?" The genuine shock in her voice matched the shock on the man's face at seeing Devon standing next to her.

The devil on his shoulder made him move in a tiny bit closer, just to jerk the guy's chain, whoever he was.

Vincent dragged his attention back to Alisha and adjusted his expression, but it was too late for any of them to not have noticed his astonishment. "Hello, sweetheart. I came to surprise you."

Sweetheart? Fuck. Devon backed out of the way as Vincent strode forward.

"Well, I'm surprised. Very," Alisha admitted. "You didn't think you should call, or let me know you were in town?"

"That's what a surprise usually means." Vincent loosened off his jacket, turning to take in Devon. "And you are?"

"I work with Devon," Alisha cut in, slipping between them and tugging Vincent toward the living space. "We did a rescue this morning and needed to grab some food to refuel. He was just leaving."

Oh, *really*? Devon didn't remember that part of the conversation. "I don't mind staying." He extended his hand toward the other man, waiting to see what response he'd get. "Devon Leblanc. And you are Vincent . . . ?"

From that little *sweetheart* comment, this wasn't an insurance adjuster for Alisha, or something.

"Vincent Monreal. Old friend of the family."

Alisha cringed, her face tight in a grimace. *Aha*, someone who actually knew the elusive Bailey family? Wild horses couldn't drag Devon away now. Not to mention there was unfinished business between him and Alisha. They had to spend time together to check that she was clear for duty, and he wanted the first time slot nailed in place before he left.

"Can I get you anything, Vincent? A drink, something to eat?" Maybe it was out of line, but Vincent pushed all his buttons. Acting as if he knew his way around Alisha's place a hell of a lot better than he did seemed the right thing to do.

Alisha gave him a dirty look behind Vincent's back and tilted her head toward the door. "Devon, you should go. I'll call you later to go over . . . the training schedule."

Good try. He got ready to argue—nicely, of course— when Alisha's expression switched to pleading.

Damn it all.

Fine, he wouldn't stick around when she obviously

wanted to be alone with *Vincent*. "Don't forget we have a session first thing in the morning."

They didn't, but this Vincent dude didn't know it, and like hell would Devon let the situation drag on even if Alisha now had a guy in the picture. Or in the picture for the first time ever, as far as he knew.

She picked up on his clues and nodded. "At the pool, right?"

Vincent watched them like a hawk, his coat now draped over a chair back and his suit jacket undone.

The man was wearing a goddamn suit and tie in Banff, for fuck's sake.

Devon had no idea why he was sticking around. Anger and frustration made him lash out the only way he could think of on the spur of the moment. If she'd planned on a lovely relaxing morning sleep-in with Mr. Suit, forget it.

"Yes, the pool. Six A.M." He ignored the flash of dismay in her eyes and turned to give Vincent a quick send-off, grabbing a business card from his pocket. "Vince. Nice to meet you. Let me know if you need a guide while you're in town."

"Devon," Vincent intoned, a hint of amusement in his voice. "I'll give you a call."

Devon grabbed his coat from the hook on the wall but didn't bother to put it on as he escaped down the stairs. His irritation only grew when he spotted the shiny rental Ferrari parked behind his junker.

Figures. Right when he finally got a break on getting to know Alisha better, it was probably too late. First time he'd ever been in her apartment, even if it was for a sucky reason, and she'd shoved him out the door as soon as some rich visitor from out of town called her *sweetheart*.

Devon kicked the tire of his truck before throwing his bag into the back and crawling into the cab. There was only one way to deal with frustration like this. He ignored the turn toward his house and headed to the gym. Lifeline wouldn't get called out on another rescue for at least a day.

One more bout of pain would be a good way to exhaust himself before he figured out exactly how to deal with the evasive Miss Bailey.

Alisha stood to one side, fighting to calm herself and not jump to conclusions.

The apartment seemed smaller than ever as Vincent paced through the living room, his dark head inclined slightly as he paused to stare out the window. It had been years since she'd seen him last, but he hadn't changed a bit. She wasn't a young, fascinated child anymore, but even as an adult she had to admit the aura of power that had always clung to him was still there.

"Vincent. You have surprised me. Bailey Enterprises has business in Banff?"

His smile made him even more handsome. "Some business, but more importantly, I wanted to say hello. It's been too long."

"Two Christmases ago, I think." Alisha had no doubts about the timing. She'd taken a rare trip back to Toronto and spent the entire visit avoiding the attempts from her parents to set her up with Vincent.

She wasn't interested, not then, not now, but as long as he didn't try to act on her parents' behalf and force the other issue regarding their supposed *deadline*, she could be polite.

He glanced around the small apartment, then cleared his throat. "It's . . . homey."

"It's more than enough room for me," she stated plainly.

"For now, I suppose. You'll find something bigger when you return to Toronto." He pulled out a chair and sat gingerly, as if he'd get cooties from her thrift shop furniture.

"My job is based in Banff. Kind of hard to live in Toronto and commute all the way across the country for rescue calls."

"Right." Vincent tapped the chair next to him. "Sit."

She was about to fall asleep on her feet. She wasn't

looking for a long conversation. "I'm actually really tired right now, Vincent. If you'd like to get together in a couple days, I can—"

"Sit." The word snapped out, before he coughed and spoke softer. "Please."

Alisha edged the chair out and farther away before she lowered herself into it, uneasy at his strange behavior.

He smiled again, leaning back in his chair and looking her over carefully. "I'm impressed, you know, that you haven't come running home sooner."

A flash of anger hit, and she lowered her eyes to the table to hide it. "I'm good at what I do, and I enjoy my job."

"Your father insists it's a hobby. A whim. Something you're doing to get it out of your system before you return to where you belong."

Oh God, she could as good as hear her father say the words. She lifted her head and forced herself to look Vincent in the eyes. "That's his opinion, but I don't agree. Did you come all the way from Toronto just to upset me?"

He reached for her hand, capturing her before she could safely pull out of reach. He nodded slowly. "You're right. I started all wrong. Causing you distress wasn't my intention. I'm interested in what you're doing here. And I've missed you."

Okay. That one was off in a new direction. "There's nothing to miss, Vincent."

"There should be." He stroked his thumb over the back of her hand and hummed gently. "You're so soft considering what you do for a living."

"I'm not made of iron. I'm trained to deal with situations." She tried to free her hand, and he let her go. Alisha took advantage of the opportunity and stepped away from the table under the guise of being hospitable. "Can I get you a drink?"

"Please. Just water."

Vincent rose and paced her apartment while she ducked into her kitchen and found him an actual *glass* glass and ice cubes.

Because *just water* meant something far different to Vincent than when Devon said it, and she knew it.

She paused in the door of the kitchen area, resting her head on the door frame as she looked around for him. Vincent had vanished—she could only wish it had been out the main door to leave her in peace. She didn't have much more to give today, not between the rescue and the shock and Devon and . . .

Alisha dragged in a deep breath and fought for control. Maybe she shouldn't have chased Devon out so quickly, but old habits of keeping secrets were hard to break.

When Vincent didn't reappear, Alisha stepped cautiously down the short hall, disturbed to discover him in her bedroom. "I have your water in the living room."

He turned from the window and nodded, stepping past her without pausing, brushing close enough their bodies touched.

She stared at the street and dug deep for the strength to deal with this. Deal until he left, and she could finally collapse.

He smiled as she joined him, his long fingers lingering on the glass as he lowered it. His neatly trimmed nails made her remember more clearly Devon's sturdy hands. The hands that had held her safely that morning, and so many times over the past years. While getting involved with Devon might have been crossed off her list for many good reasons in the past, she'd take him in a flash over Vincent, no matter how debonair and smooth the man appeared.

Devon loved the mountains. Loved excitement. He understood what made her blood thrill in a way Vincent never would.

She swayed on her feet as exhaustion rolled over her hard.

Vincent caught her around the waist. "You said you did a rescue this morning?"

Embarrassment rushed her as she stepped away, dragging her hands through her hair and fighting to stop from yawning. She wanted to present a strong, competent woman, not someone ready to fall over in a faint. "Got called out at five A.M., so I'm ready to crash."

"Then I won't keep you." He picked up his suit jacket and slipped it on. "Get some rest, and I'll take you to dinner later. We can get caught up then."

Probably needed to bring up the deadline her father had set. Convince her it was time to come home and be a dutiful daughter. "I really don't feel like going out tonight, Vincent."

He smiled indulgently. "Of course. I'm staying at the Banff Springs Hotel. Room twelve fifty-three. If you change your mind, please call. Otherwise, we'll make it tomorrow."

Drat, a one-day delay only. "Are you in town for long?"

"As long as it takes." He straightened his collar, checking his hair in the mirror by the front door.

She didn't want to know what that meant. She really didn't. Silence seemed the wisest thing as he strolled past her, again closer than he needed to be.

Vincent turned in the doorway. He stroked his fingers over her jaw, his gaze playing over her face. "You need sleep. You've got bags under your eyes."

A snort of laughter escaped before she could stop it. *Charming.* "It's been a long day."

He leaned in, and she twisted to the side so his lips landed on her cheek instead of her mouth. Cool, not warm. Nothing flaring between them to make her want to have his attentions on her, no matter that she'd dreamed about him in the past.

The current reality had nothing that made her want to explore more.

He stepped down the stairs and she closed the door. Locked the knob *and* the deadbolt, and then chastised herself for being an idiot. She was the one who'd opened the door in the first place.

Twit.

Her limbs quivered as she attempted to keep vertical. Alisha barely made it down the hall to her room, using the walls to guide her. She pulled off her clothes and crawled under the covers, praying that the physical overload would overwhelm the mental stress and allow her a few hours of oblivion before she had to wake and deal with the crap that had landed on her plate.

It wasn't the rush of water that filled her mind, though, or Vincent's unreadable expression. Thankfully, and hauntingly, it was Devon she saw as she fell asleep. The concern and caring in his eyes, the protective embrace as he clutched her to the wall.

The world might be shaking around her, but she wasn't completely alone. Even if Devon was pissed off, he had her back.

Teamwork. What they'd trained into their very hearts and souls, and as fingers of unconsciousness wrapped around her, it was Devon's blue eyes she thought of.

CHAPTER 7

||||||||||||||||||||||||||||

Dropping off to sleep at four P.M. meant she was wide awake plenty early enough to have to decide. Did she follow Devon's orders and show up at the swimming pool?

If she'd slept through she'd have felt no guilt in skipping out, but now it would be a deliberate choice, and Alisha couldn't bring herself to do that. He'd given her a break the previous day—a huge, life-changing break. He deserved a little leeway.

Still, gathering her gear together had more of a funereal sensation than the usual buzz of anticipation that came before a workout. Normally a kind of dread and desire hung over her, knowing that once she got moving the endorphins would wash through and chase away some of her blues.

Devon hadn't specifically said which pool to meet him at, so she took a chance and headed to the one at the Banff SAR school. The parking lot was fairly full, reminding her that a new class of students had recently entered their first semester of training. Sure enough, as she pushed through the glass doors into the moist air of the pool setting, the sounds of splashing, whistles, and loud shouts carried on the warm air.

Warmth—another reason the pool was so much better than open water.

Approaching the observation area took willpower. A mental bracing she'd begun as soon as she crawled out of bed. Bright overhead fluorescent lighting made the tiles underfoot shine brilliant blue and white, the morning sun only beginning to peek through the tall windows. The bleachers along the side of the pool were empty except for one broad-shouldered individual who kept his gaze fixed on the bodies splashing in the water.

Alisha walked slowly toward him, examining his face—the firm line of his jaw and his tousled blond hair. He probably hadn't done more than drag a hand through it, and he still looked good enough for a photo op. The light scruff on his chin made her itch to rub herself against it—

And this had to stop. As lovely and distracting as it was, now even more than before she needed to keep Devon in the right place in her mind. That he was willing to help her was fabulous.

She wasn't about to crawl into his bed, especially if Lana had recently been in it.

A shrill cry rang out and she turned in time to duck a splash of water flaring from the pool into the spectator area. The student who'd caused it resurfaced, his smile shining as he waved at them.

Alisha laughed, and lowered herself next to Devon. "Becki's little brother, right?"

Devon nodded. "Colin seems to be having fun."

"What are they up to?" Alisha glanced down the deck, checking for the instructor. The same man who'd put them through their paces years earlier still held sway over the water training.

Devon pointed around the pool. "Looks like stations. Some workouts, some rescue simulations. Coach Williams doesn't believe in much variety."

"If it's not broken, why fix it?" Alisha repeated solemnly.

He laughed. "God, how many times did we hear *that* over the years?"

They sat and watched for a few minutes, the familiar routine calming the nerves she'd developed walking through the doors. "We'll have to wait until they're done for our training."

Devon twisted to face her, his gaze serious as he evaluated. "Let's talk about that. You're here, which first off, I'm impressed. I didn't know if you would show."

"You told me to," she pointed out.

"Well, you had a hot date and all, I didn't know if—"

Whoa, that one was stopping right here. "No. No hot date. I crashed yesterday, and hard. Vincent is not a date, in any shape or form, so forget that nonsense."

Devon stared. Alisha wiggled.

"He's not a date," she insisted.

Devon shrugged. "I don't care if he is or he isn't. I'm saying you're here now, and that's good. You comfortable?"

Alisha ignored the comments about Vincent and considered how she felt. "I feel some stress because I'm being judged by you. It's a pool, Devon. I'm not afraid."

"So being in the proximity is fine? Take your time, think it through. If you want to strip and meditate for a bit, I won't complain."

"God, you are so annoying." She stared at the water, the gentle waves on the surface flashing in the increasing sunlight. "Nothing. It's a fucking pool."

"Sounds good to me."

Alisha had to pause for a moment to think about what she'd said, then swung her gym bag at him as he laughed. "Try really hard to get your dick under control, even though I know it's the larger of your two brains."

Devon faced the water. "Well, we're here. We may as well make it worth our while. Just to be sure." He faced her. "I thought about it more last night, and I want to make it clear what we'll do if something big comes up before we're sure you're a hundred percent. If we get a coastal call before then, I mean."

"There's not much odds of that situation arising, is there?" Alisha hated the note of begging in her voice. She cleared her throat, and spoke quieter, even though there was no way they could be overheard with the bedlam rising from the class. The students had switched exercises and were now egging each other on through an obstacle course around the pool. "Marcus said we'll extend our territory, but chances are low we'll get called out anytime soon, and even if we did, I can beg off the first situation without anyone crying foul."

Devon sighed. "So you've got a bit of leeway. But, Alisha?" He turned his blue gaze on her and she was mesmerized, like a deer caught in the headlights. "If you have to call off a rescue, that's it. That's your last chance. If we're not both confident you're safe, promise me you'll give notice. I won't demand you tell Marcus why—you could give any excuse you want so you could eventually get back into SAR, but that seems to be the only logical solution."

She swallowed around the lump in her throat. "You're right—"

His instant grin made her roll her eyes, and the awkward tension faded, to be replaced with the unending pull of competition and attraction rampant between them.

"Yeah, yeah. Laugh it up, but I mean it. I submit to your master plan—I hadn't thought it through that far, but your strategy makes sense. Only, I *am* completely fine, Devon. I won't have to quit."

"Hmm, now that sounds like the Alisha I know and love to beat at any and all challenges." He flashed his smile again, then jerked his thumb over his shoulder toward the pool. "Ten bucks says I can finish the obstacle course they're doing faster than you can."

Nice.

She faced the water. The screaming had gotten louder in the past few minutes as they talked, the last of the swimmers working through the course with their entire teams egging them on. She glanced through the challenges.

He raised a brow. "What's it going to be? You calling it quits and buying me lunch straight off?"

"Bullshit." The instant response to Devon's challenge came from a deeper place in her gut than she could stop.

Uncertainty had been her companion for a day. Her need to be the best had been in place a lot longer than that.

Devon rose and grabbed his gym bag. "Then I'll meet you on deck. I'll let Coach Williams know we want the course left out once the class is done."

Alisha nodded and followed him, breaking off to one side to hit the women's change room.

She was interrupted before she could clear the deck. Colin came running toward her, water dripping from his body. "Alisha. Good to see you."

She returned his smile, then deepened her voice. "Hey, no running. You want to slip and crack your skull?"

They both laughed, glancing guiltily toward where Coach Williams and Devon were talking. Colin wiped the water from his shoulders with the towel in his hand. "You training this morning?"

She nodded. "Once you guys are done. Are you enjoying your classes?"

Colin shrugged. "First weeks are slow. Lots of review since I took summer school, but once the rest of the group gets caught up . . . What am I saying? They'll never catch up to me."

He winked, and it was easy to see the family connection between him and Marcus's partner. "You are just like your sister."

Colin made a face. "Well, she can climb and all, but hell, I'm not old and—"

"Yes? Old and *what*?"

Becki stood a few feet behind them, clipboard nestled in her folded arms as she gave her younger brother a dirty look.

Colin didn't even blink. "Old and slow."

Alisha covered her mouth to hide her grin.

Brother and sister glared at each other for a moment before Becki ignored Colin and looked over at Alisha. "Hey, you. Heard you did an awesome job yesterday."

Alisha forced a smile. She had done well in rescuing Paul, that much was true. "Marcus has a good team. And you trained us as well."

"That must have been before I got old and slow."

A laugh escaped. "I don't think either word can be applied to you."

The students were streaming off the deck, curious glances directed their way as most of them left, whispers rising as they caught the identity of Alisha and Devon, who'd finally rejoined them.

"Coach Williams said no problem. He's using the course for another class this afternoon, so he was leaving it set up anyway. It's all ours."

"You're running the obstacle course?" Colin asked, his grin spreading wider. Alisha saw it coming from a mile away, but there was no way to stop it. With the bravado of youth and the familiarity of family, Colin poked his sister in the arm. "Bet you I can do the course faster than you."

It was in their blood. The need for competition. The urge to be the best.

Becki adjusted her clipboard to place her fists on her hips. "You and what army?"

"Boys against the girls?" Devon suggested.

Colin's face lit up. "Seriously? Dude—*yes*."

God.

Becki turned to the change room. "Fine. Just means you get to be defeated by your sister. Again, I might add."

"Damn." Colin muttered it under his breath before smiling at Devon. "So, gonna help me take revenge for the last few times she's beat me?"

Devon frowned. "How many times have you challenged her and lost?"

Colin shuffled his feet. "Five."

"Shit."

Becki called from the change room door. "Five times in the last *week*. Come on, Alisha, let's plan our strategy."

It was tough to remain nervous in the midst of this kind

of energy and enthusiasm. Alisha cast one last glance over her shoulder, noting Devon had watched her the entire way off the deck.

He was no expert in dealing with fear, but as far as he could tell, Alisha was fine. Nothing had triggered her. In fact, she'd laughed more than a dozen times in the past few minutes as she and Becki taunted Colin and they all prepared to run the gauntlet.

She'd told him the pool wasn't an issue. Wild anticipation and the drive to excel were the only emotions visible on her face. Reassured that Alisha was in control, Devon was able to concentrate on another important item.

Winning.

Lunch was on the line. He'd ignore the part of himself that dryly noted he won no matter what because he'd get to be with Alisha, no matter what.

Vincent wasn't a romantic interest? Good to know that on her side. She might not be aware the guy had other ideas, but it was obvious to another man. It was time for more than testing her nerve. Devon had had enough waiting—it was time to test their sexual chemistry as well.

He pushed those thoughts aside and focused on the course. "We running one after another for total time elapsed?"

Becki straightened the edges of her bathing cap. "I propose a free-for-all. Since teamwork is supposed to be what we're good at."

"So you and Alisha do the course simultaneously, and we compare your time with ours?" Colin asked.

Becki shook out her arms. "Hell no, little boy. That's not nearly exciting enough. I mean we all leave together, and see which two make it to the other end first."

Alisha adjusted her goggles. "Sounds good to me. Ready? Go."

The women must have discussed this in the change room, because Alisha took off with a shallow dive as Becki stepped closer to her brother and hip-checked him. Colin floundered for a moment, arms flailing in circles before gravity won and pulled him into the shallow end with an enormous splash.

Becki flashed Devon a cheeky grin before following Alisha, the surge of the dive propelling her far ahead of her brother.

The family competitiveness between them might be worse than what he and Alisha had going.

He checked that Colin was okay before following the women's example and springing outward, cutting through the water like a knife blade. The cool water wrapped around him, a blanket supporting him as his head broke the surface, and he took a breath, glancing to see where his opponents were.

Colin would have to catch up when he could. Right now? Devon needed to cause some interference or the race would be over before they'd begun.

The first challenge was directly ahead. A mesh net they'd climb up and over. In most climbing challenges he should have had an advantage with typical superior male upper body strength. Only there was nothing typical about Alisha or Becki. They were already more than halfway up the wide net, Alisha not even bothering to place her feet on the ropes. She flowed upward like a helium balloon rising on a windless day, Becki to her right moving slower, but still increasing the distance. He reached the bottom of the net and gave it a sharp tug, shaking it violently.

The women laughed.

"Nice try, Devon, but we're not rookies." Alisha swung herself over the top and began the journey down the other side. Simply dropping was an option, but more dangerous, with the possibly of getting limbs tangled in the net.

Devon swarmed upward, slowly cutting the distance between himself and Becki. Colin finally hit the station, the net swinging extra hard now that there were four of them on it at the same time. Devon took a firm grip, then reached down to his partner. "Give me your hand," he ordered Colin.

The young man clasped his fingers around Devon's wrist and they both pulled, Colin flying up the distance quicker than he could have on his own.

"Nice one. Thanks." They were over the top and headed down, Alisha already in the water headed toward second station, Becki on her heels.

Like some weird *Wipeout* setup, Coach Williams had found rollers. From one platform to the next, the only way across was via narrow, padded rollers. Devon planted his hands on the platform and pushed himself up to standing as Alisha reached the three-quarter point of her roller.

It might be evil, but it was a contest. He sprang forward and stepped on the surface, shoving the roller to the right and spinning it. Alisha struggled to keep her balance, then lost the fight, toppling to the side with a wicked splash.

Becki turned from the other side, where she'd stepped on the platform. "Dirty pool, Devon, dirty pool."

"Teamwork comes in all sorts of styles," he taunted as Alisha swam back to the starting platform to try again.

The rest of the challenges passed with a great deal of splashing and shouting, and by the time they dragged themselves up on the deck at the far side, Devon hit the bell a half second behind Alisha.

Her brilliant smile was worth losing to see.

Colin lay flat on his back on the pool deck, chest heaving as he gasped for air. Becki stood over him and *tsk*ed. "So sad to see that young people these days have absolutely no stamina."

Colin lifted his hand and flipped her the bird.

Becki laughed. She dropped Colin's towel on his face. "Six for six, brat. Anytime you want a challenge, let me know. I love having new fodder to boast about when I Skype with Mom and Dad."

Colin shot up onto his elbows. "You wouldn't . . ."

She grabbed her towel and waved evilly. She nodded at Alisha and Devon. "Nice job. Thanks for the fun. Unfortunately, I have a meeting to get to. I'll see you later."

She strolled from the deck, Colin dragging himself

upright after she'd vanished. "You won't tell anyone she beat me, will you?"

Devon held in his amusement. "I wouldn't dream of it."

Alisha nodded. "Of course not. I mean, I'd never boast about that kind of thing, or make an announcement in the middle of the cafeteria or anything, but Becki . . ."

Colin's eyes widened. "Shit. She totally would, wouldn't she?"

"Sorry."

Colin grimaced. "Well, it was fun. We'll do it again sometime."

He grabbed his gear and raced from the deck, no doubt in the hopes of cutting off Becki before she broadcast his humiliation. Alisha and Devon waited until he'd left the deck before they let their laughter ring over the water.

"I love family. They're so cutthroat." Devon hit the overhead lights to half power before tipping his head toward the hot tub. "Come on, let's relax before I buy you lunch."

CHAPTER 8

'''''''''''''''''''''''''''''''

Alisha sighed contentedly. Slipping into the water was like immersing in liquid relaxation. "God, that feels good."

"I envy Marcus his hot tub every single day. For that matter, I envy the current SAR class, who can use this every single damn day." Devon slid lower and rested his head on the pool edge. He'd closed his eyes, and Alisha didn't fight the urge to look him over closer. To admire his smooth facial features. With the lights dimmed she didn't need to hide that she was staring. He'd probably had more than enough women tell him he was good looking over the years. While she'd thought he was attractive when they were in school, he'd begun to mature in the past couple of years, the movie-star looks shifting into something she found very attractive. At least that much she'd admit.

"You did well in the challenge." Devon spoke without opening his eyes, stretching his legs across the small pool they were sharing. His shin bumped hers, and she resisted jerking away. She also stopped herself from rubbing back. Bonus.

"I'd say I did great. Notice we beat you?"

He lifted a hand from the water, water droplets splashing them both. "I meant in terms of being afraid. I didn't see a thing."

"It's a pool, Devon. It's no big deal."

He cracked one eye open. "Yeah, well, excuse me for being happy with a little proof. You didn't see yourself freak down in that cavern when the water covered us."

His words caused an instant response. No matter that the water surrounding her was hot enough to make her sweat, she had goose bumps.

Devon shot upright. "You shivered."

Oh hell. "So what?"

He narrowed his gaze. "Does thinking about the water crashing in on you make you nervous?"

Picturing it brought another shudder, but she wasn't about to apologize. "Come on, Devon. You telling me you can think of being totally covered with water, tied to a wall, and it doesn't upset you the least little bit? Because I call bullshit."

He placed one hand on the pool deck to the side of her head and the other on her shoulder. "Hey, I love the water. And tying up people is what I do for a living."

"Being tied up. Not the same thing." His gaze burned a path over her, his fingers red-hot on her shoulder. "What are you doing?"

His gaze moved as he trailed his fingers down her arm. "Making sure all your vitals are good."

Then she was lifted across the short distance separating them and rested in his lap. She barely had time to lift her gaze from the water's surface to his face before his lips met hers, and she really couldn't breathe.

He was kissing her. Hot mouth over hers, lips moving with a demand for her to respond. She opened her mouth to protest, and he slipped his tongue past her teeth, and another set of shivers took her, this time for far better reasons than fear.

He was kissing her.

He had one hand wrapped around the back of her neck, his palm wide and warm as he controlled her position. The other hand rested on the hip he'd used to tug her into his lap. His fingers were spread wide over her bare skin, his thumb stroking the edge of her swimsuit.

Under her palms she discovered she was fondling his muscular chest, fingertips exploring him as if she'd been waiting for this opportunity for years. Which she had, but *damn*. All the casual touches and fully clothed contact hadn't prepared her for this. She'd found carved living marble, his heartbeat registering hard enough she felt it through her fingertips.

He was *kissing* her . . .

She leaned into him, slipping her hands around his body and pressing their torsos together. She wasn't sure which was hotter—the hot tub water or his skin. Not to mention her skin, her breasts, and between her legs. She'd caught on fire and he wasn't putting out the inferno, but feeding the flames.

And his mouth. *God*, after one hit she was addicted. Slow and languid caresses, yet commanding enough she couldn't stop. Didn't want to stop. He thrust his fingers into her hair and pulled her head back slightly, stretching her neck. Then he kissed his way to the spot at the base of her throat.

When he put his teeth to her skin she gasped.

And came to her senses.

Alisha jerked upright, dragging her hands from where she'd had her fingernails dug into his back. She straightened, all too aware she was in his lap and he had a hard-on. There was no ignoring it, she was all but sitting on it, the rigid length pressed against her butt cheek.

He held her trapped as she met his gaze, his desire clear in the blue depths.

"What . . . what are you doing?"

It was his turn to take a deep breath, his chest rubbing hers until he slowly released his grasp and she squirmed away. "Do I really need to explain what a kiss is?"

If her mind hadn't been whirling with confusion, she'd

have made a snarky crack in response. As it was, all she seemed capable of was staring in shock. "But you kissed *me*."

He smiled. Not the full-out cocky grin she'd seen so often when they competed with each other. This one was different. More sensual. Teasing in a way that made her ache inside.

"I want to kiss you again."

A zing shot through her, like catching hold of a live wire.

He leaned forward and crowded her. "If I'm being honest, I want to do more than kiss you."

Honest made her heart pound. "Devon. Stop."

He did, instantly pulling away and reseating himself opposite her.

Fleeing seemed over the top and unnecessary, even though her heart rate was higher now than when they'd been racing. "I don't understand. I mean . . ."

His expression grew darker, not in a frightening way but as if he wanted to consume her. "What's so difficult about this, Alisha? It's been hanging over us for years. Maybe now, while we have to spend a bunch of time together, would be a good opportunity to stop fighting what we've known all along. We're attracted to each other."

"But you kissed me."

This time he cracked, amusement spreading across his face. "Yes, Alisha. I did. And you kissed me back."

"I didn't want to kiss you." Lie. Total lie, but the words spilt out from habit if nothing else. Denying their chemistry was too ingrained for her to toss it away this quickly.

"Bullshit." Devon leaned away and rested his arms on the pool edge, his biceps flexing. "You weren't complaining a moment ago. And right now, I'd bet what you'd really like, if you were honest, would be for me to start all over again and not stop."

She caught herself with her mouth gaping open, and quickly closed it. "You are one arrogant, cocky bastard, aren't you?"

"Stopped you from hyperventilating."

Shit.

Alisha pressed on the hard tiles under her fingers, curling her fingers around the edge. "You kissed me to distract me."

He nodded, then briefly shook his head. "Your pulse was rising and your breathing was accelerating, but I kissed you because it distracted you *and* because I wanted to like crazy. I've wanted to kiss you since the first day of our first class together when you walked in late and we got stuck as partners using the oldest mats in the gym."

The memory returned far too quickly. "Gee, I'd have never have known it. I seem to recall you being the center of some kind of *Devon in the middle* huddle, with all the girls using you as the football."

He pushed himself up to sit on the edge of the poolside, water running down his torso and leaving a glistening layer shining on his skin. "You remember that day far different than I do, then. I remember partnering with you for stretching. Do you have any idea how difficult it is to hide a hard-on in climbing gear?"

She couldn't stop it. Her gaze involuntarily fell to his lap, where evidence of his erection formed a mound in his board shorts.

She slipped out of the water, suddenly far too heated to stay in one place anymore.

"Alisha."

She wanted to hide, but . . . Lifting her head to meet his gaze was nearly impossible, but she'd done far more frightening things over the years. Far more frightening than to acknowledge she knew he was hot for her.

That she was hot for him?

But there was a huge deal breaker between them in spite of her raging libido. Her chin rose until they were eye to eye. "You've always had a ton of girls in your pocket, Devon. I've never been interested in being simply another toy you play with."

He nodded slowly. "I don't blame you."

"What would Lana think of us fooling around?"

His shock seemed genuine, replacing the lust. "Lana who?"

She bit back a laugh. "I saw her in your truck the other day."

Comprehension lit his eyes and the familiar, teasing Devon was back. "Oh, when I drove her to the grocery store because her car was busted. Were you jealous?"

Embarrassed was more like it. "Don't make me regret this, Devon."

"Regret what?"

They were on opposite sides of the circular hot tub, feet dangling in the water. The entire width of the pool separated them and yet she swore she still felt his touch. Bubbling and splashing carried on around them. Everything else had vanished in the wake of this new challenge.

A bit of defiance stiffened her resolve, only this time in Devon's favour. Vincent had shown up in her new backyard, so to speak. Unannounced and uninvited.

He was the last person she wanted to be involved with.

Devon had already proved he was a fine distraction. Maybe seeing him wouldn't be the worst mistake she could make. If she was careful, and didn't get her heart involved. Would it really be so bad if she let loose a little and satisfied the ache he created inside?

Devon examined her, top to bottom. Her smooth stomach, the skin showing between the expanse of her swimsuit bottom and the sports bra top she wore. She'd climbed in a top like that. He'd touched her while climbing, but this was much different. This wasn't about a professional work relationship, this was the two of them finally dealing with the itch that had been driving him crazy forever.

Her, too, if she'd admit it.

Right now, right here, all he needed was for her to agree they would be together. Time was of the essence, especially with that Vincent showing up.

Maybe there was a better way to do this, but he'd expended all his patience in the years leading up to now. "I promise I don't consider you a toy, but I do want to play with you."

Her eyes widened, and that pink tongue of hers snuck over her bottom lip.

He stood on the bench of the hot tub, not hiding his hard-on as he paced the perimeter toward her. "I want kisses, and tastes of your skin. I want to touch you everywhere and learn what kind of noises you make when you're trembling on the edge of orgasm."

"Devon . . ."

"I want to fool around with you for hours until we're both so tired we pass out, just so we can wake up and do it all over again."

The passion in her eyes—the astonishment and longing—increased as he drew closer. His cock was rock hard, tight to his body with the wet fabric of his shorts barely confining him.

He stepped to her side and slipped his hands along her thighs, loving the catch in her breathing as he made contact. Driven on by the flutter of her heart rate at the pulse of her throat, he eased her thighs apart, stepping between them as he lowered himself into the water again so their eyes were level.

Her breathing picked up. His was none too steady, either.

His hands were still on her thighs, so he skimmed them ever so slowly upward. Closer to her sex. Palms cupping the top of her limbs, thumbs dragging on the inside of her soft, smooth skin.

"I want to slip my tongue into you and eat you out until you're squirming. I want to lick your cream from my fingers after I've brought you to orgasm. Then I'll drive my cock into you until you scream with pleasure."

He'd lowered his voice, barely audible over the everyday pool noises. But she'd heard. She'd heard every word.

Her bottom lip quivered, moisture shining on it where she'd given in and nervously licked a second ago. She stared at his mouth as if she were starving.

He was. For more of her.

"Yes, Alisha? Do we give in to the heat and make both of us far happier than we've been? Or we can go back to being frustrated. You using whatever vibrators you've got shoved in your side table, and me fucking my fist, wishing I were pumping into you instead."

"*God*, Devon." Breathless. A mere whisper.

He inched his hands higher, fingertips brushing the edge of her swimsuit, thumbs hovering closer to where he needed to be.

She clasped his wrists, her strong climber's fingers squeezing tight enough to make him pause.

Devon didn't give up. "You tell me. You decide. I want you so fucking bad, but I want you to want me as—"

She let go of his left wrist and caressed his cheek, jerking his words to a stop. He was the one who gasped when she shifted their connected hands and brought his fingers over her sex. The dark circles of her pupils were so wide they nearly eclipsed the greyish blue of her irises. They stared into each other's eyes as he enjoyed the passion dancing over her face.

Alisha leaned forward, and their lips were together again.

Holy shit, yes.

Everything he'd mentioned doing to her was only the tip of the iceberg. Just the start of the adventure he wanted to take her on, but it felt so good finally beginning.

He savoured her. The sensation of her lips moving against his. The pressure as she attempted to get closer.

Even as their tongues touched and retreated, breaths intermingling, he was all too aware of her soft sex under his hand. He stroked his thumb over her suit, a gentle brush. She whimpered deep in her throat and pulled away from the kiss.

The flash of fire in her eyes—no way he wanted to miss experiencing it for the first time.

He pressed their foreheads together, left hand cupping the back of her neck to keep her where he wanted her. "I'm going to make you come, and I want to watch every second of it."

She swallowed hard and widened her legs in invitation. "Yes."

Alisha had pulled off her bathing cap earlier, and her long hair tousled over her shoulders, the ends curling around her breasts. She still wore her sports bra, and he wished they were in a better location so he could strip it from her. Leave her naked so he'd see her nipples hiding behind the long blond strands, peeking out with every breath she took. Her skin was smooth, water droplets clinging to her.

"So beautiful."

He lowered his gaze to her sex, playing again over the material, rubbing with increasing pressure as the fabric slipped between her folds. The little noises she made added to his pleasure as he adjusted his touch, varied the pressure based on her response.

He glanced around the pool area for a second, making sure they were still alone and his body blocked the instant view of what they were doing from anyone who might enter the area. There shouldn't be a class for at least another thirty minutes, but he didn't want to be interrupted by surprise.

No one around—no one to stop them from this moment. Devon slipped his fingers under the edge of her swimsuit and tugged it to one side, exposing her sex.

He nearly swallowed his tongue. "Sweet. Fucking. Mercy."

Alisha laughed. "You like?"

She was bare except for the trimmed strip of curls on her mound. "When I mentioned eating you out I had no idea. Now I can hardly wait."

Moisture glistened on her folds, not just the water from the pool, but her arousal. Her desire for him.

He shook his head to refocus and pulled his gaze to her face, staring into her eyes. The corners of her mouth twisted upward slightly as if she had a secret she wasn't willing to share. Trapping her gaze, his hand returned to her sex, circling her tender core gently. As one finger drifted deeper, her lashes fluttered.

"Look at me," Devon commanded, his voice soft but

clear. Her lids snapped open, her tongue slipping out again to moisten her lower lip. As he continued to caress her folds, a range of emotions crossed her face. Embarrassment passed quickly enough as she caught fire. Caught the need for more. Desire rising, excitement growing. Her breathing quickened as he stroked deep inside.

Devon slipped two fingers into her, pressing his thumb over her clit to continue the assault on her senses. He smiled at the soft noises she made, her face twitching occasionally when his fingers touched a particularly sensitive spot. "Oh yeah, I got you there. Right here, yes?"

He stroked with the pads of his fingers and she squirmed, a deep flush rising on her chest. She released her lower lip from her teeth to pant lightly.

Her eyes glittered as her breathing rate increased even further.

"Devon . . ."

He leaned in and whispered, "Come on, let yourself go."

Alisha threw back her head as a cry of pleasure escaped her. Around his fingers, her sex squeezed, her upper body shaking as a climax rolled through her. Devon held her, stroking through the aftershocks until she lifted her head and caught his gaze, a brilliant smile breaking free as he slowly withdrew his fingers, caressing her folds and soothing as he left her empty.

"Oh, *God*, I needed that."

Devon laughed. He met her halfway, accepting her kiss, wrapping his arms around her as she drove her fingers into his hair and kissed him with wild abandon.

The sound of voices and laughter poured through the change room door as a group of students arrived early and flipped the lights on. Devon and Alisha pulled apart slightly, but he stayed in front of her, tugging her suit back over her sex and stroking softly before removing his hand.

"Good timing." Alisha's gaze dropped to his groin, where he was still fully erect and ready for more. "We need to go elsewhere to deal with that."

"My cock and I would love to find a place to be alone

with you." She flushed so bright that he laughed. "Did I embarrass you using the word *cock*?"

Alisha swung her legs out of the water and stood. "I'm used to you teasing me, but the sexual notes feel different now. Now that we're going to . . ."

Hell, yeah. "Now that we're going to have sex?"

Man, that fire in her eyes turned him on. Funny how it had driven him crazy when for years she'd directed it at him in competition, yet now he wanted nothing more than to see it focused on him while they were both naked and able to channel it into more pleasurable pursuits.

She stood between him and the newcomers wandering onto the deck, blocking him from their view as she held out his towel. Devon didn't really care who saw that he had a hard-on, but he smiled and accepted her help, wrapping the towel around his hips.

"Where do you want to go? Want me to follow you home?"

Alisha shook her head. "If it's okay, can I . . . come to your place?"

Devon stepped in close under the guise of handing over her water bottle. He tucked his lips beside her ear and spoke softly. "I have no problems with that at all. And no plans for the rest of the morning. Or afternoon."

Alisha's eyes sparkled before she turned her back and walked away. Her ass mesmerized him before he pulled it together and got himself into the change room, rushing through a shower.

It had been a hell of a long time coming, him and Alisha, and he wasn't going to waste a minute.

CHAPTER 9

'''''''''''''''''''''''''''''''

She'd rarely done this—pulled up outside a man's house
with the intention of going in and having sex.

Not that there was anything wrong with the process, but
most of her previous sexual experiences had been spontane-
ous. A movie night at a boyfriend's house that turned into
rolling on the couch until they were sweaty and satisfied. A
party where she'd snuck away hand in hand with someone,
and they'd impulsively responded to the heat between them.
She'd had a handful of lovers over the years, none since she'd
come to Banff.

She'd never driven to someone's house deliberately for a
morning of sex. If she and Devon had simply moved from
the hot tub to the fucking, she wouldn't have had to deal
with this awkward sensation.

He'd beaten her home. He had a small place in the back
of a well-to-do neighbourhood. She parked in the second
car slot and stared at the door as she worked up the courage
to go in.

She wanted this. Wanted him, that wasn't the question.

Dammit. She was a mental wreck and needed to slap some sense into herself. When had she become this timid, fearful creature? A flash of Vincent standing over her was far too quick to rise, far too accusing, and she cursed. No. Devon was not Vincent, and the mental comparison of the two made it much easier to persuade herself to get up and head toward the house.

Devon was waiting for her, leaning on the railing outside the open front door. "I thought you were taking a nap."

"Building up my strength to jump you." She grabbed him by the shirt lapels and kissed him.

No hesitation on his part. He caught her in his arms and carried her into the house. Her bag fell from her shoulder, abandoned in the doorway as their tongues tangled. Alisha wrapped her legs around his hips, the ridge of his erection unyielding against her clit, and pleasure squeezed out a moan.

He crowded her against the wall, harder pressure in all the right spots increasing her need by the second. The door swung away from them, jerking to a stop and rebounding open as it hit something. She didn't care. Devon rocked his hips against her and she lost a little more of her mind.

She clutched them together, her strong legs helping him hold her upright. He grabbed her hair and tugged her head to the side, exposing her neck. His lips latched on, and her cry echoed into the room.

"Yes, Devon. Oh, yes."

All of the resistance she'd put up over the past years— that willpower was totally and utterly gone, replaced with a hunger like she'd never known before. He kissed her again and stole her breath until she was shaking and desperate for him to fill her.

Devon stroked her hair off her face. "Put your legs down," he ordered.

She rocked against him in protest, rubbing shamelessly in an attempt to drive herself closer to the edge.

"Alisha." He caught her hips and stilled her. "Don't pout, and trust me."

He nipped at her lip before licking it gently, and she unwillingly unwrapped herself from him.

Devon dropped to his knees, taking her pants to the floor, undies vanishing as well in seconds. She stared down, her heart pounding as he caught her under one knee and lifted her leg to the side, exposing her sex to his intent gaze.

"Oh, Devon. *Oh* . . ."

He buried his face between her legs—nothing soft, nothing gentle. His mouth in intimate contact, his tongue darting through her folds and pressing deep. Another swipe before he licked her clit hard, sending electric jolts cascading through her system. She dug her fingers into his hair and held on for dear life.

Her other leg quivered, and she fought to stay vertical. Devon kept up his devilish assault, even as he pressed his free hand over her stomach and pinned her to the wall.

Held secure by his strong grasp, she gave herself over to the sweep of sensation rocking her from top to bottom, his mouth making her pulse beat in far too many sensitive places.

Outside a car drove past, the flash of blue clearly visible through the partially open door. Alisha rubbed her fingertips against Devon's scalp, the thick fibers of his hair tangled around her fingers as she tugged him higher. Just a little higher to where—

"*Damn.*" Her head crashed into the wall, unable to hold herself steady any longer as Devon bit her clit and shot her off the edge, propelling her into a climax that removed her power to stand.

She didn't need the strength. He rose to his feet, taking her with him. Stripping off her top and humming in satisfaction. "Good girl. No bra. I'd tell you how happy that makes me, but I can't wait."

Alisha's shoulders hit the wall again as he caught her by her neck and kissed her, the taste of her pleasure on his tongue in that brief, intense moment before she was hoisted higher and his lips wrapped around her nipple.

Aftershocks continued to shake her, and there seemed to

be a direct line between her core and his mouth. He pulled her nipple in, and a rush hit all the nerve endings on the left side of her body. He switched sides and she gasped for air. "Devon. Please. Oh God, *please*."

He let go and lowered her enough that he could rest his forehead on hers, staring straight into her eyes. "Please what, Alisha? Eat you out again? Lay you on the floor and fuck you with my fingers until you're too boneless to move? Bend you over the back of my couch and—"

"Yes. All of it, but first, fuck me. Give me your cock, dammit."

He grinned. "I knew you had it in you."

"Not yet, I don't," she complained. Alisha laughed with him, his laugh contagious as he adjusted his grip.

"Wrap your legs around me again and hold on tight."

She followed his directions, and suddenly she was the one in control, clinging to his shoulders, her legs around his waist as he ripped open his zipper and pulled out his cock. She glanced down to see how he was doing, but the man was seriously talented. "How did you get that condom on so fast?"

"Desperation," Devon quipped. "Second time I promise to be more than a minute man, but dammit, I'm not going to last."

He caught her by the hips, made one slight adjustment. The broad head of his cock bumped her sex, and he caught her gaze.

Waited for a second. Watched her.

Alisha nodded, fingernails digging into his shoulders. She needed this as badly as he did. "Do it. Fuck *me*."

The final word exploded out louder than she'd planned as he thrust upward. A deep penetration, the hard width of his shaft stretching her wide.

He squeezed his eyes shut as if in agony for a second before breathing deeply through his nose and smiling. "Sweet miracle of miracles, I'm finally in your pussy."

The total satisfaction in his voice would have pissed her off if she hadn't been thinking the same thing. "Less talking, more fucking. Or you planning on leaving your cock there for a while?"

"Hush, I'm savouring."

He pulled his hips back slowly, and she couldn't stop herself from sighing happily. "Feels so good."

"I'm about three seconds away from rutting on you like a madman, so don't do anything wild," he warned.

She dug her nails into his shoulders harder. "Maybe I like madmen."

That was all it took. She was crushed to the wall, his mouth over hers again as he kissed her. His cock slammed in deep, harder and faster on each thrust until they gasped together. The tingle of orgasm that had never really left her ebbed upward, and when he adjusted his angle, cradling her knees in the crooks of his arms, she caught him by the ears and pulled him away in time to climax, her vision going blurry as she stared into his blue eyes.

Devon slowed for a few strokes as she squeezed around him, gasping for air. She was nowhere close to being on the way to recovery before he changed tempo again, palms tight to the wall, over her like a wild animal.

Alisha hung on the best she could, shocked that before he came, she'd peaked again. Or maybe her orgasm simply hadn't stopped. But when he buried himself to the root, their groins meshed together, another wave hit, pleasure encompassing her body.

Nothing left in her brain but sheer physical bliss.

Devon scooped her toward him slightly, his hands firm on her naked back as he dropped in unsteady jerks to the floor. They ended up in a compact pile, her in his lap with his cock embedded in her sex. He slipped his arms from under her knees and cradled her closer, his warmth a blanket around her as they fought to catch their breaths.

Devon pressed his lips to her temple and let out a long, satisfied sigh. "Okay, I'm good for us to start now."

She laughed. "Start?"

"Hell, yeah. That was to take the edge off. You didn't have any plans for the day, did you?"

Sex all day long sounded perfect right now. "If you feed me, I'm yours."

Devon tucked his fingers under her chin and lifted her lips to his. This time the kiss was far more tender. Still made all the hyperactive hormones in her body stand up and cheer with excitement. He brushed their lips together softer and softer until the connection between them was merely a light caress, their breaths mingling as he spoke against her mouth.

"I'll feed you. Fuck you. Maybe do them both a couple times. Sound good?"

"Such a dirty mouth." Alisha grinned. "Sounds wonderful."

What an answer to his cravings. That twist in his day had been the last thing he'd expected when he forced himself out of bed in the morning, but hell if he'd take it for granted. Or bitch about it either. He helped her up and dealt with the condom. Alisha took advantage of his distraction to snatch his T-shirt off the floor and pull it over her head.

He retrieved his sweats and pulled them on, if only to stop the semi he was still wearing from hanging in the breeze.

Alisha grabbed her bag from where it lay in the middle of the entrance, and he closed the door more carefully this time. Damn, had they really had sex with the door wide open?

He couldn't stop grinning, so he was pretty happy to see that she wore a nearly identical expression. "We're going to have to work this out of our systems before we go out in public or it'll be damn obvious what we've been up to."

Alisha paused, her bag slung over her shoulder, socks on her feet, legs bare as she clutched her clothing in a fist. "Shit. The team."

Devon waved her farther into the house. "Don't worry about them. We have other things to concentrate on professionally when we get together. They won't care if we're fooling around."

"But it's not—"

Devon wasn't going to let her even start down that path. Not after she'd finally given in and let him have a taste of how hot they were together. "It's not typical, no. When people are sleeping together it can impair their judgment in a rescue situation. But, Alisha, face it. I'm going to watch you like a hawk no matter what. Which is in no way different than what I've already been doing. We're part of a team that's been together for years. You think I haven't been willing to make the tough, snap decisions up to now? To do whatever I could to save your ass?"

She shook her head, following him into his bedroom. "You're right. Our situation is different."

"Damn right it is. There's no rule in Lifeline about sex between employees being out of line, and I'd be just as willing to take a hit for Xavier's ass as for yours."

Alisha raised a brow. "Really? When will this *hitting of asses* take place, and can I watch?"

Hell. "You know what I mean."

She tossed her bag onto the chair and grinned, crowding toward him. "I know you offered me food and fucking. Is there a particular order required to accept that deal?"

Her hands slipped over his skin, a teasing caress as she stroked her way from his waist up to his chest. Devon groaned happily as her fingernails flicked his nipples. "How about we see how long we can last before eating? I have a bit of strength left."

"Me, too." Alisha planted her palms against him, then pushed lightly. The force wasn't enough to topple him to the mattress, not if he didn't want to go.

He was no idiot. He couldn't think of anything better than ending up flat on his back, Alisha staring down at him with that naughty expression in her eyes.

"You plan on taking advantage of me?" Devon asked.

She stepped between his knees and leaned forward to

plant a hand on his abdomen. "Oh, you'll like it. Just tell me you have more condoms."

"Dresser, top drawer." He pointed. "Bring a few."

She laughed. "Cocky bastard."

"That's the point, isn't it?"

She returned before he could adjust position. Alisha examined him and the bulge in his pants while wearing a very satisfied smile. "I will admit I've lusted over your body for years, Devon. You are mighty fine."

"I aim to please. Although if you don't stop looking and start doing, I won't be the one waiting on my back for long."

"Patience. You know that rule."

His dick was at full strength again as she carefully lowered the waist on his pants, easing the elastic over his cock. "Move decisively. That's what we need at this moment. *Fuck*—"

Alisha glanced up from where she'd licked the tip of his cock. "Decisive enough for you?"

He shook his head. "Not yet, but you're on the right track."

She wrapped her fingers around his shaft and stroked. Just the right amount of pressure, not nearly enough range of motion. "You need some lube to help you with that?"

"I've got it under control, thanks."

Brain-busting, how she took control. Her tongue darted out again and again, teasing all around his cock. She hummed happily as she worked him over, slicking him up with her saliva until the pumps of her fist were smooth and far too precise to be ignored.

"In case you're wondering, I like what you're doing very much." Alisha pulled him erect and lowered her mouth over the head of his cock, wet heat engulfing him. He panted for control, grabbing hold of the quilt to stop from catching her head in his hands and taking over. "Okay, *like*? Is wrong. I fucking *love* your mouth."

He loosened his death grip on the sheets and propped himself on his elbows to get a better view. Watching and experiencing the sensations at the same time was the fast-track way to lose control, but hell if he cared. He could get it back up in record time.

He had four damn years of anticipation stored up.

Alisha held him at the base and dipped farther, the crown of his cock bumping her throat, and he swore. She did it again, but this time timed it perfectly so she opened her throat and he was completely enveloped, nothing but her mouth holding him.

Talking was impossible. Thinking was impossible. She worked him over until he forgot all his good intentions. His fingers were threaded in her hair and he was sitting up, Alisha kneeling on the floor between his legs as he guided her down his cock again and again.

A strand of blond hair fell over her forehead, and he clutched it aside, needing to see her face as she took him in. Alisha lifted her gaze, and sweet fuck, he lost it. The hard drag of her mouth, the look in her eyes, the sight of his cock stretching those perfect pouting lips—hard explosive jets shot from him as she maintained eye contact. Stared at him as his cock jerked, semen filling her. She swallowed, her throat visibly moving and he felt it all the way up his spine, as if she were sucking his brains out.

Which was fine by him. Any time she wanted to.

Alisha caught his wrists and pulled him back slightly, his cock still in her mouth but now resting on her lower lip as she licked him clean, and another shock wave rolled through him. "Holy *shit*."

She smiled, his cock falling from her lips. She licked them, rocking away to sit on her heels. "Well, that was fun."

Fun? "Hell, yeah."

He caught her under the arms and draped her over him while his heart pounded. Her bare legs tangled with his, the heat of their bodies mixing together. She lowered her head to his chest and sighed happily. Her fingertips rested on his chest and she drew small circles on his skin. "I needed that."

"Any time, any place, be my guest." Devon stroked her hair, staring at the ceiling. They might have things to work on, but right now? He couldn't bring himself to worry nearly as much as he should.

She squirmed upright far sooner than he wanted her to, straddling his waist, palms pressed to his chest as she examined him.

The colour of her eyes seemed different as she looked him over. "Are you wearing contacts?"

Alisha grinned. "No. Are my eyes blue right now?"

He nodded. "More blue than usual. Are you some kind of alien creature? Now that we've shared intimate contact you're going to take over my brain?"

Her fingers stroked his cock and he couldn't help his instant response. Her grin only got wider. "I'm already affecting one of your brains."

She got that right.

He rolled them, trapping her under him and nuzzling her neckline, nipping his way back to her mouth to take in more kisses. Soft woman under him, her willing embrace enveloping him. Arms and legs catching him close—they would have been fucking again in three minutes flat if her stomach hadn't grumbled like crazy.

They broke apart, Devon rising over her, even now reluctant to leave her warmth. "Tell me we're coming right back here after I feed you."

Alisha raised a brow. "Well, we could come back here, or we could try a few of the other things you mentioned."

Hmm, oh yeah. "Back of the couch?"

Her laughter rang as he got to his feet and pulled her to vertical. "Only if you close the door this time."

"Not into performing for the neighbours? Exhibitionism isn't your thing?"

He accepted the pants she handed him. If he'd expected to make her squirm it hadn't worked. Alisha backed out his bedroom door, staring him down as she spoke. "Well, I never said *that*."

She twisted and disappeared down the hall while his brain tried to catch up. Devon hurried to pull on his sweats, hopping forward as he pulled them up one leg. "Wait a minute, does that mean what I think it means? Alisha, don't you say something like that and then walk away."

He caught her in the kitchen already digging in his fridge. The smooth curve of her ass—God, he was fixated— wiggled at him as she pulled things from the trays. Devon laid a hand on the tight curves and stroked lightly.

She straightened and pressed sandwich fixings against his chest. "Food now, more fucking later. I don't think we need to plan the details, do we? Surprises are so much more fun."

Alisha sashayed to the right and pulled a loaf of bread forward. Devon jerked himself back to control, unable to stop grinning.

They might have had a hell of a week, but he would totally take it.

CHAPTER 10
''''''''''''''''''''''''''''''

Sandwiches were consumed, soup vanished. Small talk led to another round of sweaty, inventive sex, followed by another—why had she turned Devon down for so long?

Playboy. Notch on the bedpost.

Alisha stretched naked on the sheets, head toward the foot of the bed, her hand bumping his thigh. All of her previous excuses had melted away in the flood of desire and need he'd begun in her. Okay, this wasn't for forever anyway, and she was using him as much as he was using her.

In the big scheme of things, she was good with it.

Devon caught her hand as she trickled her fingers up his thigh, stopping her before she could touch anything important. "I can't believe I'm saying this, but we need to take a break."

She laughed. "Poor baby, did I work you over too hard?"

He pivoted her until they were lying side by side in the same direction. "When a sixty-nine makes me nearly pass out, I'd say I was low on fuel, or something. I will admit defeat if you tell me you want me to start something new."

She played her hands over his shoulders, just because she could. "No, not really. I'm pretty happy right now."

His blue eyes watched her every move. "I'm game for more later, but at some point we need to get out of bed."

"Hmm, I suppose." The sex was damn good, though. "Getting out of bed means returning to reality."

Devon trapped her fingers against his chest. "This was no sexual wet dream, Alisha. It happened. All afternoon, it happened."

"I don't think I've had that many orgasms in a day since . . . well, ever." His gloating expression prompted her to smack him lightly on the chest. "Ego much?"

"Hey, you said it, not me." Devon turned more serious. "This isn't a onetime deal. I want more of you."

She wanted more of him, so that wasn't the trouble. Only there were lines, concerns she had, and not addressing them would be stupid. "You said it earlier. We're going to spend more time together in the next while than usual. I don't mind a bit of extracurricular activity thrown in with that."

He nodded but still looked strangely somber. He didn't say anything else, though, and she was glad.

Sex had changed things. She needed time and space to raise the walls in a new manner. Before, when she'd been denying what their bodies wanted, it had been simpler to keep everything on the "do not touch" side of her brain.

Now that he'd slipped under her physical barrier, she needed to consider what other secrets she was willing to drop.

Her phone rang, the musical tones making them both jerk. When his phone didn't go off as well, relief hit hard.

Devon chuckled as she scrambled to grab her phone from the bottom of her bag. "We're going to have to be careful not to fuck each other out of rescue commission."

She put her finger to her lips to shush him before answering the call. It was impossible to look away as he sat on the mattress and watched her, the muscles of his abdomen bunched into a nice, solid six-pack. His cock far from flaccid—did the man ever lose his semi? Her voice sounded breathless, even to her. "Hello."

"Alisha."

Oh, shit. Vincent. All the lovely sexual endorphins floating through her system scurried away. She'd totally forgotten his invitation to dinner. She ignored the question in Devon's eyes and turned away, stepping toward the bathroom for privacy. "Hi, Vincent."

"I've made reservations at the main dining room. I'll pick you up in thirty minutes."

She scrambled to jerk her brain online to deal with this. "I'm really tired. Maybe we should—"

He laughed, the sound creating a far different response than Devon's. Rather than making her want to join in, the condescension put her back up. A doting older relative putting up with a wayward child, even though that comparison was wrong in about fifty ways. "You still need to eat."

She longed to tell him to fuck off, but her hands were tied, and not in a good way. "The Banff Springs is not a place you go simply to refuel, Vincent."

"If you have somewhere else you'd prefer, please, let me know. I can be accommodating."

Oh hell. She stared into the bathroom mirror, the love bites on her neck and body making her scramble for a towel to cover herself even though he was on the phone and had no idea what she'd been up to. Perhaps the best way to get rid of him was to give in this once. Get it over with. He couldn't be staying around town for long. "No, that's fine. But I'll join you there. I need to do a few things on my way."

"I don't mind stopping."

"No, this is easier," she insisted. She glanced quickly at her phone for the time. Damn, she'd never find a way to get ready in thirty minutes. "Only, could you move the reservation to seven, please?"

"Of course, sweetheart. Use valet parking. I'll meet you at the doors." He hung up with no further comment, obviously not expecting her to do anything but agree with his directions.

An hour.

An hour to get home, find a dress that would cover the

very vivid marks of her and Devon's thorough sexing, not
to mention putting on enough makeup to cover the ravages
from her recent sleepless nights.

The bathroom door opened, and Devon glanced in cautiously. "Is it safe?"

She held the top of the towel with one hand and shrugged.
"Come in. Sorry. No time for a lengthy 'you scrub my back
and I'll scrub yours.' I have to go."

Devon nodded, leaning his shoulder on the door frame.
"Hot date?"

He repeated his words from the previous day. They were
as annoying now as they'd been before.

"No," she snapped, frustration making her response
sharper than she'd intended. Devon didn't move. Didn't ask
any more questions, he only looked plenty. She sighed and
joined him, catching the waist of his sweats and leaning in
close. "Vincent works with my father. His family and mine
are old friends, and I can't just blow him off."

Devon tucked his fingers under her chin, lightly stroking
his thumb over her cheek. "You don't need to explain, but
you don't seem too thrilled."

"I'm not." For so, *so* many reasons. "But in the interest
of keeping the peace, I should go."

He stared for a moment, then nodded. "Feel free to grab
a shower here if you want."

He left the room, and all the oxygen seemed to suck out
after him.

Shit.

She followed him into the bedroom, but he was gone.
Tugging on her clothes, finding her socks—all of it strange
and far more awkward than she'd expected. She pulled her
backpack over her shoulder and fisted her keys, bracing herself to say good-bye.

He was in the kitchen, barefoot and bare chested. She
wavered for a moment, almost ready to toss the plans with
Vincent out the window, but . . . she couldn't. "Hey, I'll call
you tomorrow. Dream up crazy things for me to do, okay?"

He looked up, dropping the Tupperware container in his

hand to the counter and striding to her side. "I'll be good and assume you didn't mean that in a sexual way."

She grinned before she realized he was still staring at her with an unreadable expression.

Devon nodded. "I'll do some research tonight. See what I can find."

"Thanks."

Awkward. Teenage-crush awkward. With the tension between them now it was hard to believe he'd fucked her against the wall only hours earlier.

Devon snarled in frustration. "What the hell."

He grabbed her and laid another kiss on her, his body tight to hers, their lips crushed together. Every second that passed meant she'd have to rush more later, but she couldn't break away. Couldn't let go of where she'd caught him, her fingers fisted in his hair.

Devon was the one who jerked them apart, his grin firmly in place. "I hope you have a lovely dinner."

Her body buzzed from the kiss. From all the things he'd done to her bounding through her memory like the Energizer bunny on aphrodisiacs. "I expect the food to be wonderful and the company to suck, thank you."

He turned her to the door and let her out, patting her ass as she walked past. "You need anything, call, okay?"

"Tomorrow."

"Call," he repeated. "Tomorrow, tonight, I don't give a damn when. If you need me, let me know."

When she glanced up from the wheel, he was standing in the entrance of his house, watching her. She forced herself to wave before directing her car into the lane and heading for home.

The sight of Alisha driving away drew a frustrated sigh from him. In one massive swoop, all his admittedly dirty plans for the evening were wiped away. Hanging out by himself at home wasn't high on the agenda. Devon slammed the fridge door hard enough that everything in the kitchen rattled.

It wasn't as if he had expected her to instantly start living in his pocket. But after seeing no guys in her life for so long, now someone showed up? *Now* there was some rich friend of the family who appeared out of nowhere to take her to one of the most expensive places in town?

Fuck that.

He took some time to research possible scenarios to put her through. Only there wasn't much he could find online, and he wasn't about to go asking questions in real life because with the climbing community, anything he said would be common knowledge within twenty-four hours, and speculation would begin.

He wondered how long it would be until everyone knew he and Alisha had finally hooked up.

A snort of derision escaped him. Well, no one would suspect anything tonight, not with her gallivanting around town with Vincent.

Bloody hell, he was sitting and pouting like some hard-done-by virgin. There was no need for it. He could go out and grouch instead of staying in and being miserable. May as well spread the joy to his friends. He sent off a text, then headed to change. Distraction was the best solution, and he had plenty of people who could help him in the distraction department.

The familiar noise of the Rose and Crown crowd greeted his ears like a cheerful hello. Devon raced up the stairs, waving at a few people without stopping as he sauntered past the restaurant tables. He headed all the way to the back where his buddy Luke already held sway over a pool table. A group of women had gathered around the small, standing-only table to the right, and his name was shouted quickly enough to soothe his bruised ego.

"You on call tonight?" Kyle asked. Luke's twin brother raised a glass and the pitcher of stout in a question.

Even if he were, he could have one drink. But tonight? "Fill it and keep it full."

Kyle dipped his head and went to work, passing over a glass with a fine head of foam. "We weren't sure you'd sur-

faced yet. Saw in the paper you had another successful rescue the other day."

Devon took a good long drink before wiping his mouth
and putting his glass aside. "That's not a secret, but why
exactly are you talking so loud?"

Kyle twisted his back and pointed slyly toward the ladies.
"New to town. You can have your pick, but I get the redhead," he whispered.

"You know what?" Devon slapped Kyle on the shoulder.
"You're a dick. You can have the redhead and all the rest.
I'm not interested."

Kyle gave him the eye. "You running a fever or something?"

He shook his head and grabbed a pool cue. "Nope. Just
want a few games, is all."

"Well, me, too," Kyle protested.

"Not those types of games." His buddy flashed a smirk,
and Devon forced a laugh. It wasn't as amusing as usual. He
didn't enjoy fawning women, but he disliked even more that
he was being used by his supposed friends. "Fine, trade on
my good name if you can't get pussy any other way, but I'm
good for tonight."

His friend saluted, then strolled over to the table with a
greeting for the ladies. Devon hid his annoyance and paced
over to talk to Luke instead.

"The mighty hero has decided to grace us with his presence." Luke tilted the mouth of his bottle at Devon. "I almost
didn't recognize you without your superhero suit."

"Fuck you, too," Devon said blandly. "What are we playing tonight?"

"Nothing serious. Had a hell of a day, so it was nice to
hear you could join us."

They racked up the balls and fell into an easy camara-
derie. It was damn annoying how often he reached to check
his phone to make sure it was still on. In case Alisha decided
to call him.

Pathetic.

Kyle soon had the ladies smiling, joining in around the

table and generally getting in the way. Luke took his shots with one arm around the woman who'd picked him out. Devon had to work like a maniac to avoid the clutches of the brunette who insisted he should *teach her to play*.

The arrival of his Lifeline teammates had never been so welcome, even if it seemed strange to see Lana as a part of the group. Devon acknowledged their wave before handing his pool cue to the pouting brunette. "You can take over my spot. Gotta chat with the team for a bit."

"I could get you a drink," she offered, pressing her breasts against him before he backed out of groping range.

"Thanks. I'm good." He twisted away, ignoring the woman. He gave Luke a frustrated glance before descending on Xavier and Lana. "Tell me you've got room to hide me."

"Awww, are the dulcet darlings on the prowl again?" Xavier slid behind the table and shrugged. "No objections from me. Tripp's joining us in about an hour—Lana wanted to do the wing thing, and I said I'd show her around."

Devon waved at one of the servers to get their attention. "The wing addiction already reared its head, did it?" he teased.

"I fought valiantly as long as I could, but some cravings are too strong to be denied." Lana sighed dramatically before grinning at him. "Only, if I'm going down, I'm taking the lot of you with me."

"It's an honest way to go." Devon ordered a round. His phone vibrated in his pocket and he scrambled to pull it out. It wasn't Alisha's number on the screen, but his sister's. He offered a quick apology to Xavier and Lana, then turned to the side to answer it. "I thought I'd made this number unlisted. Damn, how did you find me?"

His sister's familiar laugh carried over the line. "You'll never escape. Face it, little boy, we have ways to track you down."

Devon accepted a glass from Xavier. "What's up? I can't talk right now."

"Short and sweet. Two weeks from now you're expected for Thanksgiving dinner on Sunday. I'll be nice—you don't have to bring anything if you bring a girl." Sandy hummed. "Or, if you plan on showing up solo again? Check the list of wines Dad posted on the family Facebook page. Shouldn't set you back too much."

The constant taunting from his siblings to grow up, get a real job, and find a *one and only* hadn't diminished over the years. Gotten worse, in fact, as they'd partnered off with true loves and started producing a copious number of rug rats. He loved his family, he really did, but there was no way he was bowing to the god of marital bliss even if they had all fallen victim.

It was his life, dammit. None of them seemed to have realized that yet. To them, he was still the little boy. The one who couldn't figure out what needed to be done.

The one who couldn't be trusted.

Frustration washed over him before inspiration hit hard enough to brighten the bleak prospect of an extended family dinner. This time he might pull one over, especially if it meant not having to put out for the outrageously expensive wines his father liked to try at holiday dinners.

He pictured Alisha's bright smile and the way she could work a room. The woman was seriously talented when it came to public speaking—he bet he could persuade her to come home with him and pacify them all. "I'll raise the stakes. I bring a woman to face the lot of you, and you have to make pecan pie."

Sandy paused. "You're not serious. Are you seeing someone?"

Devon didn't comment. "You set the rules. I'll talk to you in a couple days. Gotta run. Later." He hung up feeling damn good about the possibility of hanging out with Alisha *and* pulling a fast one on his perfect family.

Beer and wings had arrived, and the look of ecstasy on Lana's face as she licked the sauce off her fingers brought a reluctant smile to his face.

She moaned happily, slipping her tongue over her lips. "Whoever came up with the idea of coating wings in sauce should be canonized. My mouth is in heaven."

"It was probably someone in the heart and stroke profession." Xavier leaned in and nudged the basket of teriyaki closer. "Try these. They're my favourite."

She pulled one out, chatting easily with Xavier as the paramedic slowly decreased the distance between them until he was right next to her. Devon watched in amusement as Tripp arrived, and Xavier took total advantage of adjusting the chairs to place Lana's within crowding distance.

Lana smiled and flirted, her cheeks brightening as the evening continued. She twisted toward Devon, a huge grin shining out. "I like working with Lifeline. Three hot guys to hang out with in the evenings? I could get used to this."

She bumped her water glass and it tipped toward Devon. He caught it before it completely went down, about half the water sloshing over the table edge and into his lap. He swore under his breath but kept his smile in place.

"I'm so sorry." She had her hands in his lap, mopping up the moisture with her napkin.

Devon caught her wrists, pulling her fingers off his groin and back to the top of the table. "No harm done. It's only water."

"Good thing it wasn't the beer," Tripp teased before changing the subject. "Lana, tell us about yourself. Marcus introduced you and all, but I don't remember him saying specifically where else you've worked?"

She gave Devon another apologetic glance before facing Tripp. "I was on a few volunteer search-and-rescue squads before I went to school. Haven't been able to find a full-time team yet, so I thought doing the call-out desk for Lifeline would be a good change of pace. I can still be involved in an active group and maybe . . ."

Xavier nodded knowingly, glancing at Devon and Tripp. "Maybe get a shot at joining the team down the road?"

Lana hid behind her glass for a moment. She lowered it, smiling brightly. "Well, not right off, you know. You're a pretty amazing act. I need to do a lot more training to match your skill levels."

"If you ever want to join in, let us know," Xavier offered.

Devon resisted giving Xavier a kick under the table. Not only was Xav pushing it way too hard to try and impress Lana, now he was dragging the rest of the team into it? Like hell. She might have been hired for call-out duties, but that was a far cry from working a rescue. He already had Alisha to double-check on for a bit; he didn't need to babysit anyone else.

Unfortunately, Lana latched on to the suggestion like Velcro. "Anytime. I'm available, and I'd love to join you."

Tripp was making peculiar faces. Devon had to look away to avoid bursting out laughing. Instead he tried to turn the conversation to more generic topics than the meet-up times and workout suggestions Lana pushed forward in an attempt to pin them down.

Xavier topped up everyone's glass. "Important topic of discussion. I want to know. If Erin is getting a bigger bird, what equipment improvements are *we* getting?"

"My vote is for a hot tub at HQ. Or maybe a flat screen," Tripp said.

"For what? You want to hang around HQ and watch movies?" Devon shook his head. "Get a life."

Tripp lifted a wing and shook it at Devon. "I heard a rumour Marcus was considering setting up housing for us. Now tell me you wouldn't enjoy that as a bonus? Rent-free living."

"Hell, no." Devon shook his head. "Maybe the price is right, but I already train with you, eat with you, and hang out in the evenings with you when I can't find anything better to do. Why would I want to sleep with you as well?" Not to mention that would totally make the current list of activities he wanted to go through with Alisha a hell of a lot harder.

"You're afraid that you'll have to stop hauling home all the women."

Good grief. "Yeah, I use a bucket truck to scoop them up on a daily basis. Give it a rest, guys."

"I'm sure you don't," Lana objected on his behalf. "You're a type of shining prince in knightly armour. The kind to sweep the princess off her dragon and kiss her until she falls asleep."

Devon blinked in confusion, attempting to sort out her words. He peeked at Tripp, who had his jaw slightly open, eyeing Lana with distrust.

Sometime in the past couple of minutes everyone had shifted positions, and instead of having plenty of room beside him, Lana was right there, her thigh tight to his. She'd been watching the banter, her gaze darting back and forth.

Devon spotted the empty glass about the same moment Lana laid her hand on his thigh, out of sight of the guys. God, the woman obviously couldn't handle her alcohol. He grabbed her wrist, again, and lowered it to her lap, quickly bringing his hands above the table.

Fortunately, no one else noticed. Xavier laughed at her confusing statement. "That sounds like a mash-up of TV tropes. Perfect."

The instant Lana's hand touched down again, Devon shot out of his chair. "Well, thanks for the company. I think I'll be going."

He really didn't want to spend his night fending off someone he had no interest in. As a distraction, the evening had been good on a temporary basis. Other than that, it had turned into a reminder that he'd have much preferred to spend the time with Alisha, in bed or out of it.

He'd enjoyed the sex, he'd admit that, but he also liked *her.* Strange how easy that was to confess now, when he'd had a steady offering of no-strings hookups running rampant around him.

Tripp waved him off. "See you in the next couple days?"

Devon nodded, not ready to make specific training plans in case Lana took it as an invitation. She was tipsy enough to either not notice or take more offense than she should. Xavier had her laughing madly about something, and Devon took the chance to point at her secretly. Tripp rolled his eyes but nodded. She'd be babysat, but not by him this time, thank God.

On his way out of the bar he had to dodge three more

groups of women whom he'd turned down or not dated in the past while.

What a damn mess. Women everywhere, except for the one he was truly interested in. And she was busy being wined and dined by her *not-hot date*.

The temptation to go and casually stroll through the Banff Springs was huge, but he didn't need to add *pitiful* to his evening. Devon gave up and headed home, a gut full of unexplained irritation swirling inside next to a lot of sexual frustration.

The best thing that could happen tonight would be to get called out on a rescue.

CHAPTER 11

The valet took Alisha's hand and assisted her from the car, passing her off to a black-and-gold-suited doorman who had obviously been hovering in anticipation of her arrival. "Mr. Monreal is waiting for you. Right this way."

The doorman escorted her as if she were royalty, and Alisha held her frustration in check. The fawning attention was more than she wanted, but getting mad at the hotel employee would be unfair when his over-the-top courtesy was probably mandated from on high.

"How is your evening so far?" she asked him.

He blinked, as if surprised she'd noticed he was a real human being. "Um, very well. It's been quite busy."

He evaded all further conversation.

Her irritation rose another notch, and she hadn't even reached her dinner partner yet. The games that were played in the upper echelons of society pissed her off more now than when she'd been immersed in the lifestyle and had to toe the line. It was simply another reason she was thankful to have put that part of her life behind her. Hopefully for good.

A quick glance across the grand foyer placed Vincent in an oversized wingback chair on the far side of the wide expanse. The glitzed table beside him held an enormous bouquet made of dozens of pure white roses. As he rose to his feet, the contrast between the snowy white and his dark hair and suit was stark—mischief made her picture the devil fleeing from the gates of heaven. He'd switched to an even more formal suit, and she was glad she'd dressed up. Not that she wanted to impress Vincent, but the turquoise silk encasing her was like armour to counter his possible attacks.

The high-necked, long-sleeved outfit also covered the more scandalous marks Devon had left behind during their enthusiastic sex.

As Vincent approached, the reminder of Devon only made her more determined to hold her ground. She had a good idea why Vincent was here. She wasn't going to give in, though. She had far too much to lose by simply giving up and going back to being her father's little girl.

He took her from the doorman, his gaze slipping down her torso and taking in every inch from top to bottom. Calculating, judging. Smiling as she passed whatever approval rating he'd set.

"You look beautiful," Vincent breathed. He lifted her hand to his lips and kissed her knuckles.

"Thank you." She stood motionless, hoping her lack of enthusiasm could be considered sophisticated restraint.

Vincent paced around her slowly, "Come, let me take you to dinner."

As he turned her toward the main dining hall, his hand stroked her lower back, where the dress had an open keyhole in the fabric. His fingers were cold, and she shivered.

Even with the heels she wore, he towered over her. She rested her hand on his arm and attempted to create a space between their bodies as they walked, but it was impossible. He kept a tight grip, creating an illusion of intimacy that had passersby examining them with curiosity.

He seated her, ordered for them, then folded his hands together and stared for so long, even her determined attempt to remain indifferent was rocked. "Do I have something on my face?"

Vincent shook his head. "You are a blindingly beautiful woman, especially when you make a bit of effort."

Alisha fought her first instinct. She'd obviously been hanging around the rougher-edged SAR team long enough that she'd lost some of her polish. In her society days she would have ignored a compliment/insult like that. Now she wanted to bite back and at least flash him a *fuck off*.

Instead she forced herself to smile. "Thank you."

His gaze continued to burn over her. "I hope you'll have many more opportunities to shine like this in the future."

"Why would I—?" She slammed to a stop. Rethought her wording and deliberately didn't ask him a question. "There's not a lot of call for full makeup and silk when I'm involved in rescues."

"Then I appreciate it all the more that you went all out for me." Vincent caught her off guard and folded his fingers around hers. "Thank you."

So far the night was everything she'd expected it to be. Awkward, unintentionally headed in the wrong direction. Alisha attempted to pull it back to the right path. "You and my father are good friends. I'm happy to spend an evening with you."

He stroked his thumb over her knuckles, and she cursed her choice of words. With anyone else they would be considered innocent, but not with Vincent. Well, Devon would have totally turned that slip against her as well, but his type of sexual aggression didn't scare her nearly as much as Vincent's smoldering gaze.

Whoever had said *smoldering* was a sexy thing was wrong. The look didn't cause her to be lit on fire with desire like she had experienced with Devon, all energy and excitement and wild passion. *Smoldering* was a piece of kindling being held under a reluctant squatter until the billows of smoke and noxious fumes forced them to move.

Their drinks arrived, appetizers. Alisha poked at the oysters without much appetite, nodding politely as Vincent told her about the latest changes at Bailey Enterprises. She'd been gone for four years. He talked about people and deals as if she should know what he was referring to, all of it positive and flattering toward himself, of course.

All the while she waited for the bomb to fall—for the moment when he'd turn into her father's mouthpiece and start asking about her return plans for the following summer.

When it finally came it was almost anticlimactic.

"I have a friend who is selling his condo." Vincent paused as the waiters whisked away their appetizer plates and brought a soup course. "It's in a fabulous location, and I thought of you. I know you won't need a place for a number of months, but it would make sense to buy now in anticipation of your return."

Alisha shook her head. "You're working under a false assumption, Vincent. I appreciate your thoughtfulness, but I have no intention of returning anytime soon. I have a wonderful job and a great career here in the mountains that I love. It's valuable work, being the best search-and-rescuer I can be." Her enthusiasm rang out strong. "It's thrilling to make a difference in people's lives."

"I understand that." Vincent slipped his chair closer, and she twitched in her seat. "I've always known how much this mattered to you. It's why I didn't fight it when you announced you wanted to go away to school."

Why would he have fought it? "It wasn't any of your concern, not then, not now."

Vincent leaned in. "Of course it is. After all, I was the one who convinced your father to give you the time to yourself."

His cheek was close to hers, but without tilting so far to the side that she'd fall out of her seat, there was no chance to retreat. Besides, she was still trying to make heads or tails of his last comment. "You convinced my father . . . of *what*?"

"I suggested there was no harm in your coming to the school here in Banff. That a chance to try something different would do you good, perhaps help you work your unhappiness out of your system. You've done well during your time away, and I'm very proud you—I even gave a donation to your school to prove how much I respect what you've done. Only now it's time for you to make plans to move on. Put this childishness behind you, and return to where you belong."

Her shock at one part of that announcement made it tough to comprehend the rest of what he'd said. "You gave *what*?"

Vincent smiled, obviously pleased with himself. "They supported you while you spread your wings, but now that it's time for you to return home—"

"I'm not a bloody pigeon you can call home to the roost." It hadn't been her father, but Vincent who'd interfered? Anger replaced her confusion. "This is my life, Vincent. You had no right to try to organize, or suggest, or do anything in it."

"I was giving you a chance to have time to yourself. Five years wasn't a long time to wait in the big picture." He stroked the silky fabric covering her arms, the back of his knuckles causing a warning shiver to race along her spine. "Five years to sow your wild oats before returning to where you belong. Although I do hope you haven't taken the old interpretation of that phrase too literally."

Around them the tinkle of wineglasses and gold flatware on china plates combined with the live piano music playing delicately in the corner of the room. Waiters stood at discreet intervals, but she couldn't seem to catch one's eye with the invitation to interrupt, and soon.

She and Vincent must have looked far too intimate to interrupt, which was so not what she wanted.

This entire conversation was off the tracks and headed for a cliff, and she'd had enough. Alisha lifted her chin and went for broke to regain control. "It's none of your business if I've fucked my way through half of Banff. I am not going back in a year's time. I have a home here. I have a job. I . . . have a boyfriend."

Tossing the lie out was reckless and wrong, but it felt necessary.

Her fib partially worked. For the first time since the evening had begun, Vincent retreated.

"You do? One of your co-workers, perhaps?" Vincent poured her more wine, settling back in his chair.

"Again, none of your business." Alisha hauled in the last dregs of politeness she could in one final attempt to halt the confusion between them. "Vincent, I feel as if you've gotten the mistaken idea that you and I are some kind of couple, or headed that way in the future. I'm not interested in a relationship with you other than as a family friend. I came out with you tonight to be polite. Now that this conversation has crossed into far too personal territory, it's time to stop."

Her outburst took him by surprise, and he seemed to reconsider, taking time to look around the room as he rearranged silverware and fussed with his place setting. Another change of plates occurred, their main courses arriving. Alisha calculated how much longer she needed to stay, or if they had reached the point where she could simply get up and leave.

Vincent's long sigh kept her in place for another moment. He nodded slowly before carefully lowering his voice. "I had planned on waiting until you returned because I didn't want to burden you, but if you truly are planning on staying in Banff, you've left me no choice than to broach this now. I'm worried about your father."

She blinked, but the puzzle pieces refused to fall in the right direction. "What does me staying in Banff have to do with my father?"

Vincent cut into his steak, the edge of the blade slicing through the thick flesh smoothly, red-tinged juices rushing from the cut. "You know your father has controlling interest of Bailey Enterprises. He's been making unwise decisions lately, Alisha. I'm concerned for the future of the company. If he continues this way he'll end up destroying everything he's worked so hard to achieve."

Well, not a way to motivate her to change her plans. "So?"

He pulled back in undisguised shock. "Your father could lose everything. You couldn't possibly want that."

"I couldn't care less." Her father had done the cutting off up to now, not her. "I have a roof over my head, and a job. I don't need the millions that seem to be all that keeps him happy. If he can't make the right business decisions, then he'll have to lose it all."

Vincent's jaw hung open for a second before he pulled himself together. "Those are the words of an ungrateful little girl."

She shrugged. "While I'm thankful for the benefits I received from my family when I was young, since I left home everything I've done has been on my own merits. Calling me ungrateful isn't a threat."

His dark eyes flashed, this time with something more like anger, and Alisha paused as she realized if the company failed, her father wouldn't be the only one to lose.

"Oh, Vincent. I'm sorry. I didn't even consider the impact Bailey Enterprises going under would have on you. You're serious? It's gotten that bad?"

He nodded. "Within the year if his mismanagement continues."

While Alisha still wasn't highly motivated to do anything, it was a lot tougher to simply blurt that out when one of the people whose livelihood was threatened by her father's supposed incompetence was right there in front of her.

She tried to sound sympathetic. "I don't see what difference I could make, Vincent, going back to Toronto. My father does have the majority of shares, and he's not about to ask my advice in running the company even if I do return."

Vincent gave her an earnest look. "If you add my shares to yours we have more than him."

Alisha laughed. "What shares? Maybe you didn't hear the news, but I don't get my shares until I'm thirty-five. I would willingly sell them to you—I have no interest in running the company—but that antiquated requirement in my grandfather's will means you'll have to wait nine years before I can access them."

He shook his head. "Too late and too little. There is another solution, and one that I think would benefit us both."

She waited.

He raised a brow. "You could take advantage of the loophole in your grandfather's will."

Loophole?

What he'd said finally sank in and she went numb.

Oh. My. God.

Vincent sat back in his chair and smiled.

Alisha's jaw hung open until she caught herself. "You're insane," she muttered. "Did you just . . . propose to me?"

He nodded. "It's a simple solution, really. As soon as we're married you'll receive your shares, and with our joint influence I'll be able to take control. Together we could save the company."

Alisha picked up her wine and drank far too deeply. She needed something to combat the ringing in her ears that cautioned that her internal comment about him being insane had not been off the mark. She clutched the glass for a moment, staring out the window beside her at the twinkling lights decorating the thick stone balconies and tall black-iron posts. The mountains of the Bow Valley range beyond the ground of the hotel were blurred, fading into the clouds and the haze of nightfall.

This couldn't be real. She'd slipped into a dream world—*nightmare world*—and she had to say the right words to break the spell, or she'd be trapped here forever.

"I'm honoured you consider us a good match, but we're not in love."

Vincent didn't shift position. He didn't change expression. "I didn't mention being in love. I don't expect it, even though I think we'd suit each other well."

This was unbelievable. "That's a little trite, isn't it? Getting married to save the company? Because there's an important dynasty to be preserved—"

"Isn't there?" Vincent moved now, capturing her fingers again before she could pull away. "I'm going about this all wrong. I do care for you. Don't mistake my lack of gushing for indifference. I simply see no reason to pretend unnecessary emotions."

"And I see no reason to pretend this isn't some monumental joke. I'm sorry, but I'm not marrying you. Not to save the company. I've chosen a different life, and I do not want to go back to the old one." She shook her head at the impossibility of it all. "Please, Vincent. There are other options. Convince my father to change business tactics, or find someone who will sell you the shares you need so you can take control and fix things. I'd sell you mine if I could access them—but I'm not for sale."

"You think I haven't tried to find another solution?" Vincent demanded. "I've gone over all the options, and it's the only possibility. I had hoped you would agree to a short engagement and quick wedding, but if you have a boyfriend, that complicates matters. You'll have to find a reasonable explanation to call it off. Soon. Once you've done that, we'll wait a few weeks, then announce our engagement, and we could still be married by Christmas."

He hadn't listened to a single thing she'd said. "I. Am. Not. Marrying. You. Why is that so hard for you to accept?"

Vincent shrugged. "It's in your best interest."

She glared, arms folded over her chest. "Don't threaten me."

"What have I said that was threatening?" He laughed, glancing around the room in amusement, his smile shining out to the world his supposed happiness. "I offered you a proposal of marriage. Hardly front-page news." His face tightened, and suddenly he wasn't so handsome anymore. "Unless you want to tell them everything I've mentioned tonight. Wouldn't that information look wonderful splashed everywhere in the media."

She clutched the arms of the chair so hard her fingers ached.

"No, Alisha. Even if you don't mind your father losing everything, I don't see you as the type to enjoy causing his downfall." The sorrowful smile on his lips didn't reach his eyes. "Oh, that would be horrific, wouldn't it? You, announcing your father's incompetency to run the company? That kind of press would undoubtedly lead to a drop in stock value, and set off what you claim to not care about."

"I would never get involved in that manner. I simply want to be left alone." She hated that she was nearly begging.

"I agree. Forcing your father to be hurt like that would be cruel." He ignored her real concerns again and pressed the issue. "It would be so much better to take a different approach regarding the media—perhaps announcing a far more lighthearted news item. Alisha Bailey being courted by Vincent Monreal, the two of us madly in love. One call, and I could have the paparazzi here—"

"You wouldn't dare."

He motioned with both hands as if he were soothing a wild animal. "I think we've discussed this enough. You're upset, and I can appreciate that hearing about your father's incompetence has been shocking news. Once you've had time to process it, I think you'll agree that marrying me is the best—"

"Dammit, Vincent. Listen to me."

He focused on his plate as if she hadn't even spoken. "Eat your dinner, it's getting cold."

The man was impossible. "I'm not hungry," she snapped.

"You are being terribly rude." Vincent lifted the wine bottle as if to refill her glass and finish the meal. As if the entire conversation hadn't just headed off into crazyland.

Alisha left. She didn't look back. Didn't glance over her shoulder to see if he was watching her. She knew he was, though. Felt it.

His scrutiny wasn't like the constant surveillance Devon had kept over the years. This was cold. Calculating.

She pulled out her phone as she waited for her car to be brought around, her fingers hovering over the link to call Devon.

The impossibility of it all made her pause. What would she tell him?

Vincent had . . . proposed to her? Intended to use her to take over the company? The whole situation was unbelievable.

Heck, she'd *give* Vincent her shares if that were possible. She hadn't lied—she didn't want any part of her old life.

If she had to struggle to pay the bills her entire life, it would be worth it as long as she got to be in the mountains doing something incredibly valuable.

To Vincent and her father, she was nothing but a game piece to be used and moved to their best advantage. Even if Vincent had lied about the business side of things, one part was true—her father did expect her to return in a year, all her wild passions satisfied. Prepared to be a quiet, docile member of the family. She'd never intended to return. This . . . option . . . offered by Vincent didn't encourage her, either.

Only this wasn't something she could explain to Devon. How could she explain it when she could barely comprehend it?

She pushed her phone into her purse and got back into her car, the ride home colder and lonelier than she ever remembered.

CHAPTER 12

It was far too early for the phone to ring. Devon blinked through the haze in his vision as his body responded to the call-out from Lifeline faster than his brain. He was on his feet. Pouring himself into his gear, waking up enough to get himself to respond. A glance at his watch showed he'd actually slept in, which he must have needed considering he still felt like hell.

The short trip to the Lifeline building passed in a blur.

"Looks as if we've hit stupid season early." Marcus's voice carried over the speakers in HQ as they scrambled to gather gear. "Sorry I'm not there, but I got stuck in Calgary last night. I didn't expect another emergency so soon. Lana will be your contact in the office for any information you need."

Lana waved at them from behind the call desk, already on the phone with their contact and relaying flight information details to Erin.

"I'm on lead," Anders called out. "We'll be fine, Marcus.

We'll keep you posted. Now get off the line and let us do our job."

"Bastard." Marcus laughed. "Everyone stay safe and good luck."

A rush of energy surged as they got ready. Devon paused to pour an extra coffee and set it before Lana, and she flashed him a huge smile without pausing her task.

Teamwork. The smooth coordination flowing around him eased the pre-rescue butterflies that came no matter how many times they did this.

Devon hurried with the rest of them into the chopper. Alisha looked nearly as bleary-eyed as he felt, but otherwise she appeared in complete control. It had been a couple of days since their explosive sexual release, but he hadn't been in a rush to contact her, and neither, it seemed, had she craved his company. They were back to keeping their distance.

Fine. As long as she was on task right now, he'd deal with the other situation later today.

"At least it's a decent hour." Xavier's nonstop banter arrived as usual. "Daylight will make it easier for the search. Anders? What's the word?"

"Lana? Want to fill in the gaps?"

"Guide took inexperienced paddlers down the Selkirk River. There's more than one set of class five rapids and at least two impassable class six falls—and the expected happened. Guide is missing along with one other canoe, so there are four possible victims." Her voice purred over the headsets, and Devon found himself nodding—having a contact who was easy to listen to was a nice change from Marcus's far more gravelly tones.

Devon bet she was glad she'd had time to recover from her little drinking session, though.

Lana continued. "The third canoe was found trapped in a logjam. The two who were in her made the call for help. It's been three days since they started the trip—it took that long for them to find their way out of the bush."

Anders jerked a thumb over his shoulder. "There's a local SAR team patrolling the river downstream from where the canoe was found. The valley widens so they can cover the territory pretty easily. We're heading upstream into the mountains. Erin can manoeuvre through most of the canyon. If she can't clear a section, we'll have to drop in to check the territory on foot."

"Descending on the winch?" Alisha asked.

"If it works." Anders shook his hand. "We're talking narrow-gauge canyons in that area."

He pulled out a map and laid it flat. Devon leaned forward with the rest of them, highly aware of Alisha on his left, her leg next to his as she wiggled to get a better view. She didn't seem overly stressed about the upcoming rescue.

He focused on the region Anders was highlighting.

"They put in the canoes at this point. Following the river, and with the news from the two that made it out, we know they were fine until this point." Anders stabbed the map with a finger. "That's when the group got separated."

Tripp made a rude noise. "That's the first set of rapids, and it's not even technically challenging. Bunch of idiots. What was the guide thinking?"

"If they had problems with those bumps, they'd never have made it through here." Xavier tapped the map where there was a noticeable change in elevation. "Did they even know how to park the boats to portage around the falls?"

"Good question." Anders stared into the air as he issued an order. "Lana, find out if the survivors were briefed about portaging. If they were, we'll have to check the trees more thoroughly."

"Got it." Lana jumped on the line, a faint crackle of background noise from the radios in the office carrying with her words. "Weather warnings just rolled in from Environment Canada. Erin, you have high winds coming in ahead of the storm front."

"Affirmative. Thanks for the heads-up." Erin spoke over her shoulder on the chopper-only line. "So far the newbie isn't doing so bad."

Devon adjusted his collar. High-wind warnings almost guaranteed they would be climbing and going on foot for parts of the rescue. Beside him, Alisha had closed her eyes, hands folded easily in her lap.

The urge to reach over and grasp her fingers flashed out of the blue. It made him wonder.

The travel time passed too quickly. Everyone changed position to look out the windows, eyes peeled for the sight of any kind of civilization. The bright orange marker the local SAR crew had placed at the canoe site glowed like a violent gash in the greens and browns of the local foliage.

"Everyone ready?" Anders asked.

Devon gave his affirmative, his gaze meeting Alisha's for a moment. She smiled and shot a thumbs-up. Her confidence shone out even while a hint of weariness lingered in her eyes.

Which, hell, he could understand. They'd worked each other over like crazy the other day, not to mention that the previous rescue and flood incident were less than a week ago.

Erin banked the chopper, the angle hard enough that they all scrambled to grab tightly to security straps as they found positions and stared outside.

"Anything more from the survivors? Jacket colours, canoe information?" Tripp pressed his hands to the glass as he leaned into the concave window. "Tell me they all wore neon pink and make my day."

Lana clicked through. "You'll love this bullshit. The canoes are painted with camouflage—apparently the guide moonlights leading hunting parties during the duck-hunting season and figured it was a good idea to use the same craft for both activities."

Devon banged his forehead against the glass. "Idiot."

"It gets worse," Lana warned. "Looks as if your best bet will be the dry bag. As in, you heard me right, there's *one* dry bag for the lot of them in the guide's canoe. Bright red, at least."

"This guy actually have a license, or did he set up a company online and start bullshitting people?"

"Pretty much. The two who walked away from it said they were offered one place to stick cameras, phones, and wallets for the trip that wouldn't get wet. Everything else they shoved into backpacks, sports sacks, and garbage bags."

"High tech," Anders sighed. "Black garbage bags, of course."

"Of course."

Devon listened to the banter, but all his attention was on the water passing slowly beneath them. On the massive rocks lining the shoreline, the tall pines breaking their visibility as the water popped in and out of sight at random intervals. "The one good thing about this area not being a common destination for canoers—any garbage we see is probably from this incident."

"Exactly. Eyes peeled for garbage stuck in the rocks. Watch the sweepers along the riverbanks plus any low-lying branches things could get caught on. Devon, you focus on the water and the edge in this section, I'll check the trees," Anders ordered. "There's a portage coming up. On the left, Alisha, you've got the water, Tripp, the trees."

Below them the landscape changed. Instead of flying over a river that ran along a fairly level path, the elevation rose sharply to produce multiple waterfalls, each one descending no more than a dozen feet but forming a myriad of options for the water to pour over. Hidden nooks and darkened chasms created places that more than a canoe could vanish into.

"Stop," Tripp shouted.

Erin paused their forward motion. "Of course, right smack in the middle of the . . . Damn crosswinds. It won't be a smooth ride, guys. Hold on."

The chopper was buffeted from side to side as Tripp pointed. Erin fought to keep them level in the changing wind currents rushing around the pillars of rock.

"There's a bag on the edge of the scrag pile there. See it?"

Devon had found nothing on the right, so he rose to peer over Alisha's shoulder. The chopper rocked and he caught hold of her to steady himself as they both eyed the ground.

"I see it," Alisha said excitedly. "Backpack. Only . . . that's old school. It's got an exterior frame."

"Makes sense." Anders's disdain was clear. "Hunters use exterior frames for carrying out kills. I bet our wonder guide used the same gear for all of his upmarket adventure experiences."

"Can you get in closer?" Devon asked Erin. He glanced behind them as best he could, but the water remained unsearchable, with too many rocks and blocked lines of sight. "We can't see if there's anyone in the river from here."

"You'll have to go on foot. Sorry, guys. Anders can lower you to the shoreline, but there's no place for me to land soft-bodied people. The winds alone will play havoc with your descent."

Anders stepped back to his position. "Prep for action. Alisha, we'll put you down first. If you spot anything unusual on your descent, radio your recommendations for a change of drop site."

"Got it." She was out of her seat and hooking up her harness in a flash. Devon and the rest followed suit, the chopper leveling. Even with headsets on, the props were a constant buzz in his ears, the rush and pump of the massive blades creating a throb as if the chopper had a heartbeat.

"I lifted a bit so you can get ready in relative calm," Erin commented. "Let me know when you're ready."

Ropes, climbing cams, first-aid supplies. Everything they needed for a rescue was pushed into bags or attached to their harnesses. Alisha moved into position next to Anders. "Ready."

He double-checked all her attachments, fingers flying in the familiar safety check pattern they'd done hundreds of times in both training and real-life situations. "You're good."

He glanced at the others. Tripp and Xavier were clearing each other's gear.

Alisha stepped up to Devon. She tugged straps and adjusted gear, her touch skilled and professional. Then her gaze rose to meet his, and her serious expression made something inside him tighten.

She flipped his radio to a private station. "I'm fine, and ready to roll. You be careful, okay?"

It was more than the gesture of a concerned teammate. Devon nodded. "I've got your back."

The doors opened and the wind blasted into the chopper bay. The violent gust lifted everything that wasn't strapped in place and attempted to rip free everything that was. Alisha clutched the safety hooks by the door tighter, waiting for the go-ahead.

"Erin, I can't send anyone out in this," Anders complained.

Cursing carried over the line before Erin got it under control. "This is what you've got unless I take you a kilometer upstream, and even then there're no guarantees it'll calm down."

Alisha glanced outside, judging the drop. The wind was stupidly high, but there was a wide landing spot to make for, and it wasn't that far below them. "I can do this."

Anders stood beside her, staring out and judging as well. "It's crazy, Alisha."

"If I get a line set you can slide the gear and crew in less time than it'll take to hike from wherever Erin thinks is an alternative. I'm sure of it. Let me try."

He examined her face and the ground once more before nodding firmly. "Fine, if you're up for it, we'll give it a shot. Erin, Alisha's dropping. Five minutes of your best flying ever, got it?"

"Got it. Alisha, have fun, girl."

Anders caught her by the chest harness and attached a secondary cable. "If you get into trouble, call it off and Erin will lift straight up. We can have you on solid ground in less than two minutes after bugging out. Deal?"

"Deal, but we're good." She couldn't stop herself from glancing over Anders's shoulder at Devon. There was concern in his eyes, yes, but his smile was back. The cocky one that said he was having fun.

The adrenaline rushing through her veins proved she was enjoying herself far too much. Other worries faded away. Family demands. Ultimatums. Vincent's bizarre behavior, even the panic she'd felt days earlier—she knew all those issues were there, that they were real, but here and now was *more* real. More vivid and making her come alive.

She dropped from the doorway into the open air.

Icy fingers clutched her as the wind personified into an evil demon intent on tearing her from her safe connection to the helicopter. Anders managed her cable, slowly lowering her to the ground. She spun uncontrollably in the wind, twisting her head to catch glimpses of the waterfalls downstream. The wind actually decreased as she got closer to the uneven surface, and on the third rotation she slowed enough to spot something.

There, jackpot.

"We got a hit, guys. There's a paddle in the scrag pile to the right, and clothing and a black garbage bag stuck to branches on the edge of the cliffs."

"Affirmative. Ten feet. Prep for landing."

Alisha got ready to hit the ground, well aware that with the high winds Erin was doing her best, but that at any moment the chopper could change levels. While she was being lowered on the cable it wasn't as scary a thought. The worst time was at landing, when the ground could come up or down far too fast.

She kept her hand by the safety buckles, and the instant she touched land she dropped to one knee and detached the main cable. Now there was only her extended safety line connecting her to the sky. "I'm down. Hang on, Erin, ten seconds."

Even as she spoke, Alisha snapped into motion and got the gear in place. She set an anchor into the ground, looped a spare length of rope through it, and attached it to the main cable. The emergency setup she used basically created the equivalent of a giant elastic band. If Erin needed to adjust and rise slightly higher there wouldn't be any disastrous results—the ropes would expand or contract to use the slack provided.

She stepped back. "Ready for gear."

One after another, bags slipped off the edge of the chopper deck and careened down the line. Alisha was impressed all over again with Erin's ability to keep the chopper in one spot, hovering in spite of the wind current striving to push her off course. If the pressure were like a river current it would have been hard enough—a steady force that the pilot would have to fight against. But wind was even more erratic, gusting and lessening without warning. Throughout it all Erin managed to do the damn near impossible.

The bags slowed as they reached the ground, the secondary ropes Anders controlled applying the brakes so she could detach the carabiners and jerk the heavy bags off the rope and to the side. After the fourth bag, her arms were screaming for a time-out.

"Devon's in place. Prep for his arrival," Anders warned.

If looking up into the sky and seeing gear racing downward was thrilling, there was something even more exhilarating when the moving target was human. The steep cable incline meant Devon dropped rapidly but smoothly, the wind bowing out his coat before Anders hit the safety and slowed him not more than ten feet before Devon's feet hit the ground.

His grin said it all. "Holy *shit*, that was a blast."

Alisha agreed even as she prepped for Tripp's arrival.

She didn't breathe easier until they were all on the ground and she could detach the grounding cable. "You're free, Erin. And thank you, that was some amazing flying."

"Erin, you rock," Tripp agreed.

"We'll do a quick recon between here and the put-in site, since we can't help you in the waterfalls for the first while anyway," Anders announced. "Devon, you're in charge of the ground search. Everyone okay?"

They were up and out without any further discussion. Like the well-practiced team they were, everyone grabbed gear and moved to the nearest lip of the falls. Devon stepped closer to examine the drop.

Alisha paused as she dug into her bag for extra climbing cams. They were only feet away from the roaring water, the crash ringing in her ears. Her heart rate was elevated, her breathing rapid, but she wasn't panicking. It was all the emotions and excitement of a rescue, none of the icy-cold terror she'd experienced the last time out.

She rose to her feet and turned to discover Devon loaded with gear, his gaze fixed on her. She nodded and gave him an affirmative again. There was no malice in his examination, and it felt good to know that while he'd keep his word to ensure that the entire team was safe, he hadn't assumed she'd lose it again.

They moved into position, gazing over the falls. Devon pointed inland. "Trail on the side. Tripp, follow it downstream and report if you spot anything. Alisha and I will check the drops one at a time starting at the top. Xavier, you can follow the edge of the falls along the trail, but stay available for either of us calling you."

Tripp and Xavier took off as Alisha hooked up the first set point. "You want me to belay you?"

Devon shook his head. "You're good."

They tied in again, stopping for yet another of the endless checks to ensure their knots and carabiners were locked. Then Devon surprised the hell out of her by catching hold of her and kissing her briefly, the brows of their helmets clicking together.

"Stay safe." His words came out rough and off kilter.

Alisha grinned even as the shock of his kiss warmed her. "Bet I can get to the third falls in two jumps."

He rolled his eyes. "Enough with the bets. I don't like the looks of the second spray."

She nodded. "Think something's caught?"

Devon's nose wrinkled.

That was the horrid part of the job. When it wasn't a rescue, but a recovery. She pushed sorrow aside and tightened her ropes in preparation. "On belay."

"Belay on."

When she found he'd been right and the second falls were blocked with the broken bow of a canoe, her stomach turned. "Devon, trouble."

She was roped up, so moving into the current a few paces was safe, but the water crashing from above was too powerful to allow her to get a firm anchor on the wood. Her fingers could just wrap around the gunwale, but no matter how hard she rocked, nothing moved. "I can't budge it. We'll have to get Erin overhead so Anders can lower a hook."

"I'm coming down."

By the time Devon was ready to join her she'd looked around more and gathered a batch of gear that had washed onto the small rocky edge of the pool.

She finished belaying him and he turned, facing the soggy pile of personal items with sadness in his expression. "It's not looking good, is it?"

She shook her head.

Tripp's voice carried on the speakers. "I'm at the base of the falls, and we've got a DOA. There's a half of a broken canoe, and a body in the sweepers on the poolside at the base. They must have gone right the hell over that edge."

It didn't look good at their end, either. "Any sign of the second canoe?" Alisha asked.

This time it was Anders who answered. "We've got them. There's a canoe on the shoreline and people waving. Only, sweet mother of God, there's nowhere to land this baby. We're coming to get you. Alisha, you'll have to do a drop to pick these guys up on the cable."

A short time later they'd returned. Erin placed the chopper over the mangled watercraft and Anders lowered a massive hook. They tipped the canoe and a second body popped free from its trapped position. Devon caught it before it could disappear over the edge of the pool. The red dry bag that had also come loose bobbed a couple of times before vanishing into the foaming water beneath them.

Alisha fought her dismay and soldiered on as they wrapped the body for transport, hooking the harness in place and allowing Anders to winch everything into the chopper.

They returned to the main level of the falls and waited for the cable to descend for their journey up into the bay area.

Devon pulled her aside for a moment, cupping her cheek in his hand. His fingers were cold on her skin and she pressed her fingers over his briefly.

He dipped his chin. "You were amazing. As usual."

She blinked at the pure passion in his words. "Thank you."

He tilted his head toward the water. "No problems at any time, right?"

"Nothing to be afraid of—nothing more than usual rescue nerves."

"I didn't see you hesitate even once." He nodded. "I still think we need to get together when we get home to have a deep, thorough discussion of what happens next."

"Are you asking me for a date, Mr. Leblanc?" Alisha raised a brow. "Because it seems that the issue we thought we had might not be an issue."

Devon grinned. "We need to confirm you're not afraid of showers when they contain sexually excited men with an urgent need to ravish you."

It was wrong in so many ways, and yet equally right. Death's mark would accompany them as they returned to civilization. Their rush of desire was an indicator of life—of all that they strived to do. Save those they could save, and find peace for those left behind. Alisha didn't feel as if it were blasphemous or wrong for her and Devon to share the fire in their veins.

To remember and celebrate that they were alive.

CHAPTER 13

·····························

They set down on the tarmac outside HQ hours later than he'd have liked, but Devon couldn't complain. After they'd dropped the rescued victims, and the unfortunate ones who didn't make it, at the hospital in Radium, they'd crawled into the refueled chopper and headed for home. The extra time had given him the chance to replay the events of the day and come to a happy conclusion.

Alisha had done her customary flawless job. Her freak-out during the previous rescue had obviously been a onetime event, and his long-term concerns faded. Relief was quickly buried by a vigorous compulsion to grab her and kiss her senseless. The furtive glances between them had been growing harder to hide. As if once they'd let their attraction out, they were impatient to experience the fire all over again.

He sure the hell was.

Unpacking the chopper gave them plenty of opportunities to find themselves in close contact. Hips bumping at moments, rubbing past each other in the narrow passage from the storage area into the main transport bunker.

Everyone worked quickly, moving to unload gear. Tripp shouted after Anders, then raced down the path toward HQ. Devon grinned as he reversed direction and stalked to the back of the chopper to corner her outside the cargo hold, momentarily alone.

Alisha turned from the bag she'd zipped and gasped slightly, her smile widening as she took in his arms caging her on either side. "Well, it looks as if I'm not taking this equipment anywhere for the next minute or so."

She caught his face in her hands, kissing him deep and hard, pressing her body against his and rubbing shamelessly. He cupped her ass, lifting her the slight distance it took to line them up properly, his lips never leaving hers.

Excitement welled inside, anticipation at what would come next. It had been only a couple of days, and he was willing to say he'd missed her.

Wanted her like crazy.

One of the chopper doors creaked a warning, and they pulled apart, still grinning like fools.

"You coming home with me?" Devon asked quietly.

"You have a bigger shower than I do," Alisha pointed out.

The images her comment raised only widened his smile as he snatched up handfuls of gear and headed into the storage rooms.

Alisha was at his back before he could finish coiling the ropes and storing them properly. She snaked her arms around him. "You want me to grab some food on the way to your place?"

Warm body pressed to him, her hands playing over his waist—there were a whole lot of things he wanted that popped to mind, and food wasn't even on the list.

"You'd better, or I have a feeling we'll forget to eat. If by some chance you beat me home, there's a key under the mat." She dragged her hand back, stroking his groin, and he caught her wrist, trapping her fingers over his growing erection. "Now that's not playing nice."

"I'm as turned on as you right now. Does that make me a freak?"

He twisted to face her. "It makes you lucky you don't
have to hide a damn hard-on during debrief."

Alisha smiled sweetly. "Poor baby. So hard done by."

"Hard, yes. God, so fucking hard." He glanced around
to be sure they were alone before sneaking one more kiss.
Alisha pushed him away and escaped the room laughing.

Out in the main gathering space Lana grinned as she
joined them in the common area. "Sounds as if the entire
rescue was amazing."

"Thanks for your help at the desk. Everyone did a great
job today." Anders pointed at Erin. "But there's the top dog.
You did some incredible flying. We'd never have finished so
quickly without you."

Erin took a bow, then passed out bottles of sports drink.

"Hear, hear." Devon raised his in the air. He settled on
the couch, debating if making room for Alisha would be too
obvious or a straight-out bad idea. He'd managed to get
himself under control, but only so far as there was nothing
obviously showing anymore.

He didn't have to make the final decision as Lana dropped
beside him.

Alisha crawled onto the other couch next to Xavier, complete innocence on her face as she leaned in and grabbed a
granola bar off the table.

Anders took them through debrief quick enough, but
every time Devon glanced up and saw Alisha across from
him, his imagination made it tough to stay on target. He was
ready to be gone. Out of the company of the team and alone
with her. Peeling off her clothing and joining her in the
shower to scrub them both from top to bottom. He had just
the thing to do it with. He could picture the enormous puffy
scrub thing his sister had sent him as a gag gift that would
look incredible against Alisha's naked body. The peach-
coloured ball of fuzz contrasting against her smooth skin
as he stroked it along the inside of her thighs. Over the curve
of her waist and up the side of her breasts . . .

Devon shook himself to attention, leaning away from
Lana, who'd pressed closer than necessary to examine the

map on the table and hadn't adjusted back when she was done. Across from them, Alisha's brow tweaked upward as she glanced pointedly at the woman by his side.

Frustration fought with the urge to be charitable. Maybe Lana didn't realize she was nearly hanging over him? He rose to his feet under the guise of pointing out something to Anders, and then instead of sitting back down, he remained standing behind the couch.

Alisha's lips curled upward as she stared at Anders, but Devon knew what had triggered that smirking expression.

The debrief concluded, and everyone milled about for a couple of minutes before Alisha escaped, a final meaningful glance his way. Devon shot to his locker to get his keys and town coat, leaving the heavy rescue gear hanging to dry.

"You want to get something to eat?" A set of hands curled around him, reminiscent of only a short time earlier, only now all he felt was dismay. He turned quickly and backed as far away from Lana as he could.

"Thanks for the invite, but I've got other plans." Devon scrambled for a change of topic. "So, first time helping and all. Well done."

"Thanks. Maybe sometime I'll get to go out with you guys on a call. You know, if Marcus is in the office." Lana stroked Devon's arm. "You must be tired. I could give you a massage if you'd like."

Holy shit, where was this coming from?

"Um, no thank you. I've got other plans for tonight already." He glanced into the hallway, not sure if he wanted to be rescued or would prefer not to have anyone see this awkward situation.

Lana blinked, still too far into his private space. "Oh. Okay. Well, I thought we were going to do something once you were done today."

Where had she gotten that idea? "No, we hadn't talked about it."

His instinctive response about not getting involved with people he worked with froze on his tongue, because there was no way he would outright lie. Only he didn't think he'd done anything to encourage Lana, either.

She finally backed up a step, looking him up and down slowly. "Sorry, I must have misunderstood."

Devon scrambled. "I mean, you're attractive and all, but I'm not . . ."

Great. All his so-called legendary ways with the women were shown up here and now to be utter bunk. He had no idea how to turn her down without putting his foot in his mouth.

Tripp wandered around the corner and Lana backed away more.

"We'll talk again later, Devon. Some other time will work better to get together. No problem." She waved at the two of them, then vanished.

Her sunshiny response was nearly as confusing as the come-on had been.

Tripp pulled his coat from his locker, a twisted smile rising far too quickly.

"Shut up. It's not what it looked like," Devon snapped.

The dark-haired man shrugged, pulling his coat shut and tossing his keys from one hand to the other. "It *looked* as if a certain young lady is trolling through the Lifeline guys in the hopes one of them will put in a good word for her with the boss. That's all I saw. She blew it with Xavier the other night when he had to pour her into her apartment. She's moved on to you because everyone *knows* you don't think with anything but your dick."

Devon laughed. Tripp's comment was so dry it was ridiculous. "Why the hell would she do that?"

"Because some people don't rely on only doing their job to get ahead." Tripp smirked. "I can hardly wait until she hits on me. Think she'll have any luck?"

Devon didn't fight his grin. "She's missing some vital equipment if she's trying to entice you to go to bat for her."

Tripp raised his thumbs up, then glanced out the door. "Keep an eye on her. I don't trust her much, and not just because she's acting up."

Devon nodded, then got out as quickly as he could. He had better things to think about than overly ambitious call-out staff.

In his immediate future he had Alisha, a shower, and a lot of skin to scrub.

Alisha placed the take-out bag with the roast chicken on the table, then headed to search the cupboards for plates and utensils. She'd beaten Devon home—not surprising since she'd slipped out of HQ before anyone could ask her to do anything. Grabbing some ready-made meal items at the local grocery store had taken less than fifteen minutes.

Maybe the rush of excitement that hit as she let herself into his house was unusual, but it still gave her a bit of a thrill. Something as simple as having access to his private domain without him being present brought a giddy smile to her lips as much as the thought of what would happen once he got home. It was another level of trust he'd offered her, and right now she appreciated it very much.

It had been hours since they'd finished the rescue. Even longer since she'd faced the rushing water of the falls and known for certain her earlier panic attack was a one-off event. She'd thought it was, but until she was faced with another challenge, she couldn't be sure.

Vincent was more of a concern than her panic attack, and that realization pissed her off greatly.

Once the table was set, she wandered Devon's living room and waited for him to join her. Sitting on the floor by his music collection made her smile. All of her music was digital, but Devon had one of those old vertical stackers, and she pulled one CD from it after another, her amusement rising.

She loaded his CD player and hit play, the rich sounds of classical orchestration filling the house with the familiar music of her childhood. *The Mission*, *Empire of the Sun*— soundtracks with hauntingly beautiful melodies brought up the good memories she had from before her family's expectations had changed.

Alisha paced slowly through the small house. The minimal furniture was similar to her own, with a few better pieces mixed in with the thrift shop buys. The mystery of who Devon was made her wonder.

She'd kept herself and her background secret for years, and in doing so she'd blocked off sharing with others. He was the youngest of a large family, she knew that. He grew up in Calgary, he had friends in Banff . . .

He was an extraordinary lover.

The door swung open and she twisted to greet him. His smile flashed, and a rush of anticipation hit again.

He cocked his head to the side, listening. A groan escaped him. "You found the CDs my brother gave me."

"You never told me you were a classical fan. We'll have to load the chopper with a few of your selections to share with the team."

"Don't get me wrong, I don't mind the stuff, but that collection is my brother attempting to civilize me." Devon crossed the room to her side and slipped his arms around her. "Xavier listens to anything, Tripp enjoys it as well, but if you can convince Erin to agree to try something other than that pot-banging stuff she likes, you're a miracle worker."

"I'll have to tell her your opinion of her musical tastes." Alisha looked up, savouring the warmth between them.

"Trust me, she knows." Devon paused, then peeled himself away. "If I start kissing you, I won't be able to stop. Food first?"

"Everything is ready." She followed him into the kitchen and accepted the chair he held for her.

What followed was an exercise in sexual frustration. He didn't touch her. Didn't move his chair closer and lean in, or whisper sexy innuendo while they ate. He simply watched.

Every time she moved, his gaze followed her as if he were memorizing her. Stroking her skin without a touch. When she lifted a forkful of salad to her mouth he stared at her lips. She licked the dressing from the tines, and he swallowed. She picked up a piece of chicken and put her teeth to it, and the fire in his eyes lit something inside to blazing hot.

"You're making me crazy," she complained.

He lowered his glass to the table. "Eat. I can't ravish you until we're fed."

Another minute passed. Another. Alisha considered abandoning the meal to get right to the good parts, but after the day they'd had, if she didn't refuel, the ravishing wouldn't last long.

By the time she'd satisfied one hunger, though, her body was buzzing with another need. She placed her utensils across her plate and lowered her hands to her lap. "All done. I'm ready for my ravishing, sir."

Devon abandoned his plate and caught her up in his arms, "God, I'd thought you'd never finish."

Alisha laughed as he twirled them toward the back of the house, pulling to a stop outside his bedroom. "Shower?" she asked. "I never took one at Lifeline because you'd mentioned . . ."

He lowered her feet to the floor, their bodies rubbing together the entire way down. "Through that door. Strip, I'll join you in a minute. Less than a minute."

Then he was gone, vanishing into his bedroom. Alisha didn't waste any time but raced to the front door where she'd left her bag. Stripping off her clothes was first priority; sneaking a minute with her toothbrush was the second.

Devon returned when she was rinsing her mouth, and his laughter wrapped around her like a caress. She returned the glass to the counter and twisted to face him. "Good oral hygiene is important."

He breathed out a long hum of approval, his gaze lingering on her breasts, lowering down her body. "Of course it is. Now get your ass in the shower."

"Bossy." She stepped into the shower enclosure. "How did you score such an amazing house in Banff? I covet your walk-in shower."

Devon put a condom on the soap ledge in the wall, dodging out of the way as she turned on the water. "It's an old servants' quarters for the main home on the street front. The owners are friends of my parents—they had renovated this place for their son when he still lived at home, and when he moved out they offered it to me. In exchange I watch their house and deal with all the mail and bills while they snow-bird to Arizona in the winter."

"It's perfect." Alisha left the door open as she eased under the water. Heat poured over her, soothing her fatigued muscles, but the view was too fascinating to ignore. Devon stripped off his shirt, abdominal muscles flexing as he tossed the fabric aside. "You can do that slower if you'd like. There's no rush."

He paused with his hands on his belt. "You're looking for entertainment, are you?"

She slipped her hands up her torso and cupped her breasts, loving how his expression darkened, his hunger coming through clearly. "We talked about ravishing, but I feel a slow simmering event might hit the spot."

He popped his button and lowered his zipper without removing his gaze from her body. "I can do simmer. Maybe."

Alisha laughed. "Lack of control a problem for you, Devon? I'd never have guessed."

His eyes snapped up. "You want me in control?"

His tone of voice changed. Deepened. Twirled around her like a lariat and wrapped her tight. A shiver slipped along her spine in spite of the heated water caressing her. "Slow and controlled would be perfect right about now."

A wicked grin was his response. "Then I guess I'll have to dig deep, won't I?"

He opened his pants farther, his cock pressing the fabric of his boxer briefs. Alisha licked her lips and continued a slow caress over her body as she admired him. Strong thighs came into view, his calf muscles. He stepped out of his pants and edged closer, muscles flexing mesmerizingly as he stalked to the edge of the shower enclosure.

He dropped his gaze to between her legs. "Pick up the soap and lather your hands." He seemed unaware he'd low-ered a hand over his cock and was stroking it through the fabric, but as she followed his directions, that was what she focused on. The thickening length hidden from her view tantalized her. Made her mouth water.

The scent of peaches rose into the air as she rubbed her hands together, slippery and aromatic at the same time.

"Open your legs and put your hands on your pussy. That's it. Slower, though. Don't rush." He hummed approvingly as Alisha slipped her fingers through her folds, slicking briefly over her clit, then avoiding the sensitive trigger and working the rest of her sex.

Devon stripped off his briefs and joined her in the shower, grabbing the soap and coating his hands as well. She glanced at his cock, the heavy shaft full and reaching toward his navel, a bead of semen glistening on the slit before he put his hands on himself again. He fisted his cock with one hand and caressed his balls with the other.

"I could do that for you," she offered. She wanted to touch him so badly.

"Your hands are supposed to be busy," he reminded her. "Open yourself to me. I want to watch."

"You're always watching," she muttered, but she followed his directions. Widened her stance. Used her left hand to reveal herself.

Devon dropped to his knees. Alisha held her breath but he didn't touch her, just stared from inches away. She shifted uneasily, pressure inside rising as she waited for the next thing.

He grasped his cock again and stroked slowly. "Get yourself off. I want to see what you do."

She didn't wait for another invitation. Adjusted her position so the water slid over her to make her touch softer, but she was plenty slick. She dipped her fingers inside her pussy briefly then stroked her clit. Once, then again. A little harder, but just as slow. Increasing the pressure without making her motions more rapid ensured a leisurely climb to release.

At her feet Devon pulled harder on his cock and she watched in fascination as the head peeked out from his fist again and again. Without intending to, she matched pace

with him, speeding slightly, then slowing. It was impossible
to stop the little gasps and moans escaping her lips.

"That's it. Don't keep it in—I love hearing what turns
you on."

He shifted closer and she took in a deep breath as he
caught her wrists in his hands and licked her.

"Oh yeah. Again."

He laughed. "Not your choice."

His tongue flicked her clit, small circles that were more
than enough to keep her on the edge of pleasure, not enough
to send her over. Alisha tugged her hands free so she could
thread her fingers through his hair. "Please, Devon."

"You're close, aren't you?" He kissed her pussy lips,
returning to place another devastating twirl of his tongue
over her clit.

"So close," she whispered. "Please, oh, yes. *There.*"

He'd slipped a finger into her, gently playing at her opening. The contrast in sensation made tension tingle throughout her lower body, her core aching for release. Every time
she got close, though, he changed tack. Instead of circling
with his finger he pulsed in and out, the pad of his finger
brushing the front of her passage. He switched from tormenting her clit to laving all the sensitive tissue of her feminine folds.

Control. He had it all, and she was on the verge of losing
hers but never allowed to go over. It was devastating in such
a good way. Frustrating, but so satisfying.

When he stood she swayed for a second, his strong arm
curving around her body the only thing keeping her vertical.

He snatched up the condom and opened it carefully. No
frantic tearing with his teeth, no fumbling to cover himself
as rapidly as possible. Instead he rolled the latex down his
length slowly before catching her hand and pulling it over
him. Curving her fingers around his shaft and moving their
fingers together in a slow caress that made her even crazier.
"All kinds of stupid phrases just popped to mind."

"It's so big, how will it fit?" Devon tucked his fingers

under her chin and lifted her head for a punishing kiss that left her gasping for breath and her lips bruised.

When he released her she smiled, pumping him again. "We know it fits. I can hardly wait."

"You're the one who said go slow," he reminded her.

"I was delusional, and needed to be taken in hand."

Devon lifted her onto the riser at the side of the shower and caught her knee, raising her leg to the side. "Oh, so that's what that little demand to be controlled was about. You were having delusions."

He pressed her shoulders to the shower wall and adjusted his position until his cock rubbed her sex, her hand still grasping him.

"You have a step in the shower to make sex easier?"

Devon slipped the head of his cock into her, then paused. His right hand pressed to the wall beside her head, his smile dazzling her. "Previous owner. There are all kinds of modifications to the house I'm pretty sure his parents had no idea what they were for."

"Enough talk. Fuck me already." The instant the words slipped out, she knew she'd made a mistake.

Devon raised a brow.

Alisha lowered her head, fighting to keep the begging words from escaping. Then she stared up from under her lashes, forcing herself to resist pulsing her hips forward to take his cock into her body. "Please?"

Instead, he stayed like that, only partially in her. Just enough that she felt him there, needing more, desperate for him not to retreat farther.

She squeezed her internal muscles and he hummed happily against her lips, where he'd moved in for a gentle kiss. "I love women with great muscle control."

Alisha moaned in complaint. "Can I touch myself?"

"No." He flexed his hips and his cock spread her farther. "What else?"

She struggled to breathe. "Can I touch you?"

"No, hands to the wall."

Her palms slapped the tiles so fast and hard the sound echoed in the enclosure. As a reward, he moved again, rocking an inch forward before retreating.

"Oh, *yes*." Alisha closed her eyes and took a deep breath, focusing on the feel of him pulsing slowly in and out of her body. He held her right leg to the side, and with her arms wide she was perfectly braced. The only connection point between them were his hand on her knee and his cock relentlessly spreading her again and again.

She was pinned to the wall like some kind of butterfly specimen. The image made her smile as he thrust harder, burying his entire length deep.

The shower still soaked them. From the living room, the sounds of yet another musical drifted down the hall. The aroma of peaches and the lingering taste of toothpaste— everything invading her senses faded into the background, and his cock became all she could concentrate on. The orgasm that had hovered for so long drew closer, and as he quickened his pace, she lost control. Lost the desire to demand from him. Just waited for the moment when he'd take her there.

Nearly violent pleasure broke over her and Alisha called out his name. Devon adjusted his angle and went even deeper, pushing her further, taking her higher. He stopped, buried deep, and caught her behind the neck.

She stared into his face as he joined her, her climax triggering his. His eyelids fell partway as his release jolted out.

He pressed their lips together and she kissed him hungrily, twining her arms around his neck and shaking with extended pleasure. The slow buildup had brought her to a place she'd never been before, and the trip back to normality would take a while.

His caresses slowed. He lowered her limb carefully. His cock was still buried inside her as the water smoothed over them both. Heart rates dropping, smiling around kisses.

Alisha wasn't in control right now, and it had never felt so right.

CHAPTER 14

,,,,,,,,,,,,,,,,,,,,,,,,,,,,,,,

Devon wondered if he was the one going crazy. They'd fumbled through drying off, tumbling onto the bed in a nearly exhausted heap, and pulled the quilts up before passing out.

After their work that day a nap wasn't out of place, but waking up beside a naked Alisha made emotions rise he really didn't want to deal with.

He shouldn't allow himself, but he couldn't stop staring. Her hair was spread over his pillows, her fingers curled around his biceps as if she were trapping him in place. Their legs were tangled together enough that if he wanted to leave she'd probably wake up, and he couldn't bear that.

In the distance a cell phone rang, and Alisha's lashes fluttered as she woke. "Shit. That's mine."

Devon stroked away a strand of hair that had fallen across her face. "Mine isn't going off, so it's not a call-out, although they'd be crazy to try to get us out twice in one day anyway. Whoever it is will leave a message. You can call them back."

She took a deep breath and stretched, rubbing lazily

against him. "I can't think of anyone important who'd be calling me."

Her smile faded as a shadow crossed her eyes.

"What?" he asked.

She shook her head. "Nothing. Well, something, but at the same time nothing important. Not really."

Devon laughed, stroking his fingers down her body and enjoying how she arched into his touch. "That was complete and utter gibberish. Why don't you try again?"

She caught his hand and pulled it off where he'd gotten stuck on her breast. "I might have used your name in vain the other night. The phone call reminded me."

"Oh, really?" He leaned on an elbow. "Did you out me to the fashion police? Sign off your excessive drink tab in my name at the Rose and Crown like Xavier tried?"

She wrinkled her nose. "I might have told someone you were my boyfriend."

Oh, really? His mind raced as he escaped her hold and returned to teasing her skin. "Now, the other night. That limits who you might have said such a thing to. Couldn't be any of the crew, because we'd have been teased mercilessly this morning otherwise."

Alisha waited, a touch of something in her eyes that wasn't quite fear but also wasn't the bold woman he'd seen on the side of the mountain this morning.

Insight hit. "Ahhh, night as in your *not-hot date* with Vincent the Vampire?"

She snorted. "He doesn't sparkle."

"I was thinking more of the classic bloodsuckers. Wears fancy duds, has no sense of humour." Devon sat all the way up and pulled her into his arms. "Was there a reason you needed to use my name like holy oil to fend him off?"

She wrapped her fingers around his biceps. "He was being more aggressive than I wanted. I thought if I told him I was otherwise occupied, he'd get the hint and leave me alone."

Devon nodded. "Did it work?"

She grimaced. "Sort of."

"How can discouraging a guy work 'sort of'?" Then Lana leapt to mind, and Devon made a face of his own. "Wait, no, I get it. People are idiots."

"Word." She slipped from his arms and rotated on the mattress, flipping her hair over her shoulders. She was bare from the waist up, and he was going to get all distracted in a minute, so he had to make this fast.

"I totally forgive you, and I'd be honoured to be your boyfriend. Especially if it requires a lot more fucking your brains out."

"So classy." She grinned. "And definitely."

"Also, I might have thrown you under the same bus," he confessed.

Alisha blinked in surprise. "You said you had a boyfriend?" He stared at her for a second before she broke, her deadpan delivery falling apart as she crawled across the bed to straddle his thighs. "Well, in light of the *fucking* and what-all that's going on, I suppose we can use the dirty, dirty titles of *boyfriend* and *girlfriend*. Who did you out us to?"

"My sister."

She clapped a hand over his mouth. "You did not."

He nodded.

She rolled her eyes. "What made you think that was a good idea?"

"She was taunting me. You don't understand Thanksgiving at my parents'," Devon insisted when Alisha let his mouth free. "It's like Grand Central Station, only everyone milling around is related to me, and they all have short people in tow. The only positive is since I'm the only one who doesn't live in town, they don't make me cook."

"Which is probably good."

She wasn't frowning anymore, and that was good as well. "Yeah, well, it's not because they're being generous. Instead they make me bring liquor to accompany the meal, and my dad's got some high-flying idea to try all these expensive wines before he kicks the bucket. Guess who gets stuck buying those babies, since I'm not cooking or kid-herding?"

"How does you having a girlfriend mean you get to attend without bottles in your hand?" Her eyes widened. "Oh, Devon, no."

He followed her as she scrambled off the mattress and headed toward the door. "We just have to show up, make polite conversation, and eat until we're stuffed enough to satisfy my mother, and then we can escape. It's not that scary." He paused. Considered. "Okay, it *is* scary, but you're brave. You can face down your fears and help me face mine."

She dug through her bag by the front door to pull out a pair of sweatpants. When she stood, he made sure he was looking her in the eye, and not at the more delectable bits that he really hadn't had enough of yet.

Alisha shook her head. "You are something crazy."

"Hey, you did it, too."

She pulled on a T-shirt without putting on a bra first, a move he completely approved of. "I didn't invite you to join Vincent and me for a family dinner, though, did I?"

"If I had to, I would go." Devon nodded seriously.

She crossed her arms, her expression breaking into a smirk as she eyed him up and down. "I'm sure you would. Are you planning on staying naked all evening? We could pretend you're my slave boy or something if that helps you stay in character."

He didn't give a rip that he was standing in the front hallway naked. Devon stepped in closer and pulled her to him, her soft cotton clothing heating between their bodies. "Tell me you'll save my life."

She caught him around the waist. "How can I turn down that adorable smile? And I did do it to you first, so you're forgiven."

He kissed her briefly before breaking away to get dressed. "I'll be back in a minute."

She pulled her phone out to check her messages, a frown returning to cloud her expression.

It was crazy, the temptation to invite her to stay. He never let anyone stay overnight. Rarely had anyone into the house for that matter. For all his playboy reputation he had a rather sedate love life, a fact that no one believed, of course.

He hurried into the living room and found her curled up on the couch with a family photo album, the one sister number two had sent him after his parents' fortieth anniversary party. He lifted her legs and sat, lowering her limbs into his lap and tugging the album so he could see it as well.

"You went to this party in June, right?" Alisha asked. "Oh, wow, do you ever look like your father."

"All my brothers do."

She leaned forward. "How long has he had to use the wheelchair?"

For a second, the pain that never quite went away froze his vocal cords. Devon jerked himself under control and focused on the facts. Then on distraction. "Over fifteen years. Didn't you meet him? He and my mom came to our grad for Banff Search and Rescue—oh, wait, you didn't stick around for the party."

This time she was the one who paused, just for a second. "No."

Nothing more. No offer of why she'd vanished, no mention of why her family hadn't come to celebrate with her. He probably wouldn't have even noticed her hesitation if he hadn't been so keen on changing the topic.

Devon chose to ignore her lack of sharing and go back to safer topics regarding his family.

He didn't forget, however. He knew what he was avoiding talking about. It was far easier to focus on her and what she was hiding. The entire time he pointed out his siblings and the multiple offspring that crowded the pages of the album, he was thinking about her and her family. Google had finally coughed up a name and a business. Adding Vincent to the other information he'd skimmed from the Lifeline office had led him straight to Bailey Enterprises.

Only it didn't make sense, her lack of connection to her family. His family was a pain at times. There was no doubt he had his hot buttons when it came to them, but his frustrations didn't stop him from spending time with them.

Something big had to be wrong that Alisha didn't want to be known as the heiress to one of Canada's top ten companies.

He was torn between curiosity and minding his own business. She'd kept her background out of the spotlight for four years. She'd never ducked out of the sight of cameras, but all the focus had been on Lifeline, not her family status. He liked that.

Alisha put the book down on the coffee table and twisted to wrap her arms around him. "Well, they look lovely. I'll be glad to go with you and knock them off the hunt. But we could probably spring for a couple bottles of wine, now that Marcus gave us a salary increase. As long as your dad isn't too crazy with his requests."

Devon stroked his palms along her strong arms. "We can do that. And you let me know if you need help with Vincent, okay?"

She nodded. Paused. There was an awfully awkward question that had to be asked. "Are we actually seeing each other, or are we just getting the fucking out of our system? I wouldn't worry about labeling it except for, well, we need to know what to tell . . ."

Thankfully Devon caught on right away. "The team, right?"

She nodded.

It was his turn to pause. "I'm not sure how to answer. I mean, I like you, and I think we're hot together, and I don't have objections to the team knowing we've hooked up, but . . ." Devon caught her by the chin. "Being blunt, I'm not looking for forever. If you think this will end with us in a family portrait surrounded by a swarm of kids like in the photo album, I'm telling you now, no. I don't want a family."

Jeez. "That was blunt."

He sighed. "Yeah, the silver-tongued playboy scores

again with his incredibly seductive words. This is the part when you run screaming from the room."

"Or sneak off and wish you a nice life because my biological clock is ticking and I can't waste any time on a guy who's not interested in making babies and settling down?"

Devon's wary expression lightened. "Are they handing out scripts nowadays? Because I swear I heard that exact line from someone once."

Alisha rolled her eyes. "Devon, thanks for being honest, but now you tell me. Do I act like the type of woman who's waiting for my knight in shining armour to snatch me up and impregnate me so I can be fulfilled?"

"Not at all. Not that there's anything wrong with that," Devon sighed. "I'm happy for my siblings, but damn, if they project onto me one more time the glory that is parenthood, I swear I'm going to scream."

Alisha could understand the sentiment. "I don't want kids. Not now, maybe not ever, so no, I'm not expecting this thing between us to lead to the maternity ward. *God*, getting pregnant right now would be horrid for so many reasons I can't even begin to articulate."

His utter relief made her laugh.

Devon nuzzled her neck. "How about we play it by ear when it comes to the team—although be prepared to be razzed like crazy."

"I figured that."

"And while we're fooling around? I expect you to only see me."

"Ditto." Alisha kissed him, the slow tease of his lips moving over hers making her shiver in anticipation. "I assume you can do only one woman at a time."

"Please." Devon rolled his eyes. "I have no idea how I'll survive without multiple partners on a daily basis, but if you insist."

He determinedly worked his way down her jaw to her ear. Her neck. Alisha had to think hard about the other thing she needed to ask. "So, not to change the subject or anything, but are we good in terms of my freak-out the other day?"

The slick of his arms down her back to adjust her position brought her directly over his groin, intimate parts lining up nicely. "I think the fear factor in the cavern was explainable, and you've proven that simply being in a watery situation wasn't the issue. I have no worries and, as far as I'm concerned, it never happened."

She'd figured they'd moved on, but to actually have him confirm it was a relief. "Thank you."

"You did the job today," he pointed out. "The only exception would be the next time we have to go underground. I'd keep a heads-up. Make sense?"

"Totally." Alisha placed her hands on his shoulders and dug her fingertips into his muscles. "I'm in complete agreement, because there are no guarantees. Who knows what triggered the attack? Maybe I was too tired, or stressed from something else."

"Or maybe the thought of a river rushing at us in the dark with no way out of its path was enough to freak anyone out." Devon caught her by the hips and slid her over his hard length. "I was traumatized by the whole ordeal. You need to help me forget."

The solid length of his cock under her gave a hint what kind of distraction he was looking for. "Were you traumatized? Poor fellow."

He reached into his pocket, pulled out a condom, and held it in the air.

Alisha laughed. "Maybe we should do something about your fear of the dark."

She clicked off the table lamp and turned the room black.

What followed was an exercise in sensory deprivation and sexual overload. With the lights gone, there was nothing other than the pale moonlight sneaking in the windows. The small house was tucked far enough onto the back lane that there were no streetlights. No cars whipping past on a regular basis to add illumination. The faint lights from his music system. The digital clock on the microwave. That was it.

What they lacked in sight was more than made up with tactile pleasure. She tugged his shirt free, and he lifted it

over his head, and suddenly she had more sexy territory to
explore than she could cover in a reasonable amount of time.
Stroking the cuts of his six-pack made him moan. Sliding
her palms up his chest made her respond the same way, her
sigh definitely on the happy side. Then it was her turn to
remove her top, his hands cupping her breasts instantly, his
thumbs unerringly discovering her nipples.

"How do you do that in the dark?" she asked, the final
word turning into a gasp as he tweaked harder.

"They're like homing beacons." He kissed her, slow and
thorough as he teased, the pinches and tugs on her breasts
escalating in pressure, then easing off until she couldn't
stand it. She rose to her knees, her hands buried in his hair.
Even without lights she could guide him to where she
needed him most.

"Bossy." His warm lips pressed against her nipple, his
tongue slipping out to tease her.

"You know you want to take a big bite," she insisted.

Devon sucked her nipple into his mouth and she gasped,
pleasure shooting through her hard enough to shake her legs.
One side. The other, his hands supporting as he lifted her
to his mouth and greedily brought her to the point that she
was writhing.

He tugged her sweats off her ass, switching his hands to
fisting her flesh. Hard squeezes, softer circles—all the while
his tongue lashed her skin until she desperately needed him
inside.

"Please, Devon. More."

Both of them scrambled in their urge to get naked. When
she would have resettled into his lap, she found herself being
firmly placed into a new position. "Hands on the back of
the couch," he ordered.

When she grasped the fabric he slipped from under her,
muscles sliding against her briefly as he wiggled off the
couch and ended with his head between her spread thighs.
There was a pause, the sound of the condom being opened.

Only he was in no position to be using it anytime soon.
"Devon?"

"Oh man, you are wet. So fucking sexy." Devon breathed deep, and cupped her ass again, holding her so she couldn't retreat. He kissed the inside of her thigh, then licked his way up to the crease between leg and torso. She laughed and wiggled, but he held her steady. "There's no escape," he warned.

His mouth covered her sex, and she moaned. Pleasure roared through her, a tingle of tight ecstasy centered where he touched her before spreading in waves. Devon slipped a finger into her sex and stroked lightly. Not enough to send her over, but in connection with his tongue, more than enough to make her breathing hitch.

Then he switched his attention and ran his fingertips along her crease. When he stopped to tease the small, sensitive skin of her anus, she shivered.

"Yes?" he whispered against her sex. "Okay?"

She nodded, then forced herself to speak since he couldn't see it. "It's not my usual thing, but I don't mind. *Oh . . .*"

He'd sucked her clit, rapidly teasing the heated bundle of nerves. At the same time he pressed his finger in to the first knuckle. A tiny intrusion that seemed so much more.

"Oh, my *God*."

He did it again. And again, until she was quivering over him. When he finally slid his finger all the way in she tipped, the dual assault launching her past the point of no return.

She wasn't done shaking, her body still clutching around empty air as he stole from under her and heat pressed against her back, their bodies skin on skin.

"Ready?" Devon teased his cock between her labia, rubbing the sensitive nub of her clit and making her shake.

"My brain isn't working."

He dragged a hand down her back, his fingertips tracing delicately on either side of her spine as he adjusted his hips, the head of his shaft slipping into her. "Don't think, feel."

He thrust, spearing her on his cock, and soon feeling was all she had left.

Their rattled breathing was loud in the room at first, punctuated by the strangely erotic wet sounds as he plunged in deep, their hips slapping together. He grasped her tightly as he worked her over, her breasts swinging as he took her. Their bodies once again pinned together as he shortened his strokes and leaned over. Chest to back, skin rubbing, the slick of perspiration sliding them together perfectly.

Nothing was left but the sensation of touch. Being touched. Inside, and out. He surrounded her, filled her, and Alisha soaked it in. Relished it. Accepted the nearly punishing assault.

Impossibly, hovering again on the edge of release.

Devon snapped his hips forward and groaned. "So good. So tight around me."

Alisha gripped the back of the couch harder, the smooth leather under her fingers compressing as she braced herself. She leaned into his thrusts to increase the force.

Devon slipped a hand over her stomach and covered her clit with his fingertips, pressing lightly, then firmer as she panted her agreement.

"Yes. Yes, oh there. *There.*"

She squeezed her eyes shut so hard, stars floated past as she spiraled out of control and took him with her. Devon shouted her name, their hips sealed tight, his cock jolting inside her as her sex tightened around the rigid length.

Her arms quivered and he laughed, pulling her upright for a moment, twirling them both and collapsing onto the couch with her in his lap, his cock still embedded in her body.

The aftershocks continued for a long time, each one dragging a moan from her lips as he slowly gentled her, teasing his fingers over her clit, his other hand stroking up her body to caress her breasts, her neck.

He turned her head to the side and took her lips again. Breathless, openmouthed kisses followed as they gasped in an attempt to refill their lungs. Unwilling to stop in spite of their need for air.

Alisha finally broke away, resting her head on his shoulder as she stared into the darkness. "I'm seeing stars."

Devon chuckled. "I left the stars a few hundred miles back. I'm into the outer reaches of the galaxy already."

He reached out and she covered her eyes as the light came on. She wasn't sure if it was because she was feeling shy, or because she didn't want him to see that she was feeling slightly vulnerable after letting go so hard.

He kissed her temple again, then helped her upright. His cock slipped from her. "Back in a minute," he whispered.

Devon went to deal with the condom, his butt cheeks flexing nicely in the faint light as he strode from the room. Alisha grabbed her clothes from the ground and pulled them on. Found her bag, slipped on her shoes.

She glanced up to discover Devon standing nearby, his broad shoulder leaning against the wall. He'd pulled on boxers, which did nothing to hide the rest of his incredible muscles. The magnificent ridges and taut muscles she'd just had under her fingers.

Her sigh was most definitely a happy one.

Devon's grin widened. "I like that sound. You heading out?"

Alisha nodded. "I should take my stuff, and myself, home. That was awesome, though."

She stepped in closer and raised her lips.

He kissed her as he smoothed her hair from her face, his touch gentle. When she pulled back, he winked. "Anytime."

He grabbed her bag and walked with her to her car, his nearly naked body highlighted in the faint outdoor lights.

"You're insane. Barefoot outside in October?"

Devon leaned into the open window, his stomach muscles teasing her as they contracted into a perfect six-pack. "Barefoot nothing. I like to strip naked and dance sky-clad, but that one you'll have to wait a little longer to see."

He winked again, then turned and made his way to the front door. Halfway there he paused, lifted his arms, and twirled, and she laughed out loud.

Okay, this new version of Devon she was slowly getting to know was a whole lot more fun than the old one.

CHAPTER 15

''''''''''''''''''''''''''''''''''

The entire drive to her apartment she wore a grin. Not simply a smile, but an out-and-out grin.

It had turned out to be an amazing day, between the
rescue and her time with Devon. Putting the panic attack
behind her was a joy, and her body ached in all the right
spots. For the first time in days she felt totally in control.

She pulled into the parking space at her rental and a little
of that euphoria faded. The bright red-and-white FOR SALE
sign planted in the lawn hadn't been there that morning
when she left.

Shoot, no.

She grabbed her bag and slung it over her shoulder as she
headed around the back to the tall exterior staircase that led
to her attic apartment. Finding accommodation in Banff
was a pain most of the year, let alone something that would
work with her erratic hours. Now that the part-time winter
staff had poured into town, she would be in even more
trouble.

The envelope stuck between the door and jamb mocked

her with its crisp whiteness. She shoved the thin paper between her teeth, then wrestled her gear into the front entrance, leaving the bags in a pile as she hurried to open the envelope and scan the pages.

She'd been given notice. Her tenancy was due to expire at the end of October, which she knew, but the last she'd spoken with her landlords they were planning on renewing for another year with her. Obviously, something had changed.

Okay, not something she could deal with tonight, so instead she'd add it to the list of things to handle the coming week. She clicked off the front lights and left her gear abandoned in the hall.

She still had to pack a new bag before crashing, although the chances of getting called out were slim. Two disasters in a short time frame during what should be the low season was unusual enough, but she didn't want to get caught unaware.

She stepped into the entranceway of her bedroom and jerked to a stop. The streetlamp in the alley was the only illumination in the room, casting bands of faint grey across her mattress.

The bed that she'd scrambled out of in a rush that morning was neatly made, rose petals scattered on the surface.

The creak of floorboards to the right snapped her gaze over to discover Vincent rising from the old wooden chair tucked into the corner of the room. "My God, how did you get in?"

She backed up slowly as he stepped toward her.

He ignored her outburst, looking her over carefully, his face expressionless. "You're home late. I expected you hours ago."

Trapped in her own home. Alisha retreated farther, flipping on all the light switches as she moved. "You have no right to be in here, and no right to be expecting me. Get out of my house, Vincent."

"I was worried about you." He moved to the right as she reached for the door, his body blocking her escape. "Since you left on your call this morning I've been waiting to hear that you were safe. Such a dangerous field you've chosen to be involved in. I couldn't stand it if anything happened to you."

She shook her head. He knew about the call-out; he'd gotten into her home. Terror and confusion were brought under control through sheer determination. "Are you spying on me? Get out."

Vincent smiled, a horrid expression made more terrifying because it was so obviously fake. "You were with your lover. Did you tell him yet that it's over between you?"

This was not happening. Alisha eyed the window that led to the fire escape, wondering if she could cross the room and get out before he could stop her. "That's none of your business. You've gone too far, Vincent. This is breaking and entering—I didn't give you a key, and I didn't invite you in. Leave before I call the police."

He waved a hand. "I'll be gone in a minute. I had planned a more intimate evening for us, but I'm not interested in Devon's leftovers."

The thought of doing anything sexual with Vincent made her stomach churn. She held her ground and waited for him to finish.

He stepped toward her and her heart leapt. "I want you ready to return to Toronto by the new year at the latest. There's no use resisting. At some point you won't be able to hold out any longer. Once you have no roof over your head, and no friends who want to help you."

"You can't believe that you can force me to marry you. What do you think this is, the Dark Ages?"

"I believe you are a smart enough woman to see the benefits once you think them through."

She had her fingers on her phone ready to blindly call anyone in the hopes they'd figure out she was in trouble. "Get. Out."

He cast one more icy glare in her direction before he left.

A tumble of emotions swept her, and with shaking limbs she raced to lock the deadbolt. Dragging a chair under the doorknob seemed very cheesy, but necessary. How had he gotten in?

She clutched her phone as she ran from window to window to make sure they were all locked. Nothing. No indication of how he'd gotten inside. Alisha calmed her breathing and thought through her options.

Impossibly, Vincent must have a key. But if he did have a key, that meant he could get in again anytime.

Did she call someone at the wonderful hour of one A.M. to come and stay with her, or did she go crash on someone else's good nature? The warmth of Devon's bed beckoned, his comforting arms. Fleeing to him was what she wanted, but was it the right choice?

Dumping this situation with Vincent on top of everything else would complicate matters. Because Devon would expect an explanation if she showed up on his doorstep not even half an hour after she'd insisted on leaving.

But who else could she turn to?

Marcus was out of town, meaning Becki would be alone. Erin lived alone, and Alisha wasn't about to bring stalker Vincent anywhere near another woman.

The perfect solution hit. She grabbed a spare gym bag and packed clean rescue gear into it. A second bag with all the things she'd need for a couple of days, just in case she ended up gone for that long before feeling comfortable Vincent would behave.

It took two trips to get her gear all into the car, and she watched over her shoulder the entire time. She felt like a fool driving in circles, taking the long way around to her destination, but as far as she could tell she wasn't followed.

She parked down the road from Tripp's and called him, inspecting the shadows as she waited for him to respond.

"Do you know what fucking time it is?" he growled sleepily. "You okay? You need a hand?"

Her throat went tight at his instant offer. "I love you, Tripp. I need a place to stay for the night."

"No problem. Do you need me to pick you up?" His voice clearing, tone sharpening as he woke.

"I'm in my car and looking at your house. Is there room in the garage?"

"There is. I'll open the door."

She followed his progress through the three-story town house as he flipped on lights and made his way to the ground level. The garage door opened, and she eased her car in next to his truck.

Tripp was right there when she stepped out, the large overhead door closing on them, hiding them away. He checked her over carefully. "I hope I don't need to go beat on some stupid blond boy."

She choked out a laugh. "Devon? Oh God, no. He's not the cause of this mess."

"Get upstairs, we'll talk in a minute." He helped her with her bags, abandoning the one with her dirty clothes from the day's rescue in his laundry room and placing her emergency bag next to his in a safe spot. "You can have the guest room, but first, reassure me. You're not hurt in any way?"

She shook her head. "Just didn't think it was safe to stay in my apartment tonight."

He nodded. "Sleep. We'll talk in the morning."

He gave her a huge bear hug, then sent her into the spare room, the cozy quilt and soft pillows enticing her to drop all the worries and panics of the day. Tomorrow she'd figure out what to do. Tomorrow things would make more sense after hours of sleep and a good breakfast.

Only she tossed and turned restlessly. Every time she closed her eyes the darkness sent images flying at her. Sometimes it was a rush of water enfolding her in its icy grip. Sometimes it was Vincent, the ice in his stare cold enough to make her wake, shivering, whimpering in fear.

She dragged the blankets back on for the third time and tried to stop her rapid breathing. The door opened, and Tripp peeked in.

"You're not okay, and don't lie about it."

She felt about three years old. "I'm having bad dreams."

Tripp laughed softly. "Oh, girl. Fine, shove over."

"I didn't mean to—"

"I'm dead on my feet and you must be as well. Marcus is going to kick our butts with training tomorrow, so I'd like it if we could rest before then." He stood beside the bed and waved at her again. "Don't be a bed hog, though, or I'll kick you to the floor."

He crawled in beside her, a wall of warmth, and she sighed. Tripp turned his back and she snuggled up tight, only partially ashamed for taking advantage of him. "You're a good friend, Tripp."

"Shut up and go to sleep."

She laughed, and this time the warmth crowded over her fears and pushed the darkness far enough into the distance that she could sleep.

The bed was empty when she woke, morning sun lighting the sky without being high enough to show its face over the mountains yet. Alisha pulled on sweats and headed to the kitchen to find Tripp and his boyfriend seated at the table, cups of coffee in their hands as they read the paper. Cereal boxes were stacked high on the tabletop, but there was an empty place setting waiting for her, and thankfulness rushed in.

Jonah noticed her first and poked Tripp. "Your cuddle bunny is awake."

Tripp laughed, and her face heated as she stepped to Jonah's side and kissed his cheek. "Thank you for the use of the spare bed."

"No problem. Bonus? I got to have all the covers for most of the night." He winked, then pushed her toward her seat. "Tonight I get to warm you up, right? Or you know, you could crawl in between us."

"Stop flirting and finish eating," Tripp warned as he lowered a steaming cup of coffee in front of her. He tapped his wrist and stared meaningfully at Jonah. "You're going to be late."

Jonah glanced at his watch before jerking upright. "Shit, you're right."

He took a final sip of coffee before abandoning his cup on the table and rushing from the room.

Alisha smiled and drank deeply. The sleep had been welcome and needed, but now caffeine was as necessary as breathing. She looked up to find Tripp staring at her. "What?"

"I want you to tell me what happened." Tripp held up a hand. "Once Jonah's gone, though. Otherwise he'll get distracted, and we'll never get him out of here on time."

"Let me get breakfast, then I'll explain."

Tripp settled into silence. Alisha filled a bowl with cereal and fruit, relaxing as much as possible to plan what she should share.

Jonah flew into the room, darting over to kiss Alisha before stopping beside Tripp's chair. "Have fun tying things up today. I'll bring supper home with me." He turned briefly to Alisha. "Enough for three, so if you need to come back, you do it, understand?"

"Thanks, Jonah. You're the best."

He blinked happily, then kissed Tripp quickly and raced away. "I'm late."

Tripp grinned after him, with a goofy expression that made Alisha laugh. He pulled his attention back and shrugged. "What can I say, the guy's got a heart of gold."

"He's sweet," Alisha agreed. "Sorry for taking you from your bed last night. Twice."

Tripp leaned in, all amusement gone. "So spill. What happened to send you running for shelter? Not that I mind—get that straight right off the bat. I'm glad you asked for help."

"And I appreciate that I could turn to you more than you know. I had an unexpected intruder in my apartment. Someone I don't like much, but that part's not important." She shook her head. "I wasn't going to take a chance on him breaking in twice in a row."

"That would be a shocker." Tripp stared. "It was after one o'clock when you caught him. You out with the girls for the night?"

She slowed. "No. I was over at Devon's until then."

Tripp grinned again. "I knew it. About time you two faced the facts. Only—" Confusion crossed his face. "Why didn't you call *him* for help?"

That was a loaded question. Fortunately there was a logical possibility. "Coming here meant there were two guys at my beck and call if I needed you. Sounded like a smarter move to me. Plus you had the garage to hide my car in."

Tripp wasn't smiling anymore. "Sounds as if this guy really scared you."

"Would you want to discover someone in your bedroom who wasn't invited?" she demanded. "Yes, it was scary, but get real. It could have happened to anyone."

"Don't snap at me. I'm just giving you a heads-up. I bet Devon will be pissed you didn't call him. Not if you two have been fooling around. He'll feel as if you don't trust him to protect you."

"You're such a girl at times," she complained. "Going on and on about the *feeling* shit."

That made his smile return like she'd hoped. "You calling me a pussy?"

"Always." She rose to her feet and came around the table to hug him. "But I'm glad you're you. I'll deal with Devon."

Tripp nodded. "You plan on staying here tonight? You're more than welcome if you need it, you know you are."

She helped clear the table. "I'll be fine. And I will talk to Devon, if that makes you happier."

Tripp shrugged. "Not me who's going to be unhappy in the first place." His eyes lit up. "Damn, when did you two hook up? I wonder if I have time to call Xavier and double my money. I think you might have won me a tidy sum."

Oh God. "Tell me you guys didn't start a betting pool."

He tossed her a wink as he headed down the hallway. "Hey, Marcus even got in on this one, only he figured you two would cave sometime in the first year."

Idiots. She loved the lot of them.

She followed Tripp to the Lifeline building, working up the strength to face the team for the first time while the news broke. Maybe they could keep her and Devon's relationship, or whatever they were calling it, under the table for a little longer. That would work.

Alisha slipped in the door ahead of Tripp and headed to the lockers to grab a climbing belt. She jerked to a stop as she rounded the corner, Devon far too large and in charge as he buckled up his belt. He smiled, the cocky expression melting to concern as he paced forward and tilted her chin upward. "What happened? Did you sleep okay?"

"There were complications." She made to step away but he didn't release her, instead leaning closer to brush his lips past her cheek. Light. Friendly.

Not possessive or very loverlike at all, but a world removed from how they usually acted around each other.

And suddenly, she didn't give a damn about hiding from anyone. Tripp was right; she should have called Devon last night. Should have let him know right away she was frightened. She slipped her arms around his neck and gave him a real kiss. Bold as brass. A claiming and an apology all wrapped up in one.

He swept her into his arms in a flash, bodies pressed tight. Lips crushed together, brief, yet intense. Then he let her go and carefully placed her feet on the ground.

Alisha smiled at him. "Good morning to you, too."

Devon nodded. "You'll tell me what's going on later, right?"

"You can tell me what's going on now," Erin interrupted from behind him. "Because I don't think I'm seeing straight."

The pilot dodged around Devon to stand in front of Alisha, disgust on her face.

"I'm sorry if you find kissing disturbing," Alisha apologized.

"Girl, it's not that." Erin stomped to her locker and grabbed a pair of gloves. "You've got some shitty timing, you two. It's only one week to Thanksgiving. You couldn't have waited until after?"

Oh *hell*. Alisha snickered as Devon rolled his eyes.

"You lost the bet, did you?" Alisha asked.

"Over one hundred bucks I've put into that pool by now." Erin leaned in closer. "You're not just jerking us around, are you? Like you've actually done it?"

Devon laughed out loud this time and gently pushed Erin past him. "Shut up, Erin. Our fucking is none of your business."

The pilot blew a raspberry and left the room. Devon turned to Alisha and tucked her against his body, stroking her cheek. "Well, there's the first reaction from the crazies. Ready to face the day?"

"Tripp already knows, so he shouldn't be too bad."

"Great. Define 'not too bad'?"

Alisha smiled and bit the bullet. "Hey, can you come home with me after training today? I need to talk to you. Need to ask a favour." She might as well dive in full force and see what kind of situation she had. Because Tripp was right in another way. If she hadn't ended up in Devon's bed this past week? She would have called him first.

Through all the teasing and fighting of the past years, he was the one she normally would have turned to, and he deserved to know she trusted him that much.

"Where the hell are you guys?" Marcus pounded on the table in the staff room. "I hauled ass to get back here for this, and I haven't even been home yet. Let's roll, people."

Devon kissed her quickly, then set her free, and they both grabbed what they needed for the upcoming session.

Lana slipped out of the way as they joined the group in the staff area. Alisha wasn't sure why the woman tossed her such a concentrated glance, but that wasn't important now. Now was the time to wait with her teammates and pay close attention as Marcus explained the activities for the day. Devon stood at her side, but she pushed that away to focus her attention on the here and now.

They had skills to sharpen so they could save lives, and no matter what challenges she was facing in her own life at the moment, that was the more important goal—to stay strong. To be there for others.

And as she glanced around the room at Tripp, at Erin, she noted that maybe she needed to spend more time appreciating the good people she had in her life. Acknowledge that they were there for her, and she didn't have to do it alone.

CHAPTER 16

''''''''''''''''''''''''''''''''

Devon had the locks out of the door before she'd finished telling him about discovering Vincent in her bedroom. "We'll get these rekeyed today. Do you want me to stay here with you, or do you want to spend the night at my house?"

"I didn't mean to interrupt your life, Devon."

He fought to keep his frustration from showing because she didn't need more to deal with at the moment. Still, his sense of worth had gotten a major bucketload of crap dumped on it after hearing she'd gone from his bed, to being frightened, to asking *Tripp* for help. "Oh, it might sound as if you get to decide which, but those are your two options. I won't accept anything else."

He turned in time to catch her rubbing her brow. She met his gaze, more than a little guilt in her expression. "I didn't leave you out on purpose. I was frustrated and scared and just reacted."

"I get it. But now you've got time to think, and you can make a choice. Which do you prefer? If you want to stay here, good, but I need to know so I can pack a few things."

She shook her head. "There's no room here us both. I'd be grateful to bunk with you for a while. I don't understand what's come over Vincent. I mean, he's always been intense, but he's never been difficult like this before."

She collapsed onto the couch, worn and frustrated as she gazed out the window.

Devon gave himself a mental slap. She hadn't done anything to deserve this, either. "Pack. We'll talk about Vincent and his *being difficult* once we get to my house. We're still changing the locks, even if there's less than a month left on your lease. That's crazy, by the way. I thought you had an ongoing contract?"

Alisha rose and headed to her bedroom, pausing to drag a suitcase from the hall closet. "I did, only it's a yearlong one and it was up soon. They'd told me verbally it would be renewed, but we hadn't signed anything. They're not doing anything illegal."

"Just nasty."

"Yeah."

She vanished from sight. He popped the lock into his pocket and grabbed a box to load fridge supplies into. He was determined she'd stay with him until Vincent left town— there was no need for her to be afraid, or have to scoop science experiments from the fridge in a few days' time.

Once he got over his initial mad, he had to look on the brighter side. Having her in his house wasn't a hardship at all. It was a small place, but big enough that they had room to get away from each other if needed. And they didn't even have to share a bed, although he hoped that option fell by the wayside damn fast.

The reasons to have her join him sucked, but having an excuse for her to stay?

He ignored the pleasure that brought him as best he could, but the voices calling him a hypocrite were damn loud. He didn't let women stay the night. He didn't want to get attached.

He was screwed, because he *was* attached, and that was the plain and simple truth.

Settling in took far less time than he'd expected. He cleaned out a drawer in the bathroom, showed her where the extra towels were. They got a load of laundry going from the morning's training.

When he went to rearrange the tiny room that held the Murphy wall bed, Alisha caught his arm. "I could sleep on the couch."

"I want you in my bed," he admitted, pulling the mattress to horizontal. "But I want you to have your own space if you need it."

She nodded, snatching up the blankets he'd put to the side and helping him make the bed. "I can use it to lay out my gear, then."

Her wink wasn't enough to distract him from the conversation they needed to finish. "You can't make me forget I'm grilling you for details."

Her sparkle vanished. "Meanie."

"Detail-loving meanie." He straightened the pillow, then held out his hand. "Come on."

She followed him, dragging her feet as he took her to the living room and clicked the gas fireplace on. "There's not much to tell. Vincent is being . . . demanding. He wants me to marry him."

Words froze on his tongue. His face must have been a sight to see because she burst out laughing. Which was enough to snap him out of shock. "Shit, what kind of insanity is that? I mean, not that wanting to marry you would be a fate worse than death, but it sounds as if he's a touch demented."

Alisha wrapped her arms around her legs as she curled up in front of the fireplace. "He's always been like that. Talked about what he wanted, and boom, it happened. Usually it didn't matter much to me because he was this older person who hung out with my parents. I had to say hello and good-bye, and do all the polite society things . . ."

She raised her eyes to his as she trickled to a stop.

He nodded. "I figured out who you are, if that's your

hang-up. I spotted the high-society roll call with your name, and the shining tiara hovering over your head."

"I'm Alisha Bailey, member of Lifeline and a top-ranked SAR member. That's who I'm proud of, and that's who I want to be." The words came out firm and strong.

He clapped, and the tension on her face lightened. "Good for you. And you're right. If you don't want to do the family thing, then you shouldn't feel obligated. Especially if they're not firing on all pistons."

She nodded slowly. "I feel bad about my mom at times, because I think if it were up to her, she'd give me more leeway."

"Dad's in charge, is he?" Devon knew the answer before he saw her nod. "Figured."

"And Vincent is worse than my father, if you can believe that. He's definitely not going for Mr. Congeniality."

Devon picked up her foot and lowered it into his lap, rubbing his thumbs along her insole as he pondered. "If he goes home and leaves you alone, that would solve all your problems. You hoping that's what will happen?"

"Not much else I can do. He hasn't directly threatened me, and . . ." Alisha hesitated. "Okay, the reality is right now if I go to the RCMP, I'm not sure what good it would do. The ways he could use the media to twist things in his favour are scary to think about. Police reports notwithstanding, it's my word against his, and I'm a lot lower on the political totem pole. The people who would use a police report against him aren't necessarily my friends, either."

"So you're trapped into not going to the media because you'd lose." He shook his head. "You live in a damn weird world."

"Lived," she snapped. "Which is why I wanted out so bad. That, and because I really do love what we do." She groaned happily, wiggling down farther. "I'm going to melt into the floor if you keep rubbing my feet. Can we not talk about Vincent anymore?"

"Last question. Would calling your father and letting him know any of this help?"

She considered for a moment, but the misery on her face only grew stronger. "If I mention anything about Vincent wanting my shares that's going to open up the whole marriage issue. My dad would more likely ignore the suggestion it's about taking control, and insist Vincent's goal is to make a strong, political marriage—like the family suggested years ago. He'd join in to convince me Vincent was the catch of the century. He might even start his own media blitz to push us together. Those are the positive possibilities."

"Shit. Worst case?"

"Worst case, he figures out some way to make you look bad—as if you're the one who came between true love and financial happiness."

"Hmm." He exchanged her right foot for her left. "I'd be the other man, would I?"

"It's not as fun as it sounds. You don't need to be shredded in the media for something you didn't do. I doubt Marcus and Lifeline would appreciate it, either." She leaned back, glassy-eyed as she watched him strip off her second sock and start all over again. "I want Vincent gone, and I want to go on with my life. Poor, but contented."

She sighed unhappily, then pulled out her cell phone. She stared at it as if it were a snake.

"You calling your father?"

"I . . . should. You're right. He deserves a warning, and if he can help get Vincent back to Toronto, that would make me blissfully happy."

She sounded so miserable his heart ached. "You don't have to, but maybe your father will surprise you and pick door number three this time."

Devon waited as she put through the call, concentrating on massaging her feet and distracting her from the wait as it took forever for her father to come on the line.

Alisha got straight to the point. "Vincent Monreal is in Banff, and acting very strange. I wondered if you knew anything—Well, of course, I'm certain. I saw him myself."

She rolled her eyes as she listened to his response, frustration clearly rising. Obviously door number three didn't involve her father accepting information with open arms.

"I don't care if he's supposed to be in Vancouver attending a symposium. He was in my apartment uninvited last night and . . ." She broke off, and glared at the wall. "Dad. Stop interrupting. I called because I'm concerned about Vincent, who is still here in Banff whether you believe it or not, but I'm also worried about you. Is everything okay with Bailey Enterprises?"

Her father answered.

Alisha's forehead creased. "No, I'm not trying to be insulting. I heard . . . a rumour there might be some—"

She was cut off and remained silent for another thirty seconds. By the time she'd hung up Alisha was swearing lightly.

Devon sat silently, rubbing her calves as she slammed a fist against the floor. It took her a surprisingly short time before she let out a long, slow breath and pulled her arms into a yoga position of peace.

He smiled in spite of the frustration. "I take it that went well."

"Vincent is in Vancouver, you know."

"That wouldn't be hard to disprove," Devon pointed out.

Alisha waved a hand. "You know what? I tried. My father doesn't want to believe me, and I'm not going to force the facts down his throat. We'll deal with Vincent together for the few days before he has to return to Toronto. Not even *he* can pull off a magic trick that puts him in the Bailey Enterprises head office and Banff at the same time."

She shook her head, sadness clear in her eyes.

Devon leaned over and caught her before she could escape. He kissed her softly, brushing his lips over hers in a tender caress. When he pulled away, she was smiling a lot more than the moment before.

"What was that for?" she asked.

He shrugged. "Because you're the bravest woman I know.

Because I'm honoured you trusted me enough to share your concerns. Because your heart is in the right place."

Alisha beamed at him. "Oh, you are so getting lucky tonight."

"Well, if you insist."

She laughed and scrambled forward, and suddenly words were put aside, and the sexual tension that was always present between them raced back up to full. Devon enjoyed the way she crawled into the middle of the room, then knelt with her chin slightly lowered so she gazed through her lashes.

His lips curled upward as he looked her over, the kind of smile that promised all sorts of naughty things.

She shivered, trying to decide what she wanted tonight, but the first and only thing that came to mind was that she didn't want to decide. After everything that had happened, after her father had basically accused her of outright lying, she wanted to shove all of that bullshit aside and concentrate on what she knew was good and right in her world.

Concentrate on the way that Devon could make her feel desirable and wanted and passionately alive. "So you had a list of things to try with me. What's next?"

Devon raised a brow. "You're serious?"

Alisha waited. Took a deep breath. "Looks like you're in charge, Mr. Leblanc. What's the protocol for this rescue?"

His eyes lit up as he figured out her somewhat awkwardly worded suggestion. "What're your limits?"

"No means no. Beyond that?" She shrugged. "Unless you've got extreme kinks you've managed to keep secret from me during school and the time on the team, which isn't likely, I can handle and enjoy anything you want to hand out."

Devon got to his feet and stepped closer to where she knelt. He pulled off his shirt and tossed it aside. "The only one on the team who's keeping secrets is Erin. The rest of us are pretty up front about what turns us on."

He stroked her cheek, tucking her hair behind her ear before striding away to the bathroom. Alisha checked out his ass as he went and, when he returned, the bulge rising at his crotch. His comments and the visual indulgence before her were enough to distract her from wondering what his plans were. "Erin has secrets?" Alisha asked.

"Let's focus on right here and what we like instead of wondering what kinks rev our pilot's engine." The condom he'd gone to grab waited on the coffee table. He stepped in front of her again and palmed his erection, fisting himself through the loose fabric.

Alisha swallowed hard.

Devon hummed in approval even as he continued to stroke, his wrist twisting as he worked. "I love your expression. It's somewhere between panic and full-out lust. Take off your shirt, Alisha," he ordered.

She grasped the bottom and stripped the soft cotton over her head, working to slow her breathing now that there was barely anything to hide how excited she was.

Devon strolled around her slowly, giving her ample time to admire the flex of his muscles, the firm cuts of his abdominal muscles and strong curves of his biceps. "You're so delicious to look at," she breathed softly.

He trailed his fingers over her shoulders. "Delicious? I like that." His voice lowered a tone. "Lose your pants and get back on your knees."

A shiver took her as she hurried to follow his directions. She had an aching need in her core, wetness growing between her legs as she scrambled into position. Her outer clothing was abandoned on the floor by the couch. "I should have taken off my panties."

Devon lowered himself slowly as he deliberately stroked his fingertips down her torso. Over her collarbone, along the edge of her bra. Her skin tingled as he carried on all the way past her belly button. "Your panties are fantastic. They're going to come in handy."

She held her breath as he circled the tiny bow at the front of the silk covering her mound. Tiny motions that inched down so slowly, she was shaking with anticipation before he pressed over her clit.

"Oh, very nice, Alisha. So. Damn. Wet. I could slide right in, couldn't I?"

She opened her mouth to speak, but he pushed harder, and the moisture-softened fabric gave way slightly. His fingers entered her core. Just enough that he could tease, circling her pussy entrance, his thumb extended upward to graze her clit again and again.

The urge to thrust her hips forward was impossible to resist. She opened her legs wider and rocked against his hand.

He held her by the back of the neck, locking her in place as he stared into her eyes. "You're wet, but you're not wet enough. You're going to come before we do anything else. Soak your panties. I'm going to get you so wet your thighs are coated."

She gasped for air as he increased pressure, and that was when he kissed her. Rough, nearly wild. His tongue thrusting in deep and matching the rhythm of his fingers. She caught him around the shoulders and held on tight, her nails digging into his skin, his muscles flexing under greedy hands she couldn't keep still.

When he shoved aside the fabric and impaled her on his fingers, she cried out. Her head fell back as he played her, her body shaking as if she were possessed. Sensitive pressure points deep inside were stroked unmercifully, and when she couldn't take it any longer, he put his teeth to her neck and bit down.

Her climax burst like a firework, bright lights before her eyes and roaring noises in her ears. Alisha shook as Devon held her vertical and let her sheath squeeze around his thick fingers.

When she could draw a deep breath, he was smiling.

"Good?" he asked.

She nodded. "Very good."

Then she was on her back on the thick carpet, her bra being pulled forward along with her arms. Devon wrapped the loose banding around her wrists, tying her arms together in front of her.

Alisha tugged, but she was firmly trapped. "I'm impressed. That was what, five seconds? Ten?"

Devon loomed over her, his sexy smile making her heart rate keep pounding. "My turn," he whispered.

He straddled her, pressed down the top of his sweats. His cock leapt free, the thick length rising up to tap his abdomen. Alisha licked her lips.

Devon grinned wider, the blue of his eyes sparkling as he angled closer. "That's right, get your lips nice and wet. Suck my cock. Get me hard."

"I think you're hard already," Alisha teased. She let him press the heavy crown to her pouting lips, opening slowly as he added pressure.

It was worth it to hear his deep sigh of satisfaction. "Fuck, that's good."

Devon drew back and forth for a dozen slow, deliberate strokes before shuddering and pulling out. He panted a few times, his eyes closed tight before he caught her again and kissed her.

She laughed softly when he rearranged her on a cushion he stole from the seat of the couch. "Nearly lost it, did you?"

"Jesus, your mouth is a danger zone. I wasn't ready to blow."

She was going to make some comment about "blowing his mind," but he was over her again, his mouth on her breast as he sucked her nipple hard, and she decided talking was highly overrated.

It went on and on. With her hands tied together, her breasts were thrust upward, making it easier for him to palm her. To lift her nipple and play over the hardened tip until she squirmed. He'd lave it gently with his tongue. Use the edge of his teeth to the edge of pain.

Then start all over again.

She wanted to wait. Wanted him to set the pace, but it was too exquisite a torture. "Fuck me, please." The words escaped breathlessly. Aching.

Begging.

If she'd been needy before, she was throbbing now.

Devon put on the condom before he caught her by the knees and lifted her legs into the air. His gaze fixed on her sex and ass as he used one hand to hold her feet toward the ceiling, the other to slip a hand over her panties.

"Oh yes." He smiled, then pulled the fabric to her knees.

The move surprised her. It didn't allow her to open her legs, pull him to her and take his cock. She was still trapped, her legs thrust into the air.

He rose up on his knees as he pressed her limbs closer to her torso. "Oh yes, very nice."

He smiled as he rubbed the head of his cock between her labia, and Alisha shook. He adjusted his angle to fuck between her tightly closed legs, not entering her, but nicking her clit again and again.

"You're killing me." Alisha whimpered, squeezing her ass muscles. Trying to find a way to take control, but there was none. He had it all.

"Ready?" he whispered.

She didn't get time to respond before he slipped inside. Thrust all the way to the root, his cock so hard and heavy she cried out. The angle was incredible, the tilt increasing as he pushed her legs over her head and rocked his hips forward making that happy spot inside fire up again.

When he let her legs free she kept them balanced skyward. He grasped her hips, dragging her higher, holding her in place as he pounded into her. Heavy thrusts, demanding. Each one a possession, and oh so good. Another climax raced over her, and she called his name as the room went blurry.

Devon shouted, rocking in shorter and tighter strokes. Furious speed, heavy pressure exploding as Alisha's climax carried on, dragged out through the aftershocks as Devon came. His body over hers, chest pressed to the back of her thighs.

When he rolled off he was still panting. He caught her into his lap and jerked the bra from her wrists, sinking them into another kiss as they gasped for air. Striving to recover, but needing the intimacy of the contact.

Her body hummed with satisfaction and she laid her head on his chest, fingers stroking him softly as the fire bathed them in rosy light.

Satisfaction on so many levels.

CHAPTER 17
''''''''''''''''''''''''''''''''

"We're doing more training on the winch," Anders announced. He pointed at Erin. "She got a new toy, which means we all have to get in the swing of things."

Anders grinned harder as Devon groaned with the rest of them at the bad pun.

Nearly a week had passed since Alisha had basically moved in with him, and so far, things seemed to have settled into some positive patterns. Vincent hadn't shown up in person, and other than one or two politely worded e-mails that were threatening only if you put them into context, he hadn't interfered.

Alisha was slowly relaxing. They'd done a rescue. When they weren't recovering from work, the two of them were busy with wild sex. It wasn't a bad situation.

Marcus leaned on the side table as he went over the order of training for the day. "And when you're not in the chopper with Erin and Anders, you'll be on the tower with Becki. She's agreed to work you over today so I can stay with Erin while she tries her new wings."

Beside Devon, Alisha had curled her legs under her as she perched on one of the tall stools by the small kitchen counter. She gave her coffee another stir before leaving the spoon and turning with a happy sigh to face the room. "It's like early Christmas around here with all the new gadgets. Can I try some of the new gear today?"

Marcus nodded. "Sure, just let Lana know what you're using so we double-check all the gear gets a once-over before we need it in the field. I know a few of you are heading away for Thanksgiving events tomorrow—we'll do a full run-through on new equipment next week once you're all back."

Tripp stepped past Alisha and stole her personalized cup right out of her fingers before she could take a sip, ignoring her complaints as he stepped out of reach and took a long appreciative swallow of the dark liquid. "Hey, how come you get to use the new gear even though you didn't show up to help unpack?"

His accusing tease took in Devon as well, but Marcus was the one who laughed.

"You didn't have to show up, you know. Lana was willing to do the work without you. She put in extra hours the last couple of days to get the gear unloaded."

Behind the desk Lana turned from the filing cabinet to preen. Her ass-kissing had become obvious the last week, maybe because Devon was more conscious of it after having Tripp point it out. All her attention now seemed directed at Marcus. Maybe Lana had given up on the sly approach, but whatever her plans, it seemed Marcus hadn't noticed.

Only the glance Becki gave the woman proved that Lana's ploys were known to at least one of the couple. Devon ignored the urge to comment. There were times that keeping his mouth shut would be just as effective, especially if Becki knew what was going on. He didn't envy the hurt that Lana would have coming her way if she crossed a line in Becki's opinion.

Becki was more than able to defend her own.

They split into two groups, and Devon was surprised when Lana joined them, climbing gear in hand.

Xavier glanced at Devon behind the woman's back but hid his displeasure when he spoke. "You doing wall work today?"

Her grin was huge. "Marcus said I should, because then you'll have two pairs climbing at once."

"And I agreed. It's a good idea to mix it up." Becki stepped into the conversation. "Having consistent partners for climbing is positive for some reasons, but it can make you sloppy. It's good to have to concentrate and stay aware instead of falling back on familiarity."

Devon stepped into his harness. It made sense. Still, for some reason the idea of Lana belaying Alisha filled him with dread. He flashed a smile and decided to face Alisha's potential wrath later. Making sure he was the one stuck with Lana was his first priority. "Well then, can I offer you a lift?"

Lana blinked. "You want to belay me?"

"Love to." He stepped in closer and checked her harnesses, careful to keep his touch professional, but chatting on the flirty side to ensure she didn't get any ideas about suggesting to switch partners.

Alisha returned from the storage area with new body harnesses in hand. She eyed Lana and him, one brow sneaking upward. She didn't say anything, though, just turned to Xavier and flashed him a big smile. "So, big guy, you want to play with me today?"

"I thought you'd never ask." He took one of the harnesses. "This is different."

"More loops around the back. It's rated for higher weights. Thought it might be good for winter work when we've got sleds to deal with." She laid the harness on the ground and began a systematic check through all the webbing. Xavier squatted beside her and did the same for the one she'd brought for him.

The exercise was going well, he supposed, as he and Lana followed Becki's directions and worked the side of the tall tower outside HQ. There were stairs on the interior he'd run a million times during training, but here and now it was the climbing holds on the exterior they focused on.

Around the opposite side of the Lifeline yard, Erin was working her new helicopter, turning it and hovering, moving into position and waiting while Anders lowered Tripp over targets. The sound of the props was constant in Devon's ears even though they were far enough around the corner to be out of sight most of the time.

He concentrated on the wall. On Lana. On following directions instead of staring at Alisha as she and Xavier laughed and worked the kinks out of the new gear.

Lana climbed well for the most part, but she seemed to have the same trouble as him, her gaze drifting to Alisha and Xavier far more often than it should. When her feet hit the ground after one climb, Devon waved a hand in front of her face. "Hey, they aren't the ones on the end of your rope."

She blinked and turned to smile at him, all contrite. "I'm sorry. I'm just . . . curious about the new gear."

"Stay on task."

She nodded and focused a bit better for a few minutes before the side-eyed looks started again. Lana was halfway up a climb when Becki stopped beside Devon. "How're her skills, in your opinion?" she asked quietly.

Devon was honest. "I want Alisha on the end of my line when we're out in the real world."

Becki nodded before glancing up. "Lana. You're following a nice straight path, but you're using too much arms. Major muscles, remember? You'd blow up too fast on an extended climb at this rate."

"Okay. I'll remember," Lana sang back sweetly, and Devon wanted to gag.

Becki was better than him and kept a straight face. She waited until Lana faced the wall again, then patted him on the back and spoke softly. "Trust me, I want Alisha belaying you."

She stepped away to work with Alisha and Xavier as Devon hid his grin.

Lana had just landed on the ground when the unusual silence in the air caught his attention. A moment later the speaker on Becki's hip buzzed with Marcus's signal. "Sorry to interrupt, but can I steal someone from you?"

Becki frowned even as she signaled for Devon to unclip. "I can give you Devon, but what's up?"

"Tripp's not feeling a hundred percent. I'm sending him home, but Erin and Anders need more practice. That requires a body."

That was where the silence came from—the chopper was grounded. Devon dropped the rope and followed orders, waving at Alisha and Xavier as he jogged toward the main building.

Tripp passed him outside HQ doors en route to a taxi waiting in the yard. "You going to live?" Devon asked.

His teammate's face was white and he swallowed rapidly. "Stomach flu or something. Hit hard."

"Damn." Devon checked the chopper waiting for him. "Do you want me to drive your truck home later?"

Tripp nodded and passed over the keys. "I'd appreciate it. I'm too dizzy to drive—but some of that might be Erin's fault. She's got a lot of pendulum happening in the new bird. I think I set a new record for spins per minute."

Devon laughed as he escorted Tripp to the taxi. "Thanks for the warning. Don't go getting Jonah sick."

Tripp made a face. "He probably gave it to me—there's always one bug or another going around the school."

Devon's walkie-talkie squawked. "Anytime, Mr. Leblanc," Marcus drawled.

"Just tucking Tripp into bed, sir. I'm on my way." He broke into a jog and headed around the field. He hoped his stomach was ready for whatever twisted routine Erin was about to put him through at the end of the rope.

Alisha sent the e-mail message from Vincent to archives. It was another of the not-creepy-enough-to-be-useful and yet not-ordinary-enough-to-avoid-being-creeped-out variety, and she sighed.

Devon paused at a set of lights. "You're wearing that face again."

Alisha took a deep breath and looked him in the eye. "I have a face?"

"A Vincent-the-Vamp-is-annoying-me face. What'd he do now, order your bridal gown?"

The light changed and Devon was forced to turn his attention to the road, giving her a chance to consider for a moment. "The last time I showed you one of Vincent's messages, you taught me new swear words."

"I've matured since then," Devon quipped. He laid a hand on her thigh and squeezed lightly. "Let me help if you need it, okay?"

Alisha knew that. Needed that. "He pointed out that if I book my flights home now, we'd have time to attend the governor-general's Christmas ball. He has two tickets and really should RSVP soon." She didn't mention that a link to the gown he'd picked out for her was included in the e-mail.

The warmth of his palm on her thigh was reassuring and more as he slipped his hand slightly higher. "You are not required to do what he wants."

"Nope. You're right." She stared out the window at the houses passing them. "And not to change the subject, but this is where your parents live?"

Devon smirked, both hands back on the wheel. "Welcome to the family homestead."

Sheesh. She caught herself before she pressed her nose to the window to rubberneck at the acreages going past. She hadn't realized until that moment that there were details missing from what she knew about him as well.

"Devon, hit me for being an idiot, but—*ow*." Alisha rubbed her arm where he'd bumped her with the back of his wrist. "I didn't mean it literally, you jerk."

"Hey, a lady asks me to spank her, I oblige." He pulled to a stop at a massive gated entrance, lowering his window to enter the access code.

Alisha was embarrassed now at the visions she'd had about him fighting to find food during school. The starving student and the humble-living search-and-rescue worker were miles away from the enormous home with multiple outbuildings they were approaching down the long driveway. "You forgot to tell me your parents were, what? Cattle barons?"

Devon made a rude noise. "Please. You're not going to give me shit for not talking about my background, are you? Miss Sphinx?"

"Fine, I deserved that." She gave in and gawked out the window. "You have horses. Devon, oh my God, you have a whole herd of them in your yard."

"My parents' yard. And those are the family rides. I don't own a horse anymore. It would be hard to stable her in Banff."

She twisted away from the fascinating sights outside to examine Devon closer. His smooth jaw had tightened in the past few minutes, and this time she was the one who laid her hand on his arm to apologize. "I'm sorry for making assumptions."

Devon shrugged. "You have no idea."

He flashed a smile, and her worry eased. "Will you take me riding?"

"Can you ride?"

She gave him a look.

He gave her one back. "Not that fancy bullshit show stuff, but real riding."

Alisha grinned harder. "Want to see who can finish a course faster? I'm game."

The suggestion of yet another contest eased the last of the awkwardness that had risen between them, and she slipped her fingers into his until he needed his hand to apply the parking brake.

Devon walked around to open her door, then dragged a hand through his blond hair, leaving it standing every which way. "You don't have to memorize everyone's names," he reminded her. "If you forget, just ask—they'll be happy to tell you again and again. Don't accept any babies or small children out of guilt, especially not ones with suspicious scents."

Alisha laughed, stepping closer and straightening that lock of hair that always drove her crazy. "Relax. I can handle myself. I can handle your family."

He slipped his arms around her and lowered his head until their lips made contact. "Thank you for joining me."

She still had her fingers in his hair when the front door swung open, and noise enveloped them.

A deep, firm voice reached them first. "Devon. And Alisha. Welcome."

Higher-pitched feminine laughter stole out. "You're interrupting them, Dad."

"That's my job," he insisted as Alisha straightened in embarrassment.

Devon kept a tight hold on her so she was forced to remain tucked against his side. An older version of Devon peered down from the landing, his hands resting on the wheels of his wheelchair.

"It would be politer to greet guests with a drink," Devon pointed out, escorting Alisha up the stairs to the side of his dad's chair.

She held out her hand to him. "It's nice to meet you, Mr. Leblanc."

"Please, call me Stewart." He accepted her hand but didn't shake it, instead tugging her forward with a wink. "Pretty girls I insist on kissing on the cheek."

She laughed and leaned over far enough to let him plant one on her. Then she stepped back and watched as Devon shook hands solemnly with the man.

"Good to see you, son."

"I'm not pretty enough to kiss?" Devon teased.

"You got your kisses, and your lickin's, when you were younger. Now you're old enough to shake my hand and pour me a drink." Stewart eyed him closely. "You did bring wine for dinner?"

Devon made a show of regret. "Damn, I knew we forgot something."

"Oh, Devon, how could you?" Another of his sisters had stepped onto the porch, and she frowned at them in annoyance from behind Stewart's wheelchair. Her short, businesslike blond hair barely moved as she shook her head. "One thing you have to bring, and it's just like you to forget."

She glared daggers at both Devon and Alisha, and Alisha shifted uncomfortably.

Well, that was lovely. Obviously not all of Devon's family were as easy to get along with as his father.

She lifted the bag from her hip and held it out to the stern-faced woman. "Umm, actually, you'll find a couple of bottles in here. The white is already chilled, and the red can be opened to breathe if we're eating soon."

The bag was accepted none too graciously. "I don't know why Devon couldn't just say so. Everything has to be some huge joke with him."

She stormed off, leaving Stewart gazing after her. He twisted in his chair and made a face. "That one? Is a trifle high-strung. Ignore her, and make yourself at home."

Devon squeezed Alisha's fingers and they followed his father into the house.

The only possible description of what followed was *chaos*.

Children raced everywhere, from toddlers to tweens, the oldest of them eyeing Alisha with that mix of curiosity and disdain most kids that age were so good at. She stared back, poker-faced.

She was introduced to all the rest of Devon's family. His mom squeezed her in a hug and then vanished, chasing after children with a warning to stay out of the cookies until dinner was served.

It was a good thing the house was so big, because the sheer number of bodies milling around probably placed it on the maximum occupancy list. It was a strange contrast to the holidays she remembered. Gentle music playing in the background, servants ushering in the various courses of the meal. Nothing but small talk at the table, not this uproarious noise that never seemed to end.

Alisha leaned on a wall to one side of the action and took it all in, somewhere between uncomfortable and amazed.

Warm arms snuck around her. "You need me to top up your drink? You've got this glazed expression slipping over you."

"I'm overwhelmed. I guess you can tell."

"Two more hours, three at the tops, and we'll be free. We could stop on the way home and hike to Elbow Falls. Stretch our legs and work off some of the three pieces of pie I plan on consuming."

His lips hit her neck and she shivered. "Your sister will turn me into a toad if she catches you doing that. I don't think I impressed her much."

Devon stroked his fingers over her waist where he held her, his thumb gentle over the gap of skin he found. "Charley doesn't approve of me, ergo, you can't be approved of. Don't take it personally."

"I won't, but . . ."

"But what?" The words whispered past her ear, and she heated up without him even trying. "I approve of you completely."

The ringing of a bell stole the chance to explain her confusion. They were hustled to the table and placed in what were probably considered strategic positions. In fact, glancing down the long table, there was a kind of twisted symmetry to it all. The tables were slightly different heights in places—not even the giant main portion with its rough-hewn planking could hold the entire family, but the room was large enough that they had laid two more tables end to end as well. The teens were crowded around a smaller table in the kitchen, and little children seemed to be tucked one on either side of their parents, hopefully to be corralled into behaving.

Which put her and Devon close to the head of the table and the Leblancs.

The little girl on Alisha's left didn't look too terrifying, staring up unblinking with her pale hair braided into an intricate design. Alisha thought she was a Kimberly or something like that. Definitely one of Charley's girls.

Dinner itself was lovely. Bowls of homemade food passed again and again. Alisha laughed when Devon started scooping tidbits of extra stuff onto her plate, insisting she wasn't eating enough to feed a bird.

"Devon, stop teasing her," his mom warned.

Devon shrugged. "Sorry, instinct. Years of training around this table. I see an empty plate and I'm compelled to fill it."

"Have you given any more thought to the business idea I suggested?" One of the brothers shook his fork at Devon. "I'm ready whenever you are to get you up to speed."

Devon smiled, his expression tighter this time. "Thanks again for your generous offer, Mark, but I'm pretty happy with my career as it is."

"Boys. You can take this conversation up after dinner." His mom turned her bright smile on Alisha. "So, dear, tell me. What are you planning on doing once you're done in Banff?"

Devon snorted softly, and Alisha took a deep breath. "Well, I'm not sure what the question is. Devon and I are on the Lifeline search-and-rescue squad, you know. It's a solid, full-time job, and it looks like a good career for the future."

Charley frowned from across the table. "You can't keep doing that sort of work once you have a family."

Oh boy. Alisha kicked Devon's ankle under the table in the hopes he'd stop snickering. "I'll cross that bridge when I come to it."

"You're how old, twenty-one?"

Well, that would have made her a touch precocious, even in the climbing community. "Twenty-six; thank you for the compliment."

Charley seemed to be doing the mental math. Probably coming up with a number of baby-making years that were rapidly diminishing. She set her frown more firmly in place and rescued a scoop of potatoes from a toddler's fork only seconds before it toppled to the tablecloth.

And that was the introduction to the remainder of the meal. Devon got offered a job from one of his older brothers—something suitable for a family man with high potential for moving up in the world and making a name for himself. Alisha got grilled on what other jobs were interesting to her once her obsession with being outdoors couldn't support her anymore. Once she found her senses and swelled with child.

Through it all Devon kept his cool. Laughed. Lightheartedly teased his way out of committing to anything, and without actually saying the words, made it appear he agreed what he was doing in Banff was frivolous at the best and at the worst? Selfish.

Alisha grew more agitated by the minute, but she kept her annoyance hidden. Only when given the opportunity to escape, she took it.

"Devon promised to show me the horses. I hope you don't mind?"

Devon scooped the final bit of his third piece of pie into his mouth, then grabbed her hand. "It's true. Excuse us."

Dirty dishes were still being carried to the kitchen, and maybe it was rude to leave before they'd helped clean up, but Alisha was seconds away from exploding on Devon's behalf. She allowed him to guide her from the room, lips tightly pressed together to avoid saying something she'd regret.

He led her toward the fence line, the horses in the field shifting and approaching slowly. Devon clicked his tongue and called to them before turning to face her. His painted-on fake expression slid off and turned into real frustration and sorrow.

Alisha grabbed him by the collar and leapt upward, wrapped her legs around him, and clung on tight as she kissed him hard in the hopes it would consume some of her tightly compressed anger.

CHAPTER 18

,,,,,,,,,,,,,,,,,,,,,,,,,,,,,,,

He didn't care that they were on the front path to his parents'.
Didn't care that a dozen people could be gawking out the
windows at them this minute; in fact, he hoped they were.
Hoped they were watching and wishing they had the kind of
life that involved a woman like Alisha. Her fire rolled over
him and softened all the aching spots inside he'd had
clutched like a fist for the past couple of hours.

Her heated lips over his became something to focus on
rather than his frustration. The solid weight of her body
pressed tight to his anchored him.

The slick of her tongue slowed slightly as she explored,
her hands stroking his shoulder muscles while those incredible legs squeezed him tight enough to promise all manner
of wicked things.

He took the offer. Accepted it. After years training
together and moments in the field where life was on the line,
they'd learned to speak a silent language. A nearly instant
assessment of imminent danger and life-stealing hurts. They
both knew there was a give and take of necessity and

importance. The person who needed the most was provided for first, brought to aid, attended and cared for. Right now she gave and he took, and it was exactly what he needed.

Once the initial flare burned down, he cupped her face and pulled them apart, far enough so he could look her in the eyes. "Thank you."

"Please tell me we can go home. You've done more than your share of family duty time, and I'd really like to work off some of my frustrations. So either we go hiking or we find a place to fuck until we can't walk."

"How about both. At the same time if we could," he teased.

She slipped down his body but caught his hands in hers, this time tugging him to the side to admire the horses that had arrived at the fence line. "You never told me a lot of things."

"What's to tell?"

Alisha stroked the mare's nose, confidence in her touch, and Devon relaxed. He should have known she hadn't been kidding about being able to deal with horses.

"You've got the same shitty attitudes here as I have with my parents. None of them think you're good enough. That your job is a real job."

"One huge difference, though. No one laid an arbitrary deadline on me like they did to you." Devon shrugged. "After a while, I figured changing their minds would take more effort than I was willing to give. They work me over good at holidays, and the rest of the time they're, well, more subtle. It's not worth throwing a snit over."

"It still sucks," Alisha corrected him. "They might not have someone they expect you to marry . . ." When he didn't answer right away but instead stared off into space, she glared at him. "Tell me they don't have a girl picked out for you."

His laughter sounded sour in his ears. "They would have, but anyone who was on the list ran screaming when I registered for the Banff SAR School. Mountain bums aren't hot commodities in most circles. I mean, we're pretty to look at, and fun to play with, but not to keep."

He should have kept his mouth shut and gone on kissing her. That would have stopped her from hearing the bitterness that washed his words.

Alisha slipped her fingers around his forearm, her strong grip holding him in place as she made eye contact. Her wide eyes had turned storm grey. "You get dumped by someone, Devon?"

"Old news is old news, Alisha."

She rested her head on his shoulder. "I was right. It sucks, doesn't it?"

Yeah, but it was a long time ago, and he'd moved on. "I can't base my life on teenage disappointments, or the expectations of my family. I'm doing what I want, and I'm damn good at it. That's what counts."

"Still sucks," Alisha said.

And she was right.

They made their good-byes, escaping from the house without much fuss while all his siblings were busy with the family stuff. He drove them as far as the trailhead to the falls, stripping off his dress shirt in the parking lot and exchanging it for a T-shirt from his gear bag.

Alisha glanced around the parking lot. She slid beside him on the driver's side and pulled her dress over her head.

Thong. Bra. Heels. All hot red. Devon blinked hard.

"Jesus, what are you doing?" Devon stepped forward, plenty distracted from his earlier anger.

She cupped herself briefly before reaching around and pulling off her bra. "Getting changed."

His tongue was stuck to the roof of his mouth. "This is a public parking lot," he noted.

"I'll be quick." She stripped off her panties and stood naked except for the heels she wore.

He caught his cock and squeezed it in warning. "I am so making you wear that when we get home."

She dimpled a smile, then dressed quickly, covering her goose bumps, but not doing a damn thing to help ease his erection.

Sadly, Alisha also switched her footwear for more

practical runners. Then she held out a hand and he accepted it, the idea of storming down the trail to rid himself of the rest of his frustrations vanishing as she slipped into a more thoughtful mood.

The trail was wide enough that walking hand in hand was easy, and her fingers were warm in his. They strolled without saying anything for the longest time, the cool October air sweeping around them as the sun rushed too quickly toward the western mountains.

They passed a couple of groups out hiking, all headed to the parking lot. "That's the last of the cars accounted for," Alisha pointed out. "We're officially alone in the wilderness."

He nodded, the leaves underfoot crackling loudly in the quiet of the bush. "It suits, right? Last one off the trail, last one to retreat."

They reached the railing that guarded the overlook, and he stared into the swirling waters, mind twisting with snippets of conversation from the past hours. His brothers' suggestions, his sisters' well-meaning but dismissive attitudes. His parents' determined noninterference that could far too easily be construed as agreement with his siblings' opinions.

Facing them all hadn't been as bad with Alisha there, although now that they'd experienced it, he realized that bringing her along to dinner hadn't been fair. He'd used her as a diversion, but what she'd had to endure had been uncalled for.

He twisted toward her, grateful when she curled up against him, a bundle of warmth with arms.

"I shouldn't have hauled you into that," he apologized. "You've got your own family drama, although mine is nothing as bad as yours."

Alisha dug her fingers into his sides. "Stop making everything into a contest. Besides, that's one I really would prefer *not* to win."

He stroked her hair, dragging his fingers through it again and again as if he were rubbing worry beads. "The good part is I know what we're doing is valuable. Their lack of regard doesn't change facts. I don't need their approval to keep myself focused and sharp, because Lifeline makes a difference, and I want to be a part of it."

"You're preaching to the choir." Alisha slid her hands forward and jerked his T-shirt free from his jeans. She abandoned her gloves, dropping them to the ground so she could skim her soft fingers up his abdomen.

He laughed and braced himself to stop from twitching away. "Glad I could help warm your hands."

She rubbed lightly, the chill vanishing as his body heat transferred to her palms. "You'll be doubly glad in a minute," she promised.

When she put her nails to his skin and dragged lightly, he hummed in approval. When the button of his fly snapped open, he glanced down. "What are you up to?"

Alisha tugged his zipper down, her innocent smile taunting him. "Giving you something to be thankful for."

Oh hell, *yeah*. Like he was going to argue. He rested his hips on the railing and widened his stance. Alisha reached in and drew out his cock, the length thickening in her palm. She pumped slowly, rubbing her thumb over the crest on each pull, and his brain partially shut down. All the areas dealing with troubles and family judgment, at least. Those were shunted away behind a DO NOT DISTURB sign as pleasure rocked the main sections of his mind.

Alisha leaned over and licked him, the contrast of the cool air and her hot mouth making his vision blur. He pulled her hair out of the way to watch those perfect lips wrap around his dick as she sucked him in.

His involuntary hiss of pleasure was enough reward, at least to begin with. Alisha twirled her tongue over the crest again and again. Getting him wet enough that her lips slipped easily over his length. Her fist held tight to the root of his shaft allowed her to bob over him without going deep enough to choke. Deep enough to drive him wild, though, if the steady stream of words he muttered were an indication.

"Yes. Fuck, right there. So fucking good."

He stroked his knuckles over her cheek and Alisha smiled, pausing her motion to apply more suction.

"Don't stop, baby. It feels incredible. Looks fantastic, too." He slipped his finger along the seam between her lips and his thick shaft. She darted her tongue out and licked before going back to tormenting him. "So beautiful and hot."

She'd been waiting for this moment. Wanting it. Alisha found a comfortable position on her knees, lifted her eyes to his, and let herself relax. Devon stroked her cheek again, then added his other hand to her head, firmly positioning her. He tilted his pelvis and stroked in, setting the pace. The depth. The speed.

Slow. So slow, his cock sliding almost all the way out of her mouth, the heavy head resting on her lower lip.

"Lick it," he growled.

She closed her eyes and snuck out her tongue, tasting the salty seed on the crest, playing gently with the slit. A slow circle around the head made him groan and added to her pleasure.

He hadn't touched her and she was wet, an aching need in her core. Giving to him turned her on immensely, and while she wanted to slip a hand into her pants and get herself off, this was more important. This was what she wanted most.

Devon pushed deep, all the way to the back of her throat. Alisha remained still, the thick length filling her mouth. He pulled away and pumped slowly, shorter strokes now, even, measured. Nearly popping free before pressing forward with determined consistency.

The restraint was there, the determined, iron-fisted control he used during rescues and obviously when dealing with his family.

She wanted him to lose control. Wanted him to let go of the restraint and use her as he needed, but even as he took his pleasure, there was never a moment when she didn't feel he was aware of her. Of what she was giving.

Alisha looked into his face, and the tight pleasure there

made her happy and sad at the same time. What she wanted so much was to be in charge of her life. Of her situations. Why right now did it feel wrong to have Devon treating her so cautiously?

She lifted her hands to his wrists and he withdrew instantly, the hard length of his cock glistening in the fading sunlight.

"You okay?" The concern in his voice was so apparent. The focused attention. Miles away from him being an out-of-control, sexually boggled male.

It wasn't okay. It wasn't what she wanted, or what he needed. Alisha took a deep breath and let her concerns out, not caring if they sounded stupid. "I'm not breakable," she whispered. "Fuck my mouth. Be rough if you need to. I'm here for you. I'm willing . . ."

He took a moment, staring seriously into her face. "I didn't want to hurt you."

She shook her head. "You won't. I trust you."

God. His expression changed. The fear and sadness. The tension and discomfort. All of it faded away, and he nodded.

His gaze darted over her face as he adjusted his stance. Slipped his hand into her hair and tightened his fingers slightly.

The movement pulled her hair, and she couldn't stop her moan of satisfaction. *This.* This was what she wanted.

"Jesus. You're going to fucking kill me." Devon swallowed hard, his fingers wrapped around his cock as he stroked a couple of times. "You want me to stop, tap out."

"I will, but I'm not going to stop. I want this, Devon. Now, shut up, and stick your fucking dick in my mouth before I go crazy."

His lips twisted into a smile. "Potty mouth."

"What you going to do about it? You don't have any soap," Alisha taunted.

His eyes darkened as his pupils widened. "I have something better on hand."

All hesitation vanished. Devon used her hair as an anchor to tilt her head. It wasn't a violent motion, but this time there was no doubt Alisha was no longer in control. He pressed the fat head of his cock against her closed lips.

"Open."

He didn't wait for her to obey but pressed forward, the crown slipping between her lips as he thrust to the root, his groin meeting her nose. He pulled back instantly, but the difference in his touch was there. Every motion bolder, more aggressive. Full strokes that left Alisha dizzy and tingling. A network of excitement spread over her as if he had found a way to share the tension building in his body as his climax rushed forward.

Devon closed his eyes and shuddered, and the first spurt hit her tongue. He pulled her head forward as he thrust deep, and she swallowed around the head, dragging a cry from his lips as he shook, fingers tugging her hair.

He held so tightly she couldn't have moved if she'd tried, and his slow withdrawal was perfect, tension in his hands, his body, all carrying to her and showing she'd made an impact.

He gentled then, stroking the hair from her face. Smoothing his knuckles over her cheek. Lifting her to her feet and draping her against him.

They stood silently as his breathing evened out and he regained his balance. The rush of mixed emotions flooding her was confusing, and strange.

She wanted to be in control. To be appreciated for being capable and strong. She wanted Devon to take her in the most primitive and forceful ways possible.

Two sides of a coin that she had no idea how to balance.

CHAPTER 19

''''''''''''''''''''''''''''''''

"Call from the Kootenays." Lana interrupted them on the training field, papers in her hand shaking in the wind. Devon thought her dark brown eyes were sparkling far too much to be sharing an emergency call. "They have a couple of missing climbers in the Valhallas, and their last known position is in an avalanche area. The local SAR are requesting backup."

Marcus nodded, pointing to the team. "Anders, since Tripp's still out of commission, you're on lead. Alisha, when you grab those new harnesses you guys cleared the other day, make sure they're the right ones, I don't think Lana's had time to go through all the rest yet."

They were all in motion, picking up the training gear and heading toward HQ at top speed.

"I called Erin. She'll be in ASAP," Lana reported. "She said thirty minutes tops."

"Thanks." Marcus stepped around her. "Once the team is en route I'll give you a few more jobs, but for now, help them load gear. I'll take over the call desk."

Devon had to dodge around the woman as she kept pace with the team then got in the way. They were barely through the doors, and Devon had his jacket off, ready to switch to warmer gear for the high mountains.

Lana spoke eagerly. "If you want, I could join the team. Since they're one short today, with Tripp gone."

There was dead silence in the change room as the team hurried to grab their stuff. Devon glanced at Marcus, wishing there were a way to force his thoughts into the man's head, to repeat *Oh hell, no* again and again.

Lana on a rescue with them? Not fucking likely.

It seemed he wasn't the only one whose immediate opinion raced down that same line. Anders tossed a bag on the floor and stepped behind it. "As lead, I vote no. This isn't the time to have a newbie on the ropes. Sorry, Lana, we appreciate your help here in the office, but I'm not taking responsibly for an untested partner in uncertain conditions."

Marcus settled behind the desk, slipping on the headset and adjusting the mouthpiece. "There's your answer, although mine would be the same. Thank you for the offer, but we'll let the team deal with running one man short. They've done it before, and it's safer than introducing an unknown into the equation."

Alisha scooted into the change room and pulled her T-shirt off, reaching for a thicker long-sleeve shirt. Devon peeled his eyes off her, focusing on the task. "Harnesses good?"

"Got them. You want to load ropes, I'll join you in a minute and help with the rest."

She tossed him a wink and he smiled, the well-oiled gears of teamwork slipping into place in spite of the elevated voices rising from by the desk.

Lana wasn't taking no for answer.

"I'm not untried," she insisted. "I trained with them the other day. With Becki, on the wall. I'm excellent in mixed climbing conditions if they hit any ice, and—"

"No, Lana. The leader has confirmed his team, and you weren't on it." Marcus spoke firmly. He didn't attempt to hide his rising annoyance. "And I said no. One session on

the stationary wall with the team doesn't make you ready
to work with them."

"But I—"

"Enough," he snapped. "The answer is no, so get out of
the way. We'll discuss your inappropriate behavior when
there isn't a call in progress."

Devon escaped into the storage room relieved that Marcus was in charge, and perplexed that Lana had pushed so
hard, so soon.

The rescue went well, if overly long. They finally found
the climbers in a cave where they'd been trapped following
an equipment failure. Everyone on the team was thoroughly
soaked and chilled to the bone by the time they were ferried
back to HQ.

Even after Alisha showered, her lips were blue during
debrief. Marcus examined her often, and Devon was sure
she would get called up before they left.

Only Marcus tapped him on the shoulder after they were
dismissed. "I want to talk to you."

Devon nodded. "One minute." He slipped into the back
and caught Alisha by the arm. "Wait for me? I shouldn't be
long. Grab something hot to drink."

"I'm drinking, I'm drinking." She jerked on her winter
coat as another shiver took her. "I hate being cold."

Marcus looked up from his desk as Devon slipped into
the tidy office space. "Close the door."

Devon obeyed, his concern rising. "Am I in trouble?"

Marcus shook his head. "Do you deserve to be?"

"Not lately," Devon answered honestly.

That pulled a snort from Marcus. "How are things going
with you and Alisha?"

Shit. "Are you asking as my boss or my friend?" Devon
met Marcus's gaze straight on. "Because if it's as my boss
I'll tell you to butt out."

Marcus's steely gaze remained fixed firmly in position.
"How does your relationship with her affect the efficiency
of the team?"

"Makes us stronger, as far as I can tell," Devon stated

plainly. "We used to fight all the time. Now we're not putting out negative energy. I would think that's a move forward."

"So this is for the good of the team, you and her fucking each other?"

Devon had no idea what the hell was up. "Marcus, if you have concerns, tell me, but otherwise, I'd respectfully ask you to mind your own goddamn business and let me go so I can take her home and we can recover from today."

The stern, almost foreboding expression Marcus wore lightened. "Good for you. I expected you to tell me to fuck off, but that was about as close as you could get without saying it. No, I don't have any issues with you and Alisha. My trouble is elsewhere, and this is more of a warning."

Devon sat gingerly in the chair opposite his boss. "What's really the concern?"

Marcus tapped his fingers on the desk. "I had to rake Lana over the coals today for stepping over the boundaries."

Devon nodded. "She was out of line."

Marcus's gaze snapped up. "She said you'd encouraged her to try for the team. Full team, not desk work."

"What?" Of all the stupid, idiotic . . . "Encouraged her, how?"

"Climbed with her, invited her to join in during social activities." Marcus waved aside the rude noise Devon made. "I know, you were probably being friendly, but she's taken it the wrong way."

"She's trouble." Devon shook his head. "I gave the woman a ride home once. She showed up at the Rose and Crown, once. I buddied with her on the wall. Once. Right in front of Becki, I might add, and that was only to make sure no one else had to climb with her."

"I figured that was the case, but damn, the woman is good. If Becki hadn't given me a heads-up regarding her, I might have fallen for the wide-eyed innocent ploy Lana tossed at me."

Devon picked at the arm of his chair. "I need to get Alisha home. I'll be careful around Lana, but I hope you'll seriously consider getting rid of her."

"She's on probation. I have to follow rules as an employer, but I'm not pleased, and I will cut her if she doesn't smarten up fast." Marcus looked him over once more. "You're a valued member of this team, Devon. I like the maturity and confidence you bring. I don't care that you're young—you're good. I want you to know that."

Devon left the office warmer than he'd entered it. Pissed off at Lana, but thrilled by Marcus's compliments.

Alisha was curled up on the couch, blankets piled high around her. The only things sticking out were her hands and her face peeking from under her hoodie. She wore fingerless gloves, her hands wrapped around her coffee mug.

The sight of her made something flip inside. Devon pushed away the urge to scoop her up and carry her to the car. To protect her and do for her. All the urges to take control and take over—too much like what Vincent had offered, but damn if he could stop some of the impulses from rising.

She smiled as he sat beside her. "Done?"

He nodded, taking the cup and placing it on the table. "We can go."

She shrugged off the layers. "I can't believe how tired I am."

"It's the cold on top of the long day," he said. "Come on, we can crash and deal with the rest of it tomorrow."

Alisha was sound asleep by the time he pulled into his parking space. He left the engine running with the heat blowing on high while he unloaded their bags. When he finally came and tugged her arm to wake her, she didn't move.

Devon hesitated. Something was off. He reached in and took her pulse, his fingers warm against her cool skin.

Low heart rate—lower even than hers should be in sleep. "Alisha?" He stroked her cheek. "Wake up. You can curl up in bed and be much more comfortable."

Nothing. No eye flicker, no complaint about being woken.

"Shit, Alisha, wake up." Louder this time, plus he reached in and pinched her. When she didn't respond to that stimulus, he swore and flipped into action. Jumped into the car and headed for the hospital emergency room.

He hauled out his phone and called Marcus. "I don't know what's up, but Alisha is out of it. As if she's been drugged, or something."

Marcus swore. "In the fifteen minutes since you left? Take her to the hospital."

"I'm halfway there. Will you meet me?"

"On my way."

Devon glanced to the side, hovering his hand over her mouth to allow the faint stroke of air escaping her lips to brush his skin and reassure him she was still breathing. "What the hell is going on?" he asked.

The answering silence nearly killed him, and he pressed his foot harder to the floor, racing to reach the hospital.

The smell of antiseptic wrinkled her nose. A warm hand touched her arm, and she rolled over to look into Devon's noticeably tired blue eyes.

"Hey." She leaned up on an elbow, and that was when she noticed she wasn't in his bed, or her own. "Why am I in the hospital?"

Devon took a deep breath, sitting back in the chair resting beside her bed. He kept hold of her fingers. "You were drugged."

Panic shot through her in a rush. "Seriously?"

He nodded. "Don't worry. You're safe. They had you hooked to an IV for a bit to help flush your system, but pretty much sleeping it off was the best option."

She still couldn't believe it. She clung to his hand as she tried to make sense of his words. "Drugged? How did that happen? What kind of drug? When did I get it?"

"We're still trying to find the answers to some of those questions. They've tested you, now they're looking through things back at HQ. I told them you had a hot drink while you were waiting for me." Devon dragged his hand through his hair, and even through her confusion and upset at waking in the hospital, she noticed again how tired he looked.

She also realized she had to get up. "Where's the bathroom?"

That pulled a smile from him. "This way. I'll escort you."

She might have slept, but the mirror didn't hide the evidence of her exhaustion—she should probably crawl back in and sleep for an entire week. Alisha stretched, finding her balance and strength returning even though she still felt as if she'd been hit by a truck. The low-grade nausea remained, the headache.

Devon waited for her outside the door, leaning on the wall as he looked around wearily, and she smiled sheepishly. "Don't tell me you were here all night."

He shrugged. "I was worried."

He led her back to the curtained cubicle, her mind awash with curiosity at his comment. She waited to ask him anything, doing a physical check first. Trying to connect the information she could remember with where she currently was.

It still made no sense, but she couldn't seem to panic. First because she was far too exhausted, and then because . . .

She glanced away from Devon before he read her mind and figured out how much it meant to her that he'd obviously been at her side all night long.

"You know what's up? Who do I need to see to get released?"

Devon nodded. "I'll go get the nurse. Marcus talked to the doctor last night. I think you get to go pretty quick."

Alisha sat on the edge of the bed. "Marcus was here?"

"Tripp called as well. And Erin this morning."

She was touched to hear that but didn't quite know how to react. "I'm good to go as soon as possible."

She was pretty much rubber-stamped out of the hospital, Marcus having done all the paperwork necessary. She was grateful for Devon's arm as he guided her out. "Does Lifeline know I'm out of commission for a few days?"

"Marcus knows. He said with both you and Tripp

knocked for a loop, he's screening call-outs hard. He doesn't want you to worry—if it's not a three-man job, or something he can help with, he won't accept it. Not to worry."

"I'm too tired to argue." Alisha leaned on the headrest, twisting to watch Devon as he eased the car out of the parking lot. The tension in his jaw was visible even from the side. "Did you sleep at all?"

"Some. In the chair."

"Great. So comfy."

He shifted his body, easing into a better position. "I'll live. Once we're home I'll sleep for the next twenty-four hours."

She wanted to ask more details about what was going on, but he'd already told her everything he knew. The police would come talk to her later—they were already going over Lifeline to figure out if there was anything there to explain what had happened.

She accepted his hand and let him guide her into the house. Didn't complain as he helped her out of her clothes, but stopped him before he pushed her toward the bed. "I need a shower. I feel as if I've been rolling in filth for days."

He nodded and took her into the bathroom. When he stripped, she was torn between protesting and being grateful for the support of his strong arms. Leaning against him gave her a rock-solid place to rest, her hands spread on his muscular chest. "I wish I had the energy to take advantage of you."

"Some other time. Right now, let me take care of you."

When they'd fooled around in the shower before, sexual tension and high passion had driven them. It was different this time as he swayed with her under the heated deluge, the fat showerhead dropping a torrent on them like a heavy rainfall in a tropical country. Devon stroked her shoulders. Her back. His strong fingertips eased muscles that ached without a reason.

She closed her eyes and fought the rolling in her stomach, aftereffects of the drug. Devon turned them, soaking her completely. Brushing her hair off her face. Another twist, and the scent of pears filled the shower.

The slow scrub of a soft washcloth and soap drifted over her skin as Devon washed every bit of her. He supported her with his body, leaning her back and soaping her breasts, tenderness in his touch. Not lingering, but moving on to her stomach, between her legs. Smoothing up the sides of her waist and teasing the edges of her breasts. Intimate, yet his caress so natural her breathing remained relaxed and peaceful, the hint of sexual pleasures lingering, but mainly it was the caress of a friend.

Everywhere he touched tingled briefly as he chased the lingering fear from her, his touch constant and careful.

When he pulled the seat down from the wall and placed her on it, she sighed. "Decadent."

"Hmm, I've never been so happy to have this place." He rubbed his fingertips over her scalp, washing her hair, bringing up the lather as he kept the suds from slipping into her eyes. He tilted her head and directed the water to rinse the shampoo away, the side of her head resting against his firm abdomen.

Alisha felt cosseted. Pampered beyond belief. Devon used conditioner on her, working his fingers through the long strands and laying them over her shoulders before rinsing again. Water soothing and warm, her stomach settling as everything conspired to bring her ease.

The thick towel he wrapped her in appeared out of nowhere. Her eyelids refused to cooperate and open fully. "You're too good to me," she whispered, about all she had the energy for. "I'm ready to pass out again."

"Sleep is the best thing right now. Don't fight it."

But by the time he'd dried them both off, slipped one of his T-shirts over her head, and pulled on boxers, she wasn't nearly as drowsy. She stared at him as they lay in bed and he stroked her hair, his blue eyes suspiciously dark.

"You okay, Devon?"

He nodded. Paused. "I'm sorry you got hurt."

That made no sense. "You didn't do anything wrong."

"I didn't keep you safe, though."

Alisha cupped his face, the shadow on his chin rough against her palm. "The police will figure it out. I'll be fine."

His gaze darted over her face. "I hope you know I'd never do anything to hurt you."

Alisha jerked upright, the shock of his words sinking in hard enough to wake her. "Of course, you wouldn't. Who the hell said otherwise?"

"Shhh." He attempted to ease her to the mattress, but she was having none of his soothing. She pushed on his chest and he reluctantly allowed himself to be pressed to his back as she glared down.

"Did you get questioned by the police?" He wasn't going to answer her. His refusal was clear in his eyes. "You did. When you brought me into the hospital."

"It's standard procedure," Devon said. "I'm not upset. And Marcus showed up a few minutes later to clear me, but I wanted to . . ."

He trailed off, catching hold of her face. Cupping her cheeks tenderly and drawing her toward him.

What followed was exquisite. A bare, brief caress of mouths before he let her go. More intimate even than the touch of his lips was the expression in his eyes. "I was so scared," he whispered. "I never want to see you like that again. It nearly tore me in two."

Alisha swallowed hard, retreating from the intensity of his confession. Everything she'd experienced blurred together—not only her drug-induced hospital visit, but the rescue the day before, the trip to visit his family, and the hovering menace of Vincent's demands.

He smiled. "Sorry. A little out of the blue, right? It's been a roller coaster around here lately."

She nodded, stroking his skin like a worry stone, the smooth heat under her fingers reassuring her. "I do trust you. I always have, even when we were fighting to be top dog at school. I didn't want to get involved with you, but that wasn't because I thought you were terrible."

"You thought I was a man-whore," he teased, doing his

own stroking, his fingers firm on her thighs as he caressed her under the quilt. "I wasn't really. Lots of talk, not much action. I was too exhausted trying to keep up with you."

"That makes two of us, and we're still working hard." She arranged herself against him, resting her head on his chest and getting comfortable again. He had tempted her enough in spite of his man-whore status that she'd had to work to refuse him. That confession wasn't needed anymore, but she did have something else to share. "Thank you for taking care of me these past days. I don't know what I would have done without you. I think that says a lot about how much I do trust you, and I'm not the only one. You're a rock, Devon. People know what to expect with you. You might tease a lot, but your work ethic and decision-making skills have never been in question. Not by me. Not by the team."

Devon stroked her hair, his heart rate solid under her ear. "It's strange. How there are so many different circles in our lives. Family. School. Work. Friends. All of them see us as someone different."

She was fading again, the drugs still affecting her, but even washed by waves of fatigue she clued in on his issue.

Maybe the drugs loosened her tongue when she should have held it, but she laid her head on the pillow so she could look him in the eye as she spoke. "When one out of four of your circles is clearly in the minority? I'd say your family must be a bunch of idiots for not seeing what a great guy you are."

A smile appeared at her bold proclamation. "Go to sleep. I'll take care of you."

"Go to sleep yourself. I bet I can sleep longer than you."

"Always with the damn contests," he mock-complained. Then a fake snore escaped him, and she giggled as she gave in to exhaustion.

CHAPTER 20
....

It was Alisha who pulled herself from bed only a few hours later, bleary-eyed but awake. Incredibly, she was hungry.

Loud pounding on the door brought her hurrying from the kitchen to stop the noise before it woke Devon. She tightened the belt of the robe she'd pulled on, then peeked through the side window.

Shock froze her in position for an instant before she yanked the door open. "Stop making that racket," she ordered, glaring at Vincent. "What the hell do you think you're doing?"

He loomed in the doorway, and she jerked the door between them.

Vincent paused, as if shocked by her actions. "Enough. I'm through waiting for you to realize you're in over your head. I've come to take you home."

Alisha snapped her mouth shut from where she'd been gaping in surprise at his words. "I think you've mistaken me for someone you have any control over. I can take care of myself. Go away, and don't bother to come back. Ever."

Vincent rubbed his forehead for a moment, took a deep breath, then held up his hands in surrender. "Listen to me. You were in the hospital. How is that taking care of yourself?"

"How did you hear I was sick?" An even more concerning thought stuck, and she wrapped the robe front closer. "And how did you find me? What are you doing here?"

Vincent stood straighter, looking over her shoulder into the house. "This is your lover's place. He gave me his card, remember? When you left your apartment you had to have found somewhere to live, and here you are."

"Here I am, and here I stay," Alisha retorted. "Thank you for your interest in my health. I'm fine. Now go back to Toronto, and don't expect me to change my plans. I'm not marrying you, and I'm not leaving Banff. You need to accept that."

She moved to close the door, but Vincent moved faster, shoving his foot into the gap and stopping her from locking him out. He lowered his chin and stared hard, his dark eyes glittering in the afternoon light. His voice softened, but the words came out brittle like shards of glass. "No, you need to accept that you will be returning. The sooner you get that through your head, the less traumatic this will be for all of us."

"Do I need to go to the police, Vincent? Because if I have to, I will," Alisha warned. "You're threatening me."

"Of course not." Vincent took a far too intense perusal down to her bare toes and back up, lingering on her chest. "Why would I threaten the woman I love, and intend to—"

"The woman you love?" Alisha blurt out. "Damn you to hell, that's bullshit."

Vincent clicked his tongue. "Such language."

His scold broke her meager control. Alisha was furious with him, and upset that he'd attempt to order her around. She spoke clearly, enunciating every word. "You don't like my fucking language? Get your fucking foot out of the fucking door, and you won't have to fucking listen to me anymore."

He scowled harder. "That's so mature."

Her limbs were trembling and she rocked the door, hard. "Get. Out."

"Why are you making this so difficult, Alisha?" Vincent leaned on the door frame, pushing himself farther into the room. "I've been patient. I've been supportive. Be reasonable."

She came close to stuttering. "Be *reasonable*?"

His tone was nearly parental. Judgmental. "You have no home anymore, or won't in a few weeks' time. You're sponging on others' goodwill. Sleeping with one member of your team after the other to simply have a roof over your head. You don't need to whore yourself like this, Alisha."

This time words escaped her. She couldn't form complete sentences, let alone coherent ones.

Maybe the steam escaping her ears or the furious rage causing her face to heat tipped him off because he caught hold of her wrist just before she slammed a fist into him. "Don't even try. You wanted to play your little games, and flaunted your ability to turn your back on your family, and I allowed it. But that's over. Get yourself to Toronto by Christmas or you'll regret it."

"The only thing I regret is opening the door in the first place." She narrowed her eyes and stepped back, going for her phone.

"It's a dangerous business you're in, Alisha. I'd hate for something to happen to anyone who works with you." He stepped fully onto the porch. "Someone close to you. It's not impossible to influence a person's destiny. Just a tiny nudge at the right moment can make all the difference."

"Alisha, who are you talking to?"

Alisha twisted to the side to discover Devon in the hallway, blinking hard as he pulled to vertical. She glanced at the front door only to find that Vincent was gone.

Warm hands wrapped around her as Devon closed the distance between them. He tucked his head in close and kissed her neck, the heat of sleep wrapping around them both as she made a quick judgment call. Devon didn't need to know everything about the visit from Vincent. She'd just . . . downplay it.

"We had a visitor, but he's gone."

Devon jolted upright. "That's what you called your vampire friend the other day."

He stormed toward the entrance, her hands falling aside unheeded as he hauled the door open. They were in time to see the red taillights of Vincent's rented Ferrari head away down the back drive.

Devon turned, fully awake now. "Are you okay?"

She nodded. "He didn't do anything except make his usual demands for me to stop this independence charade and return to my place in the big scheme of things. As his arm candy."

Devon glanced out again before firmly closing the door. "How did he know you were here?"

She wrinkled her nose. "You gave him a business card."

He shook his head. "No, how did he know you were *here*, in my house?"

Alisha frowned. "He also talked about my trip to the hospital. And he mentioned something that makes me think he knew I spent a night at Tripp's."

Devon's lips tightened. "You said you didn't want the media involved, but in light of the drugging, you need to mention a few things when you talk to the police. If you're worried about the media finding out we can ask Marcus who's the best to discuss this with—he and Becki have contacts in the RCMP."

Alisha tugged him toward the kitchen. "After we eat. I'm starving."

"But after?" Devon hugged her close when she nodded. "Good. And next time? Don't open the door."

"Trust me, I'm kicking myself for that already."

He tweaked her nose and she blushed, and all his bare skin was far too tempting. Stupid as it was with all the other concerns, those bands of muscle wrapping around his torso were begging for her to use her tongue on them. The faint trail of hair disappearing under the elastic of his boxers teasing like a siren's song. If it weren't for the animal in her stomach begging to be fed, she'd have dragged him to the bedroom instead of the kitchen.

She ignored the lust that rose far too quickly, in spite of all her lingering concern about exactly what Vincent had been referring to in terms of someone close to her being hurt. Food first, everything else after.

Alisha had been quiet since they'd left the RCMP station. Devon figured some of that was fallout from the drugging—and even thinking about that again triggered the most astonishing sensations deep inside him.

Someone had drugged her.

Fury, frustration, fear—everything driving him crazy was bottled up with nowhere to go because the last thing she needed right now on top of everything else was him being ballistic.

When they'd placed her on the gurney he'd had a tight grip on her fingers and hadn't planned on letting go anytime soon. The sight of a uniformed RCMP officer bearing down on him had shaken him more because he'd had to allow her to slip away behind a door where he couldn't see what was happening.

So now as Devon held her hand, he was hyperaware of the warmth of her fingers in his. Aware of how she could be torn away in an instant. The thoughts that kept popping into his head were not the casual reflections of a friend, but of someone wanting more, and the idea wasn't nearly frightening enough.

They walked down Main Street, the tourists around them wandering slowly and peering into windows while he and Alisha paced quicker on the edge of the wide walkway.

Alisha slowed for a moment, and he tried to see what had caught her eye, but it was the usual shop full of knickknacks stamped with BANFF NATIONAL PARK. Cute, wide-eyed, stuffed toy beavers and chocolate-covered almonds packaged as moose droppings. Thick slabs of rich fudge and furry toques with attached antlers.

She twisted toward him and smiled, the edges a little rough, but she was obviously trying to lighten up. "You want to hit a movie or something? Mindless entertainment since I'm not ready for a workout or anything else."

Devon considered. "What about our own movie night? Pick out a few online, make some popcorn—just hang out for a while. When you've had enough, we can call it a night."

Her face brightened further. "Can we order pizza?"

"Of course. That was one of the top three menu items planned for the event." He switched direction to return them to his house sooner. "Tell me if you need a break, okay?"

She squeezed his fingers. "I'm not dying. The walk is good for me—moving around will help get the crap out of my system sooner."

They strode in silence for a while, Devon allowing her to set the pace.

She sighed, shaking her head and muttering softly.

"I hate to remind you that talking to yourself is a sure sign of trouble." Devon squeezed her fingers. "It is that bad?"

"It's not good," Alisha said. "You weren't in the office when I talked with the officer, but there's not much anyone can do about Vincent. He's not officially crossed any lines, and since I didn't want to file a restraining order or anything, unless I phone them they can't even watch him on the sly. Not that they'd have time in the first place."

"Did they find anything at Lifeline? Did they say?"

"No." Another sigh. "Turns out Becki had done the dishes after we left—including washing the mug I drank out of. She came to pick up Marcus, and while he was finishing paperwork she did some tidying. You called right when they were ready to leave. And we know I didn't have anything different from the team to eat or drink all day while on the rescue."

Which created a lovely dead end. The helplessness he felt was beyond frustrating. Another thought occurred. "Why is Vincent sticking around in the first place? He's been here for a long time."

Alisha snorted. "He said he would stay until he'd gotten the job done."

Shit. "He can't possibly have Bailey Enterprises business keeping him here. Does that mean he's only here to bother you?"

She jerked to a stop, eyes wide. "I hope not."

Now he wished he hadn't said anything. "Hey, it's okay. He can't make you do anything you don't want to. Get that straight."

All the nodding in the world couldn't hide her disgust that Vincent was still in Banff, probably on her behalf. Devon didn't blame her—the guy was a creep and an ass.

She'd barely made it through the front door when a huge yawn took her.

Devon grinned. "I saw that."

"What a shitty day. I'm going to nap for a bit," Alisha slapped her hand over her mouth to cover another yawn. "God, sorry."

"Stop apologizing and go. Sleep until you're done. I won't phone for pizza until you're awake, so there's no agenda." He tugged her against him, relishing the contact. "There's no pressure here, Alisha. We're your friends."

She stole a hug. "You are. Thank you for that."

Devon planted his feet and forced himself to not follow her to the bedroom. She was capable of putting herself to bed for a nap. She didn't need him babysitting, no matter how much he wanted to wrap her in cotton right now.

To distract himself, he pulled the pile of correspondence he'd found in the mailbox and went through it. Bills had a way of making the world disappear for a bit.

The fine envelope was out of place in the rest of the plain white ones, and he pulled it forward with curiosity. Hand-written to the main house—it had been redirected to him because of his position with the owners.

He read the letter quickly, laughing at the proposal to purchase the house. There was no way in hell the owners would want to give up the heritage home. Then he spotted the amount of money being offered and whistled softly, not wanting to disturb Alisha but needing to make some noise. Well, maybe the deal would be enticing. The offer was for at least twice the going market rate. Devon wasn't sure he'd ever seen that many zeros when a dollar sign was involved before.

While he hated the idea of potentially losing his sweet rental, there was no way he could ignore this offer. He'd have to send them a copy to consider.

Devon was about to place the letter aside when he noticed the signature and name at the bottom, and suddenly everything changed.

Vincent Monreal.

What the hell?

He double-checked the date on the letter. Examined the calendar on the wall to confirm his suspicions, but his first impressions were correct. Vincent had put in the offer only a day after Alisha had moved into his place.

Suddenly another mystery made sense. He wondered if her landlord had received a similar incentive to up and move.

Vincent was literally trying to make her homeless.

The doorbell forced Devon to leave the damning evidence until another time, but it certainly proved Vincent wasn't above using dirty methods to get what he wanted.

Discovering Tripp out on the front porch was a shocker. Devon glanced behind him, but his teammate was alone. "Hey."

Tripp slid in the doorway and glanced around. "Alisha here?"

"She's sleeping. What's up?"

"You got a minute?"

Devon gestured him farther in. "You want a drink or something?"

"Water. I'll grab it." Tripp helped himself to a glass from the cupboard, making himself at home. He drank about half before lowering the glass to the counter and making a disgruntled noise.

"You're procrastinating, aren't you?" Devon asked. "All

the signs are there. We've spent the past two years working in close quarters, and you're only twitchy when you're trying to avoid a confrontation. Just say it."

Tripp nodded. "Okay. Fine. So this is going to come out totally stupid, and I'm not sure what exactly it all means, but you know the other day when I went home sick?"

"Yeah," Devon leaned on the wall. This uncertainty was not typical Tripp—something had him tied in knots like Devon had never seen before.

Tripp made a face. "I think I was drugged."

Shock hit first, then confusion. "Wait—you had the stomach flu, didn't you?"

"I thought I did, because it made sense. I was fine that morning, though, and not even an hour into training I suddenly got dizzy and nauseated. When I got home I crashed and slept nearly around the clock, and it took a couple days to get over it." Tripp paused. "But you know, Jonah never caught it, and he catches everything. No one else on the team got sick, and I wasn't around anyone else who was sick."

"Still pushing it. I mean, public places are germ pits."

"I know, but it makes me wonder. Xavier has access to all kinds of wonderful things in his medic kit, doesn't he?"

Dread filled Devon at the direction in which the conversation had turned. "Of course he does, but why in the world would he want to drug either you or Alisha? For that matter, I can get into the medical supplies at Lifeline, and so could you."

"I know; that's why I said this makes no sense. I had to talk to someone about it." Tripp glanced down the hallway. "How is she?"

"She's going to be fine. Knocked her for a loop—she's not very big to start with, but she's damn strong." Devon cupped Tripp's shoulder. "Did you talk to Marcus about this?"

Tripp shook his head. "I got to thinking about it last night after I talked to you, but it was just this morning I clued in to the possibility. I've been going in circles ever since. It makes sense, but there's no reason for anyone to drug me, and what kind of ass would I be to make an accusation that could ruin someone's career without proof?"

Hell. "How much worse would it be to not say anything, then have someone on the team seriously hurt because we didn't mention it?"

The other man's face tightened. "I'm not eager to go pointing fingers at a teammate who's done nothing up to now to indicate any reason for him to act out of line."

Devon took a deep breath. "Tripp, this isn't something we can laugh off and wait and see what happens next. Marcus needs to know. You don't have to accuse anyone of anything, but you have to tell him you think you were drugged."

Tripp shuffled his feet uneasily.

This wasn't a matter for debate, and Tripp needed to understand that. "If you want me to, I'll go with you, but I'm serious. You tell Marcus, or I will."

"I will. You're right. I'll talk to him first thing in the morning." Tripp took a deep breath and let it out slowly. "You okay if I hang out here for a while? Jonah is gone this weekend, and I'd . . . well, I'd like to see Alisha."

Devon patted Tripp on the back and pushed him toward the living room. "You're welcome to stay. She should be awake soon. We were going to order a pizza and watch a movie."

"Don't say anything about this to her right now, okay?" Tripp turned in the doorway, holding up a hand. "I'll talk to Marcus first."

No problem on Devon's side. "I agree, let's keep things low-key tonight. Give her another day to recover before tossing anything else into the mix."

Tripp went one direction while Devon went the other, checking the fridge for food ideas.

The doorbell rang and Tripp beat him to the front door, opening it to let in Erin, who had a huge box balanced in her hands.

"Take it before I drop it," Erin ordered. "Hey, Devon. I brought dinner."

"Visitors bearing gifts. The best kind." Devon grabbed

the box, glancing behind her to see Anders and Xavier also on the walkway. "What are you, the Pied Piper?"

Erin grinned. "I'm surprised they're here already. Anders said he had to nab something. We won't stay if Alisha's not up for it, but . . ." She shrugged. "I wanted to make sure she's okay."

Devon nodded as his tiny house filled to the brim, Anders and Xavier filing through the door with their hands full as well. "I was just about to check on her."

"I'll go," Erin offered.

She was down the hall before he could answer, which was probably for the best. He herded Tripp toward the couch, forcing the man to stop staring at Xavier and causing trouble before it was time. "Pick a movie, guys. And do I still need to order pizza?"

"Of course," Anders clicked on the TV and booted up the Internet. "I mean, even if Erin cooked, pizza never goes to waste."

"It's the perfect breakfast food," Xavier pointed out. "I'll get drinks. Who wants what?"

Tripp's brows were buried in his hairline, and Devon jumped in. "I'll give you a hand."

Honestly. It was like herding cats at times, but other than Tripp's awkwardness, it was good to see them all.

Good to know they were as concerned about Alisha as he was.

She had a family here whether she realized it or not. Now he had to figure out why that thought made him uncomfortable. Or maybe he had to admit to himself that what he was feeling was more than the concern of one team member for another. More than mere sexual interest would explain.

There were some doors that were a lot harder to open than others.

Devon joined Xavier in the kitchen and pulled glasses from the shelf because that was simpler than dealing with anything else.

CHAPTER 21

〟〟〟〟〟〟〟〟〟〟〟〟〟〟〟〟〟〟〟〟〟〟〟〟

She'd already been awake when the doorbell rang and conversation began in the other room. Alisha washed her face, happily noting that she only looked half like death warmed over. By the time someone knocked on Devon's bedroom door, she'd pulled on sweats and one of Devon's oversized sweatshirts, rolling up the sleeves so her hands weren't buried in the excess length.

"Come on in." Alisha scrambled in her bag for her hairbrush, looking up in time to see Erin poke her head around the corner. "Hey you."

"Hey you, yourself. Dammit, girl, what the hell were you pulling? Hospital time? You need a vacation, you should ask Marcus for one."

Alisha sat on the edge of the bed and went to work on her hair. "Yeah, trust me, an actual holiday would be far better than the local ER. For one thing, I tend to remember holidays."

Erin shook her head, closing the door behind her and sitting in the chair beside the dresser. "You really okay?"

Alisha nodded. "Tired, but no more than when we've pulled back-to-back rescues too many days in a row. I figure one more solid sleep and I'll be up to full speed."

"Good, because while I don't want you to rush it, I need you at Lifeline before I get testosterone poisoning."

Guaranteed grin. "They are a handful, the guys." She paused, eyed Erin closer. The urge to tease was probably a sign that she was feeling a lot better. "But there's Lana now. Surely she helps fight the overload?"

Erin made a rude noise. "Don't even start me on that woman."

"Aren't you besties yet?" Alisha clicked her tongue. "I'm so disappointed."

Erin chuckled. "Sarcasm becomes you. You need to try it more often."

Alisha blinked innocently. "I wasn't being sarcastic."

They stared at each other for a moment, then burst out laughing. When Alisha could speak again she put her brush down on the side table and twisted to face Erin. "Forget Lana. She's not a part of the team. How do you like the new chopper?"

"It's awesome. Anders and I have worked out the bugs, and she's ready to roll at the next call-out." Erin pointed in her direction. "So you get better, because I want you along, okay?"

The warmth flooding Alisha wasn't only from her nap anymore. Having Erin express interest and caring was something special—something that hadn't been there the previous season. Finding a place as friends as well as co-workers was so right. "I'll do my best. Devon's taking good care of me."

Erin nodded. "I bet he is. He's totally gone on you." Alisha laughed, pausing when Erin didn't join in. The woman raised one perfect brow, her smooth dark skin shining in the soft bedroom light. "You doubt me? You need to open your eyes. I mean, I joked about losing the bet, but you two are good together. Don't miss the signs."

"We're hot together, I'll admit that. He's not half the pain in the ass he used to be."

"Hate to tell you this." Erin gave her that look again. "I don't see Devon's changed much. He's still the same *works his ass off, jokes about it* type of guy he's always been."

Alisha went searching for socks so she could think about that more before she responded. Devon had shown a new face in the past days, but had she been the one ignoring the real him? Did it matter?

Lingering effects from the drugs forced her to focus on the here and now. She looked Erin in the eye. "I like him."

"Honey, you always liked him." Erin winked, her deep brown eyes twinkling with amusement. "You just weren't admitting it to yourself."

Like a lot of things. "Hey, I have a question. A pretty awkward, personal question."

Erin smoothed her shirt and leaned back in the chair. "Ask. If I don't want to answer, we'll change topics to discuss the weather."

"You ever have someone you needed to discourage? I mean, a guy." Alisha's cheeks heated. She and Erin had gotten closer, yes, but romantic advice was not on the list of things they'd spent time discussing, even with the change in status quo. She rushed onward. "I remembered you saying something once about there being someone . . . bossy . . . in your life and that they weren't around anymore. That's all."

Erin lost her relaxed posture, leaning forward on her elbows. "You got troubles, hon? Are you in danger?" Her eyes widened. "Shit, you think you know who might have drugged you?"

The idea of Vincent being involved seemed impossible. "I've got troubles, but right now I have no idea how Vincent could have orchestrated something like drugging me. I'm . . . Devon knows. It's part of the reason why I'm living here temporarily."

"Vincent?" Erin frowned. "Who's that, and what's he been doing?"

Alisha gave a brief rundown, noting with satisfaction that Erin didn't seem ready to run from the room, but instead her spine stiffened as if she were ready to do battle on Alisha's behalf.

When Alisha was done, Erin nodded slowly, folding her fingers together and holding them to her lips for a moment as she considered. "I've had a bad relationship before, oddly enough not with the guy you heard me mention. He was . . . a different issue. As well, in a way, the solution to the first creep."

"You had a guy get rid of the first troublemaker?"

"Him, and a restraining order." Erin shifted position to sit on the bed beside Alisha. "Look, there are times no matter what you do, no matter how firm you are in handling a situation, you won't be able to deal without help. It's one of the downfalls of being a woman in today's society."

Alisha nodded. "Society can go suck eggs."

"Agreed." Erin caught her hand and squeezed it. "Thanks for telling me. I'll keep an eye out for you, but honestly? Being involved with Devon is great front-line help. On a different topic, if you need to get your stuff out of your old apartment, well, I've got room to store things. Heck, you can move in with me temporarily if you'd like—I'm not keen on a permanent roomie, because I enjoy my personal space, but the offer is there if you need it."

Alisha would be crying in a minute if she wasn't careful. "Thank you. I just want Vincent to go away. I'm not changing my mind, so I don't see what good it does him to hang around."

Erin hummed. "He's staying in Banff? How can he do that for a prolonged period of time? I thought he worked for the company your dad owns."

"I assume he's using the computer to work remotely." Alisha had wondered the same thing. "I'd call my father to find out, but the last time I asked him a question about Vincent I got nowhere. Plus, I don't need more pressure from that quarter for me to *do the right thing and come to my senses.*"

"To hell with that," Erin muttered. She rose to her feet.

"Come, grab something to eat and say hi to the guys—
they've been worried sick about you."

Alisha stood. "Thanks for the ear, Erin. I appreciate it."

"Anytime." She nodded. "And say the word, and we'll
take care of your apartment for you. I'll coordinate, get the
guys to add the muscle power. We'll be done in no time."

"I might take you up on that offer," Alisha promised.

They stepped into the hall and down to the living room.
The team swarmed Alisha. One set of muscular arms after
the other surrounded her as she was passed down the line
and hugged fiercely. Tripp's teddy bear envelopment was
followed by Anders's more casual embrace. Xavier squeezed
her extra hard before flipping into paramedic mode and
examining her eyes.

"Ambulance chaser," she joked, pressing a hand against
his chest. "Go away."

"Attention hog." Xavier patted her shoulder, then gestured toward the couch. "Put your feet up. You get to cast
the deciding vote for the first show of the night."

"*Hellboy* marathon?"

"God, no." Devon slipped onto the couch beside her.
"How can someone so sweet and innocent like you watch
that crap?"

Alisha accepted a plate of food from Tripp, leaning on the
couch contentedly. "What? You want to do the *Lord of the
Rings* again? I think you've got a serious crush on Legolas."

Tripp blinked. "Well, who doesn't?"

Anders cackled. "Or Gimli."

Devon rolled his eyes. "Yeah, right, I'm *all* about the
dwarves. But make it Thorin, and you'd be closer to the
mark."

That earned him a few hoots of laughter, and Alisha
smiled harder and relaxed into the easy acceptance of the
team as they distracted her by being themselves.

Less than twelve hours ago Vincent had threatened her.
It seemed impossible, like some drug-induced hallucination.
Glancing around the room, though, she couldn't bear to

think of not being a part of this. The smiles, the jokes. The honest-to-God caring.

Beside her Devon had balanced his plate in his lap so he could drape an arm around her shoulders. She snuggled in tight, allowing his body heat to comfort her like a living blanket.

The show began, conversation continuing over the soundtrack since they'd all seen the show a hundred times. Conversation and teasing were the order of the day, and her fears faded. How could anything tear her from something so powerful as the caring and commitment she'd found in Lifeline?

Devon couldn't stay away. The last of the team had silently slipped out once they'd discovered Alisha had fallen asleep sometime during the second movie. He'd remained motionless, her head resting on his chest, with knowing glances tossed his direction, especially from Erin and Tripp, before the door clicked shut behind them.

He carried her to the bedroom, her breathing staying even and heavy, she was so out of it. Devon arranged her on the bed, pulling off her sweats, but hesitating over the sweatshirt until he decided she couldn't possibly be comfortable sleeping in the bulky thing.

She nuzzled against him as he supported her with his body and slipped off the top, her sleep-warmed skin scalding him with the desire to consume her like a feast. Leaving the room wasn't possible—not unless he wanted to spend his evening returning every five minutes to check on her like some crazed stalker.

So he gave in and stripped, joining her in the bed. She turned and cuddled in instantly, her strong fingers skimming over his chest. A happy noise escaped her, somewhere between a sigh and moan.

He kissed the top of her head as she eased one of her legs between his, tangling them together intimately. All of it so natural, so comfortable, they could have been lovers for years instead of weeks.

The whole thing with Vincent had shaken him more than he'd thought. Adding in Tripp's concerns, he really didn't know what to think, other than that he was determined to keep Alisha safe.

How to accomplish that, he had no idea. Waves of helpless frustration swamped him harder than the sexual desire he always felt in her presence. This wasn't about wanting her, although there was no doubt that he did. It was about being there for her and not letting her down.

She'd said she trusted him, but should she?

The fear that he wouldn't be enough made him stare into the darkness for a long, long time.

He must have drifted off. It was the only explanation, because there was this incredible heat surrounding his cock. Wet pressure pulled him from dreams that involved entirely too much of Alisha's eyes—turned blue with passion—staring up as she wrapped her perfect lips around his shaft and sucked him.

Only it wasn't completely a dream. Her eyes were there in front of him, staring earnestly as the blood rushed to his cock. She'd separated their bodies far enough to wrap her fingers around his shaft as she worked him in a smooth steady pace that had his balls tightening and him blinking to regain consciousness.

"I'm taking advantage of you," she whispered.

"Sweet Jesus." Devon took a deep breath, attempting to muster up the strength to force her to stop. "Alisha, oh *hell* . . ."

She palmed him harder, her thumb skimming over the crest, slick from the come already slipping from him. "I woke up and wanted you, but I figured if I told you that, you'd offer all kinds of reasons why we shouldn't fool around."

"We shouldn't," he protested.

"See?" she asked. "I couldn't bring myself to actually make love with you before you woke up—that would be rather creepy. I hoped a little . . . encouragement would be okay."

His balls had no objections. His brain? "Alisha, hon, it's too soon."

Her lower lip stuck out slightly as she mock-pouted. "The doctor said I was supposed to go ahead and resume activities as soon as I felt up to it."

Another pump of her fist down his dick dragged a groan from him. "You know he meant work."

A devilish smile snuck over her face. "You feel *up* to it, don't tell me you don't."

Devon shook his head. "You're terrible."

"Maybe, but I want you. I want to feel you touch me and make my body come alive with pleasure. Want to feel you inside me."

The entire time she spoke she stroked, ensuring that his mental capabilities were far from full strength. Other than he'd caught that this was what she wanted, which was the only part that needed to register.

He couldn't deny her anything. And sex? Even less could he say no to her wanting some sheet-tangling, sweaty action.

Only he wasn't about to let her do the work.

He covered her hand with his own, stilling the urge to rut on her like an animal. He tightened their joint grip enough to ease off the need for release as he leaned in and kissed her.

Sweet lips met his, her tongue darting out to tease as she angled her head and pressed her torso forward. Devon soaked in her flavour, reveling in the gentle touch of her fingers as he set her hand free and she instantly set out to drive him mad. Tiny caresses flitted over his chest, his hips, her hands seemingly everywhere as she explored.

He concentrated on her mouth. On sucking her bottom lip, then biting lightly. On kissing the corners before sneaking along her jawline to her ear, the tender lobe tempting him as he rolled her under him. Every time he put his lips to her body she squirmed happily. Every nip or suck or lick elicited a delicious sound. Moans, little sighs. A fluttering gasp as he licked his way down her breast and took a nipple between his teeth.

He wanted to consume her one piece at a time. A slow, thorough feast that would let her know exactly how much she meant—

Devon froze for a second before lifting his gaze.

It wasn't right, the emotions engulfing him. They'd said this was nothing more than itch-scratching of the best sort— a kind of shared pleasure between friends.

That wasn't what he felt anymore, but damn if he knew how to tell her. Now he was scared to have her run screaming for all the opposite reasons than the other woman he'd been involved with. This was good, them together. It was more than good, it was right.

He didn't want it to end.

Alisha stroked his jaw, rubbing her palm over the stubble. "That's a serious expression."

He rapidly changed tack to avoid having to answer the question in her eyes. "This is a serious business, making sure you're satisfied."

He settled more firmly, hips between her thighs as she opened to him.

"You more than satisfy me." She arched upward, rubbing her mound against his cock, and another little moan escaped her as his hard length slid over her clit. "Hurry. We can get to the good part. I'm all warmed up."

Her cheeks flushed to deep red, the faint light from the hallway making him wonder as he skimmed a hand down her body. He eased his fingers between their torsos, slipping through her folds effortlessly as wet heat coated him. "Well, that's sweet."

Alisha lifted her chin. "I told you I wanted you."

"Were you playing with yourself, Alisha? Before you wrapped your hand around my dick and got me hard, did you put your fingers between your legs and rub your clit?"

Her eyes widened as he spoke, and then she nodded. Licked her lips. "Yes."

"And now you want my cock? You want me to hold you in place while I fuck you?"

That tongue of hers snuck out again, and he swooped in and kissed her before she could retreat, their tongues twisting together until she moaned.

Devon breathed harder as he continued, his volume on the edge of a whisper, voice deep and husky. "I'm in no hurry to get to the finale. I like going down on you. I think I'll take my time and go lick up all that sweetness you've warmed for me. Use my tongue until you're squirming and screaming my name. Maybe a few times. Then we can get to the part where I slip my cock inside you and make you shout all over again."

"Devon . . ."

She wasn't breathing as easily anymore now, either.

He worked his way down her firm body, stopping to give her breasts a moment's attention. Staying because he couldn't stand to leave. The tips tightened to hard peaks, glistening with moisture as he alternated between tasting one then the other. Alisha thrust her hands into his hair and attempted to keep him in one place. Either that, or she was trying to pull him over top of her.

He wasn't ready. Not by a long shot.

He pressed a kiss along the underside of one firm mound. Licked slowly along her ribs. He had to use distraction techniques to convince himself to leave her breasts, focusing on the treasure he headed toward next. The sweet scent of her desire drawing him onward.

His jaw brushed her belly, and she sucked in air, the rub of whiskers on his chin leaving faint red marks on her tender skin. Only she didn't seem to object. He kissed her belly button. The top of her mound. Devon slid his palms down her thighs to her knees, then gently pressed her legs apart.

Gazing up her body was the most incredible sight. Her sex open to him, wetness shining on the soft folds as they opened. Her uneven breathing shook her breasts. Wetness shone on her lips from having licked them. Her eyes—

Her eyes trapped him. The fire in their depths lit a fuse that had nowhere to burn but through them both.

Like a trigger had been pulled, Devon exploded into action. He scooped his hands under her ass, lifting her hips and lowering his head in one motion. He'd moved deliberately until this point, but now he didn't hesitate. Licked the length of her sex, drove his tongue into her. Lapped and sucked and feasted greedily as she writhed. Her volume escalated as he concentrated on her clit until she fisted the bed sheets.

"Devon, yes. Oh yes."

He was up and over her in a moment, the condom jerked from the stash in the side table and rolled over his shaft faster than he thought possible. There was only one thing he needed, only one desire driving him. Only when he pressed the tip of his cock between her folds and the slick heat welcomed him in, he slowed again. Unwilling to rush. Savouring every second of that first moment of connection.

Alisha groaned her approval, lifting her legs and wrapping them around him. The change of angle allowed him to slip deeper yet.

He pressed up on his arms, hovering over her as their eyes met. He couldn't look away, the hunger and passion mesmerizing him. He pulled his hips back so slowly his arms shook with the effort, but the fluttering of her eyelids was worth it as he hit her sweet spot. And again.

"So tight around my cock. So perfect." Devon adjusted his position to open up room between them. "Lick your fingers."

She frowned before lifting a hand to her mouth and touching her tongue to the tips.

"Wetter. That's it. Suck them until they're good and slippery."

Devon rocked his hips fast enough to keep them both on the edge. The wet heat of her sex embracing his cock was so good he didn't want it over too soon. The sight of Alisha twirling her tongue over her fingers was strangely erotic, especially since he had an ulterior motive.

"Good." The word rumbled up from where he trembled on the verge of losing control. "Now touch yourself. Rub your clit until you come on my cock."

Alisha's eyes widened as she hurried to obey, the back of her warm fingers leaving a streak of moisture on his stomach. He could tell the moment she touched the sensitive bundle—the tension in her face grew, her rate of breathing picked up. Ragged and unsteady, her hand bumped his groin as they both quickened the pace. Increased the pressure. Alisha's gaze remained pinned to his as her lips tightened into a pout, pleasure wrapping itself around her and then tearing her apart as she climaxed and took him with her.

"Alisha."

Devon buried himself as deep as possible and froze, the snug fist of her sex constricting again and again, jolting his release through his balls and into the condom so hard he worried about blowing the thing apart.

Alisha closed her eyes, squeezing them so tight that if it weren't for the smile twisting her lips he would have thought she was in agony. She dragged in a deep breath before exhaling like a runner finishing a long race.

He stared, unable to turn away, memorizing her face as she relaxed under him, fully sated. Her eyes slowly opened, long lashes fluttering as their gazes met. He wanted to say something. To make a joke to lighten the moment. Maybe tell her he was glad she was feeling better. Something.

Anything.

But no words came. None he could say aloud, because what wanted to escape was tender and caring, and far too close to telling her he couldn't stand not having her in his life.

He'd gone and fallen in love, and that terrified him more than the most dangerous rescue he'd ever faced.

CHAPTER 22

,,,,,,,,,,,,,,,,,,,,,,,,,,,,,,,,,,,,

The snow that had fallen overnight had already melted into slush in the heat of the late October afternoon sun. Beside her Devon tapped his fingers impatiently on the door frame, but he didn't say anything, not even as she took the corner too fast and had to pull the car out of a skid.

The usual heart-pounding adrenaline rush that accompanied getting a call-out had to be controlled until it could be used to a good purpose. She might have good reason to be extra excited this time around, but she was on the edge of being too riled up.

Neither of them talked—it was a short enough drive to HQ that they didn't need to chatter—and they already knew the same basics about the coming rescue. Rehashing the meager details they'd been given over the phone wouldn't change a thing.

The familiar pattern of getting herself into the right mind-set was easier in silence, and Alisha was grateful Devon seemed to enjoy the arrangement as well. Sharing a ride made sense. Showing up at Lifeline pissed off at each other? Wasn't a good idea.

It was just over a week since she'd been released from the hospital. She was back to full strength. A couple of hard days at the gym and training with the team had blown the final cobwebs from her system. Physically she was ready.

Mentally, she had to face the challenge and see.

She wondered if Devon still had his doubts. She'd caught him staring at the strangest moments over the past week, his expression somewhere between a frown and confusion. When she'd had the entire team's help loading and moving her things out of her old rental he'd been especially pensive, not to mention his constant glancing around as if expecting someone to pop out and demand they stop.

Well, that behavior she understood. Vincent hadn't shown up again. Last she'd heard he'd returned to Toronto, but it wasn't easy to believe. His ghost haunted her at the strangest moments, the echo of his words lingering in her ears.

She pulled on the parking brake and readied to open her door. Devon caught her hand before she could exit.

The expression blazing in his blue eyes messed with her heartbeat even more than the pre-rescue excitement. "Give me a kiss before we go inside," he ordered, "so I'm not tempted to maul you in front of the team."

She smiled and leaned across the stick shift to accept his caress. He cradled the back of her head and gave her a brief but firm sample of exactly how talented he was with his lips.

She gasped for air when he let her go. "Well, that was nice."

He winked and opened his door. "Watch my back, I'll watch yours."

"Oh, yeah," Alisha teased, joining him outside the car, her bag slung over her shoulder. "I watch it, sugar. Trust me, I watch it all the time."

They were both laughing as they raced through the door, Anders and the rest of the crew waving and calling out as they got into position for the updated report. Marcus stood behind the desk with Lana, the brunette waiting silently at his side.

She'd been on her best behavior since Marcus had called her out. Alisha still didn't like Lana much, but at least the other woman wasn't pushing herself forward anymore.

"Get ready for a slow, wet slog," Marcus warned. "The snow above thirteen hundred feet is sticky and thick. Chances are you'll need snowshoes or skis."

"Lovely, Slurpee season has arrived." The long tails of Anders's laces dragged over the floor as he walked. He adjusted his ski pants and sat to retie his boots. "Why do people insist on going out too early in the season?"

"Idiots determined to get their trip in no matter what. You've got bad glacier ice and crevasses—prep accordingly. I'll get more while you're en route." Marcus and Lana responded to the crackling radios in the background as the rest of the team scrambled for gear.

The rush of energy filling HQ was soothing. Packing new equipment, working to load what might be needed. Erin gave her a wink, then headed out to get the chopper in order, her bright orange ski coat visible the entire journey across the tarmac to the aircraft.

After settling into place in the transport area, Alisha took a few deep breaths before adjusting her headset and falling into conversation with the team.

Over the next hour as they flew to the base of Bow Lake, updates flooded in from Marcus. Three men had gone missing during a hut-to-hut ski trip along the Wapta traverse. They'd signed the trail book, but until they missed their expected return day, no one had known there was any trouble.

"Is there a custodian at the Bow Hut this time of year who we can ask if they made it that far?" Anders asked.

"Negative," Marcus reported. "Not until December."

"Drat, I didn't think so. Okay, best tactic. Erin will start us at the trailhead. We'll follow the usual approach to the headwall and the hut. It's a potshot until we see how far they got, or we see definitive signs of danger zones."

"Headwall is going to be avalanched, I guarantee it,"

Devon pointed out. "But in that area the snow is so unstable at this time of year, how will we know if it's the problem site or not?"

"We'll check the hut. If they stayed a night like planned, there will be signs. If they didn't show, it narrows our search zone."

Alisha accepted the map Anders passed over, unfolding the thick paper to examine the elevation markings. The edge of the known glacier ice. On her right, Devon leaned in to draw a finger along the route they'd follow.

Maybe it was terrible, but having him there made her feel . . . more at ease. She was ready, she really was, but there was something reassuring to know he had her back. He always had, even during the days before they were working together, fighting to outperform each other at school. Even then she'd never expected anything less than his best effort in terms of keeping her safe.

The realization that they'd stepped beyond the trust relationship found in the SAR team hit hard. Alisha watched Devon's hands and remembered his touch. Hard, sexual compulsions, soothing gentle caresses.

She trusted him with her life every time they came out to do a job. But this was more than that. She trusted him now on a whole different level, and the buzz of that revelation warmed her the rest of the flight to the trailhead.

"We're in position," Erin announced. "I'll parallel the creek for the first couple kilometers where there isn't another approach option. Check the snow conditions, Anders, and let me know if you need me to do a flyby on the tree route once we hit that section."

Alisha shifted to face the window, leaning in to stare down at the snow-covered ground. It was early in the ski season, so early that some parts of the creek were still open, the water flowing over the edges of ice, glasslike sections reflecting the sun in flashes. Shorter pines and scraggy brush poked up in spots along the water's edge, and through the middle lay two thin lines running parallel to each other, following the stream's meandering path.

"Ski tracks," Xavier called first. "Someone went in during the past few days, and there's no new snow over them."

"That makes the search easier." Anders stood and leaned over Xavier's shoulder. "You keep an eye on the path. Erin, looks as if we've got a straight route to the headwall. How are the conditions?"

"Wind is fine right now, but I expect it to pick up once we ascend the valley. Gusts usually roar on the glacier top."

Anders nodded. "Yeah, most nights Bow Hut shakes from the high winds. No fresh snow is great, but our chance of following these clear tracks all the way to our targets is zero. They'll have blown away or drifted over within twenty-four hours."

They passed the base of the wide half-moon wall where the trail elevation increased so rapidly that the only way for a skier or hiker to reach the top of the plateau was a series of tight switchbacks. In the summer, the steep terrain would make the average hiker's thighs burn with exertion. Now in the middle of ski conditions, there was the added danger of the snowpack on the upper slopes letting go and taking out everything below it.

"It's clear," Xavier announced. "No avalanche sign. The cornices on the peak are still hanging on."

"Swing wide to the hut," Anders ordered Erin. "Alisha, Xavier, you two will do a run in to check the daybook and see if anyone camped out during the past few nights. We'll lift up and get Erin to sweep the area while you're looking around."

Landing outside the hut proved everything she'd expected. The door cracked open and Alisha dropped to the ground, the snow underfoot hard-packed to rock solid by the wind. Any loose powder knocked free by the pressure of the props swirled icy cold around them as temperatures fell to below freezing.

"You check the sleeping quarters. I'll meet you in the cookhouse," Xavier suggested.

It only took a minute for her to look, the separate square boxlike cabin with bunks lining the walls even colder than outside. The wind caught the door and created a high-pitched whistle that echoed in the empty space. Alisha joined Xavier, glancing around the smaller hut, her breath causing puffs of steam to expand into the unheated air.

Xavier spoke into his walkie-talkie, one hand holding the hut logbook. "They were here two nights ago. Planned to head to Balfour Hut."

"Affirmative, we've spotted a faint trail line from up here. It fades, but we'll check the usual route." Anders ordered, "Prep yourselves, guys, I suspect we'll be looking in crevasses."

Alisha shivered as she and Xavier jogged to the landing site. She liked summer rescues better than winter, and crevasses were her least favourite winter rescue situation.

Lowering herself into one of the narrow cracks in the ancient glacier ice fields was mentally different from lowering into a rock cavern, and miles from doing an actual vertical climb. She checked herself, though, and while she wasn't looking forward to it, she wasn't more frightened than usual.

Fear wasn't a bad thing, especially if it kept you on your toes to stay alive.

The helicopter rose smoothly. Erin banked to the south, the pressure pressing Alisha into her seat as they moved toward the main ice field.

A soft touch on her thigh made her glance down, and she was surprised to see Devon resting his hand easily on her even as he looked out the window. She didn't say anything, just laid her hand on top of his briefly, needing that moment of connection.

Warmth rushed her. Contentment. She was here, doing what she loved, with people she . . .

Alisha took a deep breath and pushed the rest of that thought aside for now. Concentrating on the rescue was her first priority. Even though she wasn't about to deny that Devon's hand resting on her leg warmed her a whole lot.

"Head to the west." Tripp pointed into the distance. "See it? Open crevasses in the middle of a snow field."

Anders swore softly as he moved forward for a better view. "You think the idiots walked over a few snow bridges unintentionally, then hit a section of weak snow?"

Devon stared at the warning signs of a situation gone bad. Glacier ice had a tendency to crack open in long, extended streaks, exposing what looked like claw marks from the air. On the ground level, these cracks could be anywhere from a foot across or more than ten feet, and plummeting in depth from a few feet to impossibly frightening measurements. The most dangerous crevasses were the surface cracks that were three or four feet wide—narrow enough that in a strong wind, snow would cling to the edges until a cap formed over the top, creating a false level surface.

A lucky skier or hiker could cross a snow bridge without knowing it. If the pack was thick enough, and the temperatures cold enough to hold the fragile structure together. The unlucky ones broke through and fell to whatever depth before the crack narrowed and pinned them in place.

If it narrowed at all.

"We'll know in a minute," Erin offered. "I can fly you through the maze, but I can't set you down."

"No problem," Alisha straightened her collar, prepping to be lowered. "Anders can winch me."

Devon got himself ready, adjusting his harness and double-checking the new carabiner he pulled from the gear bag. He'd observed Alisha closely the entire trip out, but there was nothing about her behavior to complain about. Nothing unusual compared to before she'd had the emergency trip to the hospital.

Amazing was the only thing that came to his mind as he watched her prep to be lowered from the hovering helicopter. Brave, strong—he admired her more every day. Which made the fact he wanted to tell her that more difficult to keep silenced.

Xavier shouted. "We got a hit. Holy shit, what the *hell* did they do?"

Peering from the window, it was difficult to figure out the exact problem, until he noticed the faint lines. "They were roped together. Look. There, and there. One of them must have fallen through, jerked the other two off their feet, and they each broke through a different section."

"Alisha, get in position." Anders motioned the others back. "Set a couple anchors for the sleds before you head into the crack."

"Got it," Alisha said. While Anders checked her buckles and ropes, she glanced over his shoulder at Devon, smiling and giving him a thumbs-up.

He nodded. "Don't make me have to climb too far. I'm feeling lazy."

She snorted, then ignored him and followed Anders's instructions.

The noise increased as the main door slid open, not only the sound of the props, but the wind rushing around them as Erin hovered the chopper over one of the wider bands of solid ice. Alisha turned and leaned back, easing over the bay lip and into midair, where the cable supported her slow descent to the ground.

"She's spinning like a top," Tripp warned.

"Winds are bad. She can handle it," Anders insisted. "Damn, she's good. Look at that, right on target." He clicked on the speaker. "Lovely landing, girl. Now, set your bolts."

"On task. There's one of the men directly to the west of me. You want me to rappel down to check him while you're lowering the gear?"

"Wait for Devon," Anders ordered. He glanced over his shoulder at Devon, and Devon caught the warning. After this much time exposed, the chances any of the victims were still alive were slim.

Lowering out the door was like walking into a freezer. The wind tore through his clothing, curling around the edges of his helmet and scratching his cheeks raw in the short time he hung in midair. The new rope Alisha was tying off below him shone brilliant blue against the grey-white of the snow.

His feet touched down and she grabbed his harness to anchor him, her strong grip pulling him toward her, and he smiled. "Thank you."

She wrinkled her nose as she glanced up, undoing the cable from his belt and returning it to the chopper. "Anders thinks they're DOA, doesn't he?"

Devon nodded slowly. "It's been two days."

She sighed sadly. "I'm ready for it. You want to belay me?"

"I can go first if you want," he offered.

She shook her head, glancing upward toward where the chopper hovered above them, Xavier at the door readying to be lowered. "I said I'm prepared. You can't guard me from the awful parts, Devon."

"Doesn't mean I don't try." Like he always did.

She touched his face with her gloved hand, then reached for the ropes and tied in. Xavier joined them. Then Tripp. The four of them worked smoothly to get into the cracks and bring up the three men who'd slid in too far to get themselves out. One after another, the near-silent task continued. Recovering bodies was always the worst part of the job, even though Devon knew it gave closure to the families who'd lost loved ones.

It was so senseless. The staring eyes filled with terror even after death, or the ones who looked as if they'd fallen asleep, the cold and fatigue silently taking them to a place where they didn't hurt anymore.

He lowered Xavier to the final of the victims, carefully manning the ropes. Waiting in hope for a loud shout that never came. Xavier's quiet, "He's gone as well," was all they got.

Alisha and Tripp glanced up from where they were securing the wrapped bodies they'd pulled from below, strapping them to boards. Devon caught their sorrow, the hope for a miracle fading from their eyes. "You want a hand?" he asked Xavier.

"Nope, I'll be fine."

Alisha and Tripp finished their grim task, one at a time attaching the cable to allow Anders to winch the bodies onto the chopper. Xavier hooked on the final board and it rose straight from the depths like a somber flag against the sky.

Xavier climbed up, and they gathered gear. All of it normal and precise, pretty much like any other rescue except there was a sadness hovering over them all. The usual quips and energy were muted in a kind of respect and heartfelt sorrow.

They waited to be lifted, still tied into the safety anchors Alisha had attached at their feet to the icy surface of the glacier. The never-ending wind rushed them, stealing their breath and chilling their extremities. Alisha turned her face aside, and Devon pulled her closer, guarding her from the worst of the gale. Silence reigned—it wasn't a time for joking or fooling around.

The cable was lowered again, and Tripp gestured Alisha forward.

A brittle crack sounded, and all four of them froze. Devon held his breath, praying it wasn't ice anywhere beneath them.

"Hurry it up." Tripp motioned to Alisha again. "The sooner we get out of here, the happier—"

A sudden gasp escaped Xavier as his feet slipped on the bare ice surface. Underfoot the ice tilted, sending Xavier flying to one side. Devon lunged for him, but it was too late. Xavier slipped off the edge and into the crevasse beneath them.

Tripp swore, diving for the ropes to halt Xavier's slide. "Goddamn. Everyone, brace yourselves."

Devon eyed the safety ropes still in clear view of the surface—Alisha's, Tripp's, his own. Everything looked fine, and as shitty as it was that Xavier had fallen, his backup rope should stop him before he fell more than—

Xavier's shout of dismay changed to a shriek of fear that carried on for far too long before cutting off abruptly.

Oh God.

Tripp was on his knees, leaning over the edge. "What the hell happened?"

Devon feared the worst. Clinging to Alisha to hold her back from the edge, they cautiously peered over.

Laughing, teasing Xavier lay far beneath them, his body twisted. Utterly still.

Alisha had never tied herself in so quickly in her life. On autopilot she adjusted ropes and got herself into position to be lowered to Xavier's side. "On belay," she snapped.

Devon nodded once, his face tight with worry as he braced himself and lowered her.

It was one of her worst nightmares—one of the team being injured, and her little drug-induced trip to the hospital didn't count. This was in the field, uncertainty and confusion wanting to rush in. The only thing that would have made it worse would be if it were Devon she was climbing toward, not knowing if he was dead or alive.

"Talk to us," Anders's voice carried over the speakers. "Come on, Xavier, hang in there and give us a sign."

Nothing. Silence on the airwaves.

Anders tried again. "Answer, Xav. We're going to get you out of there. We've sent a pretty girl to come hold your hand and make you fly."

"Will she kiss me?" Xavier's words were a whisper, but everyone on the team exhaled at the same time.

Alisha gripped her rope tighter as Devon controlled her descent. She had to swallow past the lump in her throat to speak. "Well, I suppose I could kiss you, but only once we're somewhere nice and warm. I'm ready for a hot tub, what do you think?"

A groan rose from Xavier as she got close enough to brace herself on the narrowing walls of ice. "Naked hot-tubbing sounds fun, but I bet Devon would kick my ass."

"I'm there, Devon. Take." She reached for Xavier, brushing his cheek carefully. "Well, we won't invite him, then."

A couple of quick movements later she had him locked to her, safety ropes ensuring that he wouldn't slip anywhere else. She checked him quickly. His climbing belt was a mess, twisted and loose instead of snugly wrapped around his thighs and waist.

She leaned over to check his vitals, working desperately not to shake him, but in the tight space it was nearly impossible. "Xav, how you feel?'

He cleared his throat. "Actually, I don't feel much, which kind of worries me."

Oh God. No feeling meant a spinal injury. She tried to keep her face blank even as terror raced through her. She pressed her lips quickly to his. "We'll get you out of here, okay? Just hang on, and we'll get you out of here."

The next fifteen minutes were hell. Devon sent Tripp down, and he helped her get Xavier on a backboard. By the time they had him ready to transport, Xavier was passing in and out of consciousness. The board rose into the air, and a cold, icy sensation settled in her stomach.

Only once Anders had safely pulled him into the chopper did she breathe a sigh of relief. She glanced to the side at Tripp to make sure he was ready to climb out so they could get Xavier to the hospital as soon as possible.

Tripp clutched the remains of Xavier's climbing belt in his hands, the frayed webbing untwining farther as he held it in the air.

CHAPTER 23

'''''''''''''''''''''''''''''''

The subdued mood in the room was morbidly funereal, and Devon hated it with every fiber of his being. This wasn't what post-rescue was supposed to be like. They'd never had one of their own injured before. Well, bruises and bumps occasionally, but nothing so serious.

Erin had dropped the team off at Lifeline HQ before bugging out to take Xavier straight to one of the bigger hospitals in Calgary. Anders had gone along to keep everyone updated.

So far the news was skimpy and not very positive.

The RCMP had been and gone, taking their statements, asking questions that in many cases didn't make sense. Devon fumed when the authorities didn't seem to understand what the rescue had involved, and he had to repeat again and again what had happened.

By the time the last of the officers had left, Devon wasn't the only one ready to bite someone's head off. They gathered in the main room, Alisha curled up on one couch, Tripp on the other, with Marcus sprawled in the chair at the end of the coffee table.

Darkness marred Marcus's expression. "There will be further inquiries, but I want you all to know I think you're the best in the business. Accidents happen—I fucking hate that, but it's true."

Alisha wiped her eyes. "I keep going through procedure, and I swear I didn't see anything that we did wrong. He was roped in. We were all going by the book, Marcus. We—"

She broke off, and Devon couldn't stand it anymore. He left his place by the sidewall and crowded Alisha, pulling her to him as she buried her face against his neck. "I agree with Alisha. There was no reason for Xavier's accident. He was tied in, he had backup."

Tripp cleared his throat, then raised his eyes to meet Devon's. "His belt was flawed."

Marcus nodded. "That's my first suspicion. We'll check all the gear before I write it up as the cause. I had Lana pull maintenance records before I sent her home. We just bought the new shipments. Maybe one of them wasn't up to standard."

Devon rocked back, cradling Alisha. "Can we help check anything? This sitting around waiting is crap."

Marcus shook his head. "We have to go by the book now. I think you should all go home. I'll call you when I have news, or when I need to talk to you."

What Marcus wasn't saying was he'd need to talk to them individually to find out if one of them had contributed to the accident. It sucked, but Devon knew that was the reality.

Devon got to his feet and pulled Alisha with him, because sitting at HQ wouldn't help time go faster. "Call us when you need us. Call us when you hear *anything*."

Marcus nodded, giving them time to gather their things and retreat from the building.

Devon paused with his hand on the car door before motioning to Alisha. "Give me a second. I'm going to make sure Marcus is okay."

Alisha started the car and turned the heater on high. "If he needs somewhere to come, invite him over. I don't know if Becki is free."

Devon shot back through the main doors to find Marcus still seated where he'd left him. "You okay?" he asked.

Marcus snorted. "You mean between one of my team in the hospital, one of them freaking out on me, and having to deal with an emergency inquiry? Fucking aces around here."

Someone had freaked out? Devon sat opposite him and focused on the first and most important issue. "It was an accident, Marcus. A terrible, tragic accident, but we'll see it through. We're a team, and Xavier will be fine."

Marcus raised a brow. "You've been taking optimist lessons from Alisha, have you?"

Devon grudgingly cracked a smile. "She's contagious."

His boss sighed. "She'll be glad to know that the silver lining is Lana won't be around anymore. Woman went out of control when the news came through that Xavier was hurt, I thought I'd have to sedate her."

Devon had wondered where Lana had gone. "Good thing she wasn't out on the actual rescue. What the hell is that all about?"

A shrug of the shoulders was all he got from Marcus. "Seriously, I don't care how well the woman can climb, if she can't keep her head in a tight situation she's no help to a SAR team. When she heard Xav was hurt, she started hyperventilating and things went downhill from there. I sent her home. She was on probation, and this is enough to let me cancel her contract." Marcus glanced up. "And I'm sending you home. You've abandoned Alisha in the parking lot. Get out of here. We'll deal with the crap later."

Devon nodded. He paused to rest his hand on Marcus's shoulder to give it a comforting squeeze, then headed to the car to take care of Alisha. And himself.

The sight of Xavier lying in a tangled heap had broken something inside him. It had always been a possibility, but seeing it happen cut like a rusty, ragged blade.

Superimposed was another image. Another body lying

twisted on the ground, dust settling around them as his father lay silent and motionless and the horses shuffled nervously. Devon shook his head as if to clear the memory, then rejoined Alisha.

She'd been crying, but straightened as he sat. "Marcus okay?"

"He'll be fine. Let's head home."

They washed up. Ate a little. Waited for the phone to ring to find out news about Xavier, but nothing came. By the time they gave up and headed to bed, Devon was going crazy.

Alisha crawled in, her eyes filled with tears. Devon tugged her against him, and for the first time since the accident he felt something other than lost.

"He's going to be okay, isn't he?" Alisha rolled to face him, tilting her head to stare up, her eyes all the way grey, not a trace of blue in the depths.

Devon couldn't speak for a moment. He'd told Marcus some positive, happy crap, but he couldn't say the words anymore. "I don't know. God, I don't know."

They held each other tightly, the pain and uncertainty horrific, but being together making it tolerable. Memories swirled around him and he couldn't take it any longer. "I need to tell you something."

She paused in the middle of stroking his neck, her fingers gentle on muscles that had grown weary from remaining tight and clenched.

"My dad—he's . . ."

Her eyes narrowed when he didn't continue. God, how could he continue? He had to.

"You know how my siblings are a pain in the ass? They don't think I'll ever grow up. Ever amount to anything."

Alisha shook her head. "They're idiots. We've established that."

Devon shook his head. "They're not completely. They're going on what they know. On what I've done. Dad's in that wheelchair because of me, and we all know that's the truth."

Alisha leaned on her elbow, staring in confusion. "How is it your fault?"

Devon stared at the ceiling, unable to meet her eyes any longer. "I was riding with him when it happened. We were far out from the house, just farting around. It wasn't anything different than a hundred times except it was. We were the only ones riding that day." Devon laughed bitterly. "You know how often that happened in a family the size of mine? There was *always* someone else around, but that day it was me and him, and it was special. Then I decided we should have a race. I jumped the gun, you know, one of those, *ready, set* and then leave before you say *go*?"

She leaned over and he couldn't avoid her eyes unless he actually twisted away. "Go on."

He didn't think anymore, just said it. "For some reason, his horse spooked. I didn't even notice he wasn't with me until I was at the top of the next ridge. I thought he was kidding around and left him behind. Heck, I unsaddled and curried down my horse before I figured something was wrong. When I finally went to look, he wasn't moving."

Sorrow filled Alisha's face. "That must have been devastating."

"It gets worse. I went back and he was just lying there. Dust on him, his horse waiting uneasily." Pain squeezed around his heart as he remembered what came next. As he wished he could turn back the clock and change what he'd done. "God, Alisha. I moved him."

Her eyes widened.

"I didn't know how stupid it was, but I should have. Should have realized going to get help was the better solution, but no, I woke him and while he was still dazed got him to sit and then stand. He could barely stay upright, but I was all eager to be helpful after feeling guilty for abandoning him."

He'd had no idea what real guilt felt like until later.

Alisha sat up beside him. She cupped his cheek tenderly. "How old were you?"

"Ten."

She frowned. "Oh, Devon. There was no way you could have known to leave him. When I was ten, if someone had fallen down I would have done the same thing."

Devon continued. "It was one reason I went into search and rescue. I took all my first-aid courses and learned what to do so I wouldn't make stupid mistakes anymore. Working with Lifeline has been such a rewarding experience." He let out a long slow sigh. "But it doesn't change the past. Doesn't make my father able to walk, or allow the family to forgive me. They don't trust me—whether that's right or wrong, I don't know. But it was a turning point in my life. Losing their trust changed me. Changed my direction in life."

He sat up and pulled her into his arms, needing the warmth of her against him as he continued.

"I told you that to tell you this. Being a part of Lifeline was another turning point. But the bigger one was meeting you. Having you toss my lazy-ass *don't give a shit attitude* in my face? You made me take notice of the stupid things I was doing."

Alisha tilted her head to one side. "You weren't stupid."

He gave her a look.

She smiled softly. "Well, maybe a little."

"I was wasting my time. Cruising through because I had the talent to get by without working, and as my family liked to tell me, I wouldn't get it right anyway. Why should I try harder? I'd slack-assed my way through swim team, and it cost me making the national team. Even though I came to the search-and-rescue school for the right reasons, I was stuck with that shitty attitude. Putting out minimal effort, getting by. Somewhere in the top half of the class, but nowhere spectacular. You challenged me. Told me to grow up, and I did. We kicked ass at school because of you. That top placing got us on Lifeline, and for the first time in my life since my dad's accident I could honestly say I was in the right place."

He cupped her cheek, stroking his thumb along her jaw. "People trust me with their lives, and I don't let them down. And you're part of why I got there. You made a difference, and I never thanked you for it."

She blinked hard, her eyes wet with tears. "If I pushed you, you brought me up to the top at the same time. I don't think either of us would be where we are if it weren't for the competitions, and the never-ending challenge to do more. So, thank you."

They clung to each other for a moment, Alisha soaking in his warmth. The kindness of his words. She tried to put it all in perspective with the crash and the accident and the uncertainty of Xavier's future.

When Devon lifted her chin and pressed his lips to hers in a tender kiss, her heart skipped a beat. Passion flared again, heating them as he stroked a hand down her back to pull her against him as their tongues lazily explored.

It wasn't wrong, this sharing. A celebration of life and togetherness even as they were scared and nervous for Xavier. Emotion enveloped her as Devon stroked and teased and brought her to the point where she was quivering with the need for release.

Then he slowed, slipped his cock into her, and she sighed. The blue of his eyes shone like a summer's sky over her as he slowly rolled his hips and made love to her. Not frantic sex, not a ravishing, but a perfect sharing.

Devon kissed her, his tongue teasing gently. When he pulled away, it was just far enough to look her in the eyes. She was being consumed by the intensity of his gaze. By the emotions right there, undeniable and potent.

"I love you." The words whispered out as he continued to take her, their bodies intimately connected.

Alisha clutched his shoulders harder, being overwhelmed by the intensity. "Oh, Devon."

He said it again, this time against her cheek. "I love you. I love your fire, your courage. Your giving heart." He kissed her ear. Her neck. Over her face and body as he gathered her in his arms and continued to pepper her with kisses.

She knelt on either side of his hips, still connected, still rocking over him. Their bodies so tight together nothing seemed able to separate them. Tension rose; pleasure spread through her core and threaded over her body in a powerful way. When he tugged her back far enough to look into her eyes again, she held on for dear life as her climax hit and took him along, the two of them wrapped in pleasure and a type of unity she'd never expected to find.

She laid her head on his chest and let their racing heart-beats settle. Bodies slick together, panting breaths easing. Alisha had never felt this way before, and allowing the joy to spread through her as she soaked in his words and his actions—it was right.

Was it love? It was pretty incredible, whatever they wanted to call it. She didn't think she needed to say any-thing, just snuggled tight against him and slowly relaxed into slumber.

When she woke earlier than Devon, it was to warm limbs tangled with hers, his arms enfolding her as if he would never let her go. She listened to his breathing, the strong, even sound grounding her in spite of her fears about Xavier.

She slipped from the bed and pulled on a T-shirt, pacing to the kitchen to turn on the kettle. Outside the sun hadn't reached over the mountain yet, the sky bright but shadows filling the backyard. It seemed an eerie place between worlds with the light blocked from the corners, and she shivered.

It was tempting to hurry back to bed. To wake Devon and let him chase the ghosts from her mind. Only she wasn't going to wake him simply to comfort her, like some kid. She could wait.

To distract herself she checked her phone messages and e-mail, frowning to discover a message from Vincent. She'd thought she'd ditched him and the whole issue of leaving Banff. She clicked it.

Meet me at eight. My suite.

God. He was still in town? Or in town again?

She opened the attachment. Stopped in shock. It was an engagement announcement for Alisha Bailey and Vincent

Monreal. All the information organized like a press release, and the accompanying picture—them at the Banff Springs that first evening, his head intimately close to hers as if leaning to whisper secrets.

This was total and utter bullshit. Vincent's continuing to bother her when she had far more serious matters to deal with did nothing but piss her off.

There was nothing in the e-mail to take to the police in terms of being illegal, but God, it was wrong to the very core. He'd had someone secretly take a picture even way back then? Outrageous. Alisha swore a blue streak and stomped into the kitchen to make coffee, hoping some caffeine would inspire her. Help her to deal with this . . . insanity.

She checked her watch. Thirty minutes until Vincent expected her to meet him. She glanced in the bedroom. Devon was still asleep, one arm over his head as his chest moved slowly with each breath. If she woke him she knew he'd come along in an instant. Be backup support—a safety net. Part of her wanted that so badly. To allow him to be the block between her and Vincent's continuing crazy ideas.

Devon said he loved her. She was pretty sure she loved him, and the thought made her smile in spite of her anger at Vincent. In spite of her fears for Xavier.

Love. It had snuck up and wrapped around her.

Having the two men meet right now would only tangle the issues further, but she wasn't about to make the same mistake she'd made the first time Vincent had frightened her.

She dressed quickly before sitting on the edge of the bed and stroking Devon's arm gently. "Hey, wake up. I need to talk to you."

His eyelids fluttered open, his gaze sharpening as he rolled to a sitting position. "Xavier?"

She shook her head. "No news yet. I got another e-mail from Vincent, and I'm ready to kick his fine-suited ass back to Toronto."

All the sleep haze vanished. "What did he do now?"

"More of the same. Sent me a stupid engagement announcement, as if he's planning on handing it out to the media. I've had enough of the asshole jerking me around, Devon. I'm going to talk to him and tell him he can shove his threats up his ass. He can make any bloody announcement he wants—I'll deny it, and that's it."

Devon held her hands to stop her from flailing them in the air. "What about your dad? The company?"

"Nothing. I don't care." She took a deep breath and calmed herself, slipping one hand free to cup his face. "You said it last night. Focus on what's important—the people who are important. I'll call my father and give him a warning, but beyond that I don't owe any of them anything."

"I'll come with you," Devon said.

She pressed her fingers over his mouth, gently stroking his lips. "I'll meet him in the lobby, or somewhere public, but I want to do this by myself." His face tightened, and she frowned. "I mean it. I'm not being stupid, but I don't want you to come with me and have this end up some kind of public brawl."

"You don't trust me to keep my temper?"

Alisha growled in frustration. "I don't trust Vincent not to take the first swing, then find a way to pin it on you. Please, stay here. I'll be back within the hour."

She kissed him before he could protest again. He crushed her closer, his hands curling possessively around her lower back before setting her free.

"I don't like it," he complained.

Alisha backed away, letting his hands slip from hers. "I know, but thank you for letting me do this my way. I'll call you if there's any trouble. I promise."

She tried Marcus's number, but his phone went to messages. The rest of the short trip she fretted about Xavier and planned her approach with Vincent. More diplomacy was required than storming up to him and hitting him on the head with a large, blunt object.

She phoned him from the courtesy phone in the lobby. "I'm here."

"You know my suite number." Vincent spoke in clipped tones. "Stop wasting my time, and get up here."

Bullshit on that. "I'm not going into your suite alone."

He made a rude noise. "You don't trust me?"

"Not one bit. If you want to talk, it's in public."

"You risk the media discovering us before we make the announcement official," he pointed out.

Her anger shot higher. "I will not meet with you alone, Vincent."

"Very well. Wait for me in the foyer."

"No. I'll be outside the teahouse restaurant." She wanted some semblance of control headed into this façade. Besides, people passed that location regularly, but the chairs were far enough aside to allow a private conversation.

She might want witnesses, but she didn't want to be overheard.

Waiting in the elegant setting made her skin itch. Devon texted her, but she ignored it, not ready to answer him while she still had to face Vincent. Her brain ached. Her heart was equally filled with hope from her time with Devon and her fears for Xavier. With so much uncertainty before them, both good and bad, the only undeniable point was that this ongoing stupidity with Vincent had to stop.

He strolled in, suited and groomed to the nines, and she took a sadistic pleasure in having pulled on her rattiest pair of jeans, most holey runners, and an old coat of Devon's.

Alisha held up her phone with the link to the engagement announcement. "Is this your idea of a joke?"

Vincent was so smooth and calm she wanted to shake him. Or kick him, or do something physically painful and devastating. But he sat there like some untouchable statue, examining her with disdain. None of the façade of attraction he'd attempted during that first dinner meeting.

"It's no joke. You will return to Toronto with me. I need to return, and there is no cause for you to remain any longer."

"You're being an idiot, Vincent. I have a job, I have—"

"Yes, your job." Vincent leaned back and assessed her again, the fancy chandeliers around them reflecting flashes of light in his dark eyes. "How is Xavier?"

Alisha went cold through and through. Had there already been a news report about the accident? She didn't think so. "How did you know he's been hurt?"

"You were warned." Vincent ignored her question, ignored her, instead meticulously straightening the cuffs of his suit jacket to lie smoothly. "Search and rescue is a dangerous line of work. Such a terrible thing that accidents can happen in the blink of an eye."

She went to stand, but he shot forward, catching her hands and holding her in place. He tugged her to a sitting position and leaned in closer.

"Ropes failing at the wrong moment. Could happen to anyone, couldn't it?" he asked.

How could someone who appeared so sophisticated sound so menacing? Alisha glanced around, but the nearest people were too far away to hear his words or see anything other than a couple holding hands. Perhaps having a lovers' quarrel.

God, she wished Devon were with her.

Vincent didn't allow her to speak, instead sending her a hard-edged smile that didn't reach his eyes. "Or maybe the next terrible *accident* won't be on the job. Your pilot—Erin, correct? Such a lovely woman. She lives alone. She should be more diligent in locking her doors."

This wasn't making sense. "You're threatening my Lifeline teammates if I don't marry you?"

Vincent lowered his voice and darkness rasped over her eardrums, setting her hair on end. "I allowed you to make the right decision on your own, and you chose to ignore me. I've had enough, Alisha. Your time here is done."

She struggled to make sense of what seemed total nonsense. "Are you claiming you caused Xavier's accident?"

"Don't be stupid. How could I cause an accident?" His gaze tightened, his pressure on her fingers increasing to the point of pain. "I'm a businessman, not a petty thief. Not a person willing to accept money to place drugs in someone's cup. Not a desperate creature willing to damage a sturdy harness in strategic places."

The blood drained from her head, leaving an eerie echo in her ears. "Vincent—"

"I didn't want to do this, but you forced my hand, Alisha. You. Your stubborn resistance is the reason that until you cooperate, I'll find ways to *encourage* you to come to your senses. Perhaps that sweet Jonah—he's a friend of Tripp's, isn't he? He shouldn't walk to work at the school over the next while. I'd hate to have a car lose control near him and cause another tragedy."

Her chest was so tight she couldn't breathe. He knew her teammate's names, their friends, what they did for a living. What had begun as a meeting full of frustration and anger at his idiotic refusal to leave her in peace had turned into a nightmare.

"This isn't how the real world works," Alisha stuttered. "If you did something to hurt Xavier, or anyone else, you'll be caught. I wouldn't lie down and obey your insane orders simply because you've done some research into the people in my life, as infuriating as that is. You're not above the law, Vincent."

"But I am," he said. "There's nothing you can blame on me because everything is untraceable, yet I've got the resources to make accidents keep happening. What I don't have are the shares you own, and until I do, I won't stop. I'm not enjoying this—I'd far prefer to get on with our lives, and I'd imagine the rest of your team feels the same way. I'd hate for something to happen to anyone else. Especially . . . what's his name? Ah, yes. Devon."

Alisha stilled. The words escaped in a bare whisper. "No, Vincent. No."

He shrugged. "It's up to you. I need you to return to Toronto. Once you've satisfied the conditions of your inheritance, I can take the steps to ensure a smooth transfer of business matters. It's not that great a hardship, I think, marrying me. Rejoining society for a year should be a nice change of pace for you—you won't be required to do anything but act as my companion. I don't even expect you to sleep with me so long as you make the proper noises at the proper times in public." He waved a hand. "We'll arrange things in the prenuptial so once I'm satisfied the shares are permanently in my name, we can split up. You could return to your climber then." He paused and narrowed his gaze. "Or . . . you can continue to fight me, and there might not be anyone to return to."

She was going to be ill. "Xavier is lying in a hospital because you can't stand the thought of losing a business? What kind of a bastard are you?"

"One who's had enough. It's your choice. I assumed it should be an easy one to make." His eyes were cold. "If you think I'm stupid, don't. As far as any records or investigations will show, my only sin is waiting far too long for you to come to your senses and accept my proposal. I will have what I need. Now."

How had she stepped into such an impossible situation? She searched for words to deny him, but images of Xavier's broken body lying on the ice filled her head. Picturing Devon as motionless dragged a whimper from deep inside that escaped before she could stop it.

Her wrist would be bruised from his grip. "This isn't some game, and it's time you woke up. I want Bailey Enterprises. I've put too much into it over the years to allow my money to get flushed away by a fading old man or his rebellious daughter. I have the resources, and now I'm calling the shots. The sooner you cooperate, the fewer people will suffer for your mistakes."

He finally let her free and stood, pulling an envelope from his pocket and dropping it on the coffee table in front of her. His gaze drifted over her, his outside presentation still polished, which made his examination colder and more disturbing.

CHAPTER 24

''''''''''''''''''''''''''''''''

Devon paced his living room like a caged tiger, frustration and worry making it impossible to sit.

Ever since Alisha had sweet-talked him into allowing her to leave without him he'd been angry about giving in. Angry he hadn't thought to go along to protect her even if he simply observed from a distance.

Finding the balance between her need to stand on her own and being an overprotective asshole wasn't an easy line to walk. Adding in that it was now after noon and she still hadn't returned didn't make it any easier.

She'd texted him to let him know she was done talking with Vincent and she was safe. She needed "time to think."

What the fuck did *that* mean?

If it would have done any good he would have driven around town trying to spot Alisha's car, but the idea was stupid. Staying home and waiting for her to return seemed his only choice, but the longer he had to wait and keep reaching nothing but her voice mail, the more infuriated he got.

The front door opened and Alisha stepped through, lifting tired grey eyes to meet his.

"What happened?" he snapped. He stomped across to her side and pulled her against him, as she seemed nearly unable to keep on her feet. "What's wrong?"

She shook her head, pushing him away as she stumbled into the living room and collapsed onto the couch. "Give me a minute."

He'd given her all morning, but shouting wouldn't get her to talk any sooner. He followed her, eyeing her defeated body language as warning bells went off like crazy. This wasn't the confident, cocky woman who'd left him five hours ago. "Alisha, you're killing me. What the hell did Vincent do?"

A noise between a whimper and cry escaped her. "He's insane. He's completely and totally insane."

She looked up and he swore, the lost look in her eyes too much to bear. He sank to his knees and caught her hands in his. "Explain."

"Vincent pretty much admitted to sabotaging Lifeline—to causing Xavier's accident."

"What the *fuck*?"

She snorted. "Yeah, that was my response, but as bizarre as it sounds, it's true. Only he was sure to mention he couldn't be implicated in any of it. If I go to the police with this information, it will lead to nothing but dead ends. In the meantime, more accidents could happen."

Now he understood her confused expression—his must've been about the same. "This is bullshit. If he admitted to having anything to do with the accident, of course we go to the police."

"With what proof?" Alisha snapped. Her cheeks brightened as her breathing picked up. "I wandered for hours trying to figure out a way around this, but his comments are nothing but hearsay, and in the meantime, the rest of you are in danger. He threatened you. You and Erin and—God, he knew Jonah's name, and everything. Vincent's deranged enough that I can believe he'd do it. He'd *hurt* you."

Devon caught her around the back of the neck and held

on tight, his forehead pressed to hers as he attempted to calm her. To make sense of what she was saying. "He's not going to hurt anyone. Most likely he's lying in an attempt to scare you into doing what he wants. If he's really guilty, he'll be caught. The RCMP is investigating now. If you've got information, we need to tell them. Let them explore and—"

"No." The word burst out like a gunshot as she leapt to her feet, stomping away, her runners loud on the hardwood. She twirled to face him, all energy and passion again, only this time the energy stoking her wasn't sexual, it was despair. "You don't *understand*. What if in the meantime something happens? What if because I go to the RCMP something else terrible happens? I can't live with that. I just . . ."

She stared up at the ceiling, her teeth biting into her lower lip as she fought to calm herself.

Devon forced his fists to uncurl. To stand slowly, and move as if toward a skittish horse. "You have to trust nothing will happen."

Fire blazed out again. "I can't. Don't you see? You of all people should understand—the accident with your father impacted you hard, and it wasn't even your fault. It's taken years for you to move past it." Her eyes were wild. "Maybe Vincent is lying, maybe he's not causing terrible things, but what if he is? What if I can stop anyone else from being hurt, or God forbid, killed? What is one fucking year of my life compared to *that*?"

"What are you proposing?" Devon demanded. "You're seriously considering quitting Lifeline and marrying him? That won't solve anything. Not to mention if he is insane, getting married to the asshole isn't the answer. What kind of crazy abuse would you be putting yourself on the line for? God, Alisha, think this through."

"I have, dammit. He doesn't even want me, all he wants is the business." She pressed her hands against her eyes and swore. "Listen for a minute. It's stupid and wrong and like something out of the seventeenth century, I *get* all that, but it's also the only solution that makes sense. I went over it again and again after I talked to him."

"You listen to *me*." Devon wanted to shake her until reason clicked on. "Tying yourself to someone who you say has threatened others is not right in any way. You can't put yourself in danger like that."

She flicked her hands to her sides, still clenched into fists. "I know it's crazy, Devon. I *know*, but it feels as if it's the only goddamn answer there is. I don't want to do it, but . . . *arghhh*. I just want all this to go away, but it won't *stop*."

Alisha shoved past him, jerking away as he attempted to soothe her. Her feet slapped the wooden floorboards loudly as she stormed into the back of the house and slammed the bedroom door.

Devon dragged a hand through his hair, frustrated and furious and totally out of his depth.

There was no fucking way he would stand aside and allow her to offer herself up like some damn sacrifice. She'd admitted marrying Vincent was crazy. He'd give her a while to calm down before driving that point harder.

If not, he had no problem tying her to a chair to keep her safe. Or throwing her over his shoulder and hauling her down to the police station to let them know what she'd learned.

She was right about one thing. Suggesting that Vincent was involved in sabotage was a shocker at first. Even knowing in advance that the man was more than slightly unhinged, Devon had never, ever expected to hear such an accusation. Vincent's obsession with Alisha wasn't obvious at first, not until you started adding the details up. Little things showed it clearly, like the stupid ploy to buy out her residences from under her, but without that evidence it was hard to believe. Vincent would have skepticism on his side, which was the biggest bullshit Devon had ever faced.

The bedroom door creaked, and he glanced up to see Alisha cross the hallway. She stared, her face tight with frustration, before disappearing into the bathroom. The sound of running water clicked on.

His phone rang—Marcus's tone. Devon yanked it out and

answered it on the second ring, the issues with Vincent not forgotten but set aside for a moment. "Any news?"

His boss's familiar growl came through, tired and restless. "There's additional testing to be done, but preliminary reports are in. It's not good, but it's not the worst. His T10 was crushed."

"Shit." Devon closed his eyes and took a deep breath. "Chances of recovery?"

"That's the good part. You guys stabilized him properly, and he got the fastest treatment possible. They had him in surgery already this morning. He'll have therapy to deal with, but chances of walking again are higher than average."

Devon leaned on the wall to stop the room from spinning, shoving the images of his father into a corner of his mind and focusing on the here and now. "You going to see him?"

"I'm already in Calgary. Becki and I will be back in a couple days. In the meantime we're all on hiatus. I'll call everyone else and let them know. Lifeline's not taking any call-outs. I've got . . . I've got feelers out for a new paramedic for the team."

A truth that was necessary but still sucked hugely, and also meant this wasn't the time to mention Alisha's threat to quit. "I'll let Alisha know—she's here with me. You need me to do anything at the shop?"

"No. It's locked up tight. There's more investigating to do in the next week, but my RCMP contact says he's on top of it." Marcus sighed. "We'll get through this, Devon."

Marcus didn't know the half of it. "That's my line to you," Devon repeated. "Call if you need anything."

They both hung up, and Devon paced the room again, searching for the words to go and knock some sense into Alisha even as he shared the news regarding Xavier.

He picked up his coat from where she'd thrown it toward the back of the couch, more to keep his hands busy than out of a need to clean up, and an envelope fell to the ground.

The unusual texture and unusual colouring screamed

Vincent—it was the same kind of expensive envelope that had held the house offer he'd read earlier. Devon opened it and peeked inside. The plane ticket in Alisha's name confirmed part of her report. Vincent really did think he could simply take over her life.

Fury swamped him, and Devon acted on instinct. He'd been patient, he'd waited, but it wasn't time to wait any longer. He pulled on the coat and headed out the door.

Vincent wanted to make threats against the people closest to him? Devon would give him a few reasons to reconsider.

Alisha tilted her face into the shower and let the hot water cascade over her in the hopes of washing Vincent's stench away. The reek of fear.

Devon was right. She had to go to the RCMP, but horror continued to tango in her veins,

The *what if*s terrified her more than anything she'd faced in her years of rescue work. More than the panic attack in the cavern not so long ago, because not only did she feel out of control, but the chaos was deliberate. Humanly guided deceit.

A flash flood or rock slide could shatter lives. At Lifeline they fought that devastation—they brought people back safely more times than not. Man against nature followed rules she'd learned to combat during her time in school and training.

Vincent's careless disregard for human life cut harder and deeper than the smash of a rock or the icy touch of hypothermia.

Nature wasn't deliberately cruel. She was unpredictable and powerful. Most of the time she could not be tamed, but gentled. Vincent had stepped outside those boundaries, and Alisha wasn't willing to play his games. Not anymore.

If she had to leave Lifeline for the safety of her teammates, she'd do so, but she wouldn't marry Vincent. She'd go south, find somewhere to hide for a while until some proof was found of his involvement.

Devon *was* right. She needed to trust him, the way she'd trusted him with her life until now.

Going to the police was the only option. Even more urgent on the agenda, from the perspective of Vincent being more than slightly unhinged, was warning her teammates.

She clicked off the shower and hurried to dress, calling for Devon. She couldn't find him anywhere. No note, no nothing.

When his phone went to voice mail she growled in frustration. Great. Now that she'd had time to see reason, he wasn't there. It might be needy, but if she had to do this, she wanted him by her side.

Calling everyone on Lifeline individually wasn't what she wanted, either. Too many explanations—too many questions. She opened her computer and composed a short e-mail.

Maybe it was melodramatic, but Vincent's "I have the resources to make this happen," had scared her more than she wanted to admit. She had no idea if her e-mail was being monitored. Was that even possible outside television?

The less she said the better at this point.

> Potential danger. Please, stay home tonight.
> I'll contact you ASAP. Rule #3

Lifeline's rules—the ones plastered on the wall in HQ that guided all their training, rescues, and interactions. Rule three was *Trust your team*. They all understood what it meant. That she was calling on them to go without information and simply believe she was making the right decision based on information she had that they lacked.

Anders had a roommate, as did Tripp. She didn't think even Vincent would go full-out thug and try anything with them. He seemed to have gone the more devious route up to now, other than his threat against Erin.

Where the *hell* was Devon? Alisha pulled on her shoes and coat, shoved her wet hair under a toque, and headed for her car. She'd go to Erin's—at least that way there would be two of them together, and as soon as she got hold of Devon, they could all go to the RCMP station.

She set up her hands-free phone, reluctant to make one more contact, but again, it was the right thing to do. She tapped in her father's office number; the ringing seemed to take forever before going through. Of course, she still had to run the gauntlet. Hell if she'd sit around waiting for him to call back this time, though.

"Mr. Bailey's office. How can I help you?" Marilee the robot—right on schedule.

"Alisha Bailey. I want to speak with my father immediately. Don't do a callback—put me through right now, no matter what."

Marilee paused, and then, miracle of miracles, did as ordered. "Yes, Miss Bailey. One minute, I'll connect you."

God, if she'd known being a bossy bitch was the solution, she would have tried it years ago.

"Alisha?" Her father all but barked at her. "I'm in the middle of a meeting."

"I'm calling to warn you that Vincent Monreal has been threatening me. I'm going to the police this afternoon. I thought you should know so you could be prepared in case—"

"Goddamn, what the hell are you talking about?" It was sickeningly amusing to hear her unflappable father break. "Just—hold on one minute."

He must have barely covered the phone with a hand because brief speaking voices in the background were followed by the sound of motion. Only when there was silence did he come on the line.

"Slow down and explain yourself. Vincent threatened you? You're on drugs or something, aren't you? Part of your alternative lifestyle as a mountain hippie?"

Alisha clutched the steering wheel tighter but refused to give in to the urge to simply hang up. "I'm not drunk, high, or otherwise incapacitated. Not like I was last week when someone shoved enough painkillers into my drink to send me to the hospital. I'm not calling to get advice, simply as a courtesy. Vincent has been in Banff for the past month and has gone from a somewhat creepy stalker to outright dangerous. I'm going to the RCMP."

"Vincent's been here in Toronto, or on the West Coast working on deals," her father insisted. "I looked into it after you called the last time. Your outrageous conduct has got to stop now, Alisha. I'm getting tired of this twisted, attention-seeking behavior, and—"

"You know what, Dad? You know what kind of attention I want from you? Nothing. Never again. So you can just go to hell."

She stabbed the end call button and breathed out slowly. It was no use, but at least she could assuage her guilt on that account. Whatever happened in terms of fallout for Bailey Enterprises was no longer her fault. Her father had chosen not to listen or believe her, so now she'd choose her own path.

She'd choose her own family, starting with Devon.

CHAPTER 25

''''''''''''''''''''''''''''''

Anger hummed through his body as Devon pounded on the entrance to Vincent's suite. What he planned might be stupid but potentially very satisfying. It wouldn't take long. A few minutes, and he'd go home and work on Alisha.

He straightened to his full height as he waited for a response, damn near bouncing on his feet.

The thick door swung open to reveal an elegant room that probably cost as much per night as Devon paid in rent for a month. Vincent peered out, polite confusion on his face. Even in his hotel room the man was dressed in suit pants and a pristine white shirt, cuff links flashing gold against his wrists.

One brow rose as he gazed at Devon. "Well, this is a surprise. I'm sorry, did you get mixed up? I didn't book any excursions—"

Devon swung, and his fist connected with Vincent's jaw. A solid, satisfying crack that hurt his knuckles and jerked Vincent's head back. The man stumbled, fighting to regain his balance. Devon pushed into the room after him. "Shut up," Devon snapped, "You know damn well why I'm here."

Vincent rested a hand on the back of the couch to push himself to vertical. With his other hand he gingerly touched his lips before examining his fingertips for blood. "I'd suggest you reconsider before you hit me again. In your position as the enraged ex-lover I can forgive one stupid move, but if you touch me twice, I'll have you arrested."

"That's rich, coming from you. You want to go to the RCMP station, let's go right now." Devon stood just inside the door, glancing around the suite. A luggage carrier rested to one side of the door, suitcases lined up beside the oversized trolley.

"Going somewhere?" Devon asked.

"I'm headed to Toronto." Vincent shook himself, gaze tight on Devon now, far more wary than before. "The car is being brought around."

Shit. Devon didn't want him to leave, not before he'd persuaded Alisha to go to the police. "I thought your flight wasn't until Saturday."

Vincent narrowed his eyes. "You are annoying."

"I've been told that before. You have no idea exactly how annoying I can be." Devon faced Vincent head on. "Alisha's not going anywhere. I don't care what fucked-up tricks you played to convince her to give in, but it's not going to work. Leave, but don't expect her to follow."

"Our relationship isn't any of your business." Vincent straightened his tie, glancing in the mirror on the wall as if suddenly unconcerned that Devon stood before him with clenched fists. "My fiancée and I will deal with—"

Instinct won over logic. Devon hit him again, this time hard enough that Vincent staggered back and crumpled to the floor. He stared up, eyes unfocused for a moment, before blinking and grumbling his displeasure. "A prudent man would consider his actions more."

"Leave Alisha alone," Devon snarled. Warning delivered, he turned to leave.

Motion blurred toward him, a streak of blue below an unexpected but familiar face. Pain exploded in his head, the side of his skull throbbed once, and then blackness overtook him.

A heavy band of agony wrapped around his temples, and Devon took a deep breath to stop nausea from overwhelming him. He lay on his side on a smooth surface, his entire body rocking slightly from side to side. A groan escaped before he could stop it, opening his eyes to discover Vincent staring over the back of a leather seat, his cold eyes unblinking.

Devon bit back another groan of pain and glanced around as he pulled himself to vertical. He swore softly as he spotted the driver's face. The same woman who'd already made his life difficult and was probably to blame for at least one of the accidents at Lifeline.

The one who'd hit him with something hard in Vincent's room.

"You found a new employer pretty quick, didn't you, Lana?" he asked.

She adjusted her hands on the steering wheel, knuckles white she gripped it so hard, but didn't respond.

Devon did a quick physical check to assess his injuries, other than the headache that was making him see stars. His hands were tied behind his back, and an additional rope was twined around his ankles.

"Are we nearly there?" Vincent had turned his back on Devon, staring out the front window at the narrow road the rental car was skimming down. Tall spruce and rocky outcrops passed on either side. The mountaintops towered over them as Devon searched the trees trying to identify a familiar landmark so he could figure out where they were, but they could have been anywhere on the outskirts of Banff, or into the Kananaskis Valley.

There was no traffic, though, the road clear and void of all other vehicles, and Devon's confusion grew.

Lana spoke softly, answering Vincent's question. "Ten minutes to the trailhead."

"Park to one side when we get there," Vincent ordered.

"There shouldn't be anyone around. It's too late in the season for many people to want to hike the trail and too early for ice climbers." Her voice shook, her uncertainty and fear clear.

Yeah, just because she worked for Vincent didn't mean she could afford to let down her guard.

Devon tugged at his bonds, but they were seriously well fastened. Damn climbers and their knots.

All his earlier frustrations returned, only now twisted toward himself. He'd made a huge mistake in judgment, and now he was out of his league. Kidnapping had never entered his mind when he'd stormed over to the hotel. Did he tease for details? Stay silent and wait for a break?

They hadn't covered this one in SAR training.

Except . . .

They had been taught how to deal with irrational victims. Vincent might not be a victim, but he wasn't thinking straight, or not what the average person on the street would consider normal.

Don't antagonize—stay alert. Look for opportunities when they come, then act.

Devon rolled his shoulders and tested the ropes again. Tightened and relaxed his legs muscles to keep them from falling asleep. When the moment came he had to be ready to take it.

He had no idea what the hell Vincent had planned, but Devon knew one thing. He had to get out of this alive. Needed to be there for Alisha, for a future spent together discovering how much they could drive each other crazy.

Years of it.

A lifetime.

As long as he lived through the next couple hours.

The car rocked to a stop under the overhang of an ancient pine, the lowest branches high above the car roof. Gravel crunched underfoot as Vincent and Lana left the car, the shelter of the tree preventing the snow from piling up.

The trunk opened and closed. Lana appeared outside his door carrying two backpacks. One she lowered to the ground at Vincent's feet; the other she settled over her shoulders.

"Give me the keys." Vincent held out his hand. She dug in her pocket, pulled them out, and dropped them into his palm.

She stepped back quickly to face Devon's door, swinging it open.

"Get him out and ready to walk," Vincent ordered.

She swallowed hard and pulled out a switchblade, opening it to a serrated blade. "Turn and put your feet on the ground." Her words barely whispered out.

Devon took in her big eyes, the fear shaking her hands. She didn't say anything else. He took his time, careful not to scare her into anything rash, twisting uncomfortably until he'd done as she asked.

Lana knelt and put the blade against the thick fibers, sawing with large, exaggerated motions that made her right elbow swing in and out of the doorway.

Devon frowned. The knot was right there. She'd tied him tightly, but there was no reason to cut the ropes. Climbers hated to cut ropes, always preferring to loosen off and save the lengths for another time.

He glanced up at Vincent, but the man was pulling on a jacket, watching Lana from a few steps away. Her body was between Devon's feet and Vincent—all the other man would see was her back and her supposedly working like crazy to cut the rope.

Only she wasn't cutting anything. Her right hand was empty even as she continued to swing her arm. Faint hope rose as her left hand snuck around Devon's hip, and he schooled himself to not move as she slipped the closed switchblade into his back pocket.

One more moment passed before she replaced her left hand on the knot, twisting it apart and pulling the rope from him in two sections. She glanced at Devon once, begging in her eyes, before looking firmly at the ground. "He's free," she announced.

She stepped back, cautiously placing herself far enough to one side that he couldn't bump into her while trying to escape.

Vincent slipped on the second backpack. That was when Devon knew he was in worse danger than he'd first imagined. "Don't you have a flight to catch?" he asked.

The other man knelt and retied the laces of his hiking boots, and Devon eyed him carefully. The formal suit was gone. In its place was an expensive outfit, but totally appropriate for the outdoors, complete with gloves and a toque. Vincent stood and smiled, the thin line of his lips barely separating as he spoke.

"I am on the plane. Records will show I caught the flight as scheduled, and after arriving in Toronto I spent the remainder of the evening quietly at home. Tomorrow morning I catch another flight, this time to Vancouver. Oh, my whereabouts are very nicely established, thank you." Vincent pointed down the trail. "If you don't mind."

Devon stood his ground. "What do you plan to do? Tie me to a tree? Abandon me in the bush to die of exposure?"

Vincent frowned. "Well, that wouldn't make sense, would it? You're too good at surviving in the wilderness for anyone to believe you simply got lost. No. You need to have a more thorough accident. Something that might take a while before anyone recovers your body."

The casual way Vincent talked about killing him made Devon's skin crawl, but he didn't move. He didn't take his gaze off the man and crossed everything he had, hoping that what he was about to suggest would not be taken at face value. "Why exactly would I go anywhere with you, since you plan on killing me anyway? Kill me here and drag my body to where you want to hide it. I'm not making things easy on you."

Devon wasn't sure why he was surprised to see Vincent

pull out a gun. It was pretty well established by now that Vincent didn't care if his actions were illegal. Devon swallowed his fear and judged whether he could close the distance between them quickly enough to knock Vincent off his feet.

Only Vincent grabbed Lana by the arm, and the gun was now pressed to her temple. "You will walk, or she dies."

CHAPTER 26

,,,,,,,,,,,,,,,,,,,,,,,,,,,,,,,,,,,,

They'd been waiting more than an hour for Devon to show up. To call. To do something.

Alisha jiggled on the spot, bouncing on her heels before checking her phone again. She peered out the window, turning only when Erin pressed a glass of juice into her hands.

"Drink. You need to keep your energy up." The other woman wrapped her fingers around the glass and held it until Alisha finally closed her grasp. Erin crossed her arms over her chest. "If nothing else, it will help you do a few more laps in your attempt to wear a hole in my carpet."

"Where the hell is he?" Alisha growled. She made a face at Erin, who stood blocking her progress from completing yet another traverse of Erin's living room. "Fine. Drinking."

She tilted the orange juice and consumed the entire thing at one go, more to put the glass down than to cooperate with Erin.

"He's gone to burn off his frustrations. He'll be back." Erin leaned on the door frame. "You know, we could go to the RCMP station without him."

Alisha nodded. "We will if we have to. But, dammit, now I'm worried." Devon's ring tone burst from her phone, and she snatched it out in a panic, speaking before Devon could get a word in edgewise. "What kind of stupid-ass move are you pulling? I get it, I pissed you off by taking my time this morning, but now I need you and—"

A combination of crying and heavy gasps interrupted her. "Alisha, is that you? Oh God, I'm so sorry. I'm so sorry."

What the hell? That definitely wasn't Devon. "This is Alisha, who is this?"

"It's Lana. You've got to come. You've got to come now before it's too late."

Alisha froze. Across the room Erin watched with concern in her dark eyes.

"Lana? What is going on?" Confusion was rapidly followed by fear as Lana answered.

"Please, it's Devon. Vincent's got him, and he's going to kill him. There's no time."

Terror about Devon's absence flooded her, but nothing Lana said made any sense. Still, instincts kicked in. Training procedure. Gather information, *then* make a judgment call. "Why are you on Devon's phone?" Alisha demanded. "And where are you?"

"Takkakaw Falls. I'll explain everything, but you have to call the police. Get over here and save him."

Even as Lana continued to wail, Alisha made a decision and snapped into action. She gestured for Erin to join her, snatched up her gear bag, and was out the door even as she continued to speak with Lana. Erin ran ahead to open the trunk before hurrying into the driver's seat. She had them headed toward Lifeline without a single question, only she did get out her phone and make a couple of calls.

"Okay, I'm on the way." Alisha blocked out her teammate's voice, focusing on Lana. "What happened? Why didn't you call the police?"

Lana ignored the question, instead setting off on a rambling rant.

"Devon came to the hotel. He hit Vincent . . ." Lana

moaned. "I didn't want to do it, Alisha. I made one mistake, and once I fell for that, he had me. Vincent said I'd go to jail. That he had proof I'd drugged you. I wanted a chance to prove I could be on the team—that I had the skills. I didn't know he would damage Xavier's belt. I didn't know . . ."

Her voice trailed away into more crying. Alisha wished she could reach through the phone and smack the woman, partly to get her to settle down and partly because Lana obviously needed a smacking in a bad way.

"Where is Devon now? What's Vincent doing?"

"He's taking Devon into the caves by the falls. Thought it would take forever for anyone to find him, and when they did it would look like an accident." Another set of weeping interrupted her, and Alisha held on to her patience with gritted teeth. "I didn't mean for this to happen, and once I realized Vincent was crazy, I tried to help. I stole Devon's phone when he was unconscious."

The idea of Devon lying helpless at Vincent's mercy wasn't a good picture, not in light of his recent threats. "Is Devon okay?"

"He was knocked out for a bit. I gave him my knife; I slipped it to him. My God, I had no idea Vincent would go insane like this."

Yeah, Alisha could understand that one. "Are they in the caves already?"

"Not yet. Maybe. Probably not. It takes at least thirty minutes to hike, and Vincent had a gun on me, and we were only halfway to the caves when I tripped. Devon hit Vincent, and I ran. I don't know what happened then because I went down the hill and hid behind a gully, and I can't call the police because they'll arrest me."

They were pulling into the Lifeline parking lot. Alisha pointed Erin toward the chopper pad even as she attempted to talk sense into Lana.

"But if you don't help, Devon could die." She was talking to an empty phone. "Fuck." She shoved it into her pocket as she scrambled out the door.

Erin was right on her heels. "I assume you need a ride?"

"Did you get through to any of the guys?" They raced up the stairs and into HQ.

"No." Erin's face twisted as she considered. "You're not going to attempt a rescue on your own, are you?"

"Devon's in trouble."

That was all Alisha had to say. Erin smacked her palm against the wall and swore loudly.

The next moment she was settling her flying jacket around her shoulders. "Fuck it. It's all kinds of wrong, but I'll take you. I'm coming with you on the ground, and you call for RCMP backup right now, before we leave. Plus, we're taking a weapon from Marcus's case."

Alisha pulled on gear as she scrambled to put her brain in order. "Police. Yes. Ground assist, yes, but what weapon?"

Erin darted into the office, shouting over her shoulder. "I don't need long to get the chopper in the air. Just give me a second here . . . Where am I headed?"

"Toward Field town site, then north to the falls." Alisha grabbed a first-aid kit. More rope. Shoved it all in a pack. Yanked on her boots.

Something grey and metallic was thrust into her line of vision. She jerked back in protest. "Shit, Erin. A gun?"

Erin rolled her eyes even as she tucked the firearm away and headed for the door. "You don't even know where the safety is, do you?"

"God, no." For all her training, guns had never been a part of it. "I've got bear spray."

"Fucking princess." Erin's smile contradicted her insult. "Fine, I've got this. Now get your ass in gear; we leave in five minutes.

Erin slammed out the hangar door, her back visible through the opening as she ran full tilt toward the chopper.

Alisha paused inside HQ with her phone to her ear. She spoke with her contact at the RCMP and got transferred to Field in one step. Fortunately, by the time the chopper blades were going hard enough to make hearing difficult, the constable had gotten the message and she was able to hang up and sprint to the chopper.

She crawled in up front with Erin and yanked on a head-set to catch the pilot up on details.

"We'll be racing them to the cave entrance." Alisha checked her watch, calculating time frames. "RCMP has to prep, drive to the trailhead, and then hike, while we can land a lot closer to the access point. They won't be there for at least forty-five minutes.

Erin held up a hand, clicking to a different frequency for a moment and speaking to someone. She lifted them sky-ward before reconnecting with Alisha. "We owe Jason at the tower a bottle of something expensive—he got us clear-ance faster than usual."

"Done. There's a clearing above the cave entrance—you do know where we're going, right? How long will it take?"

"Takkakaw Falls? Thirty-five minutes tops. But Alisha?" A pair of dark eyes flashed a warning as Erin's hands con-tinued to dance over switches and controls. "Don't be a hero. You know the rules, and even though this is Devon and he's in some royally fucked-up situation, you do it the safe way, understand?"

Her heart was in her throat, but she got it. "Agreed."

Alisha leaned forward and stared out the window at the rapidly passing terrain beneath them, the brisk flick of the blades overhead not nearly quick enough to match the tempo pounding inside her.

Devon. She was going to tie him up and give him more than a tongue-lashing. What the hell had he been thinking?

It was a nightmare beyond anything she could have come up with. All the past weeks of caring and teasing played through her mind. The months and years before that when they'd always been there for each other, even when they'd fought like cats and dogs.

She wanted him back. God, she hadn't even had a chance to tell him she loved him yet.

Alisha shook her head as Erin took them past Saddle Mountain, the familiar outline of the Devil's Thumb out the left window. Below them the picturesque village of Lake

Louise splayed out in the level space between mountain ranges. Shining metal roofs reflected red and blue in sunshine, glorious white surrounding most of the roads and homes as winter settled over the tourist community. It was all so innocent and peaceful.

An image of Vincent's cool, sophisticated face flashed into her brain, and Alisha grimaced. Outside appearances could be so deceptive.

"Nearly there." Erin interrupted her thoughts. "You're in charge on the ground, so what's the game plan?"

Alisha took a deep breath. She'd been lead climber for more than two years, but she'd never actually had to call the shots during a rescue before. "Nothing fancy. The only issue is there are a series of caves and entrances. Chances are Vincent will go for the easiest to access, but we'll have to check the snow to confirm where they've entered. Low light on headlamps—we don't want Vincent hiding and overpowering us."

Erin nodded. "They might hear the chopper. Unless they're deep in the caverns, they'll know we're coming."

"Good," Alisha said. "That might be enough to convince Vincent to leave Devon alone. If we have enough time, backup will arrive and the RCMP can handle it."

"Cave details I need to know?" Erin asked. "And we're there in five minutes. We'll pass Mount Ogden and drop from the east. I'll have the chopper shut down in two more minutes while you go check the snow tracks."

It was time to focus on the rescue, not on memories of Devon's blue eyes shining at her as they worked together. Not on the softer, heated passion she'd seen there as he'd held her and they'd made love. Focus on the facts. Alisha closed her eyes and pulled up information from previous trips and rescues in the area. "The most likely approach is the lower loop. Upper cave closes into tight passages before leading to an eighteen-meter drop that people rappel down. The lower entrance is level with the river, and there are a ton of pools with narrow pathways along the perimeter."

Erin made a disgusted noise. "Can I vote for the water route, and not the death drop in the dark?"

Alisha didn't even want to think about it. It would be so easy to hurt someone at that point—a simple shove, and Devon would be at the bottom of the slick rocks, broken or dying. The only good part was it would take a lot longer to get up to the upper cave entrance—they had a shot at stopping the guys before they made it into the caverns.

Flying over the ridge of the falls was beautiful and horrifying. The calm waters of the glacier melt that formed the falls exploded off the granite lip into the air to fall in glittering ribbons to the earth. The sun reflected on water droplets, turning the world into a shimmering rainbow—hauntingly beautiful, considering that somewhere below them Devon's life was on the line.

Around them the treetops wavered, a fine dusting of snow off the branches filling the air and turning it white as the props whipped up wind currents. As Erin smoothly lowered them, Alisha examined the snow for clues of which direction to go. They were slightly to the north and above the cave entrances. Alisha squinted to be sure, but there seemed to be two distinct lines breaking away from the main trail. One led to the upper cave entrance, one down toward the river.

That made no sense. Vincent and Devon going in opposite directions?

A flash of alarm rang out. Was this another setup? Had Lana lied, and even now they were walking into another trap?

As the runners touched down, Alisha took a deep breath.

There was no way around it. The RCMP were on their way. Even if it did all turn out to be some elaborate hoax, no one would leave this section of the mountains without a damn good explanation.

Saving Devon came first. He'd trusted her with his life many times before.

Like hell would she let him down now.

CHAPTER 27

,,,,,,,,,,,,,,,,,,,,,,,,,,,,,,,,,

A bruised right shoulder and a slightly twisted ankle had
joined the pounding in his head.

They'd been walking single file along the narrow boardwalk that made up the first part of the trail. Lana in the lead,
Devon behind her, Vincent at the back of the line. When
Lana slipped on the snow-slicked trail, Devon reacted,
throwing himself backward into Vincent and knocking the
other man to the ground. With his arms still lashed behind
him, the only thing Devon accomplished was to temporarily
separate the gun from Vincent's hand. Long enough at least
that when Lana rolled and popped to her feet, sprinting for
the tree cover, Vincent had no way to take her down.

Vincent roared in frustration, kicking furiously and slamming his hands against Devon's face. Vincent scrambled until
he was free of Devon's body weight, snatching up the gun
and aiming down the hill, but Lana had vanished like a ghost.

Her tracks were there, though, a clear line leading away.
Vincent followed them for a few paces, sinking to mid-shin
in the deeper snow.

Devon thought furiously. While he didn't trust Lana, she was basically his only hope at this moment. "Really? You're going to leave me right out in the open to chase down some little girl who's so scared of you she can't talk without shaking?"

Vincent paused, glancing over his shoulder to where Devon lay sprawled in the snow.

It took some effort, but Devon hid the exertion it cost him, rolling and twisting and ending up on his feet in what had to look like a very impressive move, if Vincent's widened eyes meant anything.

"Yeah, you go ahead and leave me here," Devon taunted. "I'll be so far into the bush before you make it back, your head will spin. Hell, I might even make it to the highway to get the police before you can find me."

"You're very cocky for someone about to become a cave fossil," Vincent snarled. He glanced into the trees, but there were no further signs of Lana. "I'll find her after—she won't get far on foot."

For once Devon was glad to have Vincent pull his typical chauvinistic crap and underestimate Lana. The woman was probably as proficient in the backcountry as Devon, and she didn't have her hands tied. If she made the right decision and called someone, he might have a chance.

Now it was up to him to give her the time.

He paced forward as slowly as he dared, Vincent hard on his heels, that bloody gun pointed directly between Devon's shoulder blades. "If you call this off and go back to the car on your own, you might get into hiding before the authorities come down on you," Devon pointed out.

"No one is coming down on me." Vincent laughed softly as they reached the end of the easy-access boardwalk and headed onto the more dedicated climber's trail. "You're making all sorts of assumptions, as if I'm not smart enough to get the girl's phone before we went anywhere. No, I think things are going fine. If she gets lost and dies in the bush, well that adds to the mystery. Such a romantic twist—lover's spat, or some nonsense."

Vincent was breathing heavier, the increasing snow underfoot and the changing elevations taking their toll on his less fit body. Devon increased his pace, adding pressure to Vincent's already taxed system.

The man was too young to drop dead of a heart attack, but he could hope.

The trail through the trees ended abruptly, opening into a wide meadow. Devon led them forward until they were in the clear, then stopped.

Vincent pushed him forward roughly. "Move."

Devon shrugged. "You shoot me here and casual tourist sightseeing traffic will spot me from the air within the hour. You want to take me to the caves, you lead the fucking way."

Vincent stomped around him, cautious to maintain a distance between them. He waited until he had the uphill advantage to face Devon. He swung his arm and backhanded Devon across the face, and Devon rocked on his feet. "You might want to consider Alisha and what I'll do to her over the coming years. Cooperate now, and I promise to be more lenient."

Devon licked at the split in his lips, the salty tang of blood on his tongue a strong warning. "The word of a man who plans to kill me. I don't think I give a shit what you promise."

Vincent stepped back and adjusted the backpack to lie across his chest. One-handed so he could keep the gun in position, he reached in and pulled out a rope. It took him a while, but Devon had to admit the man wasn't an idiot. He vanished behind Devon again and before Devon could turn, Vincent jerked his toque over his eyes, then retreated out of harm's way.

The next thing Devon felt was a noose around his neck, the slipknot tightening. He tucked his chin to his shoulder in an attempt to protect his airway, but it was too late. Vincent slammed him between the shoulders again, and, unable to see, Devon stumbled to catch his balance, elbows jerking wide, the restraints on his wrists holding solid. The slight gap he'd maintained in the noose slipped away as the cord settled tight to his skin, and Devon's hopes fell.

Vincent had him collared like a damn dog.

His toque was pulled off along with a few strands of hair, pain jolting his already aching head. Vincent stood to one side of him, emotionless.

"Walk. Take me to the caves or I'll tie you to a tree right here and pull the fucking rope until you're blue in the face," Vincent warned.

"Gee, I'd think you didn't like me or something." Devon turned and broke trail through the pristine snow. He deliberately walked farther into the meadow than needed to leave a visible trail from the air. Heading to the caves was the only logical choice. He had to keep trying to buy more time. Every moment was one more opportunity for Vincent to fuck up.

Moving was better than simply allowing the man to choke him to death before he even got to use the knife burning a hole in his back pocket.

Devon shook his shoulders and tightened his neck muscles as he walked, thankful that when he relaxed there was a tiny bit more play in the circle. He could draw a full breath again.

He glanced back as he stepped up and over a larger rock. Vincent strode behind him, the rope between them hanging slightly, but Vincent's fingers were firmly wrapped around the excess length. The gun had vanished.

Choosing which direction to lead Vincent was simple. Devon had been in the Takkakaw caves more times than he could count—it was a favourite training ground for the SAR school. The number of hours he and Alisha had spent wandering in the dark with only their headlamps to guide them had diminished over the past two years while on Lifeline, but there were some things that were etched into his memories. Like the massive free-fall off the trail shortly inside the upper entrance. No way in hell was he leading Vincent anywhere near that. At the lower entrance he had a chance—there was nowhere good to hide a body for at least a few minutes' walking, not to mention the river and the falls to deal with. Somewhere in the growing darkness Devon would make his move.

He clung to that hope as they marched silently over the meadow, the broad face of the rock wall appearing ahead of them. The falls themselves boomed louder as they approached, the constant descent of water crashing into rocks filling his ears, a mist in the air growing as ice sparkled on the limbs of nearby trees.

They had to descend the final section. Devon was challenged to remain on his feet as he manoeuvred over snow-covered boulders, the mountain walls rising around them as they entered a natural amphitheater where the water foamed up, clouds of vapour and freezing water spray painting the rock shimmering white.

"Why are we going down?" Vincent asked, suspicion thick in his voice.

Devon snapped. "You wanted the cave, you've got the bloody cave. Look for yourself, asshole."

The rope jerked and Devon choked, bending at the waist and shaking frantically to find air.

Vincent spoke softly. "Don't push me anymore."

A thin thread of air returned as the noose loosened, and Devon dragged in a breath. He staggered for a pace, then straightened and took another step down toward where they'd have to wade through the river to access the cavern opening.

Runoff was far slower now than in the spring or summer, but the glacier melt never really stopped, the constant moisture of the falls forming into a sparkling cascade of ice in the dead of winter. Devon stepped reluctantly into the shallows, the pounding splash of the cataract covering all other noises. Icy-cold spray coated them both as they edged closer to the mountain, the falls forming a curtain to their right. Rock and water filled the sky as Devon waded forward, thigh deep in the current as the underground stream they were about to follow joined the torrent from above.

He paused as they reached the actual entrance, the warmer air from inside the opening rushing past them bringing the scents of mold and earth along with it. A moment later a light clicked on as Vincent shone the beam into the cave. Devon struggled forward, climbing out of the water onto a relatively dry path with difficulty, his tied hands pulling him off balance.

Now that they were inside, the volume of the crashing falls faded, warping into strange echoes and haunting cries.

"Which way do we go?" Vincent asked. "Never mind. I see it." He dodged around Devon, the coil of rope in his hands. "This is how this works. You stand here and wait for me. When I get where I want to go I'll call. If you choose to obey me, I'll lead you in safely. If not, I'll jerk you off your feet and push you into the water."

"Why not push me in now?" Devon would welcome it. None of the pools in this area were deep, but there were holes along the cavern wall he could hide in, and tall stalagmites he could wrap the neck rope around to give himself time to use the knife to get free.

Now that they'd reached the caves, his opportunities were better than in the open—as long as Vincent didn't shoot him. That option he simply didn't have a solution for.

Vincent stepped away another pace. "Lana mentioned a place where I could leave you. You'll never get out, not without gear, but it seems more like something she'd do, doesn't it? If we're going with the lovers' spat. Alisha will be heartbroken when they finally find your body next spring. I'll be sure to offer lots of sympathy."

Devon fought the urge to spit on the man. Vincent really thought he had Lana so cowed she wouldn't call for help when she got free?

Any mistakes Vincent made now only helped Devon. He stood silently as Vincent backed away, then turned to use the headlamp to guide himself along the narrow path at the edge of the water, the noose rope slowly falling from his hands as he moved away.

As soon as darkness closed around him, Devon had his fingers in his back pocket, the switchblade out and pressed to the ropes entangling his wrists. He cut quickly, forcing his breathing to remain calm, watching the light Vincent carried bob into the distance.

He wasn't nearly through the fibers when Vincent called

for him to move. The man shone the light toward him, the muted glow illuminating an eerie world of shadows and glistening water, ribbons of tiny streams shimmering as they trickled down the ancient cavern walls.

"Moving. Just give me time."

He kept working the blade, the occasional misdirection cutting his fingers, sliding too near to his wrists, but he couldn't afford to be cautious. Every step took him closer to Vincent, and if he discovered what Devon was doing, the knife would be gone.

Devon's chances might be gone as well.

Pressure eased slightly on every tug, but the ropes were still too tight to fall away.

A familiar sound reached his ears, echoing through the higher tunnels toward them, and Devon grinned in spite of the hellish situation. Somewhere outside the cave a helicopter was landing.

"What's that?" Vincent snapped.

"Bats," Devon lied.

Vincent paused, then swore violently. "That little bitch."

Devon wasn't sure if Vincent meant Lana or Alisha, and he didn't care. The ropes were nearly off. He stepped quicker now, hoping to catch Vincent distracted. Only the light vanished and he had to jerk to a stop before he slipped off the path or tripped over something.

The final thread snapped free, and Devon twisted his hands loose, blood rushing into his numb fingers. He bit the inside of his cheek to stop from making any noise as his eyes attempted to adjust to the even more limited lighting.

Ahead of him Vincent had fallen to his knees, frantically digging into the backpack. The flashlight in his hands focused in a narrow beam as he searched for something.

It was his only chance. Devon jerked the noose free from his neck. He tossed the rope ahead of him on the path, then stepped as close to the cavern wall as he could, crouching behind a rock and hiding.

Vincent rose, the round circle of light in his hand

blinding Devon as he endeavored to tuck himself farther out of sight.

"You bastard, where did you go?" Vincent tugged the neck rope sharply, and the free end flew through the air. "How the hell . . . ?"

Vincent flicked the light from side to side as he searched.

Even though he'd broken free, his hiding place wasn't perfect. In fact, Devon was a bit of a sitting duck. How much had Lana told Vincent about the cave system, and could he use Vincent's ignorance against him? It was a long shot, but Devon had to take it.

"If you start running," Devon called, "you might get out of the cave through the upper exit. If you go now."

For all his polish Vincent had a fairly extensive vocabulary. When the curses stopped, Vincent moved toward him. "This is your fault, you know. Alisha was far more malleable before she got involved with you."

"Bullshit. Alisha's the strongest, most opinionated person I know. You misjudged her."

Vincent took another step closer. The beam of light widened with every pace. "You're as ignorant as the rest of them."

Devon stilled his breathing and braced himself, readying to leap at Vincent if he came any farther in his direction.

The entrance to the cave glowed in the distance, the broken outline of a semicircle highlighted with the light of the wintery sky. A body stepped into view, framed by the darkness and light.

Rescuers had arrived. For the first time in ages, Devon took a deep breath and allowed himself to hope.

Vincent cursed again, then turned, the glow of his flashlight vanishing. Devon remained motionless, listening hard, forcing himself to ignore the person hesitating at the entranceway and to focus on tracking Vincent.

The other man wasn't moving.

From the mouth of the cavern a bright light flashed, streaming into the darkness like a shooting star. Brilliant red reflected off myriads of water rivulets, veins of quartz sparkling with blood-toned diamonds as the light blasted past. Another emergency flare followed it, and another, and Devon glanced over the rock to discover Vincent only feet away.

Devon leapt without thinking, pushing against the firm stone flooring and flying through the air. He slammed into Vincent and took him to the ground, a gasp of pain escaping the other man.

They rolled, Devon clutching to grasp Vincent's hands. A blow hit him in the face and another in the solar plexus. He got in a few good punches of his own, Vincent grunting as the blows landed. Around them the darkness made his eyes ache as he scrambled to subdue his target.

An ear-shattering explosion rang out as pain sliced through Devon's leg. It felt as if a raging hot knife had stabbed into his calf, but he tightened his grip on Vincent, keeping hold of him in spite of the pain.

Vincent had shot him.

Alisha was going to kill him for being stupid enough to get shot.

Something hard brushed the back of his hands, and Devon jabbed the gun away, clinging to Vincent for all he was worth. Vincent got in another lucky blow and the ringing in Devon's head got worse. The stars in front of his eyes grew brighter.

The world moved into slow motion, a blend of agony and coloured lights. Devon was seriously pissed off as for the second time that day darkness overwhelmed him.

CHAPTER 28

''''''''''''''''''''''''''''''''''

When the shot rang out, everything inside Alisha threatened to tear apart.

They'd been forced to separate, her and Erin. Two distinct sets of tracks led to the lower entrance while a lone set aimed straight for the upper, and the possibility that Lana had sent them into a trap was too great to ignore.

Alisha had promised to be careful, they both had, but there was a lot that could be accomplished while they waited for the RCMP to catch up in the next five to ten minutes.

A blend of cautious waiting and frantic rushes forward got her to the foot of the falls, where the icy-cold spray wrapped itself around her like a shroud. The pump of blood whooshing past her eardrums deafened her even to the overload of noise created by the cataract to her right.

Fear had become her constant companion, clinging like some demented devotee—a sentinel demon lusting for her to fall.

Terror skittered up her spine as she stepped into the frigid waters of the river. Images of the flash flood weeks earlier surrounded her, and the bitter taste of bile hit the back of her tongue. Alisha closed her eyes for a moment and dragged in a deep breath.

She could do this. Search and rescue was in her heart, in her soul. She'd trained and struggled and worked her ass off to be the kind of woman who could face her fears and still move forward.

Blue eyes shone into her memory—the confidence Devon had in her coming through first and foremost. The caring he showed her.

The passion they'd shared.

Fear eased—not vanished, but fading enough that she could breathe again. Breathe, and take another step forward. And another, until the rocky cave entrance loomed overhead.

The long open cavern before her held dark mysteries, the boom of the falls reverberating around her as Alisha prepared the emergency flares. The first round of flashes shot into the chasm to highlight a human figure standing two-thirds of the way down the passage. She stooped to prepare another set of flares when blurred motion caught her attention in the fading glow. She scrambled to light a flare when a gun echoed in the cavernous chamber, and Alisha's stomach rolled.

She crawled to one side and waited.

A flashlight clicked on as someone escaped farther into the cave system. Alisha waited, confused and yet eager to move forward. It had to be Vincent retreating into the mountain. Devon knew there was no way to get out that direction without climbing massive walls in the dark, impassible without a rope already in place from the top.

Unless Lana had gone in the other direction. Maybe even now she was setting up an escape route.

Alisha clicked on her walkie-talkie. "Careful, Erin. You might have company soon."

Erin's response sounded in the earbud Alisha wore—a silent solution to keep their communication from carrying to the people around them. "Got it. I'll camp outside the metal gates. Which, by the way, are open. Someone cut the chain on the lock. There's only one set of tracks heading into the caves, though."

There were definitely at least two people inside the maze of passages then. "Someone got shot. I'm going to check them out," Alisha whispered.

"Can you wait?" Erin asked.

"Negative. It could be serious."

Erin's colourful response broke off fast. "Fine. Just don't go in farther. I see the RCMP at the edge of the meadow. You'll have backup in approximately ten minutes."

Alisha stared down the passage. She lit off another flare, but there was no longer anyone moving. Desperation rushed her, the urge to move driving her forward.

The water running underfoot increased in volume as the river narrowed. Darkness closed in. Flashes of memory broke through again: the flood sweeping over her and Devon, attempting to steal her breath away, surrounding her in a trap, but that fear had been tamed. She walked quietly with her headlight on the lowest beam possible, hurrying while remaining alert in case the shooter stepped out from the distance.

Uneasiness was wiped clear by shock of a different sort as Devon's blond hair came into view, his body crumpled to the ground on the wet path. The rock was redder than usual under him, and she bit back a cry as she realized why.

She dropped to her knees, slapping a hand around his leg above the point where the blood stained his khakis. "Devon. Do you hear me?"

Her pack hit the ground. She set up a larger flashlight beside it to help her see the supplies she needed. Alisha rushed into medical assessment mode, the shallow breaths he took reassuring her he was still alive.

And when his eyes opened and he turned his face toward her and smiled, it was if the sun had risen in the cave.

"Vincent," Devon whispered. "He's got a gun."

She nodded, ripping his pant leg open with a knife and shoving a tourniquet band under his calf. "He's gone deeper into the caves. Erin's at the other end, and we think Lana as well."

"She's with him. Well, sort of," Devon warned.

"Shh, I know. RCMP are on the way. I love you."

His grimace broke into an enormous, although still pained, grin even as she tightened the band. "I love you, too. Let's get the hell out of here."

Alisha nodded, "Let me stabilize you first. We'll have help in—"

Her head jerked back as she was pulled to her feet, fingers tangled in her hair. Panic rose as she was hauled away from where Devon lay.

He rolled to his side, and Vincent spat out a warning. "Don't move, or I'll shoot her."

The light she'd set up at Devon's side clearly showed him lifting his hands in surrender. "I can't move, you bastard. Why are you doing this? Give up already."

She felt Vincent shake his head, his grip tightening as he dragged her back. "There's always a way out."

Devon's lips tightened in disgust. "Lana told you about the secret exit. Dammit, I don't believe this."

Neither could Alisha. *What* secret exit? She knew two ways in and out, and an actual loop like that was uncommon in cave systems—a third exit would be extraordinarily rare. She tested the hold Vincent had on her, but it was no use. This was one time her size was a definite disadvantage.

"Stop wiggling or I'll shoot him again," Vincent snapped. She stilled instantly. "Turn out your light. Now," Vincent ordered Devon.

Devon nodded, his gaze meeting hers. He didn't try to hide his fear, but there was a spark there of something else. Something that gave her hope. "I love you, Alisha. It'll work out, got that?"

He flicked the switch and thrust them all into darkness again. Vincent twisted her, his arm around her throat pinching off her air supply. He turned on his flashlight and shoved her forward, rapidly increasing the distance separating them from Devon. From the RCMP team who even now should be reaching the cave entrance.

Behind them was nothing but darkness. Vincent moved them in rushes, pausing at odd intervals to listen, probably in case someone was following.

"Vincent, please let me go," she begged.

He ignored her, hesitating as the path narrowed with two branches before them. "Devon said there was a secret exit. Show me."

Alisha gasped in pain as he squeezed. She clawed at his arm in an attempt to loosen his hold to get more air. She still had no idea what the hell was going on. "I thought Lana told you about the exit."

"No, Devon did. He's not as smart as he thinks. Now which way?"

"To the left." Alisha chose the direction leading away from the upper entrance.

The path narrowed before twisting to the side. The water pools and river were left behind, the light in Vincent's hand reflecting off walls that were now close enough to touch. Vincent's breathing was loud in her ear, obviously hurt as he groaned and muttered, shoving her forward into the darkness. Alisha ignored his panting as she frantically searched for a solution. Should she take Vincent to the other entrance? Wander in circles . . . ?

Oh.

She had the answer to Devon's cryptic message. One of their first searches with Lifeline. They'd rescued a couple of Boy Scouts who'd gotten separated from their troop. One of the pair had insisted they'd been looking for the *secret exit* his older brother had told him about.

Devon wanted her to make Vincent wander in circles.

"Vincent, I need to stop for a minute"—she tugged on his arm—"please."

He paused, allowing her to straighten up. "Don't try anything."

"What would I try? You've got a gun. I'm not stupid.

Only, please, stop choking me. I'll take you where you want to go."

He held the back of her coat this time, shaking her to prove he could control her movements. "Now, walk."

Being able to breathe better was a good thing. She held her hands out to stop from knocking into rocks, the light barely in front of her enough to see. "If you let me hold the flashlight, we could go faster," she offered.

"No." The words clipped. Sharp. All Vincent's smoothness had vanished.

They came to another split in the tunnel, and she took the right passage, crossing her fingers that after all this time she had selected the proper path.

The walls glittered in places as the light struck them, bands of igneous rocks mixed in with the places where running water had deposited calcium, the buildups creating waves of what appeared to be red-and-cream-coloured piles of rock-hard pudding. Sharp sounds rang out, but there was no way to tell how far away the original noise had originated, echoes carrying through the passages until the entire place became a drum chamber.

Alisha slowly worked the zipper on her jacket, careful to keep one hand pinned over the two sides to maintain the illusion of being tightly controlled. She had to be ready when . . . whatever happened, because something was sure to go off soon.

She pulled them down yet another endless passage, this one riddled with holes on one wall. Staying alert, keeping her attention focused forward, but pleased that she'd ended up exactly where she'd intended.

Vincent pushed her forward. "Faster."

"Faster and we'll trip," she warned.

Motion blurred on her right. Alisha let go of her jacket, springing forward and leaving her coat behind in Vincent's grasp. He grunted in pain, and the light in his hand tumbled to the ground. That was fine by her—in spite of the darkness she knew where she was going, at least for now.

She spread her arms wide. Her fingertips brushed wet

rock on her right, and she ducked into the first of the available alcoves she could find. The wall guided her in the darkness while she moved blindly a few steps down the passage as behind the sounds of struggle rose.

It had worked this far, Devon's trick. She'd brought Vincent in a full circle and given Devon time to surprise them. But with Devon's injury and that damn gun to worry about, they weren't finished yet.

Every sound the men made repeated off the narrow walls. Heavy breathing, fists meeting flesh. Alisha snuck back to the alcove entrance, tucked low to stay out of danger.

The flashlight Devon had knocked from Vincent's hand lay on the ground, the beam reflecting off the wall dimly illuminating the fight.

Devon had an arm wrapped around Vincent's throat, attempting to jerk Vincent to his knees. With his other hand he held Vincent's wrist, the gun gripped in Vincent's hand pointed down the passage.

Vincent roared in dismay, the sound cutting off as Devon leaned in harder. Vincent jerked up a foot and slammed his heel into Devon's leg, and Devon swore loudly, the oath bursting out in a breathless gasp. As they scuffled in the dim light Devon's face was pale, Vincent's dark eyes wide as he struggled to bring the gun around.

Alisha ripped her hiking boot from her foot. The men twirled again as Devon dragged Vincent back, closer to where Alisha was hidden. She stood and timed it as best she could, and as the men's joined hands passed in front of her she slammed the heavy heel into the back of Vincent's hand.

The gun tumbled to the ground and she snatched it up, darting into her alcove. Cold water soaked her sock as the fight continued. She put the gun down where the wall edge met the ground and hurried back to help Devon.

As she reached the opening Vincent screamed. He made a last, desperate push, sending him and Devon careening into the wall. Devon gasped in pain, and the moment was enough for Vincent to twist free, snatch up the flashlight, and race away. The sound of his feet slapping against the stone floor faded into the distance as Devon slumped to the floor.

They were left in pitch black.

A pain-filled groan rose, and Alisha slipped forward using the walls as a guide. "Devon?"

Soft hands touched his face a moment before her strong arms helped him to his feet again.

"You're crazy," Alisha whispered. "You've been shot. You shouldn't be walking, let alone fighting."

"And leave you to him? Fuck that." Devon leaned harder on the wall behind him. He took the headlamp he'd found in her abandoned backpack from his pocket, where he'd put it before leaping from the shadows. He pressed it into her hands. She twisted it on, and suddenly he could see every inch of her beautiful, worried face. "I couldn't leave you. Thank you for figuring out what I was talking about, because I wouldn't have been able to jump him otherwise."

"He can't get out." Alisha gestured down the passage ahead of them. "He's got nowhere to finish except up against the base of the first descent. If Lana is there with a rope for him to escape, Erin will stop them, and either way, the RCMP should be here soon. We're safe."

Devon tested his leg. The pain he'd ignored while tracking after Vincent and Alisha into the tunnels had lessened, probably because he was going numb. "Lana isn't on his side, at least not fully."

Alisha wrapped her arms around him and squeezed tight. "I was so scared I'd lost you."

God. "Me, too. I never want that to happen again."

"I knew better than to go to his suite by myself. Why didn't you?" Alisha complained.

Devon smiled sheepishly. "What was he going to do? Knock me out, drag me to some cave, then try to kill me?"

"Don't joke."

"Hold it right there." Blindingly bright lights hit them,

and both Devon and Alisha turned their faces away and covered their eyes. "RCMP."

Devon waved a hand toward the ground. "Lower the lights. We're the good guys."

"Opinions vary on that." A deep chuckle followed as the lights shifted to the sidewalls, making it simpler to see the team of three who crowded the passageway. Their faces were familiar—men with whom Devon and Alisha had played poker during different social gatherings in the past. One of them smirked as he stepped forward. "Devon. What's this I hear about you being kidnapped?"

God, he was never going to live this one down. "Hey, James." Devon switched footing and grimaced as pain shot up his spine. "It was all a ploy. You need to go farther in to catch your man."

Alisha tilted her head deeper into the mountain. "You know the route? Vincent's no longer armed, and he should be trapped at the headwall."

One of the other constables nodded. "We'll take care of it." Two of the team rushed past. Alisha called after them, "There's another woman at the top who might have a rope to help him, but our pilot is up there watching."

James knelt to check Devon. "We already talked to Erin, and we have a team at that entrance as well. Damn, Devon, you got yourself shot."

"Really?" Devon wanted to say something smart-assed and quick-witted, but he was having a tough time concentrating now that his adrenaline rush was fading. "Nah, this is how tough we are on Lifeline. We enjoy making rescues more challenging by first opening a vein."

James snorted, standing and patting Devon on the back. "Okay, tough guy, if you insist. You'll live long enough to hobble to the exit. I'm going to give the guys backup. You okay?"

Devon nodded.

"Wait," Alisha interrupted. "Before you go. Vincent's gun."

She disappeared down the passage for a moment before returning, holding it as if it were a rotting carcass. James took possession before vanishing, the stillness of the cavern returning as his footfalls faded.

A slow trickle of water played in the background, muted voices in the far distance, but mainly the sound of their breathing and the strange noises created by being amplified underground.

He still held Alisha's hand. Her fingers were cool in his, wet and dirty. Both of them were filthy from the mud and water covering everything. When he turned her, though, she went willingly enough, pressing against him and lifting her lips to his.

Pain that laced through his body faded at the sweetness of her kiss. The brush of her tongue, the clasp of her arms around his shoulders—he could have lost this, and the idea shook him.

Then the truth rushed in.

They could have lost each other, but they hadn't. They'd done what they had to do, both of them, and now they could move forward.

Together.

They clung to each other for another moment before pulling apart. Devon caught her under the chin, the streaks of dirt and wet mud smeared on them forgotten as he looked into her eyes. "I love you, Alisha Bailey. Thank you for saving my life."

She went teary-eyed before smiling back, the dim lantern light making them look as if they'd been painted up to play war games. "I love you, Devon. Thanks for saving mine."

CHAPTER 29

,,,,,,,,,,,,,,,,,,,,,,,,,,,,,,,,,

This time he was the one lying on the stiff white sheets of the hospital bed as Alisha parted the privacy curtains. Her smile broke over him like sunshine.

It was nearly five hours since Vincent had gone off the deep end. Under protest, Devon had been taken straight to the Banff hospital by Erin in the chopper while Alisha stuck around to accompany the RCMP. It got him medical attention a whole lot faster—he understood the reasoning, but he hated like hell that they'd been separated.

Now that he'd been poked and prodded and his wound wrapped up, he wanted nothing more than to be reunited with her and get the rest of the story. Seeing her just affirmed all over how much *the rest of the story* had to involve the two of them together.

"You clean up pretty good," he teased, keeping it a whole lot more lighthearted than he wanted to. "Tell me you've come to rescue me."

"Rescue you? I'm saving the staff. The nurses inform me you're a shitty patient, and requested I please haul your ass out of here as soon as possible." She stepped beside the bed and leaned in to kiss him.

He caught her around the waist and tugged her onto the bed, ignoring her protests and concentrating on kissing her senseless. She softened in his arms, her torso pressed tight to his, and he groaned softly, wanting nothing better than to take her home and prove all over again how much he wanted her.

How much he needed her.

She caressed his cheek, her lips against his breaking into a smile. "We should save this for later. Marcus called us all to HQ, if you're feeling up for it."

Devon sighed. "There goes the ten-kilometer hike I was going to suggest. Damn, that man ruins all our fun." His brother's familiar ring tone sounded, and Devon glanced at Alisha in surprise. "Do you have my phone in your pocket?"

She rolled off the bed. "Lana had your phone, so the police have it now. That's my phone. I added Mark to my address book and figured your musical salute was as good as any . . . I called him while you were in surgery." Devon growled, and she tossed him a dirty look even as she handed over the phone. "They're your family, and they deserved to know."

He tapped to answer the call, still giving Alisha the evil eye. "Mark?"

"Devon, oh God, are you okay?"

He couldn't resist. "You caught me on the surgery table. You want prime rib or rump roast?"

To his surprise he didn't get an instant lecture to grow up. Instead, Mark laughed with relief. "So good to hear you joking around. I'm glad to hear you made it through with only minor injuries. We're all glad—the whole family. Didn't want to keep you from your rest or anything, so I said I'd call on behalf of everyone."

Devon stared at the phone for a moment before speaking. "Well, I'm okay."

"You're more than okay. You're an amazing guy, and I'm damn proud of you. Sounds as if you and Alisha have a lot to tell us the next time you come into town. You want to come over sometime before Christmas? I mean before the big family thing? We'll do adults-only dinner, and you guys can tell us about Lifeline a bit more. It's tough to have a real conversation with the kids racing around all the time."

So this was what shock felt like. Strange—took until this phone call for it to set in. "That sounds . . . That sounds like a great idea. We'd love to."

"I'll get an e-mail loop going with everyone, so we can nail down a time and a place that at least eighty percent of us can make it."

"Okay." Devon was sure he had a stupid grin on his face, and it only got bigger when Mark spoke again.

"You've done well for yourself, Devon. Your job isn't what I would have chosen, but then you're not me. I'm glad you're doing something you love, but for God's sake, don't get shot again, okay?"

"I'll work on that."

Devon hung up and caught Alisha by the wrist, tugging her to his body and holding her close as he breathed past the emotions that threatened to make him bawl like a baby. His issues with his family weren't over with one phone call, but it was a start.

"Thank you," he whispered in her ear. "I don't know what you said to them, but thank you."

She was smiling when they pulled apart, moisture in her eyes. "We'll talk about it later. We've got a meeting to get to."

He tried to refuse the hospital wheelchair, glaring at the nurse who'd rolled it to his bedside.

"Stop being a pain in the ass, Devon, and get in," Alisha chided.

"Screw that. You get in, and I'll carry both you and the chair to the door."

"I'll deal with him." Alisha waved the nurse off. "Get in, Ironman, you can make race-car noises if that helps distract you."

He laughed and let her have her way. What he really

wanted was to go home so he could talk about Mark's change of attitude, and grill her about exactly what she'd said to his brother to kick his ass into gear. Not to mention all the other matters they still had to settle.

As they passed the waiting room, the name Bailey Enterprises blared from the television on the wall. Devon caught the chair wheels and jerked himself to a halt.

Flashing on the screen were the words *Executive Director Arrested.*

Devon glanced at Alisha. Her teasing smile faded to a blank mask as the news reported Vincent's arrest. The camera switched to follow a man who had to be her father escaping into his car as he waved off reporters with a "No comment." The next shot showed a smartly dressed employee stepping forward to smooth the waters.

"Mr. Monreal's arrest appears to be of a personal nature involving estranged family members. We at Bailey Enterprises want to assure our stockholders that this in no way will affect the company. CEO Mike Bailey is completely focused on moving toward the future in a strong and positive manner."

Damn. Devon curled his fingers over hers. She squeezed them for a moment, but neither of them spoke until they were in private by her car.

Alisha took a deep breath, staring into the sky. "Well, that would explain why he's not answering my calls. I'm obviously part of the problem, not the solution."

"You don't know that for sure," Devon began, but she held up a hand.

"It's okay. If he wants to find me, he knows where I am. Otherwise, this might just be for the best." She briefly buried her face against his chest before straightening and wiping away her tears. "Let's get to the meeting before they send out a search crew for us."

This wasn't the end of the conversation, but Devon figured he should drop it for now. Another thing to add to the discussion they would continue when they got home.

She escorted him into the Lifeline staff area and found

him a seat on the couch. Alisha curled up beside him, although she grew strangely quiet. She slipped her fingers into his, and he squeezed them reassuringly and waited for the update.

Around them the team gathered. Erin stopped to punch his shoulder lightly, Tripp and Anders nodding from across the room.

The sight of Xavier's empty place burned.

Marcus stood by the door and looked the team over carefully, his gaze pausing on Devon. His expression smeared into disgust as he glared at the leg Devon had propped up on the table in front of him, his injury raised as per doctor's orders.

Devon shifted uncomfortably. "Stop that, Marcus. You're giving me a complex."

"I can't believe you were stupid enough to get shot."

"It's better already. Nearly healed even," he lied.

Alisha made a noise, and Devon crossed his fingers that she'd hold her tongue and not mention anything about his possible concussion, or the other minor injuries the nurse had listed for him to watch out for.

He should have known he didn't have to worry. Instead she changed the topic.

"You heard from the RCMP?" she asked Marcus.

He nodded. "We're still missing details, but I wanted to let you have at least the basics. They picked up Lana on foot heading down the road from Takkakaw Falls."

"On the road?" Erin sounded puzzled. "Then who made the tracks up to the entrance I was guarding?"

Marcus actually grinned for a moment. "Some poor sod who'd decided to set up a cache for the ice climbing season. He had a gearbox he'd hauled into the cave to save himself from having to carry everything once the snow gets deep. He nearly fainted when he got rounded up by RCMP waving guns at him."

The moment of lightness passed all too quickly as their laughter died down and Marcus turned serious again.

"Lana says Vincent approached her after I'd hired her.

He suggested all she needed was a chance to make a good impression on me, and I'd willingly move her onto the team full time. She took the drugs from him—he assured her he simply wanted a chance to play the hero to Alisha while he was in town. Wipe her brow and stuff while she was ill with the 'flu.'"

"Seriously?" Tripp shook his head. "How could someone who wanted to work with the team agree to do a stupid thing like that?"

Marcus shrugged. "For whatever reason, she fell for it. And when Tripp got sick instead of Alisha without any serious repercussions, she didn't think anything of trying it a second time. Only the dose must have been higher, and it backfired. When she told Vincent she wasn't interested in helping him anymore, he turned mean."

"Who messed with Xavier's belt?" Anders asked.

"That one we have to wait to confirm. Vincent has lawyered up, although Lana insists it had to be him or someone working for him. When he threatened her, she gave him a key to the Lifeline building." Marcus paced, dragging his hand through his dark hair as he'd obviously done a lot in the past hours, if the mess was any indication. "Speaking of which, I'm getting the locks changed and a new security system put in, and if any of you say something about locking the barn after the cows escape, I'll scream."

Tripp snorted. "Not the first analogy that popped into my mind."

"You didn't grow up on a farm like Becki."

There was one question still bothering him. "Did anyone mention how I got from Vincent's room to the car?" Devon asked.

"Easier than you think. After Lana knocked you out, she and Vincent manhandled you onto the luggage cart and took the elevator to the basement parking garage." Marcus grimaced. "I'm sorry this happened. You shouldn't have to worry about your teammates being a danger, and I was the one who hired Lana. If any of you want to leave the team, let me know. I'll do everything I can to get you settled with a new SAR somewhere you feel more comfortable."

Devon barely had time to register shock at Marcus's suggestion when he was hit even harder as Alisha spoke, her usually firm voice whisper-soft.

"You didn't do anything wrong, Marcus." Alisha cleared her throat. "Lana screwed up, not you. And . . . it was my fault in the first place. Vincent was here because of me, and I should have done something sooner to stop him. I'm the only one who needs to apologize. If anyone feels uncomfortable with me staying on Lifeline, let me know. I'll understand and give notice."

Devon wasn't the only one to make scoffing noises, but he was the first to speak. "Bullshit on you quitting the team. You said it—Lana was in the wrong. Vincent was wrong. You're not taking the blame for their stupidity."

Alisha pointed to the rules painted on the wall. "This is a place we need to trust each other one hundred percent. What we do to save lives puts ours on the line every single time, and if we can't trust the entire team, that's not going to work."

"I trust you." Devon spoke clearly, catching her by the chin and forcing her to look at him even as he gestured to the others. "They trust you. This doesn't change that one bit. Am I right, guys?" He raised the question to the rest of the team.

A chorus of voices echoed his words as Erin, Tripp, and Anders all gave her their support. She swallowed hard, her eyes brightening with moisture.

"Enough talk about quitting, got it? You're stuck on Lifeline for a good, long time."

He didn't look away until she nodded.

"I'm not done with you," he whispered, stroking a thumb over her jaw as colour rose in her cheeks. "Give me a minute."

Devon let her go and stood, stepping toward Marcus, his injury forgotten in his need to slap down the bullshit. Of all the conversations they could have had, this one had been the least expected. Like hell was he going to let the second-best part of his life vanish because of guilt.

He'd dealt with enough guilt over the years. No way was he letting this one pass.

"We all trust you. You did what you had to do. Instead of cutting off someone too soon who might have become a valuable part of the team, you gave Lana a chance. I haven't always gone by all the rules, but I'd give my life for any of the team. I know they'd do the same for me. Lana chose a different route and it cost her. It's not on you."

Marcus lifted his chin slightly.

Devon wasn't finished. "Being a part of Lifeline is a huge privilege, and there's no way I want to give it up. I don't want you to feel you've let any of us down, either, and I know damn well I'm speaking for Xavier as well. He trusted all of us and gave one hundred percent, all the time. He's going to get better because of that attitude, and you were the one who beat that attitude into us."

Marcus paced away for a moment, his broad shoulders straightening as he returned to the gathering. He cleared his throat, then nodded at Devon. "Thank you."

Devon took his seat on the couch. Alisha curled her warm fingers around his arm and squeezed him tight. He took a deep breath and let it out slowly.

At the head of the room, Marcus had regained his control. "We're taking a week off. Devon, the medical reports on you look as if you had a fucking guardian angel. If you get doctor's approval, rejoin training. We'll take a look then and figure out when you're ready for active duty. In the meantime I've got three people coming in to try out for the position of paramedic. We'll work with them during training time, and either bring support onboard or only take calls we can do with limited medical on the scene. Becki has volunteered to join us until Devon is back on full roster."

There was a lot of nodding of heads as they processed the information. The meeting finished up shortly after that. Suggestions were made for activities on the days off, and a few random hugs and pats on the back given from the guys before Alisha ushered Devon to the car and took him home.

For all the planning and details they'd covered, there were still a few important personal issues to deal with.

Alisha's throat had tightened even as her sense of pride had soared. Devon hadn't only soothed her fears, he'd stepped up and been a real leader. Confronting Marcus had pulled the group tighter when the situation could have torn them apart.

Her admiration for him rose another notch, and now that they were back at his place, she couldn't take her eyes off him. He'd changed into a pair of soft grey sweatpants and a plain blue T-shirt. His calf was bandaged, but he would only need the dressings for a few days if he avoided infection.

Devon caught sight of her and strode to her side, his fingers slipping into her hair as he cradled her head and kissed her breathless.

She could get used to this far too easily.

When he broke away and scooped her up, she damn near squeaked in protest. "Devon, your leg. Put me down."

He shook his head in denial. "My injury isn't that bad, and I'm not letting you go until I know you're going to stick around and listen."

Somehow that meant being tossed on his bed, which she was totally okay with. He crawled over her and caught her hands in his, pressing them to the mattress on either side of her head as he stared down, his blue eyes shining bright.

Alisha opened her thighs and allowed his hips to settle more intimately and as usual, the sexual tension between them kicked into high gear. "You plan on ravishing me? I don't know if that was on the list of approved activities the hospital provided."

He nuzzled along her neck, pressing his lips to her skin and giving her goose bumps as he worked his way up to her ear. "I'm pretty sure the instruction paper said you're supposed to wake me every two hours all night long. I'd like to put in my request list now for the various types of wake-up calls I'd enjoy."

"I bet you would." And she'd love to fulfill each and every one of them. He lifted his head and caught her gaze again, his laughing expression shifting into something far more serious. "What?"

He paused. "I don't want you to leave."

She wiggled gently to emphasize the complete hold he had. "Doesn't look as if I'm going anywhere anytime soon."

Devon shook his head. "That's not what I mean. I mean . . . move in with me."

Alisha smiled. "I thought I already did."

"Permanently."

Her breath skipped. "Devon?"

He nodded. "I love you, Alisha. I want us to be together. We can deal with our insane families and the media, and whatever the hell else life throws at us. I want to be the one you turn to when you're sad or afraid. I want to hold you tight, and let you wash away my frustrations."

Her heart swelled with joy as he stroked her cheek. "You're a glutton for punishment, are you?"

Devon chuckled. "I dare you. I dare you to tell me you don't want that. To have adventures together, to work together and push each other to be even better than we are. I bet you can't resist the idea of getting to wake up in the morning knowing I'll do everything I can to challenge you."

She laughed out loud. "Another contest?"

"Always. Because I love you."

"I love you more."

They broke down, laughing far too hard to do any serious kissing or fooling around. Instead, they ended up in the middle of the bed, Devon wrapped around her like a safety rope.

He stroked her arm as they relaxed. "You never answered me."

Alisha twisted to face him, brushing her cheek against his. "You sure you're ready to take on a full-time, permanent relationship knowing I have Bailey Enterprises as the skeleton in my closet?"

He made a rude noise. "You're not Bailey Enterprises. You're a member of Lifeline, a kick-ass search-and-rescuer, and the only person who pushes me to be everything I can be."

"God, you're good." She was nearly floating from his praise. "You just try to kick me out."

His expression of joy reflected back and made her even happier. Then he rolled her on top and stripped off her shirt, and things weren't nearly as relaxed or peaceful as they'd been a moment before.

She straddled him, settling her fists on her hips. "How come it suddenly looks as if you have sex on your mind?"

Her bra vanished and his strong hands slipped up her torso to begin a determined assault on her senses. "It's not my mind you have to worry about."

Alisha laughed, then moaned as he went to work on making both of them very happy.

It was no contest this time. They both won.

Turn the page for the next book in the
Adrenaline Search & Rescue series
by Vivian Arend

HIGH SEDUCTION

Coming soon from Berkley Books!

A low buzz of propellers settled in his ears then inched down his spine like an eerie warning. Timothy Dextor planted his feet a little firmer on the gravel. He leaned on his car door and stared up, waiting for the first glimpse of the chopper to break through the low December cloud cover.

The whining buzz in the distance increased in volume briefly before stuttering. The noise smoothed momentarily then choked again leaving a far quieter pulse accompanied by the thin whistle of the north wind.

His skipped heartbeat changed to a rapid pulse as the bright red body of a chopper burst from the clouds. A red top, twirling as it fell, the side to side motion barely balanced by the spin.

The rapid descent could only mean disaster within the next thirty seconds. That is, if someone other than who he expected was flying.

Sure enough, the next move was not a continued free-fall toward certain death, but the re-ignition of the tail rotor. With a smooth swoop toward the clearing on the north, the chopper leveled out and glided over the treetops with scant meters to spare.

Tim grinned. Good to know some things hadn't changed. The entire time it took for the chopper to circle then land neatly beside the large industrial looking building, he was busy thinking about all the things that had changed. Like him. Like his priorities.

Changes that meant the meeting that was now inevitable would be fiery and exciting and, hopefully, far more satisfying than the last time they'd been involved. Him and Erin.

The passenger door on the chopper opened. A slim man slid to the floor before easing himself to the ground, pausing to rest his hands on his knees. His head hung low, his body language screamed he was fighting to stay vertical. As the main propellers slowed their rotation, the man finally found his feet and made his way none too steadily toward the building.

Such a typical Erin move.

Tim was too far away to see details, but he could picture her perfectly. The thick mass of hair she kept pulled back in a ponytail most of the time. Her smooth dark skin, soft under his fingers. Her long, lean body, firm under his demanding touch. Her dark eyes that would glitter at him in amusement, in passion, flashing in anger all too often.

All those images were crystal clear in his memory.

It was definitely Erin who exited the pilot's door a minute later. Confident body position, head held high. Damn near cocky in her circle of the chopper and subsequent strut to headquarters.

Yeah, that was something that hadn't changed one bit, and Tim was glad. Of course it also meant his chances of getting kicked in the nuts sometime in the next hour were at an all-time high.

The thought of the coming storm shouldn't have made him grin all the harder.

It had taken exactly five minutes longer than she'd expected to break the next applicant. Five minutes, and a spiraling descent wild enough that if Erin Tate had been a passenger and not behind the controls of the chopper, even she might have questioned their chances of survival.

Only she was the one holding the stick and adjusting controls, and that made all the difference. It was why she had avoided the fate of the wannabe newest member to the Lifeline team who was in the men's change room attempting to pull himself together after his abrupt and explosive episode of nausea.

She squared her shoulders, stared at the wall and determinedly hid the smirk that wanted to escape.

Across the room her boss tossed her a dirty look. "You realize I'm onto you, right?"

"Of course, you are. Sir."

Marcus Landers snorted his disbelief. "And don't try to hand me that ultra-polite 'sir' shit. Not now. Not after you've managed to convince all the candidates I'd shortlisted that they'd rather be stationed on Kodiak Island than join the insane crew based out of Banff. What are we supposed to do on the next call-out? Go without a paramedic?"

"I have no objection to a competent search and rescuer joining the team," Erin insisted.

"Sure looks like it to me." Marcus tossed five files onto his desk, the papers spreading like fall leaves tossed in the wind. "All qualified, all eager to move here. The longest any of them have lasted is three weeks. So I want to know. What is your goddamn problem?"

Erin eased back on her flippant mindset a notch. It wasn't Marcus's fault, and he should know that she wasn't just being a troublemaker. "I didn't like their attitudes," she shared honestly.

"Their attitudes?" Marcus's brows were near the ceiling. "This from the woman who tells me to fuck off on a regular basis, and you had a problem with their attitudes?"

Erin twisted to face him. Marcus had established their elite team years ago with the reputation of hiring only the best. He'd supported that team through thick and thin. The trouble was he occasionally focused too hard on the job skills rather than the weakest link in the people themselves. "I've never suggested you should drop to your knees and service me, though, have I?"

Instant shock registered. "You've got to be kidding."

"Took the one, who lasted three weeks, that long to corner me in the change room and suggest he'd waited long enough for a taste of brown sugar."

"Crap." Marcus took a deep breath. "Erin, I'm damn sorry."

She shrugged. "Not your fault the members of the old boys' club are threatened by a female in a position of authority. You aren't the one with the problem." Erin stiffened her spine again. "Only I won't work with the asses."

"Which means it is my problem. We need a full team in place before the winter holiday season gets into full swing." Marcus rested his one good hand on the desk, his amputated left arm tight to his body. "The medics from the hospital— they're good on a temporary basis?"

"Never had an issue with any of them."

He nodded, then made a face. "I'll arrange for more loaners while I extend the search for new members, but in the meantime?"

Erin waited as he strode to her side to poke his finger directly in her face.

"Next time just tell me instead of taking matters into your own hands. I don't doubt your skills or your ability to make a point. This is a team, however, and you're a vital part of it. Anyone who can't respect that doesn't deserve to be a part of Lifeline."

"Dealing with them is so much fun, though," she deadpanned.

He rolled his eyes. "Ten million dollar chopper, and you're using it to teach respect. How about we do it my way in the future, all right?"

Erin grinned. "I'll think about it."

She scooted out of Lifeline HQ before the fireworks started. Marcus was right. While she was more than capable of taking care of herself, there was a warm glow inside knowing someone else was about to feel the wrath for their idiotic behavior.

The parking lot held one more car than she'd expected, and she paused. Her bit of showboating must have attracted tourist attention. Better to nip any rumours in the bud and make nice—a little one-on-one conversation could hush up any potential rumours.

He was standing outside his car, staring into the distance with his profile toward her. Jet black hair just long enough to curl slightly at his neckline topped what was a lovely looking masculine build. It was a warm enough December day that she'd grabbed a light coat, forgoing the thick winter parka needed on more inclement days. This fellow wore a much faded leather jacket, collar flipped up against the wind. A scruff of beard shadowed a firm jawline, lips that were firm and slightly parted in a cocky smile.

Hmm, under the right conditions she liked a little ungroomed cockiness.

"Can I help you?"

The stranger turned from examining the airfield to face her fully. A pair of brilliant blue eyes caught her full on. There were lines at the corners of his eyes, his skin deeply tanned from exposure to the sun. A vast amount of time spent outdoors was clearly written into his skin. She stepped a couple of paces closer before her eyes and brain connected.

Her stranger was all too familiar.

"Tim?"

The slightly cocky smile bloomed into a full out grin, teeth flashing white against his skin. "Hello, love. Good to see you up to your old tricks."

The roundhouse kick that burst free was instinctive. It was wrong, perhaps, to lash out physically at someone she hadn't seen in years, but the response was as involuntary as breathing.

Her heel failed to make contact with his gut as planned, however. Instead she found her foot trapped in a strong grip, and before she could adjust her attack he'd flipped her around, catching her against his body with her arms pinned behind her back.

"Kitten, pull in your claws," he warned.

His voice stroked her nerve endings even as her blood boiled. She struggled briefly to check his hold, but unless she truly wanted to hurt him, he had her locked in position. "I'm not your kitten, and you can goddamn let me go before I call the cops."

"I was only protecting myself," he pointed out.

After all the time that had passed since they'd been together, the flash of anger that hit was far too strong. She ground out through clenched teeth, "Spider."

She hadn't expected to be instantly set free. Had thought maybe he'd forgotten what the word meant. Maybe he would simply ignore her.

Yet only a second later the icy wind was all that surrounded her.

Tim not only let her go, he retreated far enough away they were in no danger of further physical contact. "That wasn't nice," Tim growled.

"Neither was . . ." She shook her head. This wasn't the time or place for the discussion, especially since she wasn't even sure if she wanted to bring it up all over again. "Forget it. What are you doing here?"

He raised a brow. "Isn't it obvious?"

Erin opened her mouth to lambast him again for being an obnoxious jerk when it hit. Hard. "You've come to apply for the position on Lifeline."

"Right in one, love." He tilted his head toward the chopper. "Don't think you can scare me off with any circus tricks, either."

She knew she couldn't. What's more, Lifeline was important to her, and the skills Tim had were exactly what they needed. She wasn't going to chase off the best candidate for the team out of some egotistical revenge. The knot in her stomach didn't make it any easier to deal with the potential issues involved in having the man around again. "You have an interview?"

He shook his head. "Figured I'd do a cold drop in. Unless you want to put in a good word for me?"

Jeez. Bossy bastard had her over the coals, and he knew it. Was gloating over it.

She glared at him. "Push me too far, and I swear I'll find a way to fix you. As in how they fix animals. Got it?"

She didn't wait for an answer, simply twirled on her heel and headed back into HQ. The candidate she'd shaken up earlier dodged aside and all but ran for his car as she passed. One solid tug jerked the main door open, and she was back in the staff area, the familiar displays on the walls and the relaxed and yet efficient setting calming her nerves even as Tim's body only half a pace behind heated her.

Marcus glanced up from where he was working behind his desk, his gaze leaping off her to the man stepping into sight on her right. "What's up, Erin?" Marcus asked.

She took a deep breath. "Marcus, this is Tim Dextor. He's a SAR trained paramedic. The best I've ever been with." She didn't wait for Marcus to respond, just turned to Tim and poked him in the chest, staring him down, longing for a reason to smack him a good one. "Don't fuck with me again."

She ignored the question in Marcus's eyes. Avoided looking into Tim's face for fear of what she might see there.

Most of all, though, she ignored the ache in her belly that said far too strongly that working with the man was going to be incredible and horrid for all sorts of reasons.

The best I've ever been with.

As her words echoed in her brain she had to admit the comment applied to far more than his skills as a SAR.

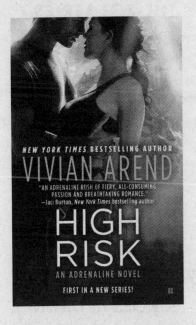

FROM *NEW YORK TIMES* BESTSELLING AUTHOR

MAYA BANKS

THE KGI SERIES

THE KELLY GROUP INTERNATIONAL (KGI): A super-elite, top secret, family-run business.

QUALIFICATIONS: High intelligence, rock-hard body, military background.

MISSION: Hostage/kidnap victim recovery. Intelligence gathering. Handling jobs the U.S. government can't . . .

THE DARKEST HOUR

NO PLACE TO RUN

HIDDEN AWAY

WHISPERS IN THE DARK

ECHOES AT DAWN

SHADES OF GRAY

FORGED IN STEELE

mayabanks.com
facebook.com/AuthorMayaBanks
facebook.com/LoveAlwaysBooks
penguin.com

M1054AS0213

Discover Romance

berkleyjoveauthors.com

See what's coming up next from your favorite romance authors and explore all the latest Berkley, Jove, and Sensation selections.

See what's new

~

Find author appearances

~

Win fantastic prizes

~

Get reading recommendations

~

Chat with authors and other fans

~

Read interviews with authors you love